Fangtabulous

"Another amusing romp in the series, this installment also sees its hardy heroine beginning to mature, adding further dimension to her character.

Reminiscent of Charlaine Harris' Sookie Stackhouse and Janet Evanovich's Stephanie Plum, Gina never fails to deliver the goods."

—*Kirkus Reviews*

"*Fangtabulous* is perfectly paced, action-packed, and a great balance or romance, suspense, and humour. If you've read the previous books in the *Vamped* series, you definitely can't miss out on this! And if you haven't started this series yet, what are you waiting for? Get to it!"

—*City of Books*

"A novel that fans of Katie McAllister's books will love and enjoy."

—*The Phantom Paragrapher*

I0658952

Fangdemonium

LUCIENNE DIVER

LORE
SEEKERS
PRESS

FANGDEMONIUM
ISBN 978-1-62268-123-5

First Printed: July 2017

Library of Congress Control Number: 2017936317

Also available as e-book. ISBN: 978-1-62268-124-2

Cover photograph by Susan Prater.

Lore Seekers Press is an imprint of Bella Rosa Books.
Lore Seekers Press and logo are trademarks of Bella Rosa Books.

10   9   8   7   6   5   4   3   2   1

This one is for my fans, especially all of those who've asked after Alistaire. I couldn't leave him (or you) hanging!

Media Tips for the Photographically Challenged Vampire:

#1. Unless it makes you happy, don't bother primping for the cameras. You won't show up, so it won't matter anyway. Yes, it sucks rocks. Worse, it sucks sweaty socks marinated in foot fungus.

#2. Practice your sound bites. Your voice *will* record, and umming and ahhing is *so* not vampiric. Just because you don't throw a physical image doesn't mean you don't have one to maintain.

#3. You're a hot commodity, so have fun with your contract. Oh not all the legalese—that's about as much fun as Great Aunt Agnes at a rave—but with the add-ons. So craft services won't do you a lot of good; maybe insist on a personal assistant or a spa day or the complete series of *Pretty Little Liars* on Blu-ray . . . Treat yourself!

#4. If word has already spread because of a series of teasers the Ghouligans (*Ghostbusters* of the real world) put out about their upcoming segment *Vampires Among Us*, insist on bodyguards to and from the recording sessions. There will be haters. Some with archery experience.

1

I'd spent months fanged and fabulous and still I took an unneeded breath as the dye packs burst open and the fans blew the brightly colored powders straight for us. I slammed my eyes shut, but not quite fast enough to prevent some dye getting in and stinging to high heaven. Blood tears—the only kind I cried—formed at the corners of my eyes to wash out the irritants. Very sexy.

I looked to Bobby on my one side, hot as all hell even streaked in blue and purple—the blue totally matching his incredible eyes—and Marcy on the other side of me in flaming red/orange, and I cringed. I remembered my color wheel from elementary art. No doubt I'd been blasted with yellow and green from the middle of the rainbow. So not my colors. I looked down to confirm and wished I hadn't.

Kill me now, I thought.

At least the cameras wouldn't catch how badly the yellow and green dye went with my screaming purple mini-dress. Or my night-dark hair. And the green *did* match my eyes, even if only the Ghouligans's studio audience would see it. That's what they were there for—neutral observers, randomly chosen, but for the background checks to keep out those who might want to end our unnatural lives. While *we* didn't show up on film, the audience did. Their testimony and reactions would help flesh out the show. The dye packs made us visible for the those watching at home. Or, at least, they made our silhouettes visible in the voids we left on the canvas behind us. Because the dyes themselves didn't help with our visibility. Whatever weird magic stole away our images also prevented anything attached to us, like clothes and dye, from showing up on camera or in mirrors. So random.

The canvas was being sent on some kind of national tour after this before being auctioned off for charity along with a bunch of other things the Ghouligans had arranged. We were making history. Vampires finally coming out of the coffin. I expected it to feel a little less . . . silly.

The audience loved it, though. They went wild. There were other tests as well, some performed previously, off-site, and edited for viewing, like the water tank test, where Marcy and I had stayed suspended without breathing for over an hour, proven only by the displacement of the water when we dipped in and when we moved, enhanced by CGI coloration of the water. Oh, and the invited witnesses. Skeptics. Experts. It was unbelievable that Marcy and I performed fully fabulous in our bikinis and yet no Sports Illustrated reps appeared to throw money and contracts at us, not photogenically challenged as we were. So not the way I'd ever pictured fame.

Ty McClellan, the Ghouligans' frontman—gorgeous with dark hair, blue eyes and that lean, wiry height that said he free-climbed on his days off or ran marathons or whatever, headed into the studio audience with a microphone and a roving cameraman to gather impressions and hype people up for our next spectacle while the three of us cleaned up backstage.

"This is crap," Bobby said. He'd managed to towel most of the dye out of his hair and off his face, except for right under his eyes so that it looked like he was sporting guyliner. Not a bad look for him, actually. Emphasized those killer baby blues.

I took the towel from him and helped—at least for a split second before one of the make-up people bumped me to the side and took over.

"Just remember what we're doing this for," I answered as she led him off.

He looked back over his shoulder with a "Help me!" sort of expression, but there was nothing I could do. We'd let ourselves in for this. The world needed to know about us—not because of the fame and fortune I'd always craved, but because there were bigger things afoot. I'd lived more and seen more in the few short months since my "death" than I had in all the years I'd been alive . . . and much of it was disturbing. In my home town of Mozulla, Ohio, my classmates had been caught up in a power struggle between vamps, getting smitten and bitten to provide cannon fodder for a war they hadn't chosen. In the small town of Wappingers Falls, NY, vamps had screwed up big time trying out a formula to make humans into sheep, figuratively speaking. In Tampa, FL, we'd discovered that the Feds who'd turned us into spies were no better than the vamps when we uncovered their horror-show hospital with vamps as victims. And in Salem, Massachusetts, where we'd met the Ghouligans, we found out that vamps were far from the only things going bump in the night.

Leaving mankind in the dark meant the baddies got to work with impunity. Immunity? One of those words. Bobby would know. But Bobby was off getting ready for his display of telekenetics. We'd decided to keep the mind reading to ourselves. We didn't need to add any fuel to crazy conspiracies about mind control and super predators. We'd gotten enough death threats already from everyone from right wing religious fanatics to our own kind. The Feds hadn't threatened us with death, but with arrest and imprisonment, possibly in one of their very special testing facilities. Good times.

The Ghouligans and their lawyers and security team had kept us safe and free so far. They'd agreed to set their researchers on finding and exposing the Federal horror hospitals we'd told them about. They got to call the shots . . . for now.

"Gina!" Marcy said, the alarm in her voice breaking through my thoughts.

"What?" I asked.

"Look!" she nudged me to face the stage, but there was no one currently on it. Ty was off interviewing audience members and . . . movement in the wings on the far side caught my eye. I shifted my gaze, only to see Maya, Agent Stick-up-her-butt, one of our former federal handlers, waving a piece of paper in the air. Only it wasn't a white flag. I had a bad, bad feeling it was an arrest warrant. Since I didn't see her partner Sid—Agent Stuffed Shirt— I had to assume he was coming up behind us. And that there'd be other agents waiting in the wings. Our time had run out. We hadn't even gotten to our reveal of the federal facilities, the experimentation, the abuse of power . . .

I grabbed Marcy and pushed her in the direction Bobby had gone. "Go, get Bobby. I'll draw them off!"

"How?"

"Don't worry about me. Go!"

She went. With my misting ability I had the least chance of

getting caught. I could go ghostly at a thought and the Feds would be grabbing air. But that wouldn't save the others. I had to get Maya and her team focused on me.

I raced onto the stage, hurdling a prop table two assistants were wheeling out with the objects for the telekinetic performance that would never happen now. The table was chest height for me, and I didn't quite clear it, catching something with the heel of my stiletto. I sent the cart crashing to the ground among cries from the props people and shouts from further back in the wings, coming down hard when my stiletto turned under me, wrenching my ankle. Pain shot through me, but it didn't slow me down.

The Feds were hot on my heels. But would they follow me onto the stage? Would they risk getting caught on camera?

I staggered to center stage, my eyes no doubt wild. Ty was three rows back with the microphone, interviewing an audience member, but they both startled at my sudden appearance. Ty whipped the microphone away from the woman he was talking to and bounded my way, leaping the stage as if he had springed heels.

"What's going on?" he asked, thrusting the mic my way. At least my *voice* would get some air time.

"They're here," I said in a rush. "They're shutting us down."

Ty looked left and right into the wings, his eyes going wide. But that wasn't the only direction of the threat. From out in the studio audience, plain-clothed people were rising up and converging on the stage. More feds? Rabid fans or foes? I had no idea.

"Agents," Ty said loudly, still looking to the wings. "Do you have anything to say to the accusations of a Guantanamo Bay for supernats? A vampire torture and testing ground?" He looked out toward the audience. "Later we'll show—"

There were screams as the lights snapped off with a pop like a breaker had just blown. Bobby? The Feds? *Bobby*, I thought. Vampires had the distinct advantage in the dark. My eyes were already adjusting.

Emergency lights flared, flickered, died. Everything fell dark again.

I didn't waste a moment; I had no idea how much time we had before power was restored. My twisted ankle protested as I sprinted back for the wings, toward the exit there. Toward Bobby and Marcy and freedom. Even with vamp healing and prowess, running in stilettos would only slow me down and probably keep my ankle from healing. I dodged the downed prop cart, then stopped just long enough to toe the stilettos off and leave them behind, running barefoot for the side exit of the stage. Agent Sid, suited and scowling, stood right in my way. He couldn't see in the dark, but he was smart enough to have planted himself in front of the door, gun out. Wooden bullets? Something else? I had no idea and didn't want to find out. I went misty and slid right through him and the door. The creepy feeling was only psychological. I couldn't feel him except as a denseness I passed through.

Once I felt the air lighten, I went solid again to get my bearings and look for Bobby and Marcy. I couldn't see a thing in mist form, not having eyes and all. I only got impressions of density, currents, temperature, so I had no idea I'd be materializing into chaos.

Outside the theatre was a mob—protesters, gawkers, people wanting to kill or kiss us. No one noticed me as I appeared. Everyone was focused inward, toward the center of the throng. Something was going on.

"Let us pass!" Bobby's voice blew forth on a wave of power. It wasn't a suggestion, it was a command. The crowd seethed backward, making room. I was about to be overrun, and then I saw an arm go up, lobbing something toward Bobby and Marcy.

I shouted a warning, but the projectile was already in motion. I dove into the crowd, ready to body surf it if I had to in order to get to my gang. I couldn't go misty in that press. There'd be no way to assure I'd have enough space to materialize again, and I couldn't help anyone in ghost form. The blow back of the bomb hit me almost instantly. Hit us all, but the humans around me didn't react to the burning droplets that rained down. Caustic like acid . . . or like garlic-infused holy water. I bit my lip to keep from crying out against the searing pain, and I'd only gotten the edges of it, but . . .

Bobby! Marcy!

I pushed aside the people in front of me, trying not to use my full vamp strength, but my focus was all on the center of the attack. I didn't know who around me was enemy and who was friend, but they weren't the ones in danger.

There were shouts from behind me now too, the Feds, probably, pouring out of the building to take us into custody.

As I forced my way into the center of the circle, there was a blast of power. I could almost feel the pain in it, the lashing out, and all of a sudden, the people around me toppled, blown down like by a gale force wind. Hurricane Bobby. I managed to keep my feet and leap over the girl toppling in front of me, coming up short in front of Bobby, his face a Freddy Krueger mask of raw, burned, pitted skin, and Marcy just as bad at his side, weeping blood tears. She must have been turned half away when the bomb hit.

Even through the pain on his face, I saw Bobby's relief as he caught sight of me.

"Come on," he called, turning for the mouth of the alleyway.

There was a screeching of wheels and suddenly a white van blocked the street where we were headed. Marcy howled her frustration. The door of the van slid back, revealing a girl about our age with wild hair in jet-black coils, café au lait skin, and the darkest, most intense eyes I'd ever seen. She was reaching out a hand to us, waving frantically. "Come with me if you want to live," she said.

"Oh, you've got to be kidding," Marcy said, then winced as her sneer pulled at her burned face.

"She's not," Bobby said, no doubt reading her mind. "She's dead serious. Let's go."

He took off running, vampire fast, Marcy and me right on his heels. We dove into the van, the feds so close behind us I heard them thump on the van door as the girl slid it shut and the driver took off, the sudden acceleration knocking us down as we tried to sit up.

"Who are you?" I asked, struggling upright, just as the van took a curb on two wheels threatening that position.

"My name is Imanyi," she said, "and that's David in the driver's seat. We're with the resistance."

2

"Seriously?" I asked, at the same time Bobby said, "You mean like in *Star Wars*?"

"I think that's the Rebel Alliance," Marcy said, prompting us both to stare.

"You like *Star Wars*?" Bobby asked, incredulous.

"Why not?" she challenged. "Even the prequels were okay . . . I mean, Amidala was like a *Project Runway* show and an extreme hairstyling competition all in one."

Imanyi looked at them both like they were crazy.

"Do you have any milk or anything we can use on our faces?" Bobby asked suddenly, and I thought that it was hardly the time for a milk bath, but I wasn't going to say anything.

"Milk?" Imanyi asked.

"It's a base. It might counteract the burn. Although, since garlic and holy water aren't acids, except to vampires, I don't really know. But Marcy and I are going to need blood soon if we're going to heal."

Imanyi shifted subtly away. "No milk. No blood. At least not from me. We'll be joining up with the others soon. Maybe then—"

I'd been watching Imanyi, just as she'd been studying us. She was like a live wire, all tension and distrust. She'd grabbed us out of that mob. Saved us, in her view. But she didn't like being trapped in the van with three vamps. She wasn't sold on us. I couldn't really say I blamed her. When facing down folks with steak knives for teeth, you couldn't help but wonder if you looked like filet mignon.

The answer was *yes. Yes, she did.*

But I didn't say that. What I did ask was, "Why did you grab us?"

I pinned her with my gaze. I couldn't compel anyone, like Bobby did, but every vamp had a certain degree of mesmerism.

And anyway, our super spy club training, back when we'd worked for the Feds, had taught me to spot truth or deception. Each was telling in its own way.

Imanyi didn't flinch from my gaze. And she didn't look like any kind of a supplicant when she said, "We need your help."

I waited for the explanation, but it didn't come. Or at least she wasn't telling.

"We?" I asked. "And what kind of help? I know you said 'the resistance'. Explain."

She blew a strand of corkscrew hair from her face, but it just fell right back out of place, so she tucked it behind an ear. "Look, I don't know if you've been in touch with anyone back in Mozulla since you left, but it's a mess there. We're talking vamps turning people to fill out their ranks. Fighting the Feds, sometimes in the streets. Sometimes to the point where people have tried to take video on their cell phones, but, of course, only one side shows up . . . unless there's collateral damage. And then . . ."

Her voice caught and stopped. *Collateral damage.* She didn't mean a sideswiped car or someone's mailbox. She meant people.

"Who was it?" Bobby asked gently.

"My sister," came a voice from the front seat. David. He sounded . . . he sounded almost computer generated, as though he'd done his very best to scour any emotion from his voice.

"I'm so sorry," Marcy said, moving forward to lay a hand on his arm. He flinched away at the contact and she pulled her hand back as if she'd been burned.

"He's not—" Imanyi started, stopped herself. "He doesn't do well with touch," she finished.

Bobby, Marcy and I exchanged glances. That could mean anything from autism to trauma to personal preference. But clearly it was need to know and we didn't. All we had to do was respect.

"And you?" Marcy asked. "How did you get involved. Why should we trust you? For that matter, why should you trust us?"

David's flinch had made an impression on her, I could tell. Or maybe it was the mob outside the studio. Or the garlic and holy water explosive. Or our close call (again!) with the Feds. I didn't have to be Bobby to read her mind. I could see it in her body language. Plus, she was my BFF. I could guess, for example, that she was already planning an exit if it came to that, making contact with her boyfriend Brent, a former Fed who'd come over to our side for love of her. He hadn't been with us at the studio. Because of cases he'd been involved with during his time with the Feds, he couldn't afford to be caught on camera. And unlike the rest of us, he'd actually show. He was human, if not exactly garden variety. Brent was a telemetric. If we were in trouble and could get word out to him, he'd only have to touch something left behind to trace us. The way we'd peeled out, the wheels of the van itself might have left an impression on the asphalt.

"I don't," Imanyi said, and I had to struggle to catch up. I'd been lost in my own thoughts. *I don't . . .* as in *trust us*.

"You lost someone too," I said.

She nodded, but didn't elaborate.

The van swerved, and we all looked to the front, to David.

"We didn't get away clean," he said. "We've got a tail. No chatter on the scanner, so they're keeping it off the airwaves."

"Feds?" Imanyi asked.

"Dark sedan, tinted windows. Looks like Feds to me. If they set up a cordon of the area, we're screwed."

"We can't meet up with the others sporting a tail. You've got to lose them."

"Tell me something I don't know." His voice was tight, like before, but this time there was a note of excitement, I thought, as if he welcomed the opportunity to thwart the feebs. In the moment, maybe he wasn't considering the consequences of failure. Or maybe he'd lost enough that those consequences didn't have any meaning. I didn't think now was the time to discuss.

One hard turn of the wheel and Bobby and Marcy careened into me, slamming me against the door of the van as we took a turn on two wheels. You would have sworn Imanyi was the one with the vampire reflexes, the way she instantly braced herself. Or maybe she was just used to David's driving. Almost immediately the van came down on four wheels again, only to torque the other way as David came to a new cross street and took the turn. I landed on top of Marcy and we all rolled to the far side of the van and then started sliding toward the back as David accelerated like he was vying for first place in the Indy 500. I alligator-crawled toward the front until I could wrap my arms around the passenger's side seat and pull myself into it.

David took another turn, a hard left and then another, and I just barely kept my head from smashing into the window.

There were emergency lights ahead of us and the red of brake lights. "Crap!" David said, yanking the car across two lanes of traffic to get to the median. The rumble strips clacked my teeth together, but I braced myself on the dashboard as David pulled a U-turn straight over the median and flew back the way we'd come. I didn't see the dark sedan in the lanes we'd left, but at our speed I'd have been lucky to recognize my own mother.

He pulled off at the first exit and hit a dead stop rather than the car in front of us at the light at the end of the ramp.

"What the hell, David," Imanyi said. "You might have warned us."

"No time."

The light changed and we took off with a roar, taking so many twists and turns that I lost track as we entered a warehouse-y area. Finally, David reached for a button attached to the shade visor and hit it, raising a garage door in a warehouse just as we approached. The door wasn't all the way up before we were in and it was closing again.

I was shocked to see a familiar face in the garage. Brent, Marcy's boyfriend, and a dark-haired girl I didn't know were loading up a gray van. Not paneled this time, but a sort of family-style mini-van. Marcy had our van door open and was spilling out of it before we even came to a full stop, leaving the rest of us to pile out after her. She threw herself at Brent, who caught her by the waist and pulled her into a tight hug before putting her back from him so he could get a better look at her face.

"We have to get you blood, stat," he said.

"Escape first, feed later," the dark-haired girl snapped. "We have to get out of here before the Feds shut down the city."

"Do you think they will?" Brent asked.

"You tell me. You worked for them."

"Okay, everybody in the van," Imanyi said as she joined us. She looked at David, "This time *I'm* driving."

"Whatever," he answered, glaring at her.

The dark-haired girl tossed Imanyi a set of keys and she motioned us toward the mini-van. There was a school sticker in the front windshield and one of those stick-figure families clinging to the back window. Two parents. Two kids. One dog. It looked like the little girl held pompoms.

"Whose van is this?" I asked.

"Don't ask, don't tell," said the new girl.

"I thought that was for the military."

"So did I," she said cryptically.

"Sanitize the van?" Imanyi said to David.

The new girl—I really was going to have to get her name—handed David something from a backpack before swinging it over her shoulder. Two somethings, actually. They looked like water balloons, only the liquid inside was cloudy.

"That's not—" I started.

But David wasn't beside me anymore. He was standing at the sliding door to the panel van, which he'd never shut. He lobbed the first of the balloons with such force it exploded on impact, and the scent hit me like mustard gas. Not garlic and holy water like the grenade someone had launched back at the studio, but a bleach bomb, splattering the insides of the van. He moved to the driver's side and did the same thing with the front section of the van. My eyes watered. Blood tears again. My nose stung.

"It won't cover everything," Imanyi said at our shocked looks, "but it'll ruin the noses of any tracker dogs and it might do enough. We can't leave anyone behind to do a controlled burn and we can't let a blaze get out of control and set fire to the building."

"Come on now," said the other girl, "load 'em up and move 'em out."

We piled into the new van, the one with the stickers. Bobby and I ended up in the back row of seats with the dark-haired girl, who was the smallest person present, about to sit between us, although she quickly scuttled over me to the other side when I suggested that Bobby needed to be fed. Seatbelts were still being fastened when Imanyi raised the garage door again and pulled out.

I offered Bobby my wrist and saw Brent doing the same thing in the middle seats for Marcy as Imanyi pulled out onto the street. She drove as cautiously as the soccer mom the van probably belonged to. My mother had never been a soccer mom. She hadn't been much of a mom at all. I'd been more like an accessory or a companion. Having a daughter meant never having to go to the spa alone. She and her Lexus had probably never driven below the speed limit in their lives. In contrast, Imanyi's driving felt agonizingly slow, especially knowing people were after us.

I tried to ignore the heat of Bobby's lips and the feel of his teeth sinking into the veins of my wrist. As always, it felt intimate. Too intimate for the confines of a van with multiple companions. I tried to catch hold of one of the many questions flying around in my head and focus on that.

"Brent, how did they get you?" I asked. Maybe I could help distract him as well. He and Marcy were much guiltier than Bobby and I of public displays of affection and I didn't really need an eyeful of all that. I did, however, keep watch on the side of Marcy's face I could see in profile, searching for the healing that I hoped for. I didn't want to think that she and Bobby could be permanently scarred by the garlic bomb.

"Much less dramatic than with you, I'm guessing," he said. "Note slipped under my door."

The Ghouligans had put us up in a hotel at a distance from the studio, hoping anyone looking for us would search closer to "home". Apparently, they'd been wrong. Or the resistance had been persistent.

"How did they convince you?" Had they known he was a telemetric and could read their sincerity on the note?

Brent reached into his shirt pocket with the hand Marcy wasn't currently engaging. He was wearing a button-up Oxford, of course. You could take the boy out of the Feds, but not the Fed out of the boy. He reached back to hand the note to me, and Marcy stopped feeding long enough to intercept it.

She took the note and something slipped to the floor of the van. I reached forward to grab it and sucked in a breath. I brought it closer to my face to be sure. It was a pencil sketch, but eerily life-like. Or deathlike, because Alistaire . . . well, he didn't look like himself. Not at all.

Alistaire . . . I still held the breath I'd taken. The moment suspended in time as I studied the sunken face of the psycho psychic I'd first met back in Mozulla. He'd been twisted into something both more and less than human—well, than vampire—by a failed murder attempt by his blood-daughter. He'd been too strong to die, and the spell too strong to leave him whole in mind or body.

Or maybe he'd been half crazy to start. I hadn't known him before his transformation, only after, when his body took on extra joints that bent every which way, giving him a spider or cricket-like appearance when he articulated to his full potential. I'd first met him when he'd menaced Marcy. The memory of his mindspeak skittered through my brain like swarming spiders.

Oddly, he'd saved my life several times over. He'd also threatened it, along with the lives of those I loved. He was nothing if not unpredictable. But still, I owed him. And no one deserved what I saw in that drawing. Tubes went into and out of him, and restraints bound him to a hospital type bed. He seemed to have become one with the mattress, making barely a dent in the sheets. The flesh of his face was nearly melted away so that his skin outlined bones and gristle. He looked like a living mummy, and I could tell the living part only because he was staring at the camera, his eyes as bat-crap crazy as ever, looking like he wanted to kill and eat something, but not before playing with his food.

"Holy crap," Bobby said, staring with me.

"What is it?" Marcy asked. "I'll trade you."

I traded her the sketch for the note. I didn't want to hold it one second longer than I had to anyway.

Dear Brent,

Go with these people. You don't know me, but the others will. Tell Gina thanks for giving me my book back, that when she first met me—that she remembers, anyway—I had ducky barrettes in my hair. I don't wear those any more. My name won't mean anything to you but will mean too much if this note falls into the wrong hands, so for now you can call me Oracle. That's what the others call me, though I'm not any kind of fortune-teller.

Gina and the others will meet you. You'll see them soon. For now, I include this sketch to show you that I was in. To show you why I got out. And to prove that I know where to find one of the Fed facilities. Quite a few of them, actually. Word is you want to take them down.

I can help.

I didn't know what in the letter would have convinced Brent to go quietly. It could have been a trick. It must have been his telemetry. All he had to do was touch an object with his bare hands to find out all kinds of things about it—where it came from, who had written it, their intentions . . . He'd have read far more on the note than the actual words.

Book. Ducky barrettes. An image started to form in my mind. A girl, maybe my age or a year or two younger—or maybe I thought that because of the ducky barrettes she'd mentioned—her blonde head bent over a book, so engrossed she never saw me sneak up to take it. We'd met in the lair of the vicious vampiress who'd mucked with Alistaire, and who'd turned Bobby and my other classmates to the fanged side of the force to form her own little army to take over the vampire council. I'd foiled that, but it had only led us to further misadventures. Anyway, I remembered the girl. If only I could remember her name. Well, Oracle now.

Oracle.

So cool. I wanted an awesome one-word name, like Madonna or Cher or Pink. It was my new life goal.

"You know her?" Brent asked.

I nodded. "She was vamped with Bobby and Marcy and the others." I turned to my boyfriend, "You have to remember her— slight girl, quiet, head always in a book, flyaway blonde hair."

"Laurel!" he said. "Smart girl. Very smart. We were always competing for top marks."

I tried to control my twinge of jealousy at his instant recognition and admiration.

"Laurel," I repeated. "Well, it seems we're not the only ones who escaped the Feds. She's out, she has information, and she needs our help."

"Laurel," Bobby said wistfully. "I wondered what became of her. I worried."

That twinge again.

"Well, don't stop worrying yet. We're all in trouble," Imanyi said, voice tight.

"Just the standard kind," I asked, "or did you have something special in mind?"

"I meant that," she said, nodding through the front window of the van.

"*Crap-crap-crap,*" David was mumbling under his breath.

There was a roadblock up ahead, and it looked as though we

were hemmed in by cars on both sides. Even if Imanyi could get us out of there, racing down the shoulder or bouncing over the median as we had earlier, we'd be conspicuous. We'd give ourselves away.

"Keep going," Bobby said.

All of us but David looked at him like he was crazy. David had eyes only for the trouble ahead.

"Are you crazy?" The dark-haired girl asked what we were all thinking.

"Not at all. Brent, change seats with me. I need to be closer to the sightlines," he said. It gave me an idea of his plans.

Brent too, because he didn't ask questions, but unbuckled his seatbelt and rose. I slid into Bobby's seat as he moved so that Brent could take mine.

As soon as Bobby sat again he explained for the rest of the class. "I can whammy the police and the Feds at the checkpoint, convince them we're nothing more than a nice family out for a drive. It helps that, with a mini-van, it's what they expect to see."

"You can do that?" Imanyi asked. I could see her tension ratchet up. "Like mind control?"

Bobby didn't look at her or he might have seen her worry for himself. He was focused on what was ahead of us. "More like the power of suggestion. All the cars but one, this one, are going to be negative for what they're looking for. They're vigilant, but at the same time, they *expect* to fail ninety-nine point nine percent of the time. Add to that a mini-van with a stick figure family and all I have to do is push them to see you and David as mom and dad and us a gaggle of restless children. Scent is the strongest sense, so if I add the suggestion of a poopy diaper, they won't be able to wave us through fast enough."

Marcy's nose twitched as if she could smell it herself at the thought. She turned in her seat to look at me. "Your boyfriend is devious."

"I know. Isn't it great?"

Imanyi didn't look like she thought it was so great. In the passenger seat, David was as impassive as a statue. "It's worth a try. We grabbed 'em for their powers, after all. Might as well test them out."

"This is a test," the dark-haired girl said, "this is only a test of the emergency escape system."

"Not funny, Paige," Imanyi said.

Ah, *Paige*! Finally a name for the dark-haired girl in the back-seat.

"Who's laughing?" Paige asked.

We sat in silence for a few minutes while we inched closer to the checkpoint. You could cut the tension in the car with a knife, though it probably would have taken the granddaddy of them. A machete, maybe.

We were only three cars back from the front of the line when Imanyi asked, "What the hell is that?"

Everyone leaned forward to see what she was talking about. The first thing I noticed about the man they were all staring at was that he could totally rock the bald thing. He had the perfect head for it. He was also tall and nearly as dark as his suit, which he looked as if he'd been made for, or vice versa. The second thing I noticed was the device in his hand. It wasn't a mirror to look under cars for explosives or hangers-on. Or a weapon of any kind I recognized. It *did* look like some kind of scanner. At the moment it was glowing white as he aimed it through the window of the white four-door at the checkpoint, but I had a feeling it wasn't going to stay that way when we got there. I didn't know what it did—find power or vampires or somehow scan DNA from a distance. There was no way of knowing what the Feds had learned from their monstrous experiments. Or from the machines they'd confiscated during our investigation of Eric, the mechanical mad scientist we'd met back in Florida. But I had the feeling that things were about to go very badly for us.

3

"What the hell," Bobby repeated.

"What do we do?" David asked.

"I don't think we can do anything," Imanyi answered. "We're blocked in."

"Bobby," I said, "isn't there something? Your telekinesis, maybe? Can you flip a switch or fry the insides or . . ."

Fear gripped me as he shook his head no. "Possibly, if I could get a good look at it and see how it worked. Or if was plugged in, *maybe* I could cause a power surge. Not that I've ever done it. But telekinesis is more like moving things around, not . . . well, I was about to say it's not magic, but I guess it is. Still, it can only do so much."

"That's it then," Brent said. "Telekinesis the damn thing out of the guy's hand and drop it to the ground just as that car drives forward. It'll be crushed under the wheels."

"Things like that don't happen on their own. The Feds will know we're here. They'll know we're in this lane. They'll swarm all over us."

"What if I can draw them off?" I asked, suddenly inspired.

Everyone looked at me.

"No," Bobby said strongly, like he was the boss of me.

"Yes," I answered. "Listen, if I ghost over there and steal one of the police cars, don't you think they'll give a merry chase? In all the confusion, it won't be anything at all for you to make sure that the scanner-thingie gets bumped out of the Bald and the Beautiful's hand and crushed to dust."

"The Bald and the Beautiful," Marcy snorted. "Perfect."

But the others were focused on the plan. "What then?" Bobby asked. "They chase you down and shoot you full of wood or holy water or vamp tranquilizer and cart you off to one of their club deads. No way. It's too dangerous."

"Not any more dangerous than doing nothing. Anyway, I'm not asking, I'm telling. I'll abandon the police car when I've led them far enough off, ghost away and mindspeak you somewhere to meet when I rematerialize. In the meantime, you should be able to do your thing and get through."

The Fed waved off the white car he'd been inspecting and now there were only three cars between him and us. We rolled forward and I got out of my seat to crouch beside Bobby's so I could grab his head and pull him down to me for a searing kiss. He resisted at first, tense with disapproval at what I was about to do, but then he grabbed the nape of my neck and deepened the kiss. It ended far too soon.

"Be safe," he ordered.

It was the kind of order I could actually live with. I hoped.

I nodded and disappeared, going misty right there beside him. I could no longer feel Bobby's hand on my neck . . . or anything else for that matter. Just the change in density where seats and people had been. I had to move quickly. I pushed myself off and out, not sure of the mechanics of it, but some part of me had to be a wee bit corporeal still, since it was like pushing off the side of the pool when swimming laps. I was out of the van then and floating, using what I remembered of everything's position to skim over the cars and cops and Feds and barriers, then going a bit further to be sure that I was far enough. I let myself sink to the ground, adjusted when I felt something solid beneath me, and then materialized when I felt the earth.

I hoped fervently I'd judged things right when I willed myself solid again. It came back in degrees—not instantaneous, but not slowly either. I was standing between two police cars. Everyone was focused on the vehicles at the checkpoints; no one was looking this way. Perfect.

I crept to the driver's side door of the cop car closest to me and tried it. The door was unlocked. I pulled it open and slid into the driver's seat. Keys, keys, keys . . . I quickly flipped the visor, checked the console. Nothing. I'd learned to hotwire in spy school, but it was going to take precious time. I looked up and saw that the van was only a single car back in the line-up now. I had to hurry. I prayed to whatever deity might still listen to a vampire and sped through the process, banging my hands celebrationally on the dash when it fired up, and then flipping every switch I could find. Lights, sirens, action! Just in the nick of time.

I put the car into reverse and whipped out, squealing tires as I took it all way too fast. I had a moment of stark terror at that, PTSD from the accident that had ended my life. I remembered squealing tires that night, being sideswiped in the rain—I forced that out of my head. No time!

I thrust the gear shift into Drive and stomped the gas pedal all the way to the floor, peeling out. The blaring lights and sirens split the night and nearly my head, but I had bigger worries. I checked the rearview mirror, adjusting it quickly. Chaos erupted behind me as cops scrambled to get into their own cars to give chase. I hoped I could draw off enough to save my friends.

The road ahead was nearly empty with all the traffic bottle-necked behind, and damn these cop cars could move! I was pushing a hundred already and didn't even feel any shimmy in the frame. But the cops were no slouches at scrambling, and they were on my butt almost before I got to my first turn. I had to slow to take it, and there they were, right behind. Lights and sirens and someone coming over an intercom insisting that I pull over or be treated with extreme prejudice.

Instead I mashed the gas pedal and the car sprang forward like a dog let off the leash. Panic gripped me, and my chest tightened around my unbeating heart. I should have thought twice before offering to lead a car chase. The night of my death was still real and terrifying. It was dark out, as it had been that night, although less so with all of the flashing lights competing with each other. If it started to rain, my panic attack might go full blown. I pushed it down. My friends were at stake. I couldn't blow this. I couldn't give in to the panic. Later, but not now.

I sped away, twisting and turning, police hot on my tail. As long as I was ahead of the game, as long as I had gas, I had no problem. But if they got someone in front of me . . . I heard the siren before I saw it, ahead and to my left. Sure enough, they were planning to cut me off, racing in from a side street. I took the first right I came to. At the speed I was going, I fishtailed even on the dry streets. I beat back my panicked reaction and tried to focus, because now the sirens were all around me.

I gunned the car through the next intersection and then a cop car pulled out of nowhere—or a side street, obviously—to cut me off. There were no turns between here and there. No driveways or loading docks or anything of the sort. Just curbside parking.

It was the moment of truth.

Hoping like hell I wouldn't actually kill anyone with my stunt, I went ghosty, rising out of the driver's seat straight through the roof of the car. I felt the rest of the auto body whip by with a blast of air, but already I was above all that, headed up and up. I floated to the side, to where I felt some density, some solidity and then when I didn't any more, I slipped over and solidified, materializing three feet above a roof. I fell fast, but landed on my feet in a su-perhero pose, knees bent, one fist down to the concrete to steady myself. I quickly rose to crouching and ran to the edge of the roof in time to see the impact of my cop car with the one that had cut me off. My car rammed it broadside with a horrible crash, blasting it several feet further down the street. The other pursuit cars con-verged around it. I wanted to stay to make sure the driver got away all right, but I knew I had to get the hell out of there before anyone could spot me on the roof.

Luckily, the buildings were close together in this part of downtown, and I leapt from one to the next until I hit a cross street, at which point I ghosted over to the next set. All this mist-ing was taking it out of me, but I couldn't stop now. I had to get away and meet back up with the others or find a safe place to go to ground before morning. Otherwise, exhaustion would be the least of my worries.

When I thought I was far enough away, I ducked down on one of the roofs and reached out to Bobby. *You there?* I sent out mentally. *Did you all get through the checkpoint?*

Bobby's "voice" came back almost immediately. *Gina, oh thank God!* I didn't know that God had anything to do with it, but I wasn't going to argue. *We're away. You do know how to create chaos! Where should we meet you?*

I didn't have the faintest clue where I was, but wherever, it was still too close to the police and the crash site I'd created.

Let me get back to you on that.

I contemplated. I could get down off the roof and hail a cab, assuming the Feds didn't have my pictures splashed all over the media by now. They wouldn't have anything post-vamping, of course, but possibly my high school yearbook photo. Anyway, it wasn't like I'd changed. Or ever would. My hair, maybe. That was a thought. But I loved my long, flowing waves. Gah, focus!

The cops might be cordoning off the area already, although why they would when I'd slipped them before I had no idea. But there were procedures. I knew that from super spy club training.

I was probably best hoofing it before anything else could happen. I misted down to street level, but then took off running in the direction that was *away* from the crash. I slowed to a less attention-grabbing walk when I came to a more active area. Closed shops, but open bars and restaurants. Slowed, but didn't stop. I kept on going for several more blocks until I came to an old-fashioned diner called Lindy's. A bar might notice I was too young and kick me out, but a diner would have no such qualms.

I sat down at a booth, hoping the others would be able to get to me before I had to order, but a waitress too old for the ponytails she was sporting was right on top of things, delivering a menu and asking, "What can I get you to drink?"

"Do you have mochas?" I asked. I couldn't drink one, sadly, but I could enjoy the scent. I missed mochas more than I could say. Almost more than my parents. At least the coffee had always been there for me.

"I can make you a cappuccino and whisk it up with chocolate sauce."

"Good enough," I answered, keeping my true feelings off my face.

She went away.

Gina?

I'm at Lindy's, I thought back at Bobby. *On . . .* I checked the menu. *1088 Market Street. How soon can you get here?*

Hang tight, he answered.

He was back before my counterfeit mocha. *Five minutes.*

Great.

My waitress, whose nametag declared her *Doris* was back shortly after, sliding my mocha onto the table without spilling a drop. "Can I get you anything else?"

Hmm, probably no time for breakfast sandwiches for the others, but, "Can you load me up with pastries? Half a dozen, your choice. To go. And then the bill. I just realized I don't have the time to sit."

"Sure, hon."

She was off again, and I was left to contemplate how my night had gone from triumphant—my television debut, sharing our message with the world—to crap.

Doris was back before I could feel too sorry for myself with two bags loaded down with sugary and greasy goodness, which I could more than smell. I could see from the discoloration along the bottom and sides of the bags. I hadn't had a donut or any other solid food since I'd tried pizza after being vamped and nearly saw myself from the inside out. Still, I hungered for the doughy treats. *Ooh, donuts.* I felt like Homer Simpson.

Instead of falling on the bags like a burner with the munchies, I gave Doris a twenty I had tucked into my cleavage, told her to keep the change, and headed toward the front entrance to wait for my friends. She approached a second later with a to-go cup of my mocha. It was torture. Coffee and donuts, and I could have none of them. Still, I thanked her, thinking that I should have ordered to-go cups for all the humans.

Too late now. I could see the van pulling up, and I walked as quickly as I could to it. The side door opened for me as I approached, and then Bobby moved aside to make way. Brent and Marcy were now sitting in the back so that I could just jump into the seat left open for me, which I did. We were off immediately, and I handed my bags toward the front of the van.

"Offerings," I said. "Oh, and I have one lonely mocha. I didn't really think things through."

"I'll take that!" said the dark-haired girl—Paige—from the back, leaning forward to relieve me of my burden. I had to keep myself from snarling. I couldn't have the mocha, and yet it was hard to surrender.

David opened the bags I'd brought and the scent almost knocked me to the floor, but I was made of sterner stuff. I'd once attended a Steve Madden trunk show without going feral. I figured I could withstand donuts. He took something for himself, read out the contents for Imanyi, handing her a chocolate glazed donut upon request, and then passed the bag to me to hand back to Brent and Paige.

Bobby gave me the side-eye, as though he too was having

lustful thoughts about pastries.

"Thank you," Brent said, when the bag reached him. The others mumbled something that could have been thanks as well through mouths full of dough.

The rest of the ride was remarkably silent. I tried to ask questions, but Imanyi shut me down, saying Laurel would explain everything when we got there. I felt like a kid being told we were going to play the quiet game to see who could keep silent the longest. I was tempted to kick her seat. But I was apparently all about self-control tonight.

Daylight was getting closer and my tension rising when David pulled into a motor lodge. He went in to register, leaving the rest of us to wait in the van. In the end, we had two rooms. One for me, Bobby, Paige and David and the other for Brent, Marcy and Imanyi. I noticed there was at least one of them assigned to each room to keep an eye on us, and two humans per room, counting Brent. I wondered if that was significant.

And then the sun rose, and I didn't wonder anything at all, but fell into unconsciousness beside Bobby on the queen-sized bed farthest from the window, which Paige had been very careful to cover.

4

Dusk hit like an uppercut to the chin, snapping my head up and me with it. I came up battling the blankets like I was fighting my way out of the grave again. I felt hemmed in. Panicked. Vampires didn't dream—at least, I never had that I remembered—so we didn't have the means to process stress or whatever while we slept. Apparently, it got pent up and sometimes exploded out of us instead.

And I was plenty stressed. There was more going on here than we were being told, with David flinching at our presence and Imanyi withholding information. I didn't have a read yet on Paige, but she certainly wasn't going to give anything away with David in the room.

Speaking of . . . she watched with interest as I calmed and took in the room, as Bobby reached out to reassure me. But as she saw me notice her, she tossed a pile of clothes onto the bed and said, "Better change. Don't know what the hotel will make of the powder all over their sheets, but we've got ourselves another ride the rest of the way into Mozulla and we'd rather keep it clean."

I'd forgotten the rainbow powder the Ghouligans had blown at us, but when I looked down at the sheets, I saw that Paige was right. They were streaked with blue and purple, yellow and green, like a bruise gone bad or one of those modern paintings I never could understand. If the Ghouligans' footage ever went out, we'd be famous. Maybe the hotel would realize what they had and we'd be immortalized in bad sheet art. Or maybe the Feds would find it and lock it away in evidence. Not that it mattered. I grabbed the bundle of clothes and headed for the shower.

"Don't dawdle!" Paige called out.

I waited to stick my tongue out at her until the bathroom door had closed between us.

I took a look in the mirror—old habits died harder than old

vamps—and then realized how silly that was. The only thing I could see was the powder that flaked off of me as I moved. I could only imagine I looked a fright, hair caked with green and gold, eye make-up probably smeared by my blood tears. Eternal youth was guaranteed with the vamping. Beauty not so much.

I made sure the sink was dry before setting the clothes down on it and then got into the shower post haste. I didn't even wait for it to heat up fully before I was lathering up my hair, watching the colors stream out of it and down the drain as I rinsed and repeated. Once I'd used up all the conditioner in the too-tiny hotel-sample bottle and scrubbed my body hard enough that I'd probably have to regrow my top layers of skin, I started on my mini-dress, doing the best I could with it and then rolling it up in one towel to soak up the moisture while I wrapped myself in another and investigated the bundle of clothes. I discovered black skinny jeans for me and a choice of shirts, both large, neither of which would do anything for me. One was plain black and the other navy blue with the Nike swoosh on the front. I went for the black, tied it into a knot at my waste to at least give myself some shape and set the other aside with the regular guy-cut jeans for Bobby, who was now knocking on the door asking whether I was decent.

I unlocked the door for him and grabbed the brush someone had left behind so that I could leave Bobby to his shower. I tried and failed not to envision it. Bobby was . . . fine didn't begin to cover it. He was tall with an incredible swimmer's build, and when those blue eyes lit with interest or intent, he was well-on irresistible. He looked at me now like he wanted to drag me back into the shower with him.

If I wasn't already dressed and we didn't have company, I might have considered it. Instead, I gave him a sexy smile, slid over and pressed up against him for a lingering kiss. I pulled away with his dye all down the front of my shirt. So much for clean. At least now my black shirt had some character.

"Whose brush?" I asked as I hit the main room. I looked to Paige, who was the only one around at the moment.

"Ours. Go ahead, we don't have cooties."

Like vampires could catch cooties. My fault for asking.

I went at my hair, untangling knots, smoothing and fluffing. Paige watched silently, playing with one spike of her dark, pixie-cut hair.

"Have any make-up?" I asked. I'd blown out of the studio without my purse or any of my things.

She cocked her head at me like a bird. "I do. Are you asking me to share?"

"Is that a four-letter word?" I asked.

"Five last time I checked." She twitched her lips, considering. "I do and you can use my stuff, but the second your boyfriend is ready, we go, whether you're primped or not."

Sounded fair enough. Anyway, I'd about perfected the art of the five-minute make-over, even without a reflection, so I was already finished by the time David let himself back into the room. "Time to go," he announced.

"We're just waiting on—"

Bobby came out then, hair all sexily disheveled from being toweled dry but not yet brushed.

"Never mind. Ready?" Paige asked Bobby.

I handed him the brush. "Ready," he said.

"Oh, one sec!" I headed back for the bathroom, grabbed the plastic lining out of the unused garbage can as a bag for my still-wet mini-dress, and was back in a flash.

"Really?" Paige said, eying it.

"Would you rather I leave it behind as evidence?"

"I think the dye is evidence enough. Whatever, let's get going."

We headed out. I expected to see the minivan from yesterday, but instead another van stood in its place, this one burgundy and completely without stickers or markings. The license plate was dirty enough that reading it would be tough but not so dirty we'd get pulled over for it. It had Ohio tags.

"You had this all planned out," I said.

"More or less," David answered. "Get in."

The others were coming out of their room now, which meant that since we were the first in, we had to go the farthest back. I sighed. At least it was easier in my skinny jeans than my mini-dress.

As it turned out, we were only three more hours from Mozulla. We hit the outskirts of town around ten and kept skirting.

"There's a curfew now," David said. "And we've just hit it. Though in reality, all the sane people are off the streets as soon as it gets dark anyway."

"Why don't all the sane people leave, if it's so bad?" Marcy asked.

Paige gave her a hard look. "We shouldn't have to."

"Plus," Imanyi chimed in, "there's a huge element of denial and not everyone can afford to pick up and leave. Not everyone has somewhere to go."

"Where are *we* going?" I asked.

I recognized the area we were in. How could I not? Mozulla had one lake, just big enough for the dozen or so houses built around it to still have some personal space. One of them was mine. Or had been mine when I'd been alive. It was only my parents there now, rattling around in those five bedrooms, their master with a great big balcony overlooking the lake. But they'd never been sentimental, and they had all their money to console them.

"There," David said, pointing ahead of us.

I'd almost forgotten the question, but the house he pointed to was almost directly across the lake from mine. It was, of all things, pink, though the owners probably called it coral, and looked more like a cottage than a house, with a cute little sun deck complete with porch swing and planters. The railings, stairs and decorative woodwork in the eves and porch rails was all an off-white that needed a bit of touch-up. The planters looked overgrown—both filled with ivy-like plants that spilled out onto the ground and stretched out across the porch, weaving in and out of the rails.

I recognized this house. It had seasonal owners. Or, I guessed, year-round owners who only used it part of the time, and had very good security. I knew because kids had occasionally tried to break in to party, but were always chased off by an alarm and police follow-up.

David reached up to something on the van's visor and the garage door of the place started to open electronically. My mind boggled.

"How did you get in?" I asked. As far as I remembered, the couple didn't have any kids, so he couldn't live here himself.

"We have patrons," Imanyi answered cryptically. "People who help the cause."

"Like—" I couldn't for the life of me remember the name of

the people who lived here, even though my parents socialized with them when they were in town. With no kids, I was generally left out of the mix except for a brief command appearance so everyone could see how I'd grown. "Like these people?" I finished lamely.

The garage door was closing behind us. The van was stopped, doors opening. Imanyi turned around to fix me with a direct gaze, "Like your parents."

She might as well have knocked me over the head. I stared, but didn't move. The others were already getting out, but Bobby, aware of the undercurrents or maybe reading my mind and my paralyzing shock, stayed behind. I thought he took my hand, but I wasn't sure. I was numb.

"Who?" I said. I sounded like an idiot. I knew that, but . . . *what?*

"Come on, Oracle will explain everything." She was out of the van and on her way into the house before I could protest.

"You okay?" Bobby asked, squeezing my hand. "I mean, that's good, right? Your parents—"

"Never cared about a thing in their lives," I cut in.

"It's easy to take for granted what's right in front of you, but once it's gone—"

"So, like, distance makes the heart grow fonder and all that? That's what you're saying?" It came out a little hostile. Well, I felt a little hostile. Not at Bobby, but he was there and my parents weren't. Like always. If they cared so much, why weren't they there to greet me. If they knew I was alive . . .

"I'm saying that maybe they didn't realize what they had until they lost it. Lost you."

"Give me a minute," I said, taking my hand back and turning away so that whether he was there or not, he couldn't see my momentary pity party. Weren't we vamps supposed to be soulless? Shouldn't that mean less pain and torment?

Bobby touched my hair, just lightly, and a blood tear started to form in the corner of my eyes. Then he was gone and I was left in the van alone. Like I'd always been. Really. At heart.

My parents had always been too busy with their own thing. And I was never interesting enough to draw them away from all that. Nothing but a pretty little doll to dress up and show off and then banish out of sight, out of mind. Once in a while to take down off the shelf and play with in beachy pictures meant to present the image of a happy family or for a day at the spa so Mom wouldn't have to eat her lunch alone. It wasn't like I'd been brilliant or intriguing or . . .

Except maybe now. Maybe that's what this was all about. Now I was a curiosity. Not unique, as far as the undead went, but certainly a talking point. Something to set them apart from their friends. *Your daughter is a neurosurgeon. So funny, mine has conquered death. Oh, you don't know? Eternal youth and beauty, an all blood diet. It's quite the thing now. They did a whole segment on her on* Ghouligans. *She's famous!*

Yup, I could see it now.

It hurt. I should have been way beyond things like that. I'd grown up a ton in the months since I'd been vamped. I wasn't a kid anymore. But this made me feel like one all over again. Back to being dependent on my parents. Back to being on someone else's crew rather than running my own. Oracle, it seemed, was in charge here.

They said you could never go home again—whoever *they* were. Apparently, they were right.

Gah, enough of this. I wiped away my blood tears and got myself out of the van. Time to put on my big girl panties and deal with it. Though, now that I thought about it, "big girl panties" sounded a lot like "mom jeans". Okay, so no. Unless those panties were lacy and high cut and sexy as sin, I was hitting "return to sender".

I felt a little more like myself when I walked into the house, straight into some kind of mudroom/laundry room combo with abandoned flip-flops, a washer and dryer and a drying rack sporting one lone hand towel. From there a door led to the kitchen, which opened onto a dining room that seemed to have become an office. Computer equipment was spread everywhere across a big, barn-style table that everyone had crowded around, filling the room to capacity. I looked around, and saw one new guy I didn't recognize—tall, whippet-thin, all angles. He had dark hair cut close to his scalp and a soul patch sticking out like a weed on a walkway. Really young. Maybe fifteen or sixteen and not yet grown into his height. He waved at the sight of me and his fingers seemed about twice as long as they should be. I wondered if he played basketball or maybe guitar.

I waved back and continued my surveillance, looking for Oracle. Beyond him at the head of the table was a blond girl glancing up from the monitor in front of her. At first all I could think was that she looked vaguely familiar. And then I looked harder. The ducky barrettes were long gone, as if they'd never been. The bookish girl I remembered from when I'd first been captured by a vampiress with plans to make my friends into her own undead army was gone. Her fly-away hair had been tamed by a handful of hair gel, slicked back sleekly against her head like she was an action-movie menace. Like a blonde Mystique from the *X-Men* or the badass German babe from *Pitch Perfect 2*. Also, she was wearing a "Fight Like a Girl" shirt with the silhouette of a woman holding a sword and axe against a red sun. And . . . was that a pile of bodies at her feet?

"Laurel?" I asked.

The dimple when she smiled ruined the intimidation effect, but it was gone almost as fast as it appeared. "Gina," she said, "you haven't changed a bit."

"You have."

"Yes," she said. That was all. And yet, there was a story there, I was certain of it. Come to think of it, people didn't end up fighting Feds and fangs without a story to tell.

"This is Silvio," she said, indicating the oversized boy with the soul patch. "If you all want to sit, I can fill you in on why I sent the gang to pick you up in Chicago. You probably also want to know what's happened with the Ghouligans."

I counted eight seats and nine of us, but that didn't bother Marcy and Brent, who shared. Luckily, the seats were large and their butts were small, so it worked for them. I was a little curvier and it would have been a challenge for Bobby and me to share a seat. Or a good core workout as we balanced ourselves. Either way, we were spared. The rest of us all grabbed chairs, and Laurel began, turning one of the multiple computer screens our way.

"First, as you know, the Ghouligans were airing live until the Feds cut the power and blocked the signal. So, the studio audience interviews, your stunt with the dye, the prerecorded audio segments with each of you—that all got aired. It's pretty safe to say the world is abuzz. Most are calling it a hoax, of course. Some are

saying the Ghouligans orchestrated the shut-down so they would-
n't have to produce proof or produce any of you for examination.
Others are true believers, thinking the shutdown was a government conspiracy of silence, which we all know is pretty accurate.
Of course, you've already experienced the range of true believers
from the studio. Some want to kill you, thinking you're a disease
something like *The Strain*. Some think you're damned and dangerous like Dracula. Others want to *be* you—us."

Everyone made a face of some sort, except for Paige, who
had about the best poker face I'd ever seen, but it was Imanyi's I
was most interested in. She looked haunted, and I really wanted to
know why.

"What are the Feds doing?" Brent asked, leaning forward,
avid for the answer. "They're spinning it, of course. What are they
saying?"

Laurel looked at him. "I'm not sure they *have* to say much.
People come up with their own conspiracies with or without
them—think of the crazy theories about how we never landed on
the moon or that the holocaust never happened or the Kennedy
assassination and the grassy knoll—okay, that one might have
something to it. *Anyway*, people are already claiming the Ghouligans could have faked the dye thing with a green screen and full
body suit."

"But the studio audience!" Marcy protested.

"The conspiracy theorists say they're either deluded or victims of mass hypnosis," Silvio put in, clicking a key on the keyboard in front of him and letting the monitor Laurel had turned
toward us play out the green screen scenario while a newscaster
with a comb-over that wasn't fooling anyone talked about mass
hypnosis, as if that was less crazy than the truth.

"In other words, those disposed to believe do. Those disposed to doubt are still skeptical, and nothing is going to change
that?" I asked, thoroughly . . . disheartened didn't begin to cover
it. Disgusted. Horrified. But not surprised. That was the worst
part. I'd seen what was behind the dark curtain and now I wanted
to rip it away, expose everything to the light—probably a bad metaphor for a vamp. But it seemed as though behind every curtain
was another. The Feds were like bad magicians with their never-
ending handkerchiefs.

"Not without us," Laurel said. She stood up so abruptly her chair wobbled back onto two legs before settling again. She made sure to meet everyone's gaze, standing as straight and tall as she possibly could at five foot two. Three tops. Still at least a couple of inches taller than me flatfooted—not that I was ever caught flatfooted.

Positioned as she was, the computer screen in front of her looked like a podium. I half expected her to launch into a rousing speech about how our ragtag little team could win the day.

"Here's the thing," she said instead. "I know where they're keeping everyone. At least, we've been able to identify most of the locations via image recognition programs."

Silvio cleared his throat. "Who's been able to identify them?" he asked pointedly.

"And who's been able to draw them so that you had something to identify?" she asked back.

Bobby raised his hand like he was back in school. "Uh, lost here. Maybe you can explain?"

Silvio cracked a smile. "Point to you. Go ahead."

"So glad I have your permission," Laurel said wryly. She looked to Bobby. "It turns out that I'm a remote viewer. It came up during spy training. Do you remember all the testing they did on us? Everything they ran us through?"

Bobby, Marcy and I nodded. It wasn't something we were likely to forget. The others watched us avidly.

"Remember the hostage situation, where we had to find where they were being held and storm the place. I could *see* it. Like a sixth sense or something. They weren't sure at first. Hell, I wasn't sure. It could have been some form of telepathy, like Bobby has. I could have been reading someone's mind. The 'hostages' had been blindfolded, but maybe someone's mask had slipped. So they separated me out. They did tests—" she shuddered.

"What kind of tests?" Bobby asked, his voice tight. I could see him bristling with the need to protect her, but from the past? Couldn't be done.

"Standard at first. They had places in mind where they'd put things or people. I was better with people. They have an emotional resonance, an awareness of their surroundings. Even blindfolded there's a sense of space, of air and movement or stagnation, sounds echoing or crunching or deadened." I knew all about that from my misting—the sense of space and place, even without visual cues. "And then came the tests. Was my ability amplified if my other senses were deprived? Could I produce images if my life depended on it? If my target's life depended on it?"

She wasn't looking at anyone now. She was lost in her memories. She no longer had a heartrate to watch, but the way she was hugging herself gave her away, her fingers digging into her arms as though to substitute physical pain for emotional.

Bobby gasped, and I knew he was reading her mind, picking up everything she left unsaid. "But you saved her?" he asked, horror quaking his voice.

Brent was pressing his lips together so hard they were flat and bloodless. He'd been one of them, one of the Feds. He was a telemetric. I wondered if they'd run him through the same tests. Would they have been as extreme with a non-vamp or would they have been more gentle with an asset they couldn't count on to come back from a near-death experience? Or . . . no, I didn't believe for a second he'd been part of *creating* such tests.

"Yes," Laurel said. "But it was a close thing. A very close thing."

She glanced up again, met Bobby's gaze and held it like it was a lifeline to the present to pull her out of the past she was trapped in. "They left Katie to bleed out in an underground vault. Alone. I don't think they really had any idea how long it would take or how much blood a vampire could afford to lose. I almost didn't find her in time. The thing with remote viewing is that you can sketch what you see, but if there aren't any identifying characteristics there then it's no use. If I hadn't figured out the drains, I'd never have found her."

Katie. There was only one Katie I knew, one of our classmates who'd been vamped with us. She was so thin, so dainty, and so pale as to be almost translucent. She looked like a prima ballerina, so light she could almost walk on air. She couldn't have that much blood to lose. To my horror, I could imagine the scene as Laurel painted it, Katie lying on ice-cold cement, hair splayed, blood draining into a vent in the floor.

"But you did find her," Bobby said.

"Yes, but by that time she couldn't come back on her own. I

had to give her blood and even then I didn't see her swallow it. You know we all look dead when we're unconscious. I couldn't tell . . ."

She shook it off. "She came back. But she didn't stop shaking for days. And then . . . I know we're not supposed to feel the cold, but she never did feel warm again. You should see her now, always swaddled in layers, as if the Feds can't get to her through them. Or as if we generate any body heat to keep close."

Her sadness was contagious.

"Where is Katie now?" I asked, afraid of the answer.

"I had to leave her behind. When I saw my chance to go, I couldn't get to her. My only choices were to stay or to get out and swear to go back for her. I went."

"So that's what we're doing now? Going back for her? Is that what you need us for?"

"It's a little more complicated than that," Silvio said, but it wasn't Oracle he looked to; it was Imanyi.

She nodded back to him and then looked all of us newcomers in the eyes, one by one. "I told you we were the resistance. I wasn't just talking about against the Feds. The vampire council here has caused trouble for too long. You were all vamped to become cannon fodder for a power struggle that ultimately failed, but that wasn't the end of it. The Feds came in. The vamps felt attacked on all sides. As if the vamps feeding on us humans wasn't bad enough—" I shared a look with Bobby. *Us* and *them* mentality never went well for anyone. "—they decided they needed to bulk up their numbers. Prepare for war. More people were turned; others died when the new recruits rose, not always under watch, and their bloodlust caused . . . what bloodlust does."

Her face had hardened. "I told you back in Chicago that you'd left a mess behind. As I see it, there are two things we have to do—take over the vampire council and stop the Feds."

"Isn't that how all of this got started—with Mellisande trying to take over the vampire council?" Bobby asked. And he should know. She'd been the one to create him because of some prophecy that he was the key and a kind of catalyst for change. She'd taken it to mean that with him she'd come out on top. Apparently, she'd been wrong.

"But we're not Mellisande," Lauren said. "We don't want

power for power's sake. We want to control the council to end the chaos. We've got to stop this brinkmanship—the Feds take some vampires so the vampires hit up humans and make more vampires, who the Feds take for their "research" and so on in a vicious cycle."

"And the Feds aren't the only ones experimenting," I said, thinking about our very first mission for them, when they'd had us checking out a smallish town in New York where the teen population had gone mad—going into sudden rages or dropping out of school and life entirely. The vamps had tried to make people passive, easy to control. Instead, they'd created a population of violents and victims.

Somewhere around the table a phone buzzed with a message. No one reached for it.

"There you have it. We can't let the Feds go on doing what they're doing. Not just because it's torture, but because we don't know what they'll do with the results. So far as I've seen, they're no different than the monsters they're supposed to fight."

Bobby tensed beside me, his eyes blazed blue fire.

"You mean us," he said, his voice as hard as David Beckham's abs. "We're the *monsters* you're talking about."

"But you don't have to be," David said.

"We *aren't*," I answered. "Not all of us. Or are you humans all alike? Hitler, Stalin and you . . . all the same, right?"

"Anyway, we *are* human," Bobby said. "There's no 'you' and 'we'. There's *us*. Got it? We're in this together or we're not in it at all."

5

Laurel was getting out schematics of the Fed facility they'd already discovered and plans were being discussed when Imanyi went into the kitchen for drinks for the 'humans', since we were thinking in those terms. Humans and vamps. Them and us.

I followed her. I was more a seat-of-my-pants kind of girl—or, more like the seat of my sassy designer dress. I'd let the others kick off the planning. I could insert my two cents later. For now, there were things going on that I didn't understand, and I didn't like having anyone at my side or, worse, at my back, who I couldn't trust. And you couldn't trust someone you don't know or who didn't trust you. At worst, they might betray you. At best, they'd hesitate, waiting to see which way you would jump. Hesitation got people killed, especially at the speed of vampire action.

I thought she'd heard me following her. I hadn't been trying for stealthy, but apparently she hadn't, and when she turned from grabbing several bottles of water out of the fridge and saw me standing right there, she startled and nearly bobbled them all. I grabbed one before it could slip to the floor, and she managed with the others, but not without a glare. "You scared the hell out of me."

"Sorry. Wasn't my intention."

"Then what was?" she hissed.

"I want to talk."

"*About?*" she asked, making a move as though she'd go past me back into the dining room. I stood my ground. She could easily have gone the other way around the island, circumventing me, and I could easily have moved fast enough to cut her off if I was inclined, but neither of us did that. Instead, she sighed, set the bottles she was holding on the island, and faced me down. "Well?" she prompted.

"I want to know your story."

"Why?"

"Because I like to know who's at my back."

"Who says I'll be at your back? Maybe you'll be expected to get mine. Or do you think humans are naturally the sidekicks?" she asked, uncapping one of the bottles of water and taking a swig.

I had to struggle not to retort. A snarky response wasn't going to get me anywhere. "I misspoke," I said, swallowing the word like it tasted bad. "I like to know who's at my side. Don't you? Do you trust *me* right now?"

She eyed me over the bottle as she lowered it from her lips.

"No," she admitted, and not like it was a hard admission.

"But you trust Laurel?" I asked. "Or Oracle or whatever you call her?"

"More or less."

"Why?"

"I knew her before. We were in book club."

"Okay, so you trust her because you knew her before. That means you must realize she's the same person she was then. Minus the reflection and meal options."

"No," she answered, reaching for the other waters again as if to end the conversation.

I thought about swiping them all off the counter and forcing her to talk to me. I couldn't do it the way some vamps could, clouding people's minds and all that. Or I *could*; I had a modicum of compulsion, but I wouldn't use it. It was totally counter to hashing out trust issues. So all I had was my charm and winning smile. Or, because I didn't think that would take me too far with Imanyi, my other secret weapon.

I gave her my best blank look. "I don't understand." People loved to fill in the blanks. It made them feel superior.

At first Imanyi only stood and stared, like she was on to me, which maybe she was. But then she said, "You want to know why I'm in this fight? My brother is one of you, okay? He was vamped."

"But then—"

"No," she said harshly, cutting me off. "No, I don't know that he's 'the same person.' My brother would never have jumped my Noni and drained her blood when she went to visit his grave."

I took a step back. I couldn't imagine the horror. Not only

losing a brother, but then her grandmother.

"Drained?" I asked. "Completely?"

She glared at me with equal parts hate and anguish. "It was either the blood loss or the heart attack that killed her. Doctors weren't sure which."

I thought about my own bloodlust when I'd risen from my grave. Bobby had been there with shopping bags to distract me, but when I'd hugged him in thanks I'd grabbed him hard enough to dent flesh with my fingers and fangs. If he'd been human . . .

"I'm so sorry," I said, knowing it was inadequate.

She took the waters and turned away. "I know it wasn't *him*. I know it was the bloodlust, but still."

"But on some level you want to help," I said. "Or you wouldn't be here."

"I don't want him running loose, but I don't want him tortured. I know he feels terrible."

"You've been in touch?"

"It broke him," she said, throwing the words at me like daggers. "I saw—I found—" a shudder wracked her whole body and ended on a sob. She disappeared with the waters and I let her go, only to find David standing in her place, his golden eyes replacing her chocolate brown but wearing the same expression—accusation.

"What did you do to Imanyi?" he asked.

"I asked her why she was here," I answered. "That's all."

"You made her relive finding her grandmother, didn't you? It was—" he shook his head as if he couldn't go on.

I didn't know what to say, so I answered his question with a question. "If she hates us, why did she join up?"

He made a sound like a cough or, if he was a cat, I'd say like hacking up a hairball. "She doesn't hate you. Or her brother. She hates what was done to him. And what he did in turn. She wants to stop it. The escalation. The experimentation. Everything. She wants us to act as checks and balances. To control things. I think that's what Imanyi wants most of all—control."

And a cure. It was Bobby's voice in my head. He must have been monitoring my situation and he must have read Imanyi when she got back to the dining room. *She thinks that the Feds might actually have a cure that they're keeping to themselves because they want the vam-*

pires for their blood and their experiments. If we raid the facilities, she might find something.

I tried to keep the shock of the mental conversation off of my face.

"And you?" I asked David.

"I want to fight," he said and turned away, ending the conversation. As punctuation, he noisily grabbed a bag of pretzels off the counter and brought it back out to the table.

I looked around the kitchen for a moment, but there was nothing here for me.

It was back to planning and ulterior motives and figuring out the people around me and what they really wanted so that I knew what they were truly capable of.

I returned to find a discussion of schematics, entryways and exits and penetration and a lot of things that sounded dirtier than they were probably meant to.

It wasn't long before I couldn't take it anymore.

"Stop!" I said finally. "Why don't I go take a look at this place?" The cat was already out of the bag about my misting ability, so there was no point keeping it quiet. "I can ghost in, look around, ghost out. I'll be able to tell you what kind of security they have and do all kinds of recon."

"Except you can't," Paige said. "What if they have more of those scanners like they had back at the checkpoint? If they go off, you'll be made. Even if they don't catch you, they'll bump up security and it'll be that much harder for us when we go in."

"But how will we *know*?" I asked. "If I don't try . . . if *someone* doesn't try then we might blow it all when we raid them. We have to test their defenses."

"Not necessarily," Bobby and Brent said at the same time.

They stopped and looked at each other. Brent motioned that Bobby should go first with his thought, which he did. "If we check it out from a distance, learn the people going in and out, we can get someone isolated. I could read him and make him forget all about it."

"Which is risky. What if he's resistant to compulsion, like Gina?" Brent asked. "He—"

"Or *she*," Marcy put in.

"Or she," Brent went on, "could raise an alarm and we'd be

over before we started. But if we play it smart and do a little sleight of hand, lifting someone's badge or wallet or whatever, I could get a read on it."

"I thought that only worked where objects had a strong emotional resonance. Who'd be that emotional about their badge or their license?" I asked.

"You'd be surprised," Brent answered.

"Okay, we'll call Brent's idea Plan A," Laurel said, like she was our leader. "It seems the least risky proposition, and if he gets a read on the person but not the facility from whatever he lifts, we'll at least have some idea whether the person is loyal or someone who might be turned, right?"

I couldn't actually argue with that, even though I wanted to when everyone started nodding along. Including Bobby. Was that it? Was I jealous because Laurel was the one calling the shots or because Bobby was agreeing with her? How silly was that?

"So tonight we watch," she said.

"Unless the opportunity for a little petty larceny presents itself," Brent said.

"And the rest of us?" I asked. "We can't all watch one place. We'll be conspicuous."

"I have an idea for you and me," Laurel said. "I'm not going to put you through what the Feds would, of course, but I think we can do some tests and maybe see about stretching your power."

"O-kay," I said, drawing it out, not actually sure it was okay. For one, I didn't like being separated from Bobby. We'd been a team ever since I'd risen from the grave. Things hadn't gone so well for the last woman who'd tried to come between us—the vampiress who'd turned him.

"What I'm wondering," she said, "is whether you've tested your limits. What can you ghost with you? What you're wearing, obviously, but what about something bigger, like a weapon or evidence or even another person?"

It was a valid question. Since I'd discovered my ability—while strapped down to a gurney and under extreme stress, something like the Feds might have arranged—I'd been either running from trouble or toward it. I hadn't taken the time to experiment.

"I see how that's something I should work on," I admitted. "Where do you come in?"

"I think that if we work together I can get a good sense of your mental resonance so that I can tune into your frequency or whatever. Then it would be easier for me to locate you or to view whatever you might have with you, whatever you're holding or touching. If we can get to the point where I can see through your eyes—"

"Bobby can read my mind already."

"But it's not the same thing. Reading your mind, he'll only know as much as you do. I'm hoping I'll be able to see and analyze alongside you. Plus, he may not always be available. This doubles our reach."

"So everyone else gets to go spy while I play guinea pig," I said. "Fun!"

"That's what we're all in this for—fun," Paige said wryly.

I stuck my tongue out at her. "Are you staying behind?"

She shook her head.

"Well then, I don't want to hear it."

The plan was set. Bobby and Brent went off with Paige and Imanyi. Bobby wore a baseball cap pulled low to hide his shaggy hair and killer blue eyes, since he was from the area and didn't want to be recognized. Brent's transformation was all about body language. As I watched, he loosened up, his shoulders dropping an inch from their always tense position. He even discovered a slouch. No one watching him would think Fed or cop. Instead, they'd think the foursome was just kids hanging out, maybe on a double date.

Marcy looked about as happy as a latecomer to a sample sale.

At least my BFF would be staying behind to watch my back, which was a strange thought, since we were all supposed to be on the same side.

"Where do we start?" I asked.

We started small and worked our way up. Utensils were no problem to transport with me. Neither were bigger things—a bowl, a tray, a laptop computer. As long as I clutched the thing in my bare hands, it misted with me through walls and everything. But if I sat in a chair or laid down on a table, and tried to mist with them, I left those things behind. It would have been awkward to take a whole table with me, it was true, but there seemed to be an insistence that something be on my person to go ghosty.

Laurel and Marcy watched with interest while Silvio and David poured over the computers.

"I wonder if it's a touch thing," Marcy said. "Maybe if you were naked . . ."

Both guys looked up at that.

"What good will it do for me to ghost in and out of places naked with furniture?" I asked.

"Well, it'd be distracting, for one," Silvio put in, a smile curving his lips, as though he could see it now.

"Off the top of my head, if you ghost in with a chair, you can tame lions," David offered. "Probably men as well. Some women. Chipmunks."

"Chipmunks?" Laurel asked, crossing her arms and staring the boys down.

"Sure, they're scared of anything. You ever seen them face down anything bigger than a sunflower seed? I didn't think so."

"I'm *not* ghosting anywhere naked," I said.

"Too bad," Silvio said with a sigh. Both guys went back to their computers, but they no longer seemed quite as focused.

"Okay, so let's table that idea for right now," Laurel said.

"Oh, a table, now that's an interesting idea," Silvio said to David, as if we weren't even there. "There's table dancing, table tennis . . ."

"Table upside the head," I put in.

"Spoilsport," Silvio said.

I growled. The guys seemed to find that funny.

Laurel cocked her head toward the next room, as if she wanted to lead me there, and I followed her into a sunken living room, Marcy right behind us. The walls were a tranquil grey-green, as if the painter was trying to capture the colors of the lake. A big oatmeal-colored sectional with overstuffed cushions took up a large part of the room with light-wood end tables, a wood-mantled fireplace and a big flatscreen television above it taking up the rest. The larger part of the couch faced the flatscreen. The loveseat faced a floor-to-ceiling bank of windows that I imagined looked out on the lake when the blinds weren't shut tight against gawkers and sunlight.

"Forget the guys," Laurel said when we stopped in the center of the room. "Let's try ghosting someone with you. Better to start with one of us anyway. Marcy and I have a better chance of surviving than one of the guys if something goes wrong."

I'd kind of enjoyed being the center of attention, but now my blood ran a bit cold. Natural for a walking corpse—not that I thought of myself that way—but this was more than just the chill of the grave. "Wrong how?"

"Well, what if we don't ghost with you entirely. Or you lose focus and we go solid in the middle of a wall or . . ."

"You're psyching her out!" Marcy protested.

She was right. On my own I didn't think much about what I did. It was natural. But then, I knew my own boundaries. I could sense where solids were—walls, ceilings, obstructions—based on air pressure, etc. I had a sense of my own space. But with someone else along, suddenly I was going to have to sense the space *they* occupied as well and make sure the obstacles I sensed were well enough away. Was I going to have to . . . *do physics*? No, no, no, not possible!

"Do we have a mannequin I can start with?" I asked, my voice squeakier than I wanted it.

"Fresh out," Laurel answered.

"Anyone you don't particularly care for? Convicted killer? Bratty child star?"

Laurel huffed. Her gelled hair didn't move. "Are you stalling?"

"Hells yeah. You've just suggested I could put you into a wall!"

"I've also said I'm okay with it."

I stared. The girl was crazy. Had she always been crazy? I hadn't known her in high school. I hadn't known her that well back at Mellisande's house of hell spawn. All I'd learned of her was that she was a bookworm who read Christopher Moore. Oh, and that she wasn't at all upset about being vamped. As a severe asthmatic from childhood, the freedom of no longer needing to breathe, let alone struggle at it, was a release.

Maybe a wall didn't seem so confining when your own body had made you feel like you had a perpetual weight on your chest.

"Seriously?" I asked.

"Seriously."

"Well then, I guess you're my first victim . . . er, test subject."

"Very comforting."

"Keeping it real. Okay, give me your hand."

Laurel reached out and I reached back and then we were holding hands. The guys would probably have gotten a big kick out of that—boys could be so silly about things.

I closed my eyes and focused on feeling a connection through our linked hands, trying to become one with her or the universe or whatever meditative crap would make this work. And then I let go of my physical self, trying to maintain a sense of my more soulful side and Laurel's as well—or spiritual side, anyway, if it was true that we vamps had no souls, as the burn of holy symbols seemed to suggest.

I wasn't sure at first whether it had worked or not. I ghosted across the room, skimming over the couch. I didn't feel any more laden than I ever did, but non-corporeal, who would know? When I felt I was clear of any furniture, I came back to myself, going solid again, and turning to look where I'd started . . . only to see Laurel and Marcy standing there gazing back at me.

"No dice, huh?" I asked, proving that I'd mastered the obvious. Now if I could just get this ghosting with friends thing down.

They both shook their heads. "Pretty cool, though," Laurel said. "I wish I could do something like that."

"I wish I could do something like—anything," Marcy said.

I rounded the couch again, on my own two feet this time. "Maybe if I try Marcy?" I suggested. "She's my BFF. We're practically one already."

Laurel shrugged. "Can't hurt."

I tried it. It didn't work.

Then I tried it again, hugging her like the sister I never had.

Nothing.

And then I had an idea. I hesitated before voicing it, but, apparently, Laurel had thought of the same thing, and she had no such qualms.

"Maybe Marcy needs to drink some of your blood," she said. "Then some of you will be part of her and . . . well, it might help."

Marcy and I looked at each other. We were blood suckers, so we knew there wasn't necessarily anything to it. I'd given my blood to people in need before, but to just offer her a vein wigged me out. Yeah, good thing the guys were in another room.

I shrugged. "We've shared clothes. Why not blood?"

"Yeah, this is a little different," Marcy commented.

"Chicken?" I asked.

"Oh, is that what you taste like?"

"Never know until you try."

Marcy stepped up to me, and I held out my wrist. Neither of us looked each other in the eyes. "Ready?" she asked.

"Be gentle with me," I teased.

I saw the flash of Marcy's teeth as she bit in, then came the strangely attractive pain of being bitten. It came with the territory—part of our magic, like mesmerism or continuing on after our hearts stopped. Make it pleasurable for our donors so they'll be willing to donate again.

Silvio walked into the room as she was drinking and stopped dead in his tracks, looking poleaxed. His lips quirked up as though he was about to make a comment, and I cut him off, "Say it and suffer."

He grinned. "It beats do it and die, which is what David's sister always said to me." The smile died. "Anyway, Oracle, we've got something, a possible match on the sketch you drew of a secondary Fed testing site."

"Great, I'll be right there."

Marcy retracted her fangs, and the bite marks on my wrist started to close up immediately. I didn't even feel the wound.

Silvio didn't head straight back to the computer. Neither did Laurel. They both stayed to watch.

I started with just grabbing Marcy's hand. I didn't feel anything different when we linked, but I closed my eyes, took an unnecessary breath and ghosted out. This time I *did* feel as though the air around me was a little more weighted. I misted above the couch and over to where I'd stopped before and this time when I reappeared, Marcy was right beside me.

"Whoo hoo!" Silvio said. "So cool!"

I looked to Marcy.

"That was . . . disorienting," she said. "It felt like that time I went on the all-grapefruit diet, kind of empty and nauseated. And then it was like the world got yanked away from me and whipped back."

"Did you sense anything else? Air currents or whatever?" I asked.

"No, but I was so startled. Try it again?"

Laurel's smile was almost as big as Silvio's. "We'll try me next. You two keep practicing." And she walked out of the room.

"Who died and made her boss?" Marcy asked.

"She did," I answered.

"Ooh, I can think of all the uses for this right now," Marcy said. "I bet I can ghost into that awesome Steve Madden dress with the broken zipper that's been sitting in my closet. And the dress with the criss-crossy straps I always get tangled up in. And—"

I laughed. "Okay, okay, I think you're getting ahead of yourself! We haven't even tried misting *through* anything together yet."

"Well, let's try it!"

"You sure you're ready? What if something goes wrong?" I asked.

"It won't."

"How do you know?"

"You wouldn't do that to me."

I wished I could be so sure.

But she turned out to be right. I didn't leave her half-embedded in a wall or a couch cushion even once.

6

A call came in as Marcy and I reentered the dining room to share our good news, and at the alarm in David's usually flat voice, we stopped dead. Well, undead.

"How do you know?" he asked. I watched for the microexpressions the Feds had taught us—the set of his mouth, the height of his brows, tension lines around the eyes. I even watched the pulse point on his neck. I had a laser-like focus for that. "No, no," he said after a pause. "Come on back. We'll be ready."

He hit the end call button and looked up at Laurel in particular, his face a bit shell-shocked. "That was Imanyi. She says we have to step up our timeline. The Feds are packing up their facility. They're planning to move out."

"What? Why? Because of us?"

"She didn't say, but Bobby thinks there's something else in the works too, like a raid on the Mozulla vamps. The guy he read was nervous and excited. He thinks the Feds want to take as many vamps as they can with them when they go. Preferably all."

"Damn!" she said, slamming a hand down on the table, but gently. The computer equipment jumped hardly at all.

"Damn, damn, damn. We still don't know where the vamps have fallen back to. How do they— But, of course, they're The Man. They have eyes everywhere."

"Not on us," Silvio said.

"That we know of."

She stared down at him, biting her lip. I couldn't help but watch and see if she would draw blood. Marcy must have taken more from me than I realized. Come to think of it, I'd fed Bobby last night. I was hungry. I was going to have to eat soon.

"Okay," Laurel said, visibly shaking off the dark thoughts. "Show me, who do we know among the vamps? There must be someone we can work with."

Silvio called up a file. Pictures and sketches showed on the screens like a mugshot line-up.

"Here's a thought," David said into the silence. "We let the Feds and fangs fight it out and kill each other off."

Laurel let her teeth show just a bit as she said, "Is that what you want? Another bloodbath? I thought that's what we were trying to prevent. What if it spills out into the streets again? What about collateral damage? No. Violence never solves problems. It just creates more. Victims, martyrs, recruiting points for more on either side, more people willing to fight for the cause."

"Wait," I said, leaning forward, as though my vamp-o-vision wasn't already perfect, as though the extra few inches would reveal anything new. "Isn't that . . . Chickzilla?" I pointed to one of the faces on the screen. She wasn't wearing her perpetual unitard, as she had when working for the vampiress who'd wanted to overthrow the vampire council and use me and my friends as cannon fodder, which was why it had taken me a second. It might have been a driver's license photo from the strained smile and plain background, but it was definitely her. I wracked my brain for her real name, because I knew she had one. Kelly, Kali . . . Carrie, that was it. But back before we'd been formally introduced, when she was nothing more to me than a mountain of a woman who could bench press me and Marcy together and not even break a sweat, I'd named her Chickzilla and it had stuck, at least in my mind. Eventually, she'd started acting human, even a wee bit helpful within the confines of her job description.

"Chickzilla?" Laurel asked. "I thought her name was Carrie."

"That was my pet name for her."

"To her face?"

"Um . . . yeah."

"And she let you live?"

"Apparently," I answered.

"Well, she's one of us now. A vampire. And she's working with the council."

I took a minute to digest that.

"What about Imanyi's brother?" Marcy asked. "Couldn't we talk to him?"

Laurel was shaking her head. "No. At least, not likely. After he . . . did what he did, he joined with the vamps too. Imanyi tried to reach him, even after what she'd seen, but he decided that he was irredeemable and completely embraced his dark side. He *might* work with us against the Feds, but we couldn't trust him."

Imanyi and the others walked in—they must already have been en route when she called. She took one look at her brother's face up on the screen and her lips pressed together so hard they created stress lines around her mouth. I followed her gaze to see a good-looking boy—dark, perfect skin, eyes that stared a challenge at the world, hair in dreads, and lips nearly as full as his sister's, though with enough sneer to keep anyone from calling him pretty because of them. I looked back to Imanyi, whose face was now completely set in stone.

"So Chickzilla—Carrie—might be our best bet," I said, turning to Laurel, trying to give Imanyi a moment to recover.

"But how do we get to her?" Silvio asked. "If the Feds are watching . . ."

"Remember misty me?" I asked. "You point me at them and I'll see what I can do."

"Me too," Marcy said. "You might need me. You're not always the most politic. And if I can't help you get through to Carrie and the council, maybe I can help you live long enough to get away."

I gave her my death glare. "Not politic?"

"Um, remember when I asked if that black skirt made me look fat and you said 'yes'?"

"Well, it did. You wanted me to lie to you?"

"A politic person might have said it wasn't a flattering style."

She might, possibly, have a point.

"Plus . . . *Chickzilla*," she added.

"Okay, fine, whatever," I said. "I prefer an entourage anyway."

"Maybe you're *my* entourage," Marcy countered.

"*Children*," Laurel cut in, as it looked as if Marcy and I might face off.

Meanwhile, Silvio cheered, "Girl fight!"

"Grow up," I said to him, and Marcy answered, "In your dreams."

"Very probably," he said.

Marcy and I rolled our eyes in unison and then grinned, face-off forgotten. "I know one thing," I said. "We're not going to impress the vampire council in jeans and T-shirts. What else do you have in the house?"

Laurel looked Marcy and me up and down. "Nothing," she said, and my heart sank. "We weren't prepared for . . . whatever you have in mind. What are you thinking?"

"Shopping," I answered. "In my own closet. My house is just across the lake. You said my parents are sponsoring you?"

"Yes, but as much as they want to see you, they can't just show up. The Feds are watching them, as you might expect."

"But if I go in mist form, no one will ever know."

"Unless the place is bugged," Silvio said.

Crap, there was that.

"We'll just have to sign to each other. Is there some way to let them know I'm coming?" I asked.

"Phone calls are too risky with the Feds monitoring everything," Silvio said. "We send spam e-mails with coded messages and links for them to follow. They can leave messages on those sites when they sign in. It's the only way to be safe, but it's not spontaneous."

I oriented myself in the direction of my parents' house and said, "Okay, then, ready or not, here I come."

I looked to Marcy. "I'll bring you back a selection," I promised. She had less in the chest but more in the badonkadonk. We'd raided each other's closets before. I had a good idea of what might work for her. I was relieved when she didn't insist on coming with me and picking out her own clothes. It took a lot out of me, misting back and forth. Maybe that was why I was already feeling the pull of the bloodlust. Even more than that, I had no idea what I'd encounter at home, but if my parents were there, I wanted them all to myself.

I took a deep breath out of habit and then faded out. I'd never gone so far in ghosty form, but with the Feds watching, I didn't see that I had another choice. I didn't know how far back the surveillance (or surveillance cameras) might be, so I didn't dare get a ride or walk closer to my parents' place before dematerializing.

I drifted right through walls and out into the open air. Solid things felt weird every time. I stayed misty, but it was as if someone compressed my mist, as if I was the same amount of stuff, just double or triple the density. The open air felt wonderful in comparison to the walls. I couldn't see, but I could feel the breeze from over the lake.

It started off just fine, but the farther I got over the water, the slower I drifted and the more effort it took. I didn't know how far I was across, but fear that I wasn't going to make it the rest of the way started to rise up. I had no idea what was going on. I was hungry and I'd already done a lot tonight, but . . .

And then it hit me—water. Vampires didn't do at all well in or over running water. I remembered that from Salem, when Marcy had gone into the ocean after a witch who was holding Bobby hostage. She'd started out fine too. While the lake didn't exactly run, it was spring fed, and the flow of that seemed to be enough.

Despite my efforts to stay high over the water, I drooped lower with every scintilla of progress I made. If I hit the water, I was sure to be shocked into solidity, at which point being seen would be the least of my worries. Vampires couldn't drown, but if I got too drained to continue on I could end up lying at the bottom of a lake for all eternity, slowly starving to death.

The fear wrecked my concentration and I dropped hard for a second, going halfway back to solid before I caught myself right above the water, one arm hanging down into it. The water felt like quicksand, grabbing fast and pulling me down. I tried to will myself lighter than air, thinking of myself as helium, floating high— so high you'd need a hook or a lasso to reel me down. It worked, and I rose slightly, but the pull of the water continued to zap me.

And zap me.

I had no way to measure distance, but I knew I wasn't yet over land. I could feel it nearby, and yet, I was so tired. So very, very tired. The water called to me like the grave. Like the softest mattress ever. Like a final resting place. I tried to fight it, but the exhaustion sucked at me. Another bit of progress and suddenly I was falling. I hit the water with a splash, which was the moment I knew I'd gone solid again.

Panic rose over me like the water. I was sinking, thrashing, but weakly. My muscles didn't have anything left in them. I was weighted. Not helium anymore, but heavy metal. Stone. Nothing buoyant for certain.

I hit the bottom, and the *Eww, gross*ness of the lakebed shocked me into a little more alertness. My eyes popped open, but

I couldn't see the soft and sucking floor of the lake, sludgy with eons of plants and animals dying and decomposing there. I couldn't see my way up either. It was so dark. Even with my vampire vision, the light wasn't penetrating where I stood.

I called out mentally to Bobby, but I had no idea whether he'd pick up my thoughts through the deadening water. Even if he could hear, there was no way he could get to me. I couldn't tell him where I was in the lake because I wasn't certain myself. Maybe . . . maybe . . . Laurel's remote viewing could tell her where I was. If one part of a pitch black lake didn't look just exactly like any other, assuming she could see anything at all *but* the dark. But any attempt at rescue would sap them too. I couldn't count on a rescue.

No, I had to do this myself. Somehow. I summoned my reserves of strength and put one foot in front of the other. It felt like the earth's gravity had quadrupled, but I got that foot placed and picked up the next despite the sucking muck that tried to hold it fast. And again. I had to hope I was headed in the right direction. My senses were busted with the water drowning them all out. Something brushed up against me—something with scales that scraped, and I gave a sudden squeak of fear that let the water into my mouth. Into me. It stung like poison. Instantly my stomach contracted, my muscles wanted to lock up. I blew the water out again, but it didn't help much. There wasn't enough air in my lungs to exhale with any force.

I tried to tune everything out then. Clear my mind, like I'd been taught in spy school. Push away the fear and the pain and the exhaustion and not allow any thought but the objective. I no longer cared if I was going in the right direction as long as I made it back to shore.

I didn't want to die this way. There were a lot of ways I didn't want to go. Spiders and other creepy crawlies ranked right up there. Captive and bound in one of the Federal facilities was another. But I suddenly discovered that alone with my senses swamped and my power sapped, at the bottom of a lake or ocean or, hell, swimming pool for that matter ranked very high up there.

One foot, then the next. Again and again, each step more difficult to take, weightier, slower.

And just when I thought it was a lost cause, that the next step wasn't even worth trying for, I caught a glimmer of light above me. Just a glimmer, like pre-dawn. I prayed to all that was good and holy or fanged and friendly that it *wasn't* dawn. Maybe . . . I hardly dared hope, but *maybe* it was the light of the moon finally penetrating the water. Maybe I was getting close to the surface. I couldn't tell if the lake bottom had been sloping up. I couldn't tell anything, but I took another step and sure enough, a breeze brushed the top of my head, chilled and so, so welcome.

I took the next step. And then the next. Slowly, my head cleared the water. And then the rest of me. It felt like I was moving a mountain and not my tiny five-foot frame. By the time I reached the shore, I was on knees and elbows, barely pulling myself forward. When I was far enough onto the grass, I collapsed, lying there in a puddle of my own creation.

Floodlights came on and I shut my eyes against the light, too exhausted even to care whether it was the Feds who had me in their sights. But when a shadow blocked out the floodlights, I found that wasn't entirely true. I cared. I forced my eyes open to see who had found me and stared up into the wrinkled face of our neighbor Mr. Mendelson, a wooden oar over his shoulder like a baseball bat.

At the sight of me he let it drop and asked, "Gina?"

I opened my mouth to answer, but all that came out was a dribble of water.

"What is it?" I heard Mrs. Mendelson call from up near the house, her voice quavering.

"It's that neighbor girl," he called back. "You know, the one who died."

He didn't seem to find anything strange in that. Maybe he knew about me? If things were as bad in town as Laurel had said, maybe he knew all about vampires.

"Well, get her inside," Mrs. Mendelson said.

Mr. Mendelson looked down at me, his faded blue eyes scanning me forehead to feet. "But my back!"

I laughed at the wonderful normality of it. It hurt. It hurt so much my whole body clenched in pain, but the muscles did move, and so I forced my elbows up under me and got my upper body off the ground so that I could reach out to Mr. Mendelson for a hand. With his help, I got to my feet, but when I tried to let go afterward, afraid to lean on him too heavily, the world swam and I almost collapsed back to the ground. Mr. M put an arm around me and together we bobbed and stumbled our way toward the house.

Mrs. M's eyes widened at the sight of me and the water sluicing off, but she opened the mudroom door for me all the same. I noticed a long metal flashlight held like a club in her other hand as she watched me squelch all the way to a bench with striped white and green upholstery.

"Sit, sit," she said before I could ask whether it was okay. Then she seemed to remember the flashlight held menacingly in her arthritic hands and lowered it sheepishly. "Sorry, dear. Can't be too careful these days. Let me get you a towel."

She hobbled off into the house, leaving Mr. Mendelson behind to watch me.

"So, you're alive again?" he asked. "Was it one of those things like on TV where you had to fake your own death? Does your mother know?"

So he didn't know about the vampires running around town. Or he didn't believe. That explained him inviting me so easily into his home. I almost felt guilty.

"Something like that," I said, smiling at his obvious excitement. He leaned in as though the closer he bent the juicier the details I might provide. He wanted a story. Maybe something to tell down at the bar. "I, uh, don't suppose we could call her—my mother, I mean? And, you know, keep this quiet. Like, just between us."

And then I remembered that I couldn't call. Not with the Feds very likely listening in.

Mr. M looked terribly disappointed at the thought of keeping things to ourselves, but he perked up as Mrs. M arrived with the towel.

"Are you in some kind of trouble, dear?" she asked, handing it over. "We could hide you out. It'd be the most exciting thing since Marge Nitchik taught us how to play Spades. Oh, the girls at cards would love this!"

"Actually, if you wouldn't tell them, I'd really appreciate it." I hadn't realized before how hoarse I'd become. That water had really done a number on me. Now that I was away from it, I was starting to feel marginally better, but I was going to need blood soon. Very soon. Mrs. Mendelson's blue veins were starting to look very, very good to me, even though it was the arteries that held all the flavor. My teeth were starting to extend, and I was afraid to speak again for fear I'd show them. It sucked that I had to trust to their failing eyesight, but I was a vampire. I was used to sucking.

"About that phone call?" I said, careful not to move my mouth any more than I had to. "Um, maybe you can make it for me? I'd rather they see me with their own eyes. Maybe you can find some excuse to get them over here, donations to a church rummage sale or something."

Mrs. Mendelson gave me a look that said I should know better. "Synagogue, dear," she said.

And, of course, I *should* have known better. If only I weren't so tired and her veins weren't so distracting . . .

"Sorry," I said sheepishly.

She patted my hand where it lay in my lap. "You've had a rough night, dear. All is forgiven. Actually, we are taking donations for this lovely family whose house burnt down. They lost everything. I should try all the neighbors. But we'll start with your family. Oh, and I while I'm inside, perhaps I should make a nice cup of tea to warm you up. Of course I should. Herb, would you like a cup as well? I can make a whole pot."

"I'll take care of it," he said, patting his wife's hand. "You stay and catch up."

He headed into the house, toward the kitchen, I presumed, and Mrs. Mendelson and I were left staring at each other.

"So," she said, "where have you been all this time? Somewhere nice? Tropical, maybe?"

With the paleness of my complexion? I had to keep from laughing out loud, knowing how much it would hurt—her feelings as well as my sore muscles. She sounded so hopeful, though, as if she wanted to live vicariously through my misadventures.

I didn't want to lie, but I couldn't exactly tell her the truth, so I was vague. I told her I'd been staying with friends, which was true, as far as it went. But when her face fell at the lack of excitement, I embellished a bit. My friends helped wayward girls, I said, victims of abuse or kids who were kicked out by families who couldn't accept them. There was a whole network.

"Ooh," she gasped, hands to her chest, "it sounds just like a movie I saw on Lifetime. The poor dears, perhaps they could use the clothes?"

I instantly felt like a heel, and not a Ferragamo, either. There *should* be an organization like this. There undoubtedly already was. I thought back to when I was first vamped, to all of those kids willing to become vampire fodder because it seemed better than the lives they'd been living. Maybe when all was said and done and I was my own vamp again, I could contribute to a better solution.

Mr. M returned with the phone—cordless rather than cell—I had a moment of . . . not exactly panic, but something strangely close to it. My parents. I didn't know how I felt about them or how they'd feel about me. Laurel had said that my parents were funding her group, so they had to know I was back in town, right? But they hadn't been waiting with open arms. Granted, it hadn't been long, but if I'd thought *my* daughter dead and then she'd resurfaced, I couldn't imagine wasting any time getting to her. On the other hand, given what I'd just been thinking, about kids on the run from their lives, my problems with my parents suddenly seemed very small.

"Something wrong?" Mr. Mendelson asked, at whatever expression had made it to my face.

I'd been staring at the phone in his hand, but now I looked up at him.

"No," I said, feeling like it was at least a semi-honest answer. "What did they say?"

"They're on their way. I had no idea your parents were so charitable. They could easily have waited until tomorrow or turned me down cold, but somehow they must have sensed it was important."

A feeling of warmth spread through me. Maybe Silvio had left them a message that I was coming. Or maybe they saw through the ruse, knowing or at least hoping that I was behind it. Mr. M had called and they were about to come running.

For me.

I wouldn't allow the thought that it was anything else, like that they were glad to have an excuse to get rid of my stuff and any final reminders of me.

7

While we waited for my parents, I pretended to sip the tea Mr. Mendelson had brought and spun a story, only slightly exaggerating my ex-boyfriend Chaz's anger the night we were sideswiped and ran his cherry red convertible into a tree. They'd probably already heard that I'd died in a car accident. It wasn't a stretch to say that I'd survived but had to fake my own death to get away from him. Or his friends who might come after me, in case they'd heard it was a double fatality. I felt a little guilty using Chaz that way, even after having it drummed into me at super spy training that the best stories always held an element of truth. And that begged the question—could a person who was already damned feel guilt? I wanted to think that it was a sign that I wasn't actually soulless as myth would have it, but really, I didn't know. Maybe somewhere in the federal archives I could find that answer, assuming I ever got the luxury of a look.

Apparently almost dying in that lake had put me in a think-y mood. I didn't usually dwell on all of this sort of stuff. I was more a take-it-as-it-comes kind of girl.

I tensed when the doorbell rang, even though it was a relief not to have to tell any more tales. I waited for Mr. and Mrs. M to proceed me before quickly dumping my tea into one of the leafy plants in their mudroom and hoping the caffeine wouldn't kill the poor thing. Then I followed them to the foyer, trying hard not to squelch.

Mr. M opened the door while I stood out of the direct line of sight of anyone looking in from outside. But I was in position to see my parents, my mother in a designer coral track suit with a deeper orange-red cami underneath, her chestnut hair in a high ponytail that gave her an instant facelift—not that she needed one. She could easily be my older sister rather than my mother. I got my night-black hair from my father, who had only a few years ago started graying at the temples. He was still in his tailored suit pants but without a jacket or tie. He even had his top button undone, which I'd never seen outside of our house. Most shocking of all, he'd begun to grow a beard, even though there was as much salt as pepper in it. Mom held a garment bag full of clothes. My father held a recycling bin overflowing with shoes.

Mr. Mendelson was inviting them in, but they'd already looked past him and Mrs. M and zeroed in on me. They were inside in no time flat. Dad closed the door behind him before they both dropped what they carried and enveloped me in a group hug that set me back, not just physically but emotionally. I couldn't remember being hugged like this since . . . maybe ever. Or maybe it had happened when I was too small to remember.

My mother's perfume washed over me. Something by Chanel that smelled of musk and vanilla, orange and jasmine. And then a second scent overwhelmed me. Polo Black. I'd know it anywhere. My father.

I pulled back before . . . No, it was too late. The blood tears had already started to form. I brushed them away before Mr. or Mrs. M could notice.

My parents let me go, but only to the ends of their arms. They held me at that length to look me over. With my mother it was almost like looking in a mirror. I had the same heart-shaped face, pointed chin, snip of a nose and eyelashes for days. My features were all hers, only painted in my father's palette—black hair, crazy-green eyes, although mine were a slightly lighter shade than his depths-of-the-forest green. I studied them back, drinking them in.

"You left," I said, forgetting about the Mendelsons for a moment. Forgetting my story. "After I died, you . . . just left."

Mom flicked a glance at Mr. and Mrs. M and I remembered myself. "I mean—"

"Can you give us a moment?" my father asked the Mendelsons, offering a gentle smile to Mrs. M, who was tearing up at the sight of our reunion. "I'm so sorry, but this is all . . . overwhelming. Maybe we can go into your study or . . ."

"Oh, yes," Mr. Mendelson said, and I thought that his eyes were a little shiny as well. "Right this way."

He led us away from the kitchen and through a set of French

doors into a gray room with darker gray accents and a sleek black desk. I'd never have thought Mr. M would go for the modern look, but then, I'd never have expected him to take my death and resurrection in stride. I wondered for a second if that should make me suspicious. Of what, I had no idea. Anyway, I instantly beat myself up for the thought. Death had made me paranoid. Or maybe it was the Feds.

Mr. M closed the French doors behind us and the next thing I knew Mom, Dad and I stood facing each other in the suddenly small room, totally at a loss for what to say.

"We didn't know you'd come back," my dad said, looking me in the eyes. "We went away after you died because it hurt too much to live with all of the reminders."

"And once the funeral was over, there didn't seem to be anything to stay for," my mother continued. "But then there were sightings. Shirl called us nearly hysterical. She said she'd seen you and that you tried to attack her. We rushed back. I still don't know why. It was such a crazy story, but I guess we wanted to believe. Only by the time we returned, you'd gone. Or you'd been taken, but we didn't find that out until later. When the craziness started in Mozulla and the Ghouligans began advertising about vampires, we remembered Shirl's story, and we hoped there was something to it all. Though we couldn't quite believe . . . not until Laurel got in touch."

Mom reached out to touch me—my arms, my shoulders, my neck, as if to assure herself that I was really there. Really real. It was freaky. We'd never been a really touchy family, so it felt a little overwhelming . . . I had the sudden childish urge to go ghosty just to hear her squeak.

"How did you get hooked up with Laurel?" I asked instead.

"She found us. I guess she knew you and thought we might be able to help."

"Which we have," my father said. "As best we can. We're told the Feds are watching, so I guess you can say we've done what we always do, throw money at things."

This, at least, was familiar ground.

"We didn't know that it would bring you back to us," Mom said, pulling me back in for another hug. If all this sweetness kept up, I was going to go into sugar shock. Really, it was almost claustrophobic. For someone who didn't have to breathe, I was suddenly doing a lot of it. Nervous breathing, I guessed. Almost hyperventilating.

"What's wrong?" Mom asked, still hugging me but sensing something of my turmoil. Maybe I'd tensed?

"I'm just . . . not used to all this," I said lamely. "I—" *Didn't think you cared* sounded so pathetic. And not entirely accurate. I always known they'd cared on some level, in their distant, convenient sort of way.

"I—" I tried again.

Mom shocked me with a sudden sob and I stopped fumbling for words. I brought my arms up to hug her back.

"We thought we'd lost you," she said, sounding strangled.

Damn, there was moisture in the corners of my eyes. Those blood tears again. I had no idea seeing my parents would have this kind of effect on me.

"You too," I answered, and suddenly I was hugging her fiercely. And then Dad was hugging us both. And then it was a good thing that I didn't have to breathe because between the dueling colognes and the strength of their hugs I might never have survived.

Finally Dad let up. And then Mom. And we were back to staring at each other, only it didn't seem so awkward anymore.

Dad put his arm around Mom, as though to stop her from launching in again. "We'd better go for now," he said. "The government people are watching us and it might seem odd if we stay longer than it would take to drop off the clothes and make polite chitchat. We don't want to get them interested in the Mendelsons. But, we want to see you again. Oracle says you have an important role to play in what's happening here, so I understand you might be busy for a bit, but you won't leave again without saying goodbye, will you? You won't be a stranger?"

I laughed, and it was a dry sound. My throat still hadn't recovered from the burn of the lake water. Or maybe it was the tears making it sting. "You don't get much stranger than me, but no, you're not going to lose me again. I promise."

I hoped the Feds wouldn't make a liar out of me.

"Is there anything else we can do before we go?" Mom asked.

I needed blood. I wasn't misting out of here again without

feeding, but there was no way—absolutely no way—I was biting into my parents. And not just because I didn't want to freak out the Mendelsons.

"No," I said, reaching out to take her hand and squeeze. "Thank you."

She squeezed back and then pulled me in for one more hug and a kiss to the cheek. "So soft," she said, touching my face. "Does the vampire transformation do that? Maybe—"

"No," my father said. It wasn't even up for discussion. "One vampire in the family is enough."

"We'll talk," my mother said as my father pulled her away. "You stay safe."

"Wait!" I said as he reached for the door. I'd called out in reaction to watching them walk away, but I knew there was something else. Something I had to tell them. Oh, right— "The Mendelsons don't know," I said. "About the whole vampire thing. They think I'm back from the dead. Or more accurately that I faked my own death. I wasn't sure how they'd feel about vampire-me."

"Got it," my father said. "Your secret is safe with us."

So funny that just twenty-four hours ago I'd been desperate to do away with secrets, to expose vampires to the world and the Feds' facilities as well. Now I was back to secrets and skullduggery.

I followed my parents to the front door where the Mendelsons rejoined us and we all said our good-byes. Then I had to watch my parents walk away, leaving me behind. But not for good. Not this time. It made all the difference.

When they were gone and I turned to thank the Mendelsons, I found I wasn't the only one brushing tears out of my eyes. Mrs. M produced a tissue from somewhere up her sleeve and offered one to me before taking one for herself, then sniffled as she gave me a great big hug for the road. Mr. M insisted that I take some of the clothes Mom and Dad had brought "for those poor girls" I'd made up on the fly. After hearing about the family who'd lost everything in the fire, taking anything for my own purposes seemed frivolous, but I reminded myself that presentation was important when talking to the vampire council. I could donate the clothes later. Or buy new clothes to donate.

Before my strength ran out or I could spin myself into a new tizzy, I went through the clothes and shoes and made a few selections. I zipped the shoes into the bottom of the garment bag and left the clothes I hadn't chosen on top of the recycling bin holding the rest of the donations. It was especially hard to say good-bye to the shoes, but they were going to a good cause and stilettos no longer fit my lifestyle—fighting, running, kicking butt. It was a sad commentary on the state of affairs.

I grabbed up my garment bag and Mr. M let me out the back door again, back the way I'd come. If I was lucky, the Feds were still watching my parents and not the lake, because I didn't have the energy to mist again. I was thankful for my stealth-black T-shirt and skinny jeans, which stuck to me like a soaky second skin. In the dark night, I hoped to be just one of the shadows. I kept as close as I could to the water without risking myself and as far as I could get away from any motion-detecting security lights.

I was beyond exhausted by the time I knocked on the back porch of our borrowed lake house. There was a minute before anyone came to answer, and then it was David who appeared at the sliding glass door, one hand hidden behind his back, concealing a weapon, I suspected.

As soon as he saw me, he brought the hand around front and I was startled to see that it held a gun. The better to protect from Feds, I guessed, since vampires had to be invited in. But really . . . *a gun*. He was prepared for a shootout. It was the first time I appreciated that we really were at war, though "appreciated" was definitely the wrong word.

"Gina!" he said. "You look like something the cat dragged in."

"Yeah, well, that seems appropriate, since we're both equally allergic to water. You going to let me in or what?"

I didn't have to be invited, since their bringing me in earlier had granted me entrance, but I *did* need the door unlocked unless they planned for me to bust my way through or pick the lock.

"You can't ghost in or whatever it is you do?"

I wasn't about to tell him I was lucky I could stand.

"Not at the moment," I said.

David unlocked the door and moved aside so that I could get past him. I was happy to see Bobby and the others when I got into the kitchen. Bobby immediately came to take the garment bag from me, not because I wasn't fully capable, but because he could see what David hadn't—that I had to sit down or fall down. At that moment, I wasn't too particular about which.

"You okay?" he asked.

I shook my head and continued on into the dining room where I collapsed into the nearest empty chair.

"Got clothes," I announced, because everyone was staring at me and I had to say something.

"What happened to you?" Marcy asked.

"The lake happened to me. Remember Salem?"

Her eyes went big and she nodded. "I never even considered that you misting over water would be the same as me swimming in it."

"Just another fun fact," I said. My hair was still dripping down my back. I hoped the chairs were well-protected from water damage. I looked to Laurel. "I need to eat. *Soon.*"

Being vamp herself, she understood what that meant, and she looked around the table at the people with us. Because while we could take vamp blood, it wouldn't sustain us for long—not unless *that* vamp had recently fed. It took fresh blood, preferably straight from the vein. Which was weird, because vamp blood did amazing things for *humans* in need.

I had a thought, so sudden it had me sitting up straighter in my chair. *What if vampires and humans were always meant to be together, like . . . what was the word? Not synonyms, but . . . symbiotes, that was it! What if we were meant to feed on people and filter their blood back to them with all the good healing stuff mixed in? What if we were never meant to be predators and prey at all?*

"What?" Bobby asked, probably reading my mind, but wanting me to share with the class.

I did. I told them my idea, and everyone was stunned silent while they digested it. I, Gina Covello, fashionista of the fanged, had literally stunned people speechless with a thought.

"Interesting," Imanyi said finally. "But it doesn't actually change anything. It's not about what we might know, but what we can get people to accept."

I slumped again. Yeah, that was the problem, wasn't it. Even in our "modern" society we couldn't get everyone to recognize racial equality or to share restrooms with the transgendered or to accept that a pentagram wasn't a Satanic symbol and a hijab did not hide a terrorist. Women had long since gotten the right to vote and held about every kind of public office and yet we had victim blaming and slut shaming and all kinds of objectification. Women still had to fight for the right to make decisions about our own bodies.

"They have to see us to accept us," I said. "Familiarity breeds . . ." and then I remembered the rest of that saying.

"Contempt," Imanyi finished for me.

But was that true? The garlic and holy water bomb lobbed at Bobby and Marcy outside the Ghouligan's studio argued for it, but word was just starting to spread. Surely with enough exposure, people would see that we weren't monsters—which would be all well and good until our first feral vamp went on a rampage, someone like Alistaire. Despite killer examples like Jeffrey Dahmer, John Wayne Gacy, Ted Bundy and BTK people didn't look at every white man and think *serial killer*, but all it took was one minority and suddenly everyone was suspect. It wasn't sense, it was insanity.

"But about that feeding?" I said, focusing on the one thing I could control right now. Sort of, anyway. It did require a volunteer.

"I'll do it," Silvio said with a grin.

"You gave blood two days ago," Laurel said. "You sure you're good to go again so soon?"

"Don't worry, I've had plenty of red meat. And iron pills. I'm good."

"In the other room?" I said, not wanting to feed in front of everyone. I was sure it was nothing they hadn't seen before, particularly the vamps, but there was always something a little intimate about it too, especially where humans were involved. There was something in our bite that made it feel good to the donors, sometimes too good.

"If you wanted to get me alone, all you had to do was say so," Silvio joked.

Bobby growled.

I rolled my eyes.

"Never mind, here is fine," I said.

Laughing, Silvio got up out of his chair to come around to me. "Suit yourself."

He held out his wrist, and I eyed it for a minute, looking for the best spot, and then I took his arm in my hands and sank my teeth in. His blood flooded my mouth, warm and heady. If caffeine was alcohol, he'd be over the legal limit. The blood rushing in made me feel zippy, like I was hopped up on caffeine and sugar. Like I used to feel after a venti mocha. I was getting a little high off of it. Silvio actually moaned.

"That's enough," someone said, though it took me a second to hear it.

Someone shook my shoulder. "Gina."

I took one more gulp and reluctantly withdrew my fangs. Silvio had a silly look on his face, like he'd just seen a girl's breasts for the first time.

I snapped my fingers in front of him. "Silvio. Earth to Silvio. All done."

He blinked and shot me a grin of Cheshire Cat proportions. "Any time," he said.

He walked unsteadily back to his seat, and I found it hard to keep mine. Now that I was all hyped up, I wanted to move. I was ready to take on the vampire council and any super villains the universe wanted to send my way. Maybe Magneto. Michael Fassbinder was *hot*.

"Okay, let's do this thing!" I said.

Laurel gave a world-weary sigh, like she was a parent or teacher or something. "First, we need a plan. Do we want the council to work with us to take down the Federal facility or just take in the vamps we free? Should we negotiate a sort of treaty so that if we release the vamps to them they won't retaliate against mankind or anything—a sort of non-aggression treaty."

"Do we want them to agree to leave Mozulla?" David asked.

"Or turn over the killers among them for justice?" Imanyi put in.

Was she thinking about her brother? Who did she want him turned over to? The police? There was no way they'd be prepared to handle a vampire. She couldn't mean the Feds, not knowing what they did. Not with us about to go up against them. Or did she mean she wanted us to deal out justice? And in what form?

"If we go in looking for treaties," Brent said, "it will take forever. Things will have to be debated, voted on, ratified and all that.

And it will only apply to the local council. Anything more far reaching would have to be taken before the general council, which means more delays, arguing, backroom deals. It could take months."

Marcy let her head thump to the table and when she raised it again, she said, "Great, vampire politics. What's the point of eternal life if you spend it in meetings?"

"Some people like that sort of thing," Brent said, a little defensively, I thought.

Marcy stared at him like he'd suddenly grown a second head. Or a pig's snout. Or pink bunny ears. Or . . . or . . . Yup, I was zippy.

"Never mind," Brent huffed. "I'm just saying we probably don't have that kind of time."

"So what then?" I asked.

Bobby was thinking so hard I could almost hear him. Almost. He was the telepath, so he had to be sending for me to receive, but it was as though his thoughts were too big to stay contained, rolling over and over each other like tussling pups.

"We can't go in as supplicants and right now we can't crash in from a position of power—not with just us nine and the Feds still to fight. We need leverage for a good bargaining position. We need the vamps that are in federal custody. That means we need to raid the Feds on our own."

"But before that, we need to warn the council vamps that the Feds are coming for them," Laurel said. "And make sure the council doesn't have plans that will conflict with ours."

"So it's parlay now, treaty later," I said, pretty proud of myself for that word, parlay. I'd learned it from *Pirates of the Caribbean*, Jack Sparrow being *very* memorable.

"Um, yeah," Laurel answered. "Are you still game? As far as I know, the council hasn't called off that Kill or Capture order on you."

"Pah, that old thing!" They could try to enforce it. I'd just mist right out of their hands. What were they going to do, spray holy water on me? The advantage to dealing with people with the same weaknesses was that, well, they had the same weaknesses. Vampires weren't going to wave around UV lights or hurl crosses and garlic at me. They couldn't.

"I'll take Marcy with me, since we've already practiced going ghosty."

"Take me instead," Laurel insisted.

"That doesn't make any sense. Marcy's already taken my blood. We know what we're doing and we've already been a team, so we can each predict what the other will do. With you—what if I zig and you zag?"

"That's what I'm worried about," she mumbled, which didn't work at all with vamp hearing, which she would know. Meaning, she meant for me to hear her.

"What?" I asked, trying not to jump to conclusions, but as *Buffy the Vampire Slayer* had once said, "I took a small step, and there conclusions were." (Yeah, I wasn't thinking about the irony of quoting a vampire slayer when I was one of the fanged.)

"You're already on the council's bad side," she said. "I just don't think you should be the one playing ambassador."

"I get it—you need me to get you out if anything happens, but otherwise I should be seen and not heard, be a dutiful little foot soldier and let you take the lead. First, I've never been much good at that. And second, if you are our leader," I was going to leave that open to debate, "do you really want to put yourself in their hands if things go wrong? Aren't you needed here?"

"I'm counting on you to make sure things *don't* go wrong."

"So you trust me to get you out, but not to handle things on my own?"

"Yes."

There was dead silence in the room. And I mean *dead*. If anyone had so much as taken a breath, they were holding it now.

"*Whatever*," I said finally. "Set it up. But I want to talk to Chickzilla."

Breath whooshed out of several mouths, and I smiled. I'm not sure it was reassuring. It wasn't really meant to be. I'd go with the flow as long as I agreed with it. After that, well, Alistaire had called me chaos. So far he hadn't been wrong. The cool thing about chaos was that it was by nature unpredictable and that meant you couldn't plan for it. Or pin it down.

"Done," Silvio said, typing a number he read from his screen into a phone. It looked like a cheap model, maybe a burner. He let it ring once before handing the phone to Laurel.

She walked into the kitchen, maybe for greater quiet, but I was interested to hear what she had to say, so I followed. Vamp hearing was an amazing thing, but if everyone started talking behind her, I'd still have trouble weeding out the phone conversation from the background noise.

"Carrie," she said, in such a way that I thought maybe she'd gotten Chickzilla's voicemail, "you won't remember me, but I'm one of Mellisande's former recruits. I have another recruit here you might remember—Gina Covello. She certainly remembers you. And she—we—want to talk. We have very important information to share, but will only trade it for our safety, which given the council's feelings means it's better if you come alone. Offer's off the table at sunrise."

Laurel looked at me as she hung up. "I hope you're right about her."

I shrugged. "She follows orders, but she isn't always happy about them. I figured we could maybe work with that. Better the devil you know, right?"

8

Chickzilla called back, and the meet was set up for one hour later in a park not far from the elementary school. Not enough time for us to scout in advance and set up any kind of ambush—or for them either. Or that was the hope. We'd chosen the time; Chickzilla had chosen the place. That meant it was suspect.

I'd pawed through the clothes in the bag and found a deep purple top with bling at the bust and my favorite pair of designer jeans, which should do for a walk in the woods. I didn't have anything with which to replace my soggy sneakers, since Mom had chosen the best of the best of my shoes and while I'd forgone the spiky stilettos, I'd kept my Grecian-style sandals and my wedge heels. I did like my extra height.

"Blow dry the sneakers," Marcy suggested.

"Or put them in the dryer," Silvio said.

I'd done the latter, since I had better uses for the blow dryer after taking the world's quickest shower (learned in spy school) to wash out the lake water.

I had one more thing to do before we left—the blood exchange with Laurel so that I'd be able to whisk us away if we were in a tight spot. Silvio, of course, wanted to watch, but we shot him looks sharp enough to kill and took it into the living room.

Not long after, I stood at the entrance to the park with Laurel, my toes getting pruny in my still-damp sneaks. So stylin'.

Sunshine Park brought back memories. I remembered going there with my nanny as a kid, climbing around on the jungle gym, waiting my turn for the slide—after she'd gone over everything in sight with disinfecting wipes. I remembered screaming gleefully when one of the older kids played monster and chased the rest of us around, giving Nanny Truesdale fits. And heaven forbid someone should cough or sneeze or wipe their nose on their sleeve! Nanny T was always a nervous wreck by the time we left. And by then my face stung from the frequent and enthusiastic application of her handwipes. Ah yes, good times.

The playground was at the center of the park. There were also hiking trails, picnic tables, a field for playing frisbee and tossing a ball around. Aside from the chance for ambush along the way, the park was a good choice. It closed at sundown. There were no video cameras and no one to see us.

Chickzilla waited for us on one of the swings, toeing the wood chips that covered the ground in a protective layer and swinging desultorily as she watched for our approach.

It was so weird to see her there, as though no time had passed. Her bright blonde hair was still pulled back into her ever-present ponytail and glowed like a halo in the streetlights at the four corners of the playground. The only difference was that it seemed Chickzilla had finally given up her unitards in favor of bicycle shorts and a T-shirt, though it was possible the T-shirt just thrown *over* the unitard. I wondered, but not enough to ask.

She studied us as we came up the walkway, a smile forming on her face at the sight of me.

"You haven't changed a bit," she said as we breached the entrance to the playground, close enough to talk without shouting.

"Neither have you," I answered.

"Well, actually . . ." she broadened her smile and I caught the flash of fang.

"Right. I heard about that. Um, congratulations?"

"It was about damned time. Literally, I guess. And, hey, I got vamped at the peak of my performance." She flexed, and I thought of She-Hulk. Laurel and I had a close up view of the gun show, and I had to admit it was something.

I wondered whether all the work she'd put into her body before being vamped made her a super-super strong vamp or whether our strength was sort of baseline, which would piss me off if I was her.

"Impressive," Laurel said, reminding us both that she was there.

"Thanks."

Chickzilla motioned to the other swings like she was offering us a seat. "So, you wanted to talk?"

I took the swing next to Chickzilla and used it for its intended purpose. At least, I used my toes to swing myself just a touch.

What I really wanted was to twist myself round and round until the chains on the swing wouldn't go any farther and then let them unravel and spin me out like I had when I was a kid. Maybe I'd get one of those in before we left.

Chickzilla was looking at me and I was looking innocently up toward the sky. This was Laurel's show, for now.

"We wanted to touch base and see what plans the council has for dealing with the Feds," Laurel began.

"Why?" Chickzilla asked, cocking her head like a bird.

"Because—"

"Wait," Chick said, holding up a hand. "Strip first."

Laurel's eyes about fell out of her head. "What?"

"So I know you're not wearing a wire. Strip. Down to your skivvies. Bras and panties are fine. Nothing I wouldn't see at the beach."

Chickzilla waited, rocking on the swing as if she had all night. She paused when we didn't start immediately. "Shy? I wouldn't have thought that of Gina here, but as good faith, I'll go first." She released the chains of the swing to grab the bottom of her T-shirt and whip it over her head. So that answered that question—she still wore her trademark unitard underneath, lime green today. Muscles bulged, straining the stretchy fabric, but only muscles, as far as I could tell. That didn't mean we didn't have directional mics or anything else aimed our way, but I couldn't see why we would—unless Chickzilla was working with the Feds, in which case they'd be closing in already rather than simply eavesdropping.

I sighed and lifted the edges of my shirt. I didn't pull it over my head, but I did pull it up long enough for her to see there wasn't anything underneath. I glared pointedly at Laurel as I undid the button of my jeans. If I was stripping down, so was she.

Laurel glared back and started undoing the buttons on her top. She flashed us at lightning speed before buttoning up again and Chickzilla laughed as she did. "Oh, honey, if I wanted to see boobs, I'd look in a mirror."

That didn't seem to make Laurel feel any better. "Okay, enough," she said. "We're not dropping our pants." Well, yay for that! "We've got serious business here and we're burning night. What are your plans?"

"Can't tell you," Chick said, resuming her swing.

It didn't take vamp-o-vision to see the steam coming out of Laurel's ears.

"How about this," I cut in. "Can you tell us if you have any plans to move on the Feds over the next few days?"

Laurel kicked me in the shin. I kicked back.

Chick laser-focused on me. "Why?"

"You don't get to answer a question with a question. Or, you *can*, but that's no way to get answers out of me."

Chick huffed. "Fine. No, not at the moment. We're still doing recon. There are indications that they're preparing to bug out. We figure they might be most vulnerable on the move. Your turn."

"There are also indications they want to take more of you with them when they go," I answered.

I could see the words hit home. Chickzilla's lips flatlined.

"You mean more of *us*?" she asked.

"You, us, vamps, whatever. They don't intend to leave you behind. You'd better be wary."

"Why are you telling me this?" she asked. "I thought you were against the council. You've certainly screwed with them enough."

Neither of us were looking to Laurel now.

"I want us all working together, not against each other. I don't want the federal facilities, but I also don't want the killings, the disappearances, the turf wars. I don't want anyone to have an excuse to fear us or lock us up. I want things to change."

"So naive, to think things will change just like that." She snapped.

"They certainly won't if we don't try. I want to negotiate. Tell the council we're coming to them in good faith. Tell them we want to talk."

"You can tell them yourself," Chickzilla said, shoving her fingers into her mouth and giving a high-pitched whistle.

Laurel and I glared around and sure enough there were vamps coming from every direction, converging on the playground.

I swung my gaze back on Chickzilla and we locked eyes. "Not cool," I said.

"Don't worry, I got them to agree to capture rather than kill."

I surged up out of my swing to grab Laurel, but Chickzilla was now just as inhumanly fast and had me by the back of the jeans before I was fully upright. She swung me around hard, away from Laurel, letting me go as maximum momentum would send me flying. Laurel jumped on her as I was flung away, down to one knee, skinning it on the wood chips that covered the floor of the playground. The knee would heal, but my temper . . .

I jumped to my feet again and lunged for Laurel, who was flying back from Chickzilla's fist to her face, but I was caught up short by a vamp who'd come up fast and now had a fistful of my shirt. I heard the seams start to rip in his grip, but as I whirled toward him anyway. My fangs flashed and my fingers curled into claws aimed at his eyes. I didn't recognize the bristly-faced beast I was facing. He looked more Mountain Man than Mozulla, but his eyes gouged like anyone else's, and he growled, but didn't let go, using my shirt as a fulcrum to swing me into the swingset pole, which clanged like real iron.

My vision doubled, but I hugged all the poles until they resolved into one and used the leverage to kick back, catching him, I hoped, in some sensitive spot. This time he grunted and when his grip started to loosen on my shirt, I ripped myself away regardless of my beleaguered seams. Hell, any vamps who'd been in hiding had probably gotten an eyeful already when Chickzilla checked us for wires.

Momentarily free, I grabbed for Laurel, who'd fallen to the ground not far from me, and as soon as I had a hand on her, I ghosted us both out.

Something dense came crashing down where we'd been—a foot, a body? I could only tell that it displaced a lot of air and shot me through with an uncomfortable sensation of compression before we misted through and around. I didn't let it screw with my focus, but concentrated on bringing us up, up and over the swings and the ambush party below, out over the rest of the playground and onto the path just outside the park. It was familiar enough to me that directions and distances were no issue at all.

When we rematerialized, Laurel punched me in the arm. "So much for your great contact," she said.

"So much for your great plan," I answered.

"At least we know that the coast is clear with the Feds for now."

"So success then," I said.

She eyed me. "Is that what you call it."

"We're alive and we're free. You've got to look on the bright side."

9

It had been a long night full of learning experiences. I'd learned I could tandem mist. Running water kicked my forever-firm behind. Mom and Dad gave a damn. And being vamped hadn't imbued Chickzilla with supernatural fashion sense. Or any other kind of sense that I could determine.

It was almost dawn and I was ready to sleep like the dead. Literally.

There were four bedrooms, and luckily by the virtue of us vamps needing absolute dark and the huge windows throughout the rest of the house not offering that option, Bobby and I got one of the rooms, which had been fitted with black-out shades. I wondered if that had been part of my parents throwing money at the problem or whether they'd been there all along. But I was too tired for questions. Not quite too tired, though, to appreciate when Bobby curled around me, spooning me against him, his head resting on my shoulder and his arm wrapped around me. He didn't try anything, not with the sun being minutes away from rising. We just lay there snuggled until the sun came up and our eyelids snapped down like the shutters on a coin-operated viewer at a tourist trap.

We woke hours later—woke being a euphemism for snapped back to the land of the living. Seriously, the movies all had it wrong. Anyone who encountered us during the day wouldn't think "vamps," they'd think "bodies." Probably call homicide. Maybe even open the blinds for a better look and make it a reality, burning us to a crisp. Maybe that was how rumors of spontaneous human combustion started.

Fun thoughts for first thing in the evening.

Tonight's awakening seemed to be brought to us by the letter B for Breakfast. It didn't take vamp senses to pick up on the smells of coffee and bacon. Bobby's arm lifted from around my waist and he propped himself up on one arm, looking down at me.

"I miss bacon," he said dreamily. So romantic.

"Me too," I answered, not surprised to find my fangs extended. It seemed to be the vamp version of salivation.

"Maybe someone will let us bite them after breakfast? Bacon-flavored blood? Do you think that's a thing?"

"We could find out."

He smiled down at me like I'd just said something wonderful. "You're cute when you're mussed from sleep."

I wrinkled my nose at him. "Aren't you supposed to think I'm perfect? I don't do *mussed*."

"But you are perfect," he said, staring into my eyes.

My heart flipped. It wasn't doing much else anyway. Certainly not beating. I pulled him down for a kiss that felt so good I kept at it. Bobby shifted for a better angle, and—

A hard knock at the door surprised us apart. "We're burning night here, people," someone said. Silvio, I thought. If I had a hit list, I'd seriously consider adding him to it.

Bobby threw a pillow at the door and leaned down to kiss me again, but the moment was lost, and we got up before too long, me staggering to the door like I was more zombie than vampire. Bobby always seemed to wake up more easily. Maybe he'd been that way in life too. He might even have been—the horror!—*a morning person.*

I had to know the truth. I gave Bobby the side-eye and said, "You were a morning person, weren't you?"

He stopped short of pulling open the door to look back at me. "Kind of. That a problem?"

I considered. "Not unless you start humming or, worse, whistling. I'm pretty sure whistling is a killing offense."

"Wow, they play rough in the United States of Gina."

"Damn straight. Don't even ask me the penalty for spitting tobacco. Or wearing polka dots with plaid."

"What?"

"Seriously, don't ask." Because I couldn't think of anything appropriately heinous.

Bobby smiled, and it was a little lopsided and a lot endearing. "After you," he said, opening the door for me.

"You just want to watch me walk away."

"Yup."

The smell of coffee and bacon was stronger than ever. There was also egg and cheese and sausage.

I might have moaned.

"You okay?" Bobby asked.

I looked back at him.

"Oh . . . *oh*," he answered.

He closed his eyes and took in a big breath himself. "I miss it too," he said, repeating his waking statement.

I led the way to the kitchen and tried not to drool as David loaded plates with scrambled eggs and cheese. There were serving plates already heaped with bacon and sausage, I guessed so that people could help themselves. There was another with toast, already buttered.

When I'd been alive, breakfast had been my favorite meal of the day, whenever I got around to it.

Imanyi, Silvio and Paige were already there as well, taking the proffered plates the second they were available. I wondered if that meant they'd slept over and were keeping vamp hours. It seemed so.

Laurel appeared a second later, rubbing sleep out of her eyes and smoothing down her blonde hair, which had been kinked all out of sorts on one side—no doubt the side on which she slept. There was no sign of Brent and Marcy, and if I knew them like I thought I did, there might not be for awhile, long enough to get up to something.

I glanced at Bobby, wondering whether we had time to roll around while the others ate. He smirked back at me like he was thinking the same thing.

Laurel gave up on her hair and glanced around at the others, catching us up in her gaze before we could put our idea into action. "You're all here. Who had day shift?" Silvio looked up from his plate and said with a mouth full of eggs, "Me." He chewed and swallowed. "I'm skipping the coffee. I'm going to catch a catnap while you all do the recon, the bump and grab and whatever else you need to do to get ready to break into a federal facility. I'll be up in time for backup. You know me, I don't need a lot of sleep. Couple hours will do."

"I don't know that it's going to be as easy as you all think," I said. "For one, a keycard alone won't do a thing. They use fingerprint scanners and stuff like that. Might have even upgraded to facial recognition or retinal scans. The last time we broke into one of their facilities, I ghosted in and we used an electromagnetic pulse machine to wipe out their tech. They're bound to have learned something from that break-in, though. Tightened security. Plus now they have those hand scanners we saw back at the checkpoint. I don't know what they alert on, but the supernatural for sure, which means there's a good chance they'll see us coming."

"What do you suggest?" Laurel asked—not like she thought I actually had a suggestion, but like she'd catch me out.

"Chickzilla seemed to think they'd be most vulnerable when they move. That's when they break people out in all the prison movies."

"And if they move during the day?"

I didn't have an answer for that.

"Okay, so we do this my way," she said when I didn't respond.

Marcy and Brent came in silently. I'd barely registered their presence before Marcy was whispering in my ear, "I have a bad feeling about this."

I nodded back, but didn't say a word. Laurel was already watching us. Well, I was watching her right back. And the plans and prep. Until we actually went in, it wasn't too late to pull the plug.

She set Marcy and me to do surveillance on the facility—who and what went in and out, shift changes, any unusual activity. I thought about protesting. It seemed like busy work to me. They'd already have studied the place; they ought to have formed a pretty complete picture. But the truth was that I wanted to see it for myself. I didn't want to trust myself to someone else's perceptions. Bobby, Brent and the rest were divided between staying here in the nerve center of things (Silvio and Paige), shopping for supplies (Imanyi and David), and waylaying known workers at the federal facility (Laurel, Bobby and Brent). I would have been jealous about the shopping if they were planning to hit anything but a home improvement store. I *was* jealous of Laurel working

with Bobby, especially since she was in shiny black leggings that
looked like leather but weren't and a long black T-shirt that with
her slicked-back hair managed to make her look chic instead of
casual. She looked like a runway model prepared to fight for her
place on the catwalk.

Marcy and I exchanged a look, as though she was thinking
the same thing, only replacing Bobby with Brent. Laurel hadn't
done anything but be gorgeous and smart. *And bossy as hell*, my
mind added. But neither Brent nor Bobby were the types to be
turned off by a strong woman. If so, they'd never have been with
Marcy and me.

I now knew exactly how Bobby had felt when Ulric, a goth
guy who'd been along on a few of our adventures, had flirted with
me mercilessly and I hadn't minded as much as I probably should
have. Damn, turn-about did not seem fair play at all.

Marcy and I were armed with binoculars, because we weren't
going to be able to get anywhere close to the facility, so even our
vamp vision wasn't likely to do us any good. We had a few other
tricks up our sleeves, but mostly we'd be there to watch, not en-
gage. Unless we got caught. If surveillance was boring enough we
might hope for a little action.

The facility was at the top of one of the few hills around with
only one road leading up. We couldn't take the road or we'd be
seen—video cameras would catch the car if not us—so the gang
had to drop us at a distance from the road at the base of the hill.
Marcy and I were going to have to trudge through trees to get
there, just in case said cameras were armed with special sensors
like the one we'd seen back at the checkpoint in Chicago. There
were two or three houses built on the hillside as well, but they
were set apart from each other and even if we could just go from
yard to yard, we'd risk exposure. So it was underbrush and over-
brush, branches slapping us in the face, vines threatening to trip
us up. Spiders and snakes and ticks, oh my! Did ticks like vamps?
Did they sense kindred spirits or did they prefer their blood fresh
as well? An interesting question I didn't want to learn the answer
to. Marcy and I could mist through the trees and avoid the first-
hand experience entirely.

We did just that, though I stopped us when I could feel the
trees thinning. Laurel said that the Feds had occasional patrols

scanning the woods and the area surrounding the facility. I didn't blame them. I wouldn't trust electronics alone to warn of an upcoming threat, especially not after we'd defeated them back at their Florida facility.

I materialized us, but a few inches too high, and so Marcy and I fell to the ground. She landed on a twig that snapped with a crack that seemed to pierce the night.

"Sorry," she whispered.

I held up a finger to shush her, to listen for guards or that patrol Laurel had mentioned, but I didn't hear anything.

Apparently, neither did she. A second later, Marcy asked, "What now?"

"I guess we get to the edge of these trees and look for the entrance to the facility."

We did that, but it was about as exciting as watching paint dry. Unlike the facility in Florida, which had looked to be a burntout medical center, this place looked like a fortress or a high security prison. A cement wall ran all around the facility with spiky metal pinwheels of doom all along the top, as if someone had taken throwing stars, strung them along a pole like someone might string popcorn for holiday garland, and mounted them on top of the cement. Fun stuff. The only entrance stood at the end of the road in, made up of two solid metal doors—or perhaps metal sheeting over some lighter core—large enough to allow in a tank if need be. They looked as though they'd swing inward with the proper clearance, which, of course, we didn't have.

Marcy and I climbed a tree at an angle to the entrance hoping to see over the walls, but it was a no-go. The trees were tall enough, although the branches were so thin toward the top that if Marcy and I weighed an extra ounce they might not support us, but there was some kind of camouflage netting over the top of the facility, almost like a giant mosquito net. Apt, I supposed, if they were trying to keep out us bloodsuckers.

"We need to see inside," I said to Marcy.

"Hush," she drew it out into a hiss.

"Don't shush me," I said.

"No, really!" She pointed down the way and sure enough one of the patrols Laurel had warned us about was headed our way. Marcy and I pulled farther back into the tree canopy, using the leaves and branches as camouflage of our own. Then we stayed deadly still, no rustle at all to give us away. Before I'd ducked back, I noticed there were three in the patrol, all armed with guns. I didn't know what ammo they used, but it didn't really matter. Even regular bullets, strategically aimed, could take us down long enough for capture. And wooden bullets well aimed could really ruin our eternity.

There was no chatter from the patrol below. No monologuing, which would have been helpful. A simple, "So, Biff, when are you and your team heading out, leaving the facility totally vulnerable?" or "Yo, Jake, you're on that first transport, right? The one with all the vamps tomorrow evening at nine?" Nope, nothing like that. We had to count on the boys and Laurel for intel.

Or did we?

If Marcy and I could only get a closer look at everything . . . I schemed while the patrol went past. I could have misted us out of there at any time, but the sudden release of our weight on the tree limbs would have caused some backlash and might have tipped the Feds off that we were there. I didn't want that.

I'd been to a Renaissance Fair a few years ago with Marcy and our friend Becca, and a song we'd heard some pirate wenches sing was playing through my head now. *"Get in, get out. Quit screwin' about. Yo ho, yo ho, yo ho."* It seemed like a pretty good mantra to me. This surveillance stuff was for the birds. Given our current perches, I meant that literally.

As soon as the patrol passed, I whispered to Marcy, "Your phone is on silent, right?"

The rebels had given us throwaway phones to keep in contact, in case Bobby wasn't tuned in to us mentally when we had a message to send.

"Of course."

"Okay then, let's go."

"Where?" she asked.

I wasn't giving her the chance to argue. I wrapped one arm more firmly around the branch I was holding and reached out with my other hand to grab Marcy. Then I willed us to go ghosty. It was a little harder than before, as though my blood was already being broken down by her body, but hard was not impossible. Not by a long shot. More slowly than I'd have liked, we faded out, going insubstantial, and I willed us to rise above the canopy of the trees and mist over and beyond the walls of the federal facility.

When I sensed the lack of free-flowing air beneath us, I knew we were over one of the buildings. I drove us a bit father, to a position I hoped was about central within the facility. Then I lowered us down until we misted right through their camo netting. When I felt more serious resistance, the density of floor beneath our feet, I materialized us again, bracing for an alarm just in case they had weight or motion sensors on the roof.

No alarm sounded. Marcy was practically shooting daggers at me from her eyes. She pulled her arm out of my grip the second she was corporeal and hauled back to give me a slap. Not at full vamp strength. Barely enough to make much of a sound, but enough to let me know she was *not happy*.

"What?" I asked, barely above a whisper. "Like curiosity wasn't getting the best of you too."

"Curiosity killed the cat," Marcy whispered back.

"You saying you're not tougher than any old cat."

"*They* have nine lives," she said.

"Yeah, and we're already into our second, which could last well on forever if you'll just shush."

Glaring. Daggers.

I'd seen the look before. I was unimpressed.

We had to keep low to avoid bumping the camouflage netting and setting off a ripple effect. And the lighting wasn't good with the netting blocking out the moon and no lights wasted on the roof that wasn't being used, not at the moment anyway. But vamp eyes adjusted quickly to the dark and it didn't take me more than a second to realize that this particular roof was broad and flat and painted with a design that looked something like a bulls-eye. A helipad! There was some chance the vamps wouldn't be evacuated by van or truck or tank or whatever at all. Not if the Feds chose to airlift them out.

In which case, there'd be nothing we could do. It only reinforced the idea that we couldn't wait for them to make their move. We didn't know how close the Feds were to bugging out, but it could happen at any time.

I pointed to the pattern, drawing Marcy's attention to it, and her eyes widened as she came to the same conclusion. The glare dissipated into determination, and Marcy nodded at me to continue, on board now. We crept low to the edge of the roof and slowly, cautiously, peeked our heads over to survey the ground below us—and immediately pulled our heads back and flattened ourselves against the roof to avoid being seen. Then I gave in to that cat-killing curiosity again and peered over, just a bit. Below us were two guards, one man, one woman, both smoking. Real cigarettes. The smell of burnt tobacco and acrid smoke rose up to tickle my nose despite the fact that I didn't have to breathe.

"Better hurry it up," the woman was saying. "It's long enough after dark now. They could come at any time."

The guy breathed out a couple of smoke rings, probably thinking he was hot stuff. "You really think they're that stupid?"

"I think they're that desperate. We have their people. We've made sure they know we're moving out. You think they're just going to let us go?"

The guy threw the end of his cigarette down, ground it under his foot, then picked it up, wrapped it in a napkin he took from his pocket and tucked it back in, stub and all. "You ready?"

"As I'll ever be," the woman said, slinging her gun around to a better angle so that she could squat and bury her stub in the ground outside the back door.

"Don't let Cobbs catch you doing that," the man said.

"Hasn't yet."

Then they were headed back inside and Marcy and I rolled to stare at each other. "It's a trap," she said. "They're expecting us."

"Don't we expect them to expect us?"

"I don't know, do we?" her brow wrinkled up. I wondered if mine was doing the same.

How had they "made sure" we knew they were leaving? Had the guy Bobby read let something slip intentionally or was there more to it? Had they planted the suggestion with one of our people? And had that person passed it on unwittingly or knowing it to be a trap

"Did you notice whether the smokers propped the back door?" I asked.

Marcy shook her head. "Not that careless. They used a keycard to get back in."

Interesting. Maybe this facility was well enough protected by the walls and whatever else they had going on that keycards were all that were necessary once inside. Maybe we could use that.

I started to say something to Marcy when alarms suddenly blared and sprinklers rose from the edges of the roof, coming on with a sputter and a pop. Pain hit me with the first drops. Instinctively, Marcy and I rolled away from the edge of the roof, trying to outpace the spray. From the burning pain, this wasn't any garden variety sprinkler. They were using holy water. They knew they'd been breached.

A crazy commotion rose from down below, complete with cries of pain. What the hell? Were we not the only vamps caught in the watery scattershot? Had Chickzilla lied to us that the council vamps weren't ready to go on the offensive? Had they come raiding just like the Feds hoped?

Twisty, tied-up thinking. But one thing was crystal clear—we were in trouble. The Feds were more than ready for us.

10

Rolling away was no solution. A second set of sprinklers shot up, lashing Marcy and me with the acid spray of more holy water. I screamed and grabbed Marcy, shoving the pain away like an unwanted advance so I could focus on going ghosty. Next thing I knew we were dropping right through the roof and onto the floor below. I made us rematerialize before we could drop through that as well, hoping and praying that the top level of the building was used as storage or offices and that we wouldn't reappear in a guardroom.

As usual, I put us a bit above the flooring rather than risk burying us in it. Marcy and I both dropped to our feet in a ready stance, prepared to take on whatever came. The alarms were blaring inside as well, but the three occupants of the room weren't coming at us any time soon. They lay deadly still in their beds—no breathing, no rising and falling of chests. Just the faint shushing sounds and occasional beeps of the huge machines they were hooked up to. I stepped toward the closest bed, taking in the emaciated form of the vampire there and the fact that she was strapped down to the bed with wide leather straps. They wouldn't hold a vampire under normal conditions, but clearly these were anything but normal. These vampires had been starved. And the machines they were hooked up to seemed designed to keep them that way, sucking blood out and trickling the faintest bit back in. Pale pink rather than robust red.

In horror, I made myself look at the faces of the three vamps strapped down this way, searching, I realized, for Alistaire, despite the fact that he was a homicidal lunatic. There always seemed to be a method to his madness, a kind of crazy cunning that made me think he was on our side. Maybe I was delusional. Maybe now wasn't the time to analyze it, especially since he wasn't here. I didn't know these vampires.

"What do we do?" Marcy asked.

"Free them," I said. "Maybe while the council vamps have everyone distracted we can do what we came here to do."

"But we can't take the whole place down. We don't have any explosive charges to set or video we can leak or . . ."

"Video of what? That's the genius of it—we can't record the victims. They won't appear on camera. All we have are the machines."

Marcy didn't like that. Neither did I.

"Call the others," I said. "Let them know what's going on. I'll see if I can figure out how to get everyone free."

"And then? We don't have any kind of exit plan."

I racked my brain. Nope, she was right. No plan.

"I laugh in the face of your plans," I said, hoping to reassure her with snark. "We had one—surveillance and then infiltration. Look at how well that's gone. Besides, I've always been more of a pantser."

"This from the girl who used to plan her wardrobe weeks in advance?"

Damn, she had me there. "Whatever. I got over it."

A fierce grin spread across Marcy's face. "So, we're winging it?"

"Damn straight."

"Whoo hoo!" she gave a little fist pump into the air and then realized she'd gotten a little loud.

Her head snapped toward the doorway in fear that she'd attracted attention, but the clamoring of the alarm had drowned her out. I hoped it would cover any other noise we might make. And that the guards were fully occupied elsewhere. If the council vamps hadn't infiltrated this far, there'd be no reason to conduct a room-to-room search. Not with the captive vamps in the condition they were in and unable to aid in their own rescue.

I studied the first machine, trying to figure out whether there was any good, safe shut-off switch, but it had a touch screen controller what wouldn't do a thing without a badge to activate it. I was going to have to do things the hard way. The Gina way. I grabbed one end of the tubes and pulled as slowly and steadily as I could. I didn't want to rip open anyone's veins and make it twice as hard for them to heal. Not when I needed them to follow us under their own steam. Immediately, the touch screen started to strobe red, and an alert bloop started up, quietly at first, but growing louder and louder as though frantic for someone to notice.

The vamp's eyes snapped open and fluttered closed again, her lashes dark against ashen skin, her hair dry and brittle from starvation. When I got to the second set of tubes, her hand twisted in its restraint and grabbed my wrist, squeezing to the point where she would have broken bones if she'd been at full strength. As it was, I could barely feel the pressure.

"Friend," I said, prying her fingers off my wrist. "We're getting you out of here. If you behave. Can you walk?"

Her eyes fluttered open again and stayed that way, though it took a second longer than it should have for her to focus on my face. Her lips moved, but nothing came out. She flicked out a tongue so dry it rasped against her lips, trying and failing to wet them.

She tried again to speak, and this time succeeded in a voice like that of a two-thousand year old mummy with a smoking problem. I had to lean in to hear her over the sound of the machine's frantic alert. "Maybe," she said. "If . . . have blood."

Marcy was doing the same thing I was over the body of another vamp, only she'd made the mistake of undoing the restraints first, and she squeaked as he grabbed her with both hands, pulling her down for a bite. She fought him off, pulling away and throwing herself halfway across the room and up against the third bed. The vamp there didn't even rouse.

"Trade?" I said.

Marcy nodded, and went to work on my vamp while I manhandled hers back into his restraints. It wasn't hard. He was as weak as a garden variety human. I stared down at him once I had the cuffs around him again. "You going to play nice or do we have to leave you behind?"

"Nooo," he said, his nearly colorless eyes beseeching me. "Just . . . so . . . hungry."

"I'll give you a bit of blood. You prove to me you're not a threat and the first guard we come across is yours. You attack my friend or me and I put you down. Got it?"

He nodded and, like the first vamp, tried to lick his lips with a cracked tongue, doing nothing to wet them whatsoever. He nodded agreement rather than try to talk again.

I looked to Marcy. She'd already cut her wrist with her own teeth and was letting a bit of blood trickle into the female vamp's mouth. Smart. As blood deprived as they'd clearly been—maintenance doses, it seemed, just enough to keep them alive—they couldn't be trusted to stop drinking at a safe point. I'd been there. I understood far too well.

I bit into my own wrist, hardly feeling it, and held the open wound over the vamp's mouth. He reminded me of a baby bird, straining to get at the worm his mother had brought back for him. But that mental image grossed me out, and I had to look away, straight into the gaze of the third vamp, who was now awake and fixated on us, eyes wide and riveted on the blood dripping from my wrist.

Damn, damn, damnity damn. We didn't have time for this. It was going to take too long to free everyone this way. To feed them, and then be slowed because they weren't at capacity and would maybe stop to feed on others. How were we going to get everybody out? I couldn't mist them all. I doubted I had enough blood or energy to go around.

I pulled my wrist away from the vamp I was feeding when I thought he'd had enough and left it to Marcy to free him when she finished with hers. I went over to the staring vamp. His gaze hadn't left my wrist, which was already healing.

I ripped it open again. I had this much blood anyway. I let a stream trickle into his mouth and tried not to watch his Adam's apple bob up and down as he swallowed greedily. I started to feel a little woozy and stopped. It had been a crazy few days. We had to find some guards to replenish the hungry vamps.

I froze as soon as I thought it, raising my wrist up and wrapping it with my hand to staunch the blood that much sooner. The vamp on the table lifted his head as though he could chase the blood back to its source.

What was I thinking? I'd essentially promised one vamp a nice, juicy guard if he behaved. When had I started bartering humans? Was I on my way to becoming one of *them*—the council vamps, putting fangs first? The Feds treated vamps like lab monkeys. Here I was treating humans like take-out, raiding a federal facility. And not my first.

Had I already chosen sides? What would the rebels do to me if they thought so?

Not the time for deep thought, I told myself. You can't free the vamps and fight them at the same time. There will be casualties. Their captors will go down, replacing the blood they've taken, like it or not.

I didn't like it.

I looked to Marcy, wanting confirmation that we were doing the right thing, and found the first two vamps already freed, leaning against the walls to hold themselves up and eying us like we were bloody steaks thrown into a puppy pound. Too late to go back.

I freed the third, and he lunged for me the second his restraints fell away. I hit him, hard, and he slammed into his bed, sending it sliding and the machines crashing to the floor. Someone would certainly know we were here now.

The attack-vamp was back up, snarling, and the other two had come away from the walls, watching us intently, waiting to see if their roommate distracted us sufficiently so that they could close in and feed. We had to get out of here.

"Do it again and you die," I told him. I turned my head slightly to address the other two without taking my gaze off the first. "That goes for all of you. You have a death wish? Call my bluff."

"Moving out?" Marcy asked me. She was having the same doubts I was, I could tell. But we either stayed here facing off with the starving vamps until someone discovered and locked us up or we carried on with our plan.

"Moving out," I confirmed. "Get the door? I'll watch your back."

She nodded, and I shifted to cover the whole room. All three vamps eyed me, but none gave it a shot.

Marcy went to the door into the hallway and looked out. She moved her head out of view almost instantly. "Two guards coming," she said. "Stakes and sidearms."

"Got it. Go!"

Marcy swung open the door, and the three starving vamps bolted past her, bursting out into the hallway. We jumped out right after them to see one guard already down on the floor, covered by two vamps. The second guard fired his gun dead center of mass at the third vampire, who went down before we could do a thing. Marcy caught the vamp as he fell backward, leaving me to vault them both and land in front of the second guard as he fired again. I tried to go ghosty, but wasn't quite fast enough. I felt the pain rip into me, but then nothing as I turned to mist and the bullet blasted out my now-insubstantial back.

I rematerialized as quickly as possible, shocking the shooting guard by appearing right up in his grill. I chopped the blade of my hand down on his gun-hand, and the weapon clattered to the floor. He bent for it, and I slammed the crown of my head into his nose, hearing it crack as I connected.

I dropped to the ground as he staggered back clutching his nose and grabbed the gun myself. I came up with it leveled at him.

"Marcy, you okay?" I called.

"Yeah."

"Come and take this."

I heard the vampire she'd caught hit the floor as she came to grab the gun, holding it on the guard whose blood was dripping over his hands and now drawing the attention of the two vamps squatting over his fellow guard.

I grabbed them both by the necks of their shirts, twisting them up into nooses that wouldn't do a thing to stop breath they weren't using but which gave me the leverage to lift them to their feet.

"Enough!" I said. "Look to the other vamp." He'd been shot, which wouldn't under normal circumstances be fatal, but it had been center of mass, and if the bullet had shredded his heart, he didn't have enough blood in him to heal from it.

I threw them toward the downed vamp and hoped that Marcy could cover them too if they chose not to listen. They'd fed enough now that they could be a threat. I squatted beside the female guard, the one I'd seen smoking earlier. Her throat had been ripped out on one side and her shoulder torn down to tendons on the other. She wasn't getting up again.

I glared back at the vamps who'd taken her out. "This is your last human, understand? You feed, but you don't kill. You owe me your lives now, and I *will* collect."

They snarled, and the male vamp spat, "We owe you shit."

Wrong answer.

I grabbed the downed officer's gun out of her holster, swung it around and fired in the same movement. Spy training had made me a crack shot. The bullet grazed his head, taking with it the top of his ear.

"You might want to think again." I kept the gun on him as I raided the guard's Batman-style utility belt for her stakes and lockback knife and, most importantly, her key card. I already held her only side-arm.

"Now, move. Next room, you can feed and free the vamps, we'll guard the door."

But I was already seeing a problem. Right now the odds were three against two. They were going to get steadily worse. And that was when we *weren't* up against the Feds with unreliable vamps at our backs.

I could ghost Marcy out now, make it the council's problem—except I wasn't actually sure I could. Not with holy water coating the roof. Not with that much more time passed with her system breaking down my blood that she'd taken in. I could always refresh that, but felt too much like retreat. We couldn't leave the Feds to recapture their captives and add the council vamps to their numbers. And I couldn't leave without Alistaire. Not knowing he was here and having seen his condition in Laurel's drawing. We headed for the next room, and I used the guard's key card to get in. Marcy kept watch on the others in the hallway while I peeked inside, but the space was currently being used as a storeroom, everything boxed or shoved up against the walls, ready for the move. Empty of Feds or fangs.

As soon as I stepped back into the hallway, I felt it, the sense of an army of insects invading my brain, legs tickling all the dark corners.

Morsel, came the voice that went with it. *Here, chick, chick, chick.*

Alistaire. I hated when he did that.

"Jeez, ever heard of women's lib?" I said out loud. "I don't answer to *chick.* Or morsel for that matter." I ignored the fact that I thought of Carrie as Chickzilla. That was different. At least I'd given her a tough name, not one that screamed *prey.*

You prefer chicken *then? That is the grown-up form, yes?*

Something happened then, and it was like the call was disrupted. The spiders in my head momentarily stopped skittering.

No time to play. COME!

My body moved two steps before I even knew what it was doing. I commanded myself to stop, but it was no use. I'd been resistant to mesmerism all my vampiric life. Except that with Alistaire I actually had to fight it. This time, even as weak as he must be, his compulsion was somehow stronger than ever.

"Marcy!"

Her gaze shifted momentarily from the freed vampires to me, but her gun never wavered. "A little busy here!"

But then she really looked at me, caught by whatever look must have been on my face.

"It's Alistaire," I said. "He's in control."

"What?"

"No time. I need back up!"

"I thought I was providing that."

I was two doors away from her now, and she had to decide fast, because her divided attention was going to get her killed. I opened my mouth to warn her when she whirled to full-on face the vamps creeping up behind her.

"Halt," she said, leveling her gun like she was some old-timey gunslinger. "You don't want us here and we're about to get gone. Nothing you need to do about that. Free the rest of the vamps. Make a run for it yourselves. Do what you've got to do, but spare as many humans as you can. You won't want to mess with us on this. You know Alistaire? Well, he's like Gina's creepy old uncle, and he'll be *seriously* disturbed if you cross her."

Alistaire was seriously disturbed with our without help, but I wasn't going to nitpick.

I headed toward a set of emergencies stairs, Alistaire's compulsion pulling me along, Marcy followed, but turned around, watching our backs just in case. I hit the door to the stairs and had just raised a hand to the pushbar when I felt a rumbling coming up through the floor. It seemed the staircase was already occupied, and from the rising sound of running feet, the occupants were headed our way.

Still, my hand started to push on the door.

"Dammit, Alistaire," I said out loud. No, I didn't say it, it burst out of me like an explosion. "Let me go. I'm coming already! But we have company."

Marcy looked at me like I was crazy. She didn't have Alistaire talking in *her* head, lucky girl.

"Company?" she asked.

My arm dropped as Alistaire let me go, and I instantly threw myself back against the wall, out of sight of the window onto the stairway. Marcy flattened herself against the wall on the other side, gun now aimed at the stairwell.

A guard burst through, and I stuck out a foot to take him down. No spy club training needed. The second guard coming through didn't have time to pull up before falling over the first. Marcy covered both with her gun, but I made the mistake of watching them go down and didn't see the third guard or the stake coming at me until it was buried in my shoulder. Pain cracked through me like forked lightning, spasming my muscles and making me drop the gun I held.

The guard followed the stake with another, coming at me while I was stunned, but it didn't last. I had vamp reflexes, and I used them, whipping my other hand up to knock away the stake and lashing my foot toward his knee. I connected solidly, felt the crack of bone and the buckling of the leg and bashed the guard over the head as he went down, hoping to knock him out and keep him there.

Three guards down on the ground. Five still-hungry vamps drawn by the bloodshed. The woman in front had her fangs full-out and glistening from the blood she'd already consumed. Ready to go for more. There was no one home but hunger in her eyes. The others looked only marginally more in control.

"Escape now, feed—" *later* I started to say.

But she never let me get to the end of the sentence before she was on me, aimed like a missile at the blood coating the stake through my shoulder. I grabbed her straight out of the air and hurled her into the wall, but she bounced right back at me, teeth still thrashing and hands extended like claws. A shot rang out, shockingly loud, and I knew that Marcy was fending off the other vamps. We didn't have frickin' time for this. If Bobby were here, he'd issue one mental command and have them stopped in their tracks or following along like well-trained puppies.

Marcy's attention diverted, the downed guards who hadn't been knocked out were scrambling back to their feet, weapons at the ready.

I quickly snapped the neck of the female vamp I was grappling with—she'd get over it—and yanked the stake out of my shoulder, ignoring the blinding, world-annihilating pain. As soon as it was out, I reached for Marcy, latching onto her leg and willing us to go ghosty. It was a struggle, but I was determined, and I misted us through the wall into the stairway, leaving the guards and the vamps to battle things out now that each side had a fighting chance. We had to get to Alistaire.

"Come on!" I said to Marcy, and we thundered down the stairs, trusting the sound of the fighting around us to cover the sounds of our descent.

Morsel, Alistaire said again, and I felt a pull out into the hallway. This was the right floor. Alistaire was somewhere off to the left. Marcy and I blew through the door from the stairwell out into the hall and dropped into ready stances, but nothing came at us. The floor was dead silent. The fighting either hadn't made it this far or hadn't left any survivors.

A hallway stretched out from the staircase in both directions, flanked with closed doors to either side. Based on the pull of the compulsion, we turned left, and Marcy nodded that she'd take the doors on the right side of the hallway, leaving me with the rest. We peered into each room as we went, alert for signs of an ambush, making note of how many vamps needed freeing, but we didn't do a thing about them. Not yet. That pull toward Alistaire was getting stronger, drawing me toward the double doors at the end of the hallway. We couldn't risk starving vamps at our backs and Alistaire at our front.

As if I'd summoned him with the thought, my brain once again crawled with insects and I heard *Morsel!* This time with a frantic edge that would have sent my heart racing if it was still online. Anything that sent Alistaire into a panic terrified me.

We reached the double-doors and I swiped the keycard into the reader. The light turned amber. *Amber!* Not green or even red.

"What the hell does that mean?" I yelled at the reader, as if it could answer. I beat at the door with the heel of my hand in frustration and the pain reverberated all the way up my arm. Those were some serious doors. Reinforced metal. Fire doors maybe. No way to break them down. As tough as the last double-ghosting had been and as drained as I was, I didn't dare risk it again and trap Marcy and me within them.

"Maybe this door is different," Marcy said. I barely contained my *duh*! "Maybe someone on the other side needs to swipe as well," Marcy said. "Or push a button to admit us or something, but—"

The doors jumped suddenly as something on the other side knocked against them. Or was thrown. Suddenly, a twisted face appeared in the window, looking like that famous painting *The Scream*, only instead of strokes of paint, this face was brushed with blood. The woman mouthed something at us, and then lurched to the side. The light on our reader glowed green so I presumed she'd swiped her card and that Marcy had been right. She grabbed me out of the way as the double-doors started to swing open in our direction, and then released me almost instantly to catch the woman as she fell through into Marcy's arms.

Her mouth was still going, as though she wanted to say something, but her throat had been half-ripped out, and was still gurgling blood, turning her lab coat into a red Rorschach test pattern. The blood on her face came from a head-wound near her hairline that looked deep enough that stitches might be the least of her worries. It was a miracle she'd made it this far.

"You help her," I said to Marcy. "I'm going after Alistaire."

"Alone?" she asked, not taking her eyes from the stricken woman. Or maybe all that blood.

"We'll need someone on this side to open the doors," I said, tipping my chin toward the woman's keycard. I still held the card I had, but I was going to need both hands free. I tucked it quickly into my cleavage and was through the doors before Marcy could argue. The doors were already starting to close again, and I wasn't going to miss my moment.

Once through, I noted an abandoned nurse's station—or guard station—and just three closed doors, to the left, right and straight ahead. I followed the trail of the woman's blood to the right. Even without the strange compulsion that drew me toward Alistaire like a tractor beam I knew that in the event of Alistaire and carnage in the same vicinity, one was the likely cause of the other.

When I heard the sudden impact and rattle of a body meeting metal, I knew I was right. I reached for the door as a body slammed against it. A *huge* body, so big all I could see was back and shoulders, the head above window height. *Not* Alistaire, thank all that was good and . . . well, holy might be pushing it.

I swiped the key card and waited. The red light blinked three times and went back to steady. It was a no go. I must need a higher clearance beyond those double doors than the guard I'd stolen the key card from.

Dammit.

Maybe I could manage one more misting, since I had only myself to get through.

Another slam at the door, and it jumped in its frame. This time a face appeared in the window looking outward, a familiar face, bones subtlely wrong, jaw too long and looking like it might unhinge, which I knew to be a real possibility. Alistaire. His crazy eyes sought mine, burrowing in.

Help? he said in my head. Then, *What the hell are you waiting for?*

Then he was gone from the window, but not my head.

I didn't waste any more time but closed my eyes and thought of going insubstantial, letting go of my sense of physical self long enough to fade into my mist or molecule form. The compulsion that had been with me since Alistaire made contact pulled me into the room, but the door wanted to stop me. I could feel it. There was something about it that wanted to hold me there like flypaper. Panic almost had me going solid so that I could fight against it, use my arms and legs to scrabble at the walls or floor or ceiling or *anything* to help pull me through, but I struggled against the instinct. If I went solid now I'd be trapped, and I didn't know what that would do to me. Supposedly, I was eternal. Would I live out my unnatural life trapped in the entryway of this federal chop shop?

I couldn't tell what was going on. Had garlic been mixed into the paint? Some kind of spell cast?

It didn't matter. I had to get free. I fought and strained as best I could, but I was caught in a trap. With no body, I couldn't physically help myself and with a body, I'd be bisected by the door.

I threw out a mental rope. Alistaire already had his hooks into me psychically. Maybe I could use them to get me through. I focused on that tractor beam feeling, let it draw me along, letting go of the urge to fight—against him, against my entrapment.

Morsel! he called. Even in mental-voice it sounded strangled. He needed my help, and I needed him to hold out long enough to pull me through.

Slowly, I felt it working. Everything tingled as I went through, pricking like a thousand pins. Or burning like a thousand fire ants. But I felt the burn travel, sliding over me and finally past. It was as though something wanted to hold onto that last little bit, like I was caught by my big toe or something. I rematerialized, but I imagined kicking off hard as I did. I managed to rip free—most of me anyway. It felt like I'd left a little bit of flesh behind.

I couldn't look to see how bad it was, because the grappling men were about to fall right on top of me. I rolled like my life depended on it, which, given the size of the behemoth Alistaire was fighting, it just might. I came up against the bed, which had been thrown against the back wall by the struggle.

Quickly, I sized up what was going on. Alistaire had unhinged all of his extra joints and now stood looking like a praying mantis about to get his head ripped off. His jaw unlocked and his face elongated, fangs extended, even those oversized compared to run-of-the-mill vamps. Not quite saber-teeth, but my fangs looked downright dainty in comparison. His opponent, as I'd noticed through the window, was *huge*. A mountain of a man. If The Rock and Andre the Giant had a love child who'd joined the marines and been issued a standard training uniform one size too small (green crew-neck shirt and matching shorts), it might look something like this guy. His hair was so closely cropped to his head, it was little more than a five o'clock shadow. Veins throbbed in his neck and at his jaw. Muscles bulged at his arms, chest and legs, straining the seams of his clothing as he tried his best to rip Alistaire's head from his body.

"Hey!" I yelled, trying to distract him and give Alistaire an opening. "Hey, Hulk!"

The behemoth barred his teeth and growled, but he didn't look my way. Well, crapcakes, I was going to have to do this the hard way.

I exploded away from the wall, moving, I hoped, too fast to track. Vamp fast. I came up behind him—or so I'd expected—but he was somehow equally fast. Anticipating me, he'd whirled so that Alistaire was now his shield against me. I didn't miss a beat. I jumped up onto Alistaire, bracing myself on his hinged limbs like I was climbing him to perform a human pyramid. Instead, I sank my fangs into the oversized hand gripping the side of his head. I was not gentle. This was no feeding; it was an attack. I pierced and ripped, tearing away as much of the Hulk's flesh as I could.

The monster roared, and his hand came free from Alistaire's head to lash at me, swatting me like a fly. The blow rang my head like a bell, battering my brain against the side of my skull and doubling my vision. I slipped from Alistaire's back even as I felt all of his muscles coil to spring into action.

I landed on my feet, whirled, waited for the world to come back into focus and watched Alistaire punch with all of his strength right for the beast-man's solar plexus. It knocked him back a few steps, but he barely oofed. I didn't wait for his counterattack to launch my own. I came in with a kick to where all men were vulnerable, but he grabbed my foot in mid-launch, twisting and sending me spinning in the air before crashing to the ground. He shouldn't have been fast enough to stop me. Not a man against a vamp, not someone so muscled I wondered how it didn't limit his motion. How did he scratch his back? Or his balls, for that matter?

Clearly that first blow had knocked the sense out of me. These were not the questions I should be asking.

I looked harder at him. Not at the bulk or the build, but at those bared teeth. At the canines . . .

Triple-damn. The man was a vampire. His fangs weren't as impressive as Alistaire's, not by a longshot, but they were out. Fully extended. All things being equal, little five-foot nothing me didn't have any chance against a marine-trained monster man. From the fact that Alistaire had been in dire straits when I arrived, I doubted he did either. Maybe together . . . Or maybe I needed something to level the playing field.

I looked around for a weapon as Alistaire and the monster man engaged again—Alistaire launching an attack, the man blocking, striking, relentless.

There was an IV pole not far from me, and I grabbed it, waited for one of the monster man's blows to knock Alistaire halfway across the room and ran at him, using the pole as a battering ram. Or a lance if I was strong enough to drive it right into his massive muscles. He saw me coming, and grabbed the end of the pole before I could do either one. His shredded hand didn't seem to be slowing him a bit. Damned vampire healing. Not so awesome when it was turned against you.

He started to tilt the pole upright, as though I'd be stupid enough to hang on and let him raise me into the air. As soon as I let go, he changed his grip and started swinging the pole like a baseball bat, right at my head. I ducked, came up under his swing and was finally right where I wanted to be, level with a certain tender part of the male anatomy. I slammed my fist right into his dangly bits and winced as he dropped the pole he was holding onto my back. But it was a glancing blow and the pole rolled right off. Meanwhile, he started to buckle, curling around his bruised man parts.

Alistaire chose that moment to launch himself right over me, aiming for the behemoth's head, wrapping his arms around it and knocking him over backwards, taking them both to the ground. The behemoth's head hit hard, and I scrambled out of the way of his lashing feet. I grabbed the pole as I rose back to standing, holding it like a lance in case I needed to wield it again, but Alistaire's fangs were now latched firmly on the monster man's neck, and he was sucking hard, his Adam's apple working as he swallowed his blood down in great gulps,

Gross.

"Enough!" I told him. "We've got to get out of here. It was all a trap. The Feds are on to us."

Alistaire tore his fangs out of the marine's throat, not caring that he ripped a chunk of flesh out with them. The man would heal. I wasn't sure that was a good thing, but I couldn't kill him while he was down. A tiny bit of sanity bled back into Alistaire's eyes, and as I watched he started to fill out, his eye sockets no longer so pronounced, his cheeks no longer so sunken I could dive them for buried treasure. Also, his fangs retracted back to normal vampire length. Enough so that he could talk, and not just in my head.

"We can't leave yet. We have to destroy everything."

"Everything?" I asked. "You mean like bring the place down around us? I thought you said *I* was chaos."

Alistaire launched himself up from the ground and grabbed me by my shirt, his crazy-eyes hard-staring into mine. "If that's what it takes," he said. "They took something from me. From everybody, but from me in particular. This muscle-head you met . . . he's only the prototype."

Crap. Crap. Crap.

"There are more of them?" I asked, just to be sure.

"If not yet, there will be. We have to destroy all the science— the testing and the data. Follow me."

He thrust me away from him and was out the door before I could give him an answer. Probably it didn't matter. He was a man on a mission, with or without me.

I chased Alistaire down the hallway, to the door at the far end of the hall. He stopped short in front of it, so I used my keycard in the reader. The color of the light—red—didn't change, but it gave three angry pulses, and I wondered if an alarm was ringing somewhere because we'd tried an unauthorized swipe.

But Alistaire had already moved to plan B, which seemed to be beating the crap out of the door. Even as weak as he must be, he dented the door, but I could tell from the sound of the blows that it was steel reinforced just like those out into the hallway. He wasn't going to get anywhere. I didn't want to risk misting us in if I was going to get us stuck. Anyway, doing the blood exchange with the psycho-psychic—I'd had nightmares only half as scary. Already I didn't know where his ability to compel me had come from. In the good old days I could shake him off, so either he'd grown stronger or I'd grown weaker, and I didn't like either possibility any more than a sandpaper facial.

Somehow, we had to get in.

I left Alistaire battering the door and went to the deserted nurse's station, hoping someone hadn't logged out of their computer. There was a screen up, a schematic of the whole floor, our area flashing red. If there was a similar screen somewhere else and someone was watching, we could have company at any moment.

I studied the schematic, used the mouse to maneuver the pointer over the options menu and scrolled through. There was a manual override listed. Score! I clicked on it and up popped a window asking for the confirmation code.

"Alistaire, code!" I yelled.

He was a psychic. It ought to be good for something more than vague predictions.

"What?"

"Don't think. Just do!" I said.

I didn't expect it to work. I expected retaliation for daring to order him about, but in a voice different from his usual—calmer, deeper, almost sane—he started reciting, "C9XO673Z8."

I typed as he talked, and sure enough, the lights on the screen went from blinking red to green. I clicked on the schematic for the door we wanted, chose the door release option and, miraculously, the light on the reader changed and there was an audible click. I hit the button for Marcy's door, the one out into the hallway and clicked that as well. I had the override now. I hoped that meant it was safe to let her in. I didn't like leaving her out there without backup.

She raced through the doors when they opened and immediately started to yank them closed behind her, like she could hurry their pneumatics. "Company coming," she yelled. "Close them. Lock them down!"

I reclicked the button to close them, but the doors didn't move any faster. It scared me to think I might not be the only one with an override code. Almost certainly wasn't.

From the other set of doors that Alistaire had been frantic to get through, he gave a huge bellow, like a wounded bear. Marcy and I looked at each other and took off in that direction. If worst came to worst, at least we could all make a stand together.

We rushed through the doors into that formerly locked-off section at the end of the hall and saw Alistaire in the midst of chaos. And not of his own creation. There hadn't been time. All around were upended chairs, an explosion of shredded paper that had missed its receptacle, dust bunnies that had been dragged into the light by the yanking of cords that had once been strung from computers and other electrical equipment. Some of the cords remained behind. But not the computers. Those and the people they belonged to were all gone. Hastily evacuated, it looked like.

Alistaire was standing in front of two huge units with glass fronts, something like double-sized convenience store refrigerators, only they were empty.

"It's gone," Alistaire said, voice shaking with disbelief. "All of it."

"What's gone?" Marcy asked.

But there was no time to answer.

Our company burst into the room—or at least a vanguard of three security guards. There were more behind them.

"Stop right there!" called the one front and center.

He wasn't messing around. He wasn't armed with a gun, holy water or otherwise, but with a crossbow armed with a deadly wooden bolt. And he was sighted in on Alistaire. His compatriots to either side of him were focused on me and Marcy, armed the same way. They stepped into the room and fanned out, allowing the others behind them to come through.

I liked being the ma'am with the plan, but I was fresh out. "What do we do now?" I asked Alistaire.

"We fight. We can't let them take me alive."

Me, not us. Crazy speak? Something more? No time to tell. The three guards who'd come in first stayed central, crossbows aimed on us. The other four with them were fast-approaching, guns in one hand, cuffs in the other. Bullets would put us down long enough to take control while leaving us alive for their little experiments. I didn't intend to spend the rest of my unnatural life hooked up to their machines.

Alistaire leapt, his crazy-jointed legs propelling him like a grasshopper, higher and further than should have been possible. In awe, I watched for a millisecond longer than I should have, long enough to hear the first guard's startled cry and panicked firing of the crossbow bolt, which pieced Alistaire's side. And then the guard closest was reaching for me with the cuffs. Hell with that. I leapt back out of reach, then came in with a whirling kick of my own. Unlike the monster marine, she wasn't fast enough to counter my kick, and it caught her dead center of mass. She caved around her stomach, giving the guard behind her a clear shot at me. His gun was already raised, and he fired before I could even think to move, the blast loud in the reinforced room, immediately eclipsed by the pain of the bullet shredding my shoulder. Same shoulder as before, damn it!

It blew me back half a step, and I went with it rather than fight it, whirling all the way around so that I was no longer where I had been, which was a good thing, because a second shot followed the first, pinging off the floor and shattering tile. I'd taken the room in at a glance when we burst through. I knew what I had to work with. I dove for the floor, rolled, and came up with one of the cords that had been left behind. It was a good one, thick and heavy, with a power strip still attached at the other end. I swung it like a lasso, twirling it around once for momentum before sending the power strip end smacking into the gun-arm of the second guard. He dropped the gun with a yelp of pain, but I didn't have time to revel in my victory. The female guard had recovered from her belly blow. She wasn't standing entirely upright, but she was steady enough to have a gun aimed at me at point blank range. She fired and I arched back, like I was trying to pull a Matrix-worthy move. The bullet skimmed me breast to shoulder, but kept going, and I came up again whirling my lasso-computer cord like a pro and sent it spinning straight at her. The power cord slammed into the female guard's temple and dropped her to the ground.

The other guard dove for the gun I'd knocked from his hand and came up with it, aiming from his knees. He fired again before I could get my power cord lasso back into the proper arc, and pain flared in my side to match the pain in my shoulder. I staggered, but forced myself back under control and sent the power cord swinging straight for him, ready to do to him what I'd done to his cohort. I was a little sloppy, and it caught him in the jaw rather than the temple, but I heard something crack, and he went down just the same.

Quickly, before either could recover, I used the cable end of my weapon to lash the two downed guards together back to back. I kicked their guns far away into the corner with the dust bunnies of doom and finally acknowledged the searing pain in my shoulder. I'd given away enough blood that my wound wasn't quick to heal up on its own. I needed to feed. My bloodlust burned almost as brightly as the pain. I had to drag my gaze away from the pulse points of the captive guards to look around the room to see whether anyone needed help. I had to fight now, feed later.

Marcy had downed one of her attackers, but the second was aiming for her. I threw myself at one of the guns I'd kicked away and we got our shots off simultaneously. Luckily, the guard's went high, but mine was right on target, and she dropped like a stone, clutching her gun arm. I swung my aim and my gaze toward the door, toward Alistaire and the crossbow guards, but I needn't have worried. Two were down, one alligator-crawling toward a weapon, both legs twisted at horrific angles. The third was clawing at Alistaire's hands as he held the man by his shoulders, coming at him with those monstrous teeth. The guard's terror was so clear that I thought his heart would give out.

I ran for the crossbow the downed guard was crawling for, stepped on it and aimed my gun at him so the consequences of reaching for the weapon would be clear. Then I shouted, "Alistaire!" And again when he didn't immediately answer. "Hey, psycho. No playing with your food. We've got to get moving!"

Alistaire didn't respond. He was staring crazily into the terrified guard's eyes, and I felt a wave of power reach out from him. "Where did they go?" he snarled, barely decipherable around the fangs. That wave of power, I was sure, was to compel the guard to answer the question.

The guard whimpered, trying to resist, squeezing his eyes shut as though Alistaire's power was all in his gaze. It wasn't.

"Don't make me ask you again," Alistaire said, voice dripping with menace.

"Away," the guard said, and then howled with pain when the compulsion wasn't satisfied. Or maybe it was Alistaire himself, hands tightening on the guard's shoulders as if he could squeeze right through.

"A new facility," he added, panting. "I can't . . ."

"You *can*," Alistaire said, and a new wave of compulsion nearly knocked *me* over. I suspected that if Alistaire hadn't been holding the guard upright, he'd have been floored.

"New Orleans, okay?" the guard said, face a rictus of pain, every vein standing out, every muscle straining. "That's all I know. Relocating . . . all the facilities . . . consolidating."

Alistaire released the guard's shoulders and the man dropped like a stone, crumpling to the floor and mewling in pain.

The guard by my feet made a move, and I returned my attention to him, refocusing the gun. He stopped.

I pulled a pair of handcuffs out of my waistband and tossed

them at him. "Put these on," I ordered.

He glared and snarled, but it wasn't nearly impressive after Alistaire's snarl, and I didn't react. Just watched until the cuffs were in place, then put my gun away to check them. I did the same for all the guards in the room, using their own handcuffs against them.

Then I did my trick with the computer and got us the hell out of there. The rest of the floor was deserted except for whatever vamps were left in the rooms. I veered toward one of them and Alistaire snapped, "Leave them!"

"But—"

"No buts. They're slow and useless. *We're* important," he said. "*Us* and our information. We know where they're going. We need to stop them *there*. With an army. And a plan."

I didn't like his thinking—not at all—but I followed it. We had information that couldn't die or stay trapped with us. It had to get out.

Then I nearly hit myself upside the head. I mentally called out to my boy Bobby, wanting to send out the info in case we got caught, but he was the one with the mental mojo, not me, and if he wasn't tuned in or if he was out of range, I was SOL. He didn't answer my call.

Alistaire was already headed toward the stairs, assuming Marcy and I would follow. Or not caring. I followed, mostly because he needed a watcher. I didn't trust him on his own. I pulled out my phone, though, trying to text and run. I had no idea what fun things autocorrect had made of my mistypes. I hit send on my message to Bobby without reading it over, but it didn't matter. The phone flashed "Send failed" at me. Were the Feds jamming?

Crud puppies. We had to make it out, just like Alistaire said. When the psycho psychic started making sense, I worried.

He raced down the stairs, skipping the second floor and stopping at the door to the first. He held a hand up to halt Marcy and me, as we would have crashed into him, expecting him to keep going through the door. If it weren't for our vamp reflexes, we'd never have stopped in time.

"What is it?" I whispered.

Alistaire turned those creepy, soulless eyes on me, and they were even more vacant than usual. A thousand miles away. "It's almost over," he said, as if he was seeing something in his head, a movie just before the end credits started scrolling.

"What is?" I asked.

"The round-up."

Okay, so it was a Western film then. Great. Lovely.

I edged around him, ready to go for the door myself, but he grabbed my hand, clamping down on it as if his fingers were made of iron. I gasped in pain and froze. And suddenly he released me, jerked his head in my direction and focused on my actual face instead of his mental movie. "Now."

I reached tentatively for the door, afraid that maybe I misunderstood him, but this time he let me do it. The stairs let out into a hallway off the foyer just beyond the elevators. I took three steps toward the exit and then stopped as I peeked into the central reception area and caught sight of what Alistaire had been talking about—the round-up.

The rest of the fight was already over. The council vamps had been captured, and guards were herding them using crosses and crossbows. I looked for Chickzilla, going right past her and then back when I realized that the girl in the black knit cap and ninja-black long-sleeved tee with the black stripe under her eyes like a football player was actually her. She spotted me too, and I tensed, waiting for her to give us away and ready to run, but all she did was mouth, *Help us.*

Help us. She'd lied to me and Laurel, arranged for the council vamps to close in on us at the playground. And now she wanted our help.

Wait, I mouthed back. *We'll come for you.*

And then one of the guards thrust a cross in her face to turn her around and move her on. She hissed and flinched away, but she didn't look back toward me. She didn't give us away.

I wanted to help now, but we were outnumbered. We had to hold off until we had some hope of winning the day and freeing them all.

I pulled back out of sight. "Is there any other way out?" I asked Alistaire, as if he'd had the run of the place and hadn't been kept a prisoner this whole time, which begged the question of how he'd gotten free before we got to him. But explanations would have to wait.

"Windows?" Marcy suggested, when he didn't immediately answer.

"Barred," Alistaire said, gaze distant, as though he was looking at sights only he could see. "Crosses in the ironwork."

Brilliant. And also damn.

Suddenly, those crazy eyes were pinned on me, pupils so large they swallowed his irises so that his eyes were, literally, black holes. He grabbed me by the shoulders and shook me as though to get a point across. I nearly passed out as his fingers dug into my still-healing stake-wound. "You are chaos," he said. "Hear you roar."

The only roaring I heard was in my ears, but that wasn't going to get him to let me go. "Okay," I answered, worried about the shakiness in my voice. "We'll just—"

My head exploded with a vision of the Feds and fangs as we'd just seen them, but with weapons jumping out of hands, federal flunkies suddenly spilling to the ground as though they'd been tripped or pushed by invisible hands. By *my* hands.

"Got it," I swore, ripping myself out of his hold. "You two get ready to run. I've got this."

I had to, didn't I? It was our only chance for escape. *Their* only chance for escape. As weak as I was from blood loss, I didn't have the juice to mist us all out, even if I had the means. I probably couldn't ghost through doors or walls myself right now, soaked as they were by the holy water sprinklers.

I closed my eyes for a second and focused on something I'd learned in a woo woo class my mother had dragged me to once. I took a deep breath, lifting my shoulders all the way up to my ears and tightening everything up. Then I gave one great whooshing exhale, expelling all the negative, all the tension and pain, dropping it to the ground when I dropped my shoulders, letting it flow out through my fingertips. I didn't know why it worked, but it did. Before any other awareness could crowd in, I thought insubstantial thoughts—until all I had left was a vague sense of myself fading out, ghosting away. Of air density and the general positioning of things.

I sent myself misting out toward the Feds corralling the vamps. When I felt the air tighten with tension—there was no other way to describe it—I focused on solidifying again. Just a bit, enough to catch a glimpse of my targets and enough that when I reached for the closest weapon and batted it out of the guard's hands, I made actual contact. The crossbow went flying and a cry went up.

Other crossbows turned in my direction, but I'd vanished. Whisked myself away, misting right through one guard to the next. He cried out like a girl, by which I guessed he could feel me, maybe like the chill of the grave. But then I was out again, going semi-solid to pull a taser out of next guard's belt and depress the button. He jittered and went down as the probes struck, and I willed myself to fade again, but not before I saw the vamps they had surrounded start to bristle.

If I discombobulated the guards any more, we might have open rebellion. Could I do it? Could I free them all?

I whipped myself across the room, blowing through three or four others, at least half of them undead. I couldn't say how I knew that except that they felt different. Colder. Less dense somehow, maybe because their substance had been so wasted away by all the Feds had done to them.

When I sensed I was free from the pack, I let myself go semi-solid again and ended up staring straight into the frightened eyes of one of the guards. Not so frightened that she forgot the crossbow she held, which unluckily was pointed straight at me. She hit the trigger, and I vanished. I didn't feel any pain, only a swift pressure as the bolt blew through me.

Then something was sucking at me, almost like a vacuum, pulling me away from the fight, away from the Feds and the fangs. Toward the exit, unless I was mistaken. Alistaire's mesmeric tractor beam?

I wasn't in my physical body to dig my heels in against it. I wasn't even sure if I should. If Alistaire had foreseen my death . . . That crossbow bolt had been a little close for comfort.

The beam pulled me all the way to the door, and then started to yank me through. That was when the burning started, as though someone had lit a chemical fire at my core that raged out of control. As if my every molecule was tinder and had gone up in an instant. I was no longer solid or vapor, I was a living blaze.

And soon, I was sure, a dying ember.

11

It was the blood I noticed first. I gulped it down as though I was starving. Then the hunger came roaring to life, and I realized that was it exactly. I was starving, empty, flattened. I needed the blood to fill me out.

And then I realized that the blood *tingled*. Like it had been super-charged. Taser-blood. It jolted through me, ripping everything open—pain centers, awareness, all the chemicals my body made for whatever purpose, dumping a crazy cocktail into my system. I felt like I was vibrating. *No,* I felt like I could feel *every molecule in my body* vibrating. And not necessarily to the same frequency.

My eyes snapped open, and I was suddenly staring into the shark eyes of the psycho-psychic, who had one arm around me while he watched blood drip from the other into my mouth.

I snapped it shut and sat up, all of me screaming in pain at the movement. I didn't let that stop me from scuttling away as fast as I could. I didn't get far before my butt hit something rough. That something was a tree. We were in the woods. Marcy was staring at me. Alistaire was staring *into* me. And I was staring back.

"What the hell was that?" I asked, hyperventilating even though I didn't even need to breathe.

"What?" Alistaire asked, but not like he didn't know. More like he asked out of clinical curiosity. As if he was one of the Feds and I was his experiment.

"Screw that, you know exactly what I'm talking about. Your blood, it's . . . charged."

"Let me taste!" Marcy said, licking her lips. "I'd love something with a little kick."

"It won't last," Alistaire said. "And we need to get out of here while we can."

Right, we were still too close to the compound. We could still be captured.

"Marcy, do you have any idea where we are?" I asked. I sure didn't. One tree looked like another to me, and I hadn't been in any condition to note landmarks on what I presumed was our mad dash away from the federal facility. I didn't remember a thing. Had whatever coated the door at the federal facility knocked me back into my body and out of my mind? Had Alistaire carried me? Oh hell no.

"I think so," Marcy answered. "This way."

She veered off through the trees, then looked back to make sure we were following. Alistaire still had his gaze on me, making sure I could move. I was determined. I bucked myself away from the tree and rose to my feet. Dizziness swept over me. And nausea. And, *damn, damn, damn*, every single one of my molecules was vibrating. *Every single one!* I wanted to tell them all to get it together and stop pinging off in different directions. It was as though they wanted to break me apart, all the various parts of me exploding like fireworks.

But I made my legs move and, thank all that was holy—or *un*—at least I could convince *them* to go in the same direction. The pain in my body burned up as I ran, but so did the taser-blood. By the time we burst out of the woods at our rendezvous point, my body had healed, but all the blood had been eaten up in the process, and I was once again on empty. When the van door slid open to let us in, I threw myself into a seat and collapsed.

Imanyi stared at us from the driver's seat. Well, stared at *Alistaire*, really, as Marcy yelled, "Go, go, go!"

She whipped her head back around, wrenched the car into gear and we shot forward like a rocket. David took up staring where she's left off, jacked around in the passenger's seat. "Who the hell is this?" he asked.

I noticed that his hands were out of sight. Maybe on a weapon. I couldn't blame him. Alistaire was a scary dude.

"This is Alistaire," I said. "He's a vampire and a psychic and, yeah, a little psycho, but he's with us. Laurel knows him."

"She'll vouch for him?" Imanyi asked without turning around.

I hesitated, but it was barely noticeable by human standards. "Yup."

I didn't actually know what she'd do. Definitely she didn't want the Feds to have him or for him to continue to be tortured, but whether she'd want him in our midst I couldn't even guess. I know I'd rather have him where I could keep an eye on him. I just wished I could keep a cross by my bed in the event that he got out of hand.

"Okay now, important question," Marcy chimed in, "What the hell?" She was looking at Alistaire, her gaze boring into him. If he was a bug, she'd have him pinned to a board.

"What the hell *what?*" asked David. He was clearly uncomfortable with the whole thing. "What happened in there and where did he come from? You were just supposed to observe."

"Yeah, about that," I said, "wasn't our fault." Well, technically it was. We could have let the council vamps go in and get captured, which was what had happened anyway, but then we wouldn't have our inside man. Or menace, anyway.

"Report," Imanyi ordered.

"Marcy, you want to take this one?" I asked. I was tired. So, so tired. Even moving my lips took effort. Finding words was asking much.

She didn't need the prompting. She launched in immediately, "The council vamps lied to us. Or they changed their minds. *Whatever.* They broke into the facility. The Feds were ready for them. Gina and I decided to go in while the vamps were creating a distraction." I loved that she'd glossed over the part where I'd ghosted us onto the roof pre-council vamps. "We found and freed Alistaire, and we came back with intel. We reconned the hell out of this mission."

"What intel?" Imanyi asked, tone still grudging, but she was staring to cave. We were safe. We hadn't rained destruction down on them . . . yet . . . though we were inviting the fox into the hen house. No, terrible analogy. For one thing, Alistaire was way scarier than any fox. For another, we certainly weren't hens. I imagined the guys in particular might take offense at that.

"You already knew they were bugging out," Marcy said. "Well, now we know where—New Orleans."

Imanyi and David exchanged a glance. They looked less than impressed.

"New Orleans is a big place," David said, still twisted around in his seat to watch us. "Can you get a bit more specific?"

"That's all we've got," she said, tone defensive. "But I'm sure your precious Oracle can remote view you a lead."

"Let's hope," Imanyi said.

Alistaire suddenly jerked forward, and David reared back, bringing his hand up with a stake in it. "Whoa, far enough!"

Alistaire's shark eyes looked at him in distain, as though he could take the stake and use it on David in an instant, which I knew he could. "We've got to stop them. Ask Gina. She saw."

I saw what? Empty refrigeration units? Carnage? Yes and yes. But that wasn't what he was talking about.

"You mean the monster man?" I asked. "The guy who looked like a flesh-toned Incredible Hulk?"

"He's one of *them*," he said. "And one of mine."

He was speaking in riddles again. Damn psychics. Was there something that came with the power that scrambled their brains?

"Explain," I said.

"Think back to when you were first vamped. Why did Mellisande," *the woman who'd vamped Bobby and warped Alistaire almost beyond recognition,* "want Bobby so much?"

"Because of *your* prophecy."

"No, no, no," he said, agitated. "Think, *pretty, pretty.* Use your head for something other than a fangholder. The prophecy was because of him. Not the other way around."

"His power," I said, a lightbulb going on. "She wanted him for his power. *And* because you said he was the key."

"Because that kind of power in vamps is scarce. Usually the transformation burns out any other abilities. It turns off the potential. That's why you don't see vampire witches running around. Can you just imagine all that power in one place?" he said that with avarice, with a gleam in his eye like Gollum would look at the One Ring. Gah, there was Bobby, poisoning me with his geekdom again. "But in some cases, the vamp transformation turns a switch to On instead of Off."

"Okay," I said, because it was. I got that. I wasn't thick, even if my brain felt so at the moment. "What does any of that have to do with the monstrous marine or stopping the Feds."

"Magic, *morsel*," he said. "In my blood. Haven't you noticed that my get tends to develop powers?"

"But Mellisande—"

His gaze pinned me to my seat. "Mellisande was a witch before she was turned. Literally. I vamped her to turn her with me rather than against."

"That worked out so well for you."

Alistaire looked down at himself and smiled a creepy smile, showing teeth still bloodstained from his feedings. "It did, actually. She wasn't able to kill me. She had just enough residual power to twist me up. But my bloodline, through Mellisande, through your boy—how would you say it? The force is strong with this one?"

Was Alistaire really quoting *Star Wars*? Really?

"Huh?" was all I said. Brilliant.

"You, Bobby, the little blonde girl—"

"Laurel?"

"If you say so," he answered.

He turned his black-hole gaze on Marcy. "You?" he asked.

"Not so far," she said bitterly.

"Are there others?" I asked. It hadn't occurred to me how strange it was that we'd developed powers, even after the big deal Mellisande had made over Bobby's. I'd taken it in stride. If there were others, maybe they could help us in the fight against the Feds. If we could get to them.

"Maybe," Alistaire answered. "Could be. We'll see."

"Oh, you're rhyming now?"

He just grinned his bloody grin.

"So, when you say the monster marine was one of yours, you mean you transformed him."

"The Feds did the deed. They didn't want wild cards. Standard vampires. They wanted soldiers—disciplined, designed to follow orders and respect the hierarchy."

"In other words, so not us," I said.

"But he was only a prototype. Obsolete already."

"He seemed pretty kick-ass to me." I hadn't forgotten being hurled across that hospital room.

"There is another like me," Alistaire said, his smile disappearing.

The mind boggled. *Another like Alistaire?* No one was like Alistaire, and I appreciated the hell out of that fact.

"Who?" Imanyi asked.

He turned his psycho-gaze on her, letting Marcy off the hook. She seemed to deflate a little, to relax, as though she'd been at attention and on edge the whole time she'd been central to his focus.

"We haven't had the pleasure. But I heard them call her Ophelia. They wanted to find out what would happen if they mingled our blood."

I sat up suddenly in my seat. I was no psychic, but I knew where this was going. Knew it. "That's how you escaped, isn't it? They gave you her blood and it made you stronger."

He turned to me, put his face right into my personal space. Close enough that I could smell the coppery tang of blood on his lips. "And I fed our commingled blood to you. You felt the power. You know what it can do."

My eyes widened. "But we've got you now. And anyway, the effect was temporary."

He huffed, and it blew a gust of that fetid breath into my face. "The effect of *drinking* it was temporary. The effect of a transformation using both our blood, that will be permanent."

Marcy's eyes went as large as dinner plate. "They're going to out-vampire us vampires?"

"Worse, they're making daywalkers," I said. "Remember, they've already developed that potion that allows vampires to stay awake during the day and gives them some protection against the sun. Couple that with some industrial grade sunscreen, and they're pretty much unstoppable."

"There are still stakes," David said. "And beheadings."

"Holy objects, holy water, garlic," Imanyi added helpfully.

"Great, *you* get close enough to stake these guys," I said. "I think we need a plan B."

"Crossbows?" Marcy contributed.

"They'd be a start. But we're not winning against these guys one on one. Alistaire, are you saying they've already created these super soldiers or just that it's in the works?"

He turned those black void eyes on me. Or maybe they hadn't left me, but I'd been too busy seeing future horrors in my head to notice. "I see wretches locked in their own torment."

"Meaning?" Gah, this psychic thing was for the birds.

"Success without sanity. Such a fragile thing, sanity. Not for the faint of heart."

"Great, so we've got insane super vampires. What are you doing next, David?" David asked himself. "I'm going to Disney!"

"Speaking of sanity—" Imanyi said.

"Well, look, it's pointless isn't it? There's no way we can win. Might as well get working on our bucket lists. Live a little before we die," David said, raking his fingers through his hair and leaving it standing on end.

"Nearly impossible," Alistaire said helpfully. "But not pointless."

"Gina says you're a psychic," David said. "Do you see us succeeding?"

"I see possibilities."

"And?"

"In desperation and destruction, all things are possible."

David was silent a second. "Destruction. Now there's a thought."

I didn't ask what he was thinking. I was afraid I might already know. Scorched earth policy. Burn it all to the ground. And everyone with it. No more Ophelia. No more blood supply. Assuming they kept Ophelia at their new facility. Assuming the super soldiers were on site as well, along with all the research. No off-site backup. That was a lot of assumptions. Even if they were right, we couldn't bring a whole building down with everyone in it. If the end justified the means, how were we any better than the Feds? We couldn't even pretend to be the good guys.

"How about we find the place, then come up with a battle plan?"

"It's not up to you," Imanyi said.

"No, you're right. You can decide to go the terrorist route and we can start fighting each other."

You could cut the resulting silence with a chainsaw but it was a toss-up which would win.

Imanyi parked the van in the garage, and we all waited for the automatic door to lower before getting out so that no one would see us. *Gina!* Bobby said into my head as soon as he heard the engine shut off.

Bobby! I said back, so glad that his mental speech didn't have the spiders-swarming-my-brain feel of Alistaire's.

As if Alistaire sensed my thoughts, he gave me a huge pointy-toothed grin. I stuck my tongue out at him.

Bobby was waiting when we got inside the house and wrapped me in his arms. I let myself relax into him. Yeah, *let*—as though my body wasn't ready to collapse and I wasn't leaning on him for support. He walked me into the living room and we practically fell together onto one of the couches.

"What the hell happened?" he asked, putting a finger through the stake-hole in my blood-soaked cami. "You were just supposed to be there for surveillance."

"The council vamps had other ideas."

The rest of the rebels had appeared—Brent hugging Marcy much the same way Bobby was holding me. Silvio smirking, Paige wide-eyed at the sight of Alistaire, and Laurel looming in the be-tween-space connecting the dining and living room, arms crossed, staring Alistaire down. Wasn't a fair contest.

He stared back. "Hello, *chick, chick, chick,*" he said, like she was a puff-feathered little peep running around a farmyard.

"Freak," she answered.

Alistaire laughed, and it was the sound of madness. "Ah, even a chick will peck if you squeeze."

Laurel shifted her gaze to me, then leveled it at Marcy. "I send you out for recon and *this* is what you come back with."

"First," I said, settling myself better on the couch so that I had a little more dignity and a little less wilt in my posture, "you didn't *send* us. We went. Second, Alistaire *is* our recon. He was on the inside. And things have changed. By tomorrow that facility might be a mere shell. We knew they were bugging out. We didn't know they're as good as gone already. And now that they've rounded up the council vamps, they're not going to stick around long enough for us to bust them out."

Her arms dropped from their adversarial position, down to her sides. "What?" she asked, stunned.

"You might want to sit down for this," Marcy said.

Laurel did, shuffling her steps until she hit one of the chairs in the living room and then perching on the arm.

"Go," she said, and I had flashbacks to our federal handlers, Agent Stuffed Shirt (Sid) and Stick-up-her-butt (Maya) telling us to report.

Whatever. I wasn't getting into a power play. Not until it mattered.

I let Marcy take it. She told Laurel and the others essentially what we'd told Imanyi and David in the van, only with more detail, talking about the empty lab with the raided refrigerators, about the defenses they had in place, and what Alistaire had told us about Ophelia and the super serum.

Finally, she wound down, and Laurel sat there with her face frozen in a look of *oh shit.* "Wow," she said. "Wow."

"This changes everything," Silvio contributed.

"Thanks, Captain Obvious," Paige answered.

"Do you think the council sent *all* their vamps up against the Feds?" Marcy asked.

All heads swiveled to her. "What?" Laurel asked.

"I saw Chickzilla." I put in. "I can't speak for any others, since I don't know their whole team."

"But now that you mention it," Marcy said, picking up where I left off, "it doesn't seem like they'd leave their home base unguarded. It's like when we used to play capture the flag at recess. You always leave someone behind to guard your flank and your . . . stuff."

"But if the Feds were expecting them, they'd also have been prepared to strike while they were divided. I can almost guarantee they sent a team out to round up whoever remained."

"We need to find out," I said, rallying the strength to keep on going. "Also, we need to contact the Ghouligans. Let them know we're all right, but also see what they've learned. They've been searching out the federal facilities for weeks in prep for their programs. Maybe they can give us a head start on the mega lab the Feds are fortifying."

"You can't go to the Ghouligans," Laurel said. "It's too dangerous. The Feds will be monitoring them. Any communication will be tracked back."

"We made a plan," I said. "In case the worst happened. Ty McClellan has a burner phone. We have burner phones. We can make this work."

Silvio produced a phone from his back pocket, the cheap one I'd seen before. "You mean like this?"

"How about something fresh?" I asked.

Laurel eyed me. "Okay, but keep it short."

As if I didn't know that. As if she and I hadn't gone through the same super spy club training. I knew how long it took to trace a call.

She went into the kitchen, came back a second later with a phone still in its wrapping and tossed it to me. "Has to be activated," she said.

I handed it to Bobby to fiddle with. Too tired to wrestle with plastic wrap. My normal vampire strength was down to nothing.

Alistaire yawned. "Interesting and all," he said. "But you got anyone to eat?"

David flinched, and I saw his hand twitch instinctively toward the stake tucked into his belt. He didn't yank it out, but he was ready at a moment's notice.

"What about the morsel there?" Alistaire asked, staring at Imanyi.

"Over my dead body," she answered, pulling her own stake.

Alistaire tsked. "Not the same. Blood goes bad so quickly."

Imanyi looked as if she was going to be sick.

"I'll do it," Paige said with only the slightest quaver to her voice. "You can stake him if he gets fresh."

"No one is feeding him," Laurel said, crossing her arms back over her chest. "Or, I mean, *I'll* feed him and one of you can replenish me when I need it. On a volunteer basis. I don't trust Alistaire."

Alistaire looked absolutely gleeful at that. Not at all offended. "By all means," he said. "I'm looking forward to it."

Her face did *not* indicate that she shared the sentiment.

Alistaire rose, and instinctively the humans still standing backed out of his way, but closed in behind him as he approached Laurel, ready to go stabbity-stabbity if he got out of hand.

Bobby handed me the burner phone, and I took it into the kitchen to make the call so that I didn't have to watch Alistaire feed. I had to lean against the kitchen counter to stay upright. There was no answer from Ty or anyone else on his burner phone, so I left a message, short and sweet. "All okay. New developments. Call me."

Then I went back through the living room, where everyone still sat or stood in a frozen tableau, staring at or looking fixedly away from the feeding. I grabbed the power cord from Bobby's lap and slunk into the room that had been assigned to us. I plugged in the phone, collapsed down onto the bed and my body shut down. I became one with the mattress, one with the covers. I couldn't have moved for anything short of a zombie apocalypse. Maybe not even then. They'd mistake me for a corpse. They'd move on and I could get some much-needed rest. I needed to feed myself, but after Alistaire . . . well, I could wait.

I went out like a light.

Gina, a voice said in my head. Not at all skittery. More warm and enveloping, like a blanket fresh out of the dryer. I snuggled in.

Gina, wake up.

Gina!

I bolted upright, ready to find that voice and put it down, and found myself staring into the most amazing pair of blue eyes, the color of the sunlit sky I no longer got to see.

"What?" I asked, but my crankiness was already receding. I could tell from the way I felt that it was full night, and there'd been an edge of fear to Bobby's mental voice. I must have slept past sunset. Probably by a not-insignificant amount.

"You need to feed," Bobby said, gaze roaming all over me as though to assure himself that I was all right, even though he'd vamped me himself and knew that we'd survive whatever didn't kill us outright.

"You offering?" I asked. And yeah, there was a slur to my words. I was tired. So tired. In answer, Bobby rolled back his left sleeve. After he'd jolted me awake, I'd sunk back down into the pillows. They'd accepted me as one of their own. I didn't really want to move for a better angle from which to feed, but I didn't see that I had much of a choice.

When I did move, I discovered, to my horror, that I left a blood smear behind. The blood all over my clothes had still been tacky when I passed out the night before. It was dry now, though, and flaking off a bit as I shifted on the bed. Such a waste.

Bobby eyed it too, but he didn't say a word. At least he'd gotten to sleep in the dry spot. I caught his wrist in my hand, and drew in the scent of his much fresher blood lying in wait just beneath his skin. I licked him once for taste, savoring the spice of his skin before digging in.

The hot rush of his blood took over then. If most of the world was drive-through coffee, then Bobby was like a fine rich French roast. Or high quality Columbian. Or however people rated coffee. Something rich and dark with chocolate overtones. Smooth, but with a nice bite. A kick to it. It hit me hard and my body woke up, starting in my core and exploding outward to my extremities. Until I was buzzy.

Fingers threaded through my hair, fingernails scraping along my scalp. I moaned against his wrist. Then those fingers tightened and pulled, yanking just hard enough to get my attention.

"Gina, that's enough," Bobby said, out loud and in my head.

I didn't want to let go. Bobby tasted good. Felt good. But I couldn't leave him weakened.

Reluctantly, I withdrew my fangs and kissed the punctures I'd left behind. They'd close, but I hated seeing them all the same. I lifted a finger to my lips just to be sure I hadn't left a drop or two behind, and then met Bobby's gaze.

"Thank you," I said. "You taste good."

His dimples appeared, and if I had a heart rate, it would have sped up. "So do you," he answered, leaning down to kiss me.

I sank back onto the bed, and Bobby came with me, our lips locked, and hands exploring each other before the bedroom door sprang open, and Alistaire stood in the doorway, eyes flaming red and beating at his head. "You buzz like insects," he said, then his hands came flying our way. Bobby and I reared back, uncertain what he was going to do. Alistaire snapped his fingers all around our heads. "Pop, pop, pop," he said for emphasis. "You pop like bugs in a zapper. Like Pop Rocks. You explode."

"What the hell?" I asked. "Alistaire, *get out.*"

Bobby repeated it, unleashing some of his mental mojo. I felt it blast out, hit Alistaire like a storm wave, but he was a rock in the face of the blast. He slow blinked back at Bobby, but somehow there was a menace to it, like a monster who knew he could take you any time he wanted. No rush.

"Aren't you going to answer it?" Alistaire asked.

He'd lost it. Absolutely and completely. He'd never been stable to begin with, and now—

My phone rang, loud in the sudden silence.

I looked at it, then at Alistaire, who made a shooing motion with his hands and nodded significantly. I guessed that was the call I was supposed to answer.

I glared at Alistaire as I picked up the phone, first looking at the caller ID, which said, "Restricted".

"Hello," I answered.

"G?" Even with just that—presumably we weren't using full names—I recognized the voice on the other end of the phone. Tyler McClellan, Ghouligan extraordinaire.

"T?" I said, just to be sure.

"Moody monkeys make marvelous messes," he answered. It was the call sign we'd agreed on. I had a moment of panic that I'd forgotten the response. It seemed so silly at the time.

"So do inglorious gibbons."

He laughed. "Great to hear your voice. I want to know everything, but I suppose we have to keep this short. I'm sending you what we've been able to find about real estate sales in the New Orleans area. After Hurricane Katrina, there was so much destruction, so many properties abandoned. The Feds or shell companies bought up quite a bit, but in a lot of cases it was tough—houses had been passed down through generations with no clear chain of title, or the owners disappeared . . . Sorry, not relevant. Just sad. Anyway, I've starred the most likely. I don't think the Feds will set up in the city center. Maybe an outlying area with the most blight and least reclamation. I've focused on commercial properties."

"Thanks so much for doing this," I said, already mentally delegating the search through the property records to Brent and Bobby. They'd probably even get a kick out of it. Bobby could get his geek on. "You guys okay? The Feds haven't dragged you in?"

"Well, they did. We had our big interrogation and all, but the studio sent their people. Have you ever tried arguing with entertainment lawyers?"

"No."

"Don't," he answered. "Very ill-advised. Anyway, we're holding our own. You worry about you. And if you need anything else—back-up, a camera crew . . ."

"You're the first one I'll call."

"And we still want the exclusive. As soon as you're safe and we can get around all this red tape."

"Done. I'm going to send you some info back. Don't know what you'll be able to do with it. The place will probably be sanitized shortly, but . . ."

"Send it. We'll do what we can."

"Thank you, T."

"Any— Gotta go."

And he was gone, just like that. I pulled the phone away from my ear and stared at it like it might have answers. Since it didn't— *duh*—I turned it off in case Ty's sudden emergency had anything to do with the Feds. I didn't want them tracking me by the new phone. Damned global positioning systems, cell towers and the whole nine yards. Without them, we'd be back in the dark ages, but with them we were all way too damned traceable.

Bobby and Alistaire were staring at me, waiting.

"So?" Bobby asked.

Alistaire's eyes just glittered like he already knew.

I started to fill them in, but Bobby vanished as soon as I mentioned that Ty had sent us material, headed, no doubt, for Silvio's computers. I wasn't staying behind in the bedroom to lose a staring contest with the psycho-psychic. He never even blinked unless it was to make a point.

"Out," I told him. I needed to change clothes, and for that I needed him gone.

He slow-blinked at me as he had at Bobby earlier.

"Out!" I said more forcefully, and when he didn't move a muscle, I made myself put a palm on his chest and push. It was risky, and I was fairly certain I couldn't take him if he decided to make an issue of things, but all he did was lick his lips and then turn for the door. I had no idea what the lip-licking was about and no urge to find out.

As soon as he was out the door, I closed and locked it behind him. I turned once again to the clothes my mother, bless her, had brought. More blood flaked off me as I changed, and I scratched at the rest to shed it, but I still needed a trip to the bathroom afterward to clean off what remained. I desperately needed a shower, but I settled for a quick wipe down.

The kitchen and dining room were packed with people, some with typical breakfast things littered around them, plates with bread-based edibles in various states of being devoured—bagels, toast, English muffins—glasses or mugs filled with things other than blood. The smell of freshly brewed coffee was sharp and pungent in the air, making my nose twitch. I missed my mochas, but the undoctored battery acid of brewed coffee didn't hold any appeal, especially with my enhanced vamp senses.

Sure enough, Bobby was in front of Silvio's screens with Silvio hovering, standing over them protectively. Brent had the chair at Bobby's right side, leaning into his personal space as they read from the same screen.

We'd arranged drop folders with Ty, to be erased upon reading. Or downloading. I didn't know how it worked with erasing our digital footprints, but I trusted the guys to know. Brent had been with the Feds a lot longer than we had before he'd bugged out for love of my BFF. I was sure he'd picked up a trick or two on the inside. And no one had come right out and said that Silvio had hacker tendencies, but all the signs were there.

Brent was scribbling notes on some printer paper he'd nabbed—actual physical notes. Bobby, I knew, had a nearly photographic memory. He probably didn't need notes at all.

Silvio cut through the silence, "You'll never get answers that way. Calculations, guesses, sure, but we need more input."

Bobby craned his head to glance up at him. "Like what?"

"Like man-on-the-street kind of input."

"Which would be great, only we don't have a man on the street."

"We could," he said cryptically.

Brent looked sharply at him. "If you have rebel boards or 'vampire resistance' sites or whatever, I can guarantee you, the Feds are monitoring them. If you've said anything—"

"Duh," Silvio answered. "Do I look stupid to you? Wait, don't answer that. I'm just talking about people I know on-line. Gamers, prop board guys, sci-fi enthusiasts. Some of them are from New Orleans. Or Orleans Parish, anyway."

"So you'd say what, 'Hey, guys and gals, let me know of any suspicious activity in the New Orleans area'? First, there's no way we could sort through *that* kind of deluge. Second, if you put that chatter out there, there's a better than even chance the Feds will pick up on it. And if you send civilians skulking around, they could be in danger."

Silvio chewed his lip, thinking about that. "What about if I just lurk? Not those boards, necessarily, but local news or mysterious sightings blogs in and around New Orleans. If trucks are going in and out of a formerly abandoned site, *someone*'s going to have noticed. If there's no 'Future Sight of—' signage, people will be talking."

"Knock yourself out," Brent said. "But be discreet."

Silvio rolled his eyes. "This isn't my first rodeo."

Bobby left him to his screens and opened a laptop further down the table, typing faster than I could follow.

In the meantime Laurel came up to Marcy and me where we hung back, afraid that if we got any closer we'd be roped into research. I couldn't say what Alistaire was thinking. Dark and skittery thoughts, I was sure.

"I want to try something with the three of you," she said.

"Can I watch?" Silvio called from the other room.

Laurel shot him a death glare that didn't quell his interest in the least. "Hey, someone's got to hold the video camera," he added.

She turned back to us, not dignifying that with an answer. "You were all there, at the federal facility with the guards and the researchers. It's possible that physical contact—not *that way*—" she yelled over her shoulder to Silvio, "—might help me focus my remote viewing."

"We could try it," Marcy said, "but we never saw the place ourselves."

"If you could give me someone to focus on . . ."

Marcy was shaking her head. "No one we saw will have made it to the new facility yet, even if they bugged out instantly. Unless maybe they were air lifted."

"I can give you somebody," Alistaire said. "The head lady. She bugged out early. Not a job for her, a calling. Eats, sleeps and breathes blood and bondage." He licked his lips. "Come to think of it—"

"Eww," I said. "Just eww. Do you have to work at being this

creepy or does it come to you naturally?"

Alistaire's smile was full of nightmares.

"Fine, whatever," Laurel said. "We'll set up in the living room."

"And we'll keep watch," Imanyi said, bringing her breakfast plate, which now contained nothing but crumbs, into the kitchen. Paige was right behind her. Hence, I assumed, the "we".

"Great," I said. Any time Alistaire was someone else's problem was a good time. "We'll, ah, go help the boys."

Or maybe not. Marcy put a hand to my arm before I could head into the dining room and hours of deadly dull research. Instead, she dragged me toward the living room after Laurel and her gang, but slowly, lagging behind the others so that we'd have a second to talk.

"You okay?" she asked quietly. She studied me way too closely, as though looking for cracks.

"Why wouldn't I be?"

"G, you collapsed last night before the sun even rose. Like face down, no personal grooming. Pretty sure that's one of the signs of the apocalypse."

That brought a smile to my face. She was probably right. "It was Alistaire's blood, mixed with that other vamp's—Ophelia, I guess. It was like a drug. Crazy high and then a crazy crash. I don't recommend it."

"But the high—"

"Even the high was scary—like I could feel every molecule vibrating. Out of control. I felt like . . . not me."

"But—" she started again and then stopped dead just before we hit the living room and the others. She picked at a nail, an old habit she'd tried hard to rid herself of. Something was bothering her.

"Spit it out," I said, grabbing her hands so that she'd stop picking at them. So she'd have to focus on me instead.

"Do you think that if *I* took the blood it might . . . activate something in me?" Marcy asked. She glanced at me quickly and then away, embarrassed.

I rocked back on my heels, surprised. It hadn't occurred to me how left out Marcy must feel. Bobby had his telekinesis and telepathy. Brent, human as he was, could read objects just by touch. Laurel had her remote viewing. I'd come to my power a little late, but I could mist or ghost or whatever the technical term might be. Now we had Alistaire, the psycho-psychic.

Marcy hadn't manifested any special power beyond the vamp speed and senses. And now that she knew from Alistaire that his line had a habit of developing powers beyond the norm, she must feel terrible, like the last person picked for teams.

I let go of her hands and pulled her in for a hug, but she pushed me away. Hard. If I was human I'd have been thrown half-way across the kitchen. "I don't want your sympathy. Don't you dare pity me."

I stared at her. "Mar, you're the toughest girl I know. Why do you think we're best friends? Not everyone could stand up to my fabulosity. You *are* a super power."

She let out a puff of air that said she wasn't buying it for a second and turned away. "You are so full of crap," she said. "You don't want me to develop a superpower. If I get one too, you're no longer special. You don't get to boss me around."

It felt like she'd punched me in the heart. My chest hurt. Was that how she saw it, that I lorded things over her?

I thought back to the night before. I *had* pushed her into moving in on the federal hospital of horrors, and I hadn't thought twice about it. It seemed like the thing to do, so I did it. *Of course* Marcy would go along.

Which she did.

But . . .

But . . . "How long have you felt like this?" I asked.

Marcy eyed me from our new distance. "I don't know. It's been growing. This isn't high school anymore. We're not the same people. You need to start treating me like my own person and not an extension of you."

"Don't I do that?"

She went from not looking at me at all to staring me down, eyes laser-like in their intensity. "No."

She shot the word like a bullet, and it hit home. "You know the first time I really felt like me in forever? When we infiltrated those vampire lifestylers back in Florida, and I joined the steam-punk gang. My doomsday dress was kick-ass. And that poison ring. You were surprised, I saw it on your face. You didn't know whether I was playing a part or I had hidden depths. *And you never asked.*"

I stared at her without really seeing. Maybe that's how I'd been the whole time. What I was seeing now was myself in a fun-house mirror. Not at all flattering, but still my own reflection.

"In my defense," I said. "There hasn't exactly been a lot of downtime between fighting the fangs and the Feds. And when we haven't been fighting, you've been off with Brent."

"Or you've been with Bobby," she said.

She was right. I was right. She was maybe *more* right, but I couldn't bring myself to say it.

"I'll do better," I said instead. "I really do care. You're my best friend. I just . . . I never realized you minded."

"I didn't used to so much," she admitted. The setting on her stare had been dialed down from incinerate to stun.

I opened my arms, hoping we'd hug it out like we used to when we fought, but massively unsure. I wasn't used to the feeling. I didn't like it one bit. It felt crappy and vulnerable. Her hesitation seemed to last forever, but then she slipped into my arms, hugging me back, at first lightly and then harder when I squeezed her.

"You suck," she said without heat.

"So do you."

"Yeah, but I make it look good," she said, pulling back so that I could see her smirk.

I gave her that one.

"I'm glad we've got this worked out," Marcy said. "You're all the family I have."

My heart rose from the dead to give a great leap at that. "But your family—" I realized even as I said it, and the rest of the sentence ran away from me.

Marcy's face was set, though. Not in pain, but in stone. "You know how religious they are. They'd think I was of the devil. They'd lock me up and probably organize an exorcism, and you know how well we do with crosses and holy water."

I hurt for her.

"Damn," Silvio called from the other room. "If you've given up on the idea of a girl fight, you could at least keep hugging it out. Maybe with tongue?"

"You're a pig," Marcy told him, scorn dripping from her voice. But at least her face was no longer set in stone.

"Pigs are cute," he answered.

"You keep telling yourself that," she said.

"If you're done in there," Brent cut in before Silvio could answer, "Bobby and I could use some help. We have a few possibilities narrowed down. You two could get aerial imagery on them while we finish going through real estate, see how isolated they are."

I blew out a breath. "How on earth are we supposed to access aerial imagery?"

"Google Earth to start," Brent said. "They won't be recent pictures, but they'll be images of the property. It'll help narrow the list to something more manageable."

"Can't," Marcy said with faux regret. "We have to go help Laurel. I think I hear her calling us now!"

"Me too," I said, wondering whether it was the first time I'd ever spoken those words.

Marcy grabbed my arm again, and this time she didn't have to drag me toward the living room. I happily followed her lead.

We entered the room quietly, in stealth mode so we wouldn't disrupt Laurel's concentration. Marcy moved up behind her, and as much as I wanted to do the same thing, I was afraid that two of us looming would be too distracting. Laurel sat so straight in her chair, her feet flat on the floor, lap desk balanced where it belonged, that it was as though she was a puppet and someone was holding tightly to the strings. Her lids were lowered, but I presumed she must have them cracked enough to see the sheet of paper she had anchored with one hand and was drawing on with the other, but maybe not. Maybe her eyes *were* all the way closed and she was staring at an image in her mind's eye. Alistaire was leaning over from the couch, two fingers and a thumb pressed to Laurel's temple as though he was performing a Vulcan mind meld.

Alistaire was definitely looking down at the page, staring at the picture forming on the paper. I was close enough to see it now myself, but it took a second to make any sense. The sketch wasn't architectural at all. It wasn't a *what*, but a *who*. A tall man, which was a funny thing to think, because the image only showed him from mid-chest on up, but somehow the sketch gave him the impression of height. Maybe it was the perspective. Everything about him seemed to loom, from his posture, which was bent slightly forward, over the viewer, to his glasses, which seemed perched on his nose like a bird of prey on a rainspout—which was just what his nose reminded me of, jutting out from his face and slightly down-tilted. I wouldn't have been surprised to see a drip at the end of it. His hair didn't so much loom out of his head as sprout forth like wheat grass.

The image looked familiar. Eerily so. It nagged until I got it, and then it startled a laugh out of me. If Beaker and Dr. Bunson Honeydew from the *Muppets* had a love child and that love child had merged with Lurch from the Addams' Family, it might be this guy. The sketch was all charcoal, but I *knew* his hair was red. Just knew it.

Everyone in the room was staring at me, even Laurel, who'd stopped drawing, startled out of her trance.

I met everyone's accusing gazes. "I'm sorry, but seriously, look at that guy. He looks like a Muppet gone bad. Doesn't he?"

Marcy's hand flew to her mouth as she tried to stifle a laugh of her own. "Now that you mention it, he does look a little like a badass Beaker."

"Right?" I said.

Laurel eyed the drawing, seeing it rather than the image in her head for the first time. She held the drawing out a little farther, studying it at the ends of her reach. "Maybe mixed with Sam the Eagle," she admitted.

"I can see that."

Laurel angled the paper toward Alistaire. "Do you recognize this guy?"

His eyes burned into the paper to the point where I was afraid it would literally catch fire. "No, but—"

His eyes flipped up into his head, and he fell back against the couch cushions, body twitching, arms suddenly flailing, looking like he was having a seizure. Could vampires get seizures? Our crazy transformation seemed to heal everything else.

Laurel lunged from one side to grab the closest arm and pin it before he could hurt himself or anyone else. I hurdled the couch to get at his other side, but I no sooner touched him than he went still. Dead still.

I looked into his eyes to see if he was conscious, to see if he was all there. I found him staring back at me.

No, I found *someone* staring back at me. But it wasn't him. There was no crazy to it. No glimmer like he wanted to open me up and play with my innards. Just a kind of agelessness, as though these eyes had seen everything for always.

"Hurry." The words came out of Alistaire's mouth, but it wasn't his voice, any more than it was him staring out at me through his eyes. The voice belonged to a woman. Not a young one from the sound of her voice—old and rich, but full of strength and a patois. Whoever this voice belonged to hadn't been taken to New Orleans, she'd started out there. "Hurry," she repeated.

"Ophelia?" I guessed. "Can you tell us where you are? Or who the guy is in the drawing? Can we trace him to you?"

"Find Renata," she said, her voice fading. "Tell her—"

Alistaire's eyes rolled up into his head again, and this time when he fell against the backrest of the couch, he stayed there, boneless. Ophelia was gone.

The rest of us stared in silence, waiting to see if he or Ophelia would rally. Neither did, at least not right away. If Laurel had looked like a puppet at play earlier, Alistaire now looked like a puppet whose strings had been cut.

"Ophelia?" Laurel asked the room at large. "Renata? So who's this guy?" She held her drawing up.

She'd been upstaged by a possession. So much showier. Probably why Hollywood didn't make any remote viewing horror flicks.

"On it!" Marcy said, leaning over to pluck the picture out of Laurel's hand. "Facial recognition software? Do we have anything like that?"

"Silvio might. Maybe."

Very reassuring.

Marcy took off with the picture, leaving me, Imanyi and Paige behind with Laurel.

"Don't look at me and Imanyi," Paige said, a big yawn splitting her face nearly in two. If I didn't know better, I'd swear the girl could unhinge her jaw. I knew Alistaire could for certain, but then vamp/human. No contest. "We took second half of the day shift, and it's now way, way past our bedtimes. I could research, but I'd miss something for sure. Probably fall asleep at the keyboard."

Imanyi started to say something. Looked as if it was going to be a protest that she didn't need sleep. I didn't think she wanted to be left out of a thing, but Paige's yawn had been contagious, and she caught it. "Fine, whatever," she agreed. "But wake me up if anything happens."

"Will do," Laurel promised.

"Okay then," I said, as Paige and Imanyi headed off to sleep, "I've got Ophelia and Renata. The names can't be that common. And together . . . I'm sure to find something."

"I'll help too, whoever needs me most. But what do we do about this guy?" she asked, nodding toward Alistaire. "We don't dare leave him unattended."

She was right. If the possession made him peckish, Paige and Imanyi were far too vulnerable, and with Alistaire's speed and stealth they could be drained before we even knew to act.

"Be right back."

I disappeared into the dining room and came back hefting a tiny laptop and even smaller tablet. "Choose your poison," I said, holding one in each hand for Laurel to choose.

"Tablet's mine, so I'll take that."

I tossed it to her, trusting her vamp reflexes to nab it out of the air. I wasn't disappointed.

Marcy popped a head back into the room. "Silvio is sending a scan of your drawing as well as some addresses from their list to look up. Bobby's handling the others. He and Brent are still going through real estate. Not just recent sales, but federal facilities already owned. Some were sold due to military cutbacks, like the Naval staging yard, but others are still government owned. Anyway, they're on it."

"Thanks," Laurel said, already focused on her screen. Typing and waiting while the tablet booted up.

I looked around for a decent place to sit. Laurel had the easy chair. Alistaire was sprawled all over the couch, which left me the uncomfortable option of pushing his legs aside and joining him. The single other option was the rocker, and looking at it, I could tell my feet wouldn't hit the floor—the perils of being five foot nothing—which meant I'd have no stability or comfort.

I sighed. Loudly. Laurel didn't even glance up. Sacrifice unremarked, I went to the couch, shoved Alistaire's left knee over toward his right and sat down. I turned on my borrowed laptop and asked "Passcode?" when the prompt came up. She looked over, probably spotted the alien-head sticker on the back of the screen and said, "Soylent Greens."

"Huh?"

She spelled it out for me, and I typed along, repeating, "Huh?"

"Soylent Greens is people," she said, as if that made it all clear.

"Oh, sure. Makes perfect sense."

I tried to open the search browser before the computer was fully ready for me and wasted another sigh at the delay. Whirly, swirly, wait-a-minute graphics were the bane of my existence. Those and garlic. And stakes, holy water, and running water, apparently. Also, white after Labor Day, mismatched patterns, clashing colors and any shade of neon. Okay, so my existence was basically a minefield and I was some kind of *gorram* hero for surviving. Gah, there was Bobby and his geek-speak infecting me again. *Firefly* this time—which, okay, wasn't *so* bad. Actually, Inara was sort of my new fashion crush, and I liked Kaylee's spunk. And—

I hit my hand against my head to knock sense back into it, and at that, Laurel *did* look up. "You okay?" she asked.

"Five-by-five," I answered.

Good enough for her. She went back to what she was doing, and my swirly thing had stopped, my browser now up, set directly to Google as a homepage. I typed in Ophelia and Renata and New Orleans, and got about a million hits, but none of them actually seemed on point. After the first five, I wasn't even sure why they'd all come up. They seemed to mention one name *or* the other, but not both. There were obituaries—a lot of those—and company or academic type directories. There were some crime reports—a stabbing, an arson, financial malfeasance. None of it seemed very promising. Nothing proclaimed, for example, "Renata and Ophelia Blank, two sassy-ass women, living at So-and-so Court, key under the matt." *That* would have been helpful. Unlikely as all hell, sure, but helpful.

No point in another sigh. I settled into a better position and prepared to slog through all the obits and articles, searching.

I finally found the two names in one place, in the offerings of an occult shop on Dumaine Street. Renata—no last name, like Madonna or Cher—was a card and palm reader, a fortune teller. Ophelia Dubray had been a spiritualist, who specialized in contacting the other side, conducting séances and the whole nine yards. *Had been* because the advertisement I was looking at was an old one for the shop. When I went looking for something more recent, Ophelia's name no longer appeared. But now that I had it in full, I went back to the search engine and back to the obituaries. I knew I'd seen Ophelia Dubray before.

Sure enough, I found her, but I wasn't sure how on earth it would help us. Our Ophelia had "died" over a year ago in a house fire. We knew she hadn't, not really, but that might have been the end of her mortal self, after which she rose again as a vampire. Or she might already have been a vampire, which could have allowed her to escape the fire.

I tried to find an address for Renata, but with no last name, it was an impossible task. At least we had a place to start, the Occult Outpost. To me it seemed an odd name for a shop, like a Trader Joe's for the supernatural set. Maybe that's what they were going for. Something that would invite the tourists in rather than scare them off.

"Got her," I said, turning my laptop around so that Laurel could see the shop's website. "Renata works at the Occult Outpost. And I think Ophelia is Ophelia Dubray. She used to work there as well."

"Dorian Gray," Alistaire burst out, suddenly awake, arms and legs flailing. One arm hit the laptop and nearly sent it spinning to the floor. If I hadn't reacted whip-fast, it would have been a shattered mess.

I stood with it and moved toward the rocker, even if my feet weren't likely to touch the floor.

"What?" Laurel asked, impatient.

Alistaire beat at his head. "No. No-no-no. That's not right, but Dorian . . . *something*. That's the doc's name. Ophelia heard that much."

Laurel responded only with hands flying across her tablet keypad. She looked up after a few seconds, "Anything else?"

Alistaire looked at her with psycho-eyes, and she actually shuddered, but she didn't give up. "Is he a scientist? A doctor? Anything at all? Just *Dorian* doesn't give me enough to go on. I keep coming up with links to the show *Penny Dreadful.*"

"I don't know," he practically shouted, twitching all over, so agitated I thought he was going to raise his fists again, either to Laurel or his own head.

"Okay," I jumped in. "It's okay." I'd never tamed a lion in my life, but I wondered if the trainer used this same kind of tone. Probably not. Probably the trainer had to show the lion who was boss. With Alistaire, that seemed like a good way to get eaten. "We've got enough to start."

And we did. It was time to get with the others and see what they had. It was time to talk strategy. Also, we were probably going to need a bigger war chest. Whatever they'd gathered for going up against one measly little federal facility wasn't going to work for storming a fortress.

Laurel and I rose at the same time, and she quickly skirted her chair and the side table next to it to get to the step up to the dining room before I could. Like we were having a race. I thought about what Marcy said about me always expecting her to follow, and I let Laurel have her victory. I tried to tell myself that I could be a team player, but I wasn't so sure that was true unless I was the one leading the team.

I let Laurel tell them what we'd found so far on the Occult Outpost, even though *I'd* been the one to find it. (*Doesn't matter, there's no I in team,* I told myself, thinking what a really stupid statement that was.)

When she ran down, the guys admitted that they still had a long way to go. Too much real estate, too little information that could be found without all the Feds' privacy-violating sniffer programs. Brent sounded particularly bitter about no longer having access to that software.

Silvio linked his fingers, twisted his hands outward and cracked his knuckles—loudly. "So, when do we leave?" he asked.

Laurel looked around at the guys, since the other girls were sacked out. "That's up to all of you. You don't have to come. It's going to be dangerous. And we won't exactly have the home field advantage."

"Screw that!" Silvio said. "You get to the good part and you want to leave us behind? First of all, road trip! Second of all, New Orleans. Third of all, fighting the big bad. Do I need to go on?"

One side of Laurel's lips quirked up. I thought her face would crack. "You do not," she answered. "But, are you sure?"

David rolled his eyes. Loudly. Yes, humans could roll their eyes loudly. So could vamps, for that matter. It was more attitude than amplitude. "We're sure, already. Jeez. Do you think vamps know their own minds but we poor little humans have to check ourselves before we wreck ourselves?" Now *there* was some malice. He hid it in sarcasm, but I wasn't entirely sure I wanted David watching my back. We were getting out of his town, taking the fight off the streets and onto . . . well, potentially other streets. Maybe his motives were pure. Still, I'd be watching him. Just in case.

"Okay then. We just have to hear from the girls—"

"Hear what?" asked a voice from behind me.

I turned to see Imanyi, wild hair all flattened on one side and rucked up on another. Bed head. Behind her Paige gave another one of those face-splitting yawns.

"I thought you were asleep," Laurel said.

"Who can sleep with all this noise? First your uber-vamp starts with the 'No, no, no' and then Silvio starts up about a 'road trip.'"

"To New Orleans," Silvio added.

"To fight feds and free vamps," David said with significantly less enthusiasm.

"Yay?" Paige said. "No, wait, I mean *yay!*" She looked around. "Right?"

"Absolutely!" Silvio said.

"We'll have to take two cars," Imanyi said practically.

"Or more," I chimed in finally.

Everyone looked at me.

"Come again?" Laurel said.

"We still need to check in on the council vamps to see whether the Feds really did round everyone up. We slipped through their fingers. There are bound to be others. Maybe we can find reinforcements."

Alistaire was no longer beating at his head, but shaking it sadly. "No," he said, leaving out any *morsel* or *pretty, pretty*, "we can't. They're gone. All gone. I see desolation and death. It's waiting for us all, unless we stop this thing."

"*All* of us?" David asked, as if weighing acceptable losses.

Alistaire's gaze bored into him.

"All," he said, with the weight of worlds.

12

It was thirteen hours to New Orleans and only a few hours left until dawn. The drive could be done in a day, but that left us vampires out. The humans—Imanyi, Paige, David, Silvio and Brent—all went to catch a couple hours of sleep, leaving Laurel to supervise the loading of supplies and the rest of us as her workforce.

A little more than an hour before dawn, Bobby kissed me and turned to Laurel. "There's something I have to do before we leave."

I was surprised. We'd worked side by side all night and he hadn't said a thing. Maybe he'd been lost in thought.

"Oh," Laurel said, sounding equally surprised. "But, dawn isn't far, and what we're doing is too important to lose you on an errand."

Bobby's lips quirked, "Gee, thanks for your concern."

"What I mean—"

"I know what you mean. I'm going anyway. You don't have to risk anyone else. I won't be long."

He turned toward the door, and I caught his arm. "Bobby, where are you going? You could be seen. I know you said you won't risk anyone else, but do you need backup?"

He looked into my eyes, his own sad but determined. "I have to see my parents before we go. Don't worry, they won't see me. That would be too cruel. What if we don't come back? But to be this close and not see them . . . I can't just leave."

I understood. I'd gotten to see my parents. Better, they'd seen and accepted me. Marcy couldn't even attempt it, and Bobby . . . I didn't know his parents. I'd never met them. We'd come together on prom night, and I hadn't survived to tell the tale. I'd woken three days later in my coffin, clawed my way out of the grave—totally ruining my manicure—to face a life without tanning options but with eternal youth and an all-liquid diet. Bobby had already been dead to the world at that point. We'd never gotten to the meet-the-parents stage in our relationship. Now—

"I'm going with you," I announced.

"No," Bobby and Laurel both said at the same time with varying degrees of adamancy, if that was even a word.

I didn't spare Laurel a glance. "Why not," I asked Bobby. "If you want to get in and out unseen, I'm the way to go."

"I just . . . it's something I have to do on my own. I need some privacy."

That means he might cry. I hadn't known Silvio very long and already I could hear him in my head. I shoved the thought aside.

"I'll give you all the privacy you want. I promise."

Bobby looked at me then—*really* looked at me. He opened his mouth to say something, but Laurel spoke first, "No, we can't spare one of you, let alone two."

I turned on her. "Look, let's get something straight. Just because I don't challenge you at every point, doesn't mean you're the boss of me. Or him. Or anyone else. If you see this as a dictatorship rather than a democracy, we're out. We can take the Feds out without you."

"Can you?" she asked. "Really? Because from where I'm standing, we're not even certain to take them out together. We're vastly outnumbered, and they'll have all their defenses in place, reinforced because they won't have to spread out their resources over various facilities. Are you saying your personal wants outweigh the needs of the many?"

That struck me, much like Marcy's comment earlier in the night. She had a point, and it hit me right in the feels. That didn't mean that I thought she was right, only that I couldn't put into words why she was wrong.

Bobby took care of that. "No, we're saying that if you run over personal freedoms for the needs of the 'many' then you haven't actually gained anything at all. Then you lose any distinction between us and them. I'm going. If Gina wants to, she'll come with me, because I'm not going to tell her she can't."

Laurel's lips were pursed. She closed her eyes and seemed to count to five. "Fine. Go. But don't get yourselves killed or captured."

Is that an order? I wanted to ask, but I thought it was more along the lines of *break a leg*, so I kept the comment to myself.

Bobby gave a tight nod, and glanced my way. "Ready?" he asked.

Misting out was the best way to go unseen. There was only one problem. "Uh, I don't know where you live . . . *lived*."

Bobby sent it to me telepathically. I already had his blood running through my veins—assuming anything "ran" without the heart to pump it. I wasn't really sure what kind of supernatural craziness kept us going, but now wasn't the time for analysis.

I grabbed him by the wrist, dragged him into a private corner of the living room, and offered him my neck. He'd need to have some of my blood for the mutual misting to work.

I'd already pulled my hair back for him, but he brushed a few strands I'd missed away and tucked them in with the others, letting his fingers rake through my hair, caressing my scalp. I shivered as he stepped nearer and kissed the expanse of skin offered to him, then nibbled it, sending waves of heat and sensation sparking through me. When he bit down, I nearly exploded. I wanted to sink down to the floor with him, but he held me firmly by the waist, and so I stayed riveted by the sensation of his body against mine and the sharp pleasure of him sucking at my neck.

He drew away far too soon, and yet not really. Not if I wanted the strength to get us to his parents' place and back before dawn.

He dipped his head back down to lick at the wounds he'd made, maybe lapping up the one last swelling of blood before the holes closed as if they'd never been.

"Wow," I said.

"I know," he answered. "Every time."

We looked at each other in wonder for a second, and then I said, mouth dry, "I guess we'd better go."

I guess.

I grabbed him, hugged him hard to me and then mourned as I ghosted us both and I could no longer feel him against me.

I drifted us out and away from the houses, toward the road that led away from the lake and toward the south side of town, but it was too far to go in ghosty form. For one, it would take too long. We didn't exactly have propellers or engines or anything to move us in the right direction at greater speed. For another, the right direction was a pretty general thing and we needed specifics.

Unfortunately, precision wasn't something I could do in mist-state. So, I materialized us and promptly screamed like a girl when a pick-up truck honked right behind us. Bobby and I dove into the bushes, the truck blowing past, missing us by bare centimeters. We lay there for a second, stunned.

"Any better ideas?" he asked.

I shook my head. "You?"

"We could steal a car."

I thought the pick-up truck breezing by my rump had given me the shock of a lifetime. I'd been wrong. *This* did it. My white knight, Bobby, proposing grand theft auto . . . The mind didn't just boggle, it gave out entirely.

"Well, we can't hitchhike," he said, defensively. "I'm sure the Feds have splashed our pre-death photos all over the news. And if they didn't, the Ghouligans promos probably did."

"Don't you think stealing a car might attract a little attention?" I asked.

"You're right." Like every woman ever, I wished I'd had my phone out to record that for playback the next time he doubted me.

"Of course I'm right."

He eyed the long stretch of road in front of us and we missed out on the chance of a really sweet ride. A night-dark Mustang GT sped past us going probably twice the posted speed limit.

"I don't like doing it," Bobby said, "but maybe we'll have to hitchhike after all. I can always whammy someone into forgetting about us."

I hadn't even been thinking about Bobby's awesome mental powers. Of course he could erase all memory of us. Unless who-ever helped us out was immune to his mental mojo, like me. I guessed it was a chance Bobby was willing to take, because he stepped toward the road, his thumb out in the universal sign. I stepped up beside him, and we both started walking in the direction we wanted to go. Laurel hadn't wanted to spare anyone or anything else, but really, it would have made a ton more sense for her to have offered one of their vehicles . . . although, loaded down with all the fire power we were bringing up against the Feds, maybe not. And maybe it was best not to take a vehicle that could be traced or followed back to the lake house. If the Feds were watching my parents, surely they were watching Bobby's as well.

"Move," I said to Bobby, pushing him to the side, farther away from the road. I took his place. "Let me." Partly, I needed a more active role right now to take my mind off things. And partly, I was smaller by a good half a foot and less intimidating than Bobby.

The next car . . . the *very* next car . . . stopped for us. It was an old Cadillac, like from back in the days when they made them boat-sized, tan on the outside, though the dealer probably called it *champagne* or *sandstone* or something like that. I heard the locks disengage, and a pale hand mottled with liverspots reached over to pop the passenger door open for me. I had a sneaking suspicion even before I bent down to see Mr. Mendelson in the driver's seat.

I looked back to Bobby. "We're okay, it's Mr. M."

Bobby quirked a brow at me, and I realized he had no idea who that was, but he moved for the backseat anyway, willing to trust me.

"Thank you so much," I said, as I slid into the passenger's seat. "We're headed to Park Lane. Any chance you can take us there?" I didn't want Bobby to have to whammy Mr. M for the ride. Now that I thought about it, I didn't want him to whammy Mr. M at all. I had no idea what that might do to a person, especially someone his age. Was that age-ist? I didn't know, but my feelings were my feelings.

Mr. M patted my arm before putting his hand back on the wheel. "Absolutely. Headed near there myself."

He put the car into gear and we started rolling down the hill, significantly slower than that Mustang GT had been going.

Bobby leaned forward from the back seat. "What are you doing out so late?" he asked. Mr. M might not have heard the suspicion in his voice, but I did.

I sighed loudly enough for him to hear me in the back seat. "Mr. M, this is my . . . boyfriend, Bobby." I didn't hesitate because of the state of our relationship, but because of the story I'd told Mr. and Mrs. M the other night. Plus, there was something about Mr. M that screamed old-fashioned, and it made me worry he'd grill Bobby on his intentions.

"Nice to meet you," he said, glancing briefly in the rearview mirror and then nearly swerving off the road. Oh, crap! Bobby wouldn't show up in the mirror and Mr. M must have noticed. I reached over, ready to take the wheel if necessary, but Mr. M righted the car and continued on as though nothing had happened. "To answer your question, young man, it's not late, it's early. Ava and I are early risers, especially when she's got that nerve thing going on. There's an all-night pharmacy on Cardinal Lane just past Park, and that's where I'm headed. Now, you answer a question for me." It was a demand, rather than a suggestion. I braced for the question.

"Are you like her?" Mr. M asked, looking in the rearview mirror again. I knew he couldn't see Bobby, which meant he must want Bobby to see *him* and his serious-face. I stared at him in shock. He couldn't mean what I thought he meant.

"*Like me?*" I asked, because Bobby, just as stunned, hadn't said a word.

"I know you think I'm old and out of touch, but I can still put two and two together and come up with four."

I stared at him. "And what is four?"

He gave me an *oh come now* look before glancing back to the road. The turn into town was coming up. He didn't have much choice.

"That story you told me and the Missus, it was good, but there's been some pretty weird stuff going on around town lately. Not really safe to go out at night anymore. I figured this close to dawn the coast would be clear, but here you two are. You're going to be all right, right? I can give you a ride back as soon as I pick up Ava's prescription."

I was dumbstruck.

"Also," Mr. M added, "you said your boyfriend was abusive and you had to fake your own death and yet here he is, looking as nice as can be. You'd better be as nice as you look," Mr. M said, his voice totally no-nonsense. "You treat this girl right now or you answer to me, fangs or no fangs."

I teared up. Honestly. Blood tears.

"Mr. M—" I started. Stopped. I didn't really know what I wanted to say except *thanks*, so that's what I said. "Thank you. So much you have no idea. You sure you're okay with this? We're kind of on the run right now. I don't want you getting into trouble for aiding and abetting."

Mr. M laughed, but it turned into a cough at the end. "You think they're going to arrest an old man like me? You thought you had me fooled. I'm sure I can convince anyone who comes asking about you. I've learned a thing or two in my time on this earth."

I wanted to hug him, but he was driving. He turned onto Blackthorn Road. Next turn would be Park.

"You can just drop us off here," Bobby said, at the end of the road. "We'll walk it the rest of the way."

Mr. M pulled over to the side of the street, but instantly engaged the child locks. I tensed up, ready for . . . what? I couldn't seriously believe Mr. M meant us any harm, and if he did, could I really hurt him?

He turned in his seat and looked back at Bobby. "Okay, but I'll need an address. If you're not back here in half an hour, I'm coming to get you."

My eyes nearly bugged out. In that moment, Mr. M didn't sound like an old man. Or if he did, he sounded like an old man with a lot of fight left in him. I'd always liked him. Now I respected him times a thousand.

"Number 77," Bobby said. He didn't argue that Mr. M wasn't tough enough to handle things, and for that I respected *him*. "But give us a little wiggle room, okay. Might take us thirty one minutes."

"Fine, one minute grace period. That's as far as I go."

Bobby reached forward a hand and Mr. M shook it. I put a hand overtop both of theirs and met Mr. M's watery gaze. "Thank you," I said. Maybe it was my gaze that was watery. I looked at him through a red haze. Damned blood tears.

"Go on, get out of here," he said in response. He sounded choked up. "Clock's ticking."

He disengaged the locks, and Bobby and I bolted. We heard gravel spit out from under the wheels of the Cady as Mr. M got back on to the road, and we booked it, keeping to the shadows as we approached Bobby's house. Luckily, this close to dawn the streetlights had gone out, so there were a lot of shadows, but predawn was starting to light up the sky, so there was also very little time.

Bobby slowed nearly to a stop two houses away, and I asked, "What's wrong."

"I don't recognize the car in the driveway."

It was a dark sedan, and knowing it didn't belong and that it was the style preferred by government types made it seem especially ominous.

"Damn," I said.

"We still have to go in," he said, "check on them."

"Of course."

"You ready to go ghosty?"

I nodded, grabbed Bobby and thought insubstantial thoughts. The world faded out—or really, *we* faded out and with that my perception went as well. I mentally pushed off of the spot we occupied and drifted us toward Bobby's house, feeling the change in the air as we passed the two houses intervening and adjusting as we hit his place.

I misted us through a wall or a door or something substantial and then I stopped. I didn't know which way to go, and didn't have much perception in our current form. We couldn't see or eavesdrop. We couldn't check on Bobby's parents. The only way to spy risked discovery.

Suddenly, I—we—seemed to jog to the right, and I wondered if Bobby was able to exert some kind of control. Maybe his mental powers let him tweak the reins. Despite my automatic instinct to take them back, I let go. This was his house, he knew it best. I focused on staying insubstantial and let him handle the directions. Such a guy thing.

When he had us where he wanted us—or so I assumed because we'd stopped—I felt a kind of . . . pulse, like someone squeezing my hand. Slowly, feeling for a panicked reaction in case I was wrong, I let us rematerialize until I could feel Bobby's hand in mine. I could also feel something pressed into my back and something else chunky and squishy at the same time under my feet, nearly twisting out from under me as I shifted. I grabbed him harder to keep from slipping and making a sound.

Where are we? I asked mentally.

Coat closet.

Awesome. Last time I'd been stuck in a closet with Bobby I'd been vamped.

Now, shhhh!

I bristled, but I stayed still and silent. It hadn't occurred to me that with Bobby's mental mojo, he could probably eavesdrop without ever leaving our hiding spot. He knew his mother and father well enough that he could get into their heads, see and hear the conversation from their side. The idea made me a little squirmy. I knew I didn't want to get into *my* parents heads, but that was me. And surely his parents weren't thinking squicky thoughts about each other with the Feds visiting.

He opened up the channel into my mind too, so that I could also hear if not see.

"A death cult," his mother gasped. "And you're saying that our Bobby is part of it. That's why he . . . he ran away? Why he was implicated in the disappearance of those bodies from Shady Pines Cemetery?" The same night Bobby and I'd had our broom closet tryst, I'd been killed in a car accident. When I'd risen from the dead three days later a night watchman had seen Bobby and me run off together. I'd forgotten that Bobby had been implicated in . . . well, the news people hadn't known what to call it. Grave robbing didn't really fit when the corpse was your accomplise.

"We've been hearing talk of vampires—" Bobby's father added.

"That's what they call themselves," a voice said. It was deep, it was deadpan, and it wasn't one I recognized. So not Agent Sid. Definitely not Agent Maya. Maybe they'd failed at grabbing us one time too many. Or maybe these were their reinforcements. "You've probably heard of the zombie drug that's been in the news. Lowers your heart rate and paralyzes your body for a time to the point where any pulse or breathing are undetectable. It appears the person has died. It's terribly dangerous, and some kids never do come back. We're trying to crack down, which is why we need to find your son. We need to find his supplier."

Bobby's mother started to cry. "I can't believe he's mixed up in anything like this. He was an A student. Scholarship material. It must be *that girl.*"

That girl was me. I tried not to bristle, especially because if anyone had gotten anyone into anything, it was Bobby who'd sucked me into his unlife style.

"Very possibly," a new voice said. Also male, but softer, scratchy. As though he had laryngitis or his vocal chords had been damaged and this was as loud as he could go. "It's very important that you let us know right away if you see or hear from him."

"Of course," Bobby's father said. "If you'll leave your number . . ."

There was a pause, during which surely there was a passing along of cards, and then Bobby's father showed them out.

I expected Bobby to squeeze my hand again, to signal that he was ready to go, but he stayed frozen, and I didn't push him.

After half a minute, I heard his father again, back in the living room. "Come on," he said to his wife. "Let's get you back to bed."

"How can I sleep after that?" she asked, her voice harsh. "How can you even think about it?"

The next words were so soft, I was sure only Bobby with his mental mojo could even hear them. "They're lying," his father said, close to his wife's ear if I had to guess. "You don't make pre-dawn house calls for a drug investigation. A bust, maybe, but . . . Come on, we'll talk somewhere else."

Somewhere the Feds hadn't been and wouldn't have potentially planted listening devices. Bobby was brilliant. It seemed the apple hadn't fallen far from the tree. His father was no slouch. If his mother hadn't been so upset, she probably would have realized the truth as well. And there must have been other clues. Both Imanyi and Mr. M had said there'd been a lot of strange things happening in Mozulla. Fighting in the streets. Not everyone would have accepted the easy explanation.

It wasn't the first time we'd heard the zombie drug idea bandied about. Plenty of conspiracy sites had touted it when the Ghouligans started with their program promos. Maybe the Feds had even started the rumor, had bots or trolls spreading it far and wide. Not that the drug would explain our failure to appear in mirrors and on film. Or many, many other things. Not that reality had much bearing on what people would believe. Not in the era of "alternative facts". Bobby squeezed my hand. I looked up at him—not that there was anything to see in the deep dark of the closet. *Follow them?* I asked mentally.

Not tonight, he answered. *It's enough to know they're all right. They know I'm alive . . . or at least, they believe. Let's keep it that way. If I don't come back, I'll live on for them. If I do, all this madness will be behind us. I'll see them then.*

I squeezed his hand back. *Gotcha. Let's go.*

I could feel his pain through our link, but also his resolve. The feelings winked out with us when we went ghosty again, thoughts and senses equally fuzzy as we misted through the walls and back onto the street. Then I drifted us down the road, afraid the Feds might still be watching the house.

It was impossible to tell light from shadow in this form, but I pushed us along until I thought we were far enough away, then rounded the corner of the density to our right and let us rematerialize. We were about five houses down, sheltered by the side of the house. Still the brightening pre-dawn light sapped my strength, and I could feel sleep starting to pull at me. Bobby still held my hand, and now guided me toward the road where Mr. M idled his car, waiting.

"Everything go okay?" he asked as we poured ourselves into the back seats.

I nodded. It was all I had the energy for.

Mr. M didn't waste any time putting the car into gear and getting us underway, back toward the lake and the safety of shelter.

"Okay," Bobby said, sounding as tired as I felt. "But the people after us—they're here. I hope you stay out of their notice."

"Don't worry, young man. I told you I can take care of myself. You just take care of you."

I leaned into Bobby, resting my head on his shoulder, and he put his arm around me and angled his head down to lay on the top of mine. We rode the rest of the way in silence.

We ducked down as we hit the lake road, in case anyone was watching. "Park in your garage?" I asked Mr. M. "We can take it from there."

He turned to look at me and I waved him back around. I hadn't seen any surveillance on the road, but I didn't want to take any chances.

He didn't ask questions, though, just hit the button on his garage door opener as we got to his driveway, drove in, and clicked the button to shut it again as soon as we were clear. Bobby and I waited for the garage door to close before opening our car doors.

"Want to see something cool?" I asked Mr. M, who looked at us like *now what?* He'd earned it, and anyway I couldn't do any less for him than I'd have been willing to do for the Ghouligans studio audience.

I took Bobby's hand again and waved to Mr. M as I ghosted us out. The shock on his face was priceless. I wished I could use my phone camera to capture it.

The sun dragged at us as we misted through his walls and rounded the lake toward our house. I wasn't crazy enough to try to skim over the lake again. But around had its own risks. Dawn was very close now. I could feel the sun as though it was super-heating the air, like we were in danger of being flash steamed or spontaneously combusting or something. I willed us faster, but I had no idea if it had any effect. All I could think about was the burn. If I had a body, no doubt there'd be pain. As it was, all I had was panic.

I tried to shut it away, to focus on distance and density, to sense when we'd hit our target, but my awareness narrowed to the heat and the fear that Bobby and I might burn off like morning mist. And then we were passing through something a lot denser than air. As soon as we hit the other side, it all became too much. Pain propelled us back into our bodies, and Bobby and I collapsed together into a heap right there on the back porch, crisping as the sun nearly broke the horizon. Someone ran out from inside the house and threw blankets over us, the shade blissful, but the weight of them pain itself. It hurt even more when they wrestled us to our feet and guided us inside, but we made it probably an instant before the sun rose completely and incinerated us on the spot. Then all I knew was oblivion as we fell away into the sleep of the dead.

13

The whole world was shaking when sunset snapped open my eyes. I startled out of sleep, throwing both hands out to catch myself, one scraping against hard, gritty metal and the other catching flesh. I was baffled by both the quaking and the sensations, but as my sight seeped back, it cued me in that we were rattling around in the back of a van and that the flesh I'd touched was Bobby's.

He clutched me back, twining his fingers with mine. "Good morning," he said with a slow smile. "Or, I guess, *good evening.*" He gave the last two words the bad Romanian or Russian or Hungarian accent Hollywood had chosen for movie vamps.

There was a masculine groan off to the side, and when I looked over, there was Brent, blinking sleep out of his eyes. Brent, but no Marcy. I kept looking, unable to process.

"Where's Marcy?" I asked, like he'd know. He'd just woken up, same as us.

I scootched myself up against the wall of the van so that I could sit against it and get a better angle on what was going on. It didn't really help. We were in the back cargo area, and between us and the front of the van were a pair of thick black-out curtains that went along with the blacked-out back window. Probably not street-legal, but I had bigger concerns.

Brent propelled himself toward the black-out curtain and whipped it aside. "What the hell is going on?" he asked. "Where's Marcy and the others?"

Now that the curtain was out of the way, I could see David in the passenger's seat. I couldn't see who was driving, until Imanyi took her attention off the road to answer Brent.

"Hello to you too. They're in the other car. We had to take two. We hit some traffic on the way, but we should be to New Orleans within half an hour. An hour max."

"You put her in another car with that . . . that . . . *Alistaire?*"

Imanyi turned back around, and it was David who answered. "Hey, calm yourself. Someone had to ride with him. Laurel and Marcy can take him. It's two against one. Plus, Silvio thinks he's Rambo with all his weapons. If Alistaire gets out of line, he's got water pistols, garlic bombs and stakes."

He didn't know Alistaire very well if he thought all that made anyone safe, especially in such a confined space. Luckily, Alistaire was on our side . . . for now. But one crazy vision and who could say?

"No," Brent said, commanding, like he was one of the Feds again. "It won't do. You have to pull over. Exchange me for Marcy."

"Can't do it," Imanyi said, equally fierce. "You're needed. All of you. The others are headed straight for the guest house."

"Guest house?"

"Somewhere we can all stay. Totally private, totally secure and completely sun-proof. Well, they call it paparazzi-proof. It's meant for famous people who value their privacy, but it'll work great for us. Gina's parents set it up," Imanyi said from the front.

"Are you sure it's safe? Untraceable?" I asked.

"That's what they tell me. I guess famous people are big on anonymity as well. I don't know all the details. Only that they put it in the name of S. Surrus."

I felt like the Grinch at Christmas—my heart grew three sizes. Su Surrus was my all-time favorite performer. The fact that my parents knew that . . . well, I'd never thought they were paying that much attention.

Bobby climbed through the curtain and took the passenger seat behind Imanyi. That left one passenger seat and two of us, unless we all wanted to get really cozy, which I did. I shoved at Bobby's leg to move him over toward the window so I could share his seat. About half my backside fit. I figured it would be a balancing act to stay put. Probably a good work-out. The whole vamping thing had given me eternal youth and all, which probably meant nothing was going to give out, but I wasn't taking any chances. I waved Brent into the other passenger seat.

It gave us all a view out the windows, now that the sun was safely down, not that there was much to see. We were on the highway, traffic slowing to a crawl as we approached the city, so it was cars, cars and, oh look, more cars. Oh, and Jeeps and SUVs and even a banana-yellow Hummer that had to be burning gas at an absurd rate. From where I was sitting, it didn't look like things were going to clear up any time soon. There was a line of vehicles in front of us longer than the holiday check-out queues at the mall.

"Taking a detour," Imanyi announced.

"Got it," David said. He fiddled with his phone, no doubt having his GPS recalculate, and announced. "Get off at the next exit."

"Already in the plan."

It took fifteen minutes to go the single mile to the next exit, and we couldn't see the cause of the back-up. An accident, almost certainly. What we *did* see shortly after getting off the highway was a neighborhood that was a study in contradictions—newly reno-vated houses, no doubt restored after Hurricane Katrina damage, and storm-ravaged houses, boarded up, defaced with graffiti, or with political statements spray painted all over the boards. Some had front-door access blocked by branches or in one case a fully uprooted tree. Others had roofs caving in or the black scarring of mold. Still. After all this time. In contrast, the houses around them were mostly painted cheery colors. Yellow and green were pop-ular, but there were also blues and purples, some with contrasting trim on the windows and door jambs.

They were almost without fail one story, long and narrow.

"Shotgun houses," Bobby said, and I braced for an explana-tion. Bobby never missed a teaching opportunity. He'd have made such a great dad some day, boring his kids on road trips with in-formation they could someday bore others with in turn. But he'd been vamped. The dead—or undead—weren't able to create the living, as far as I knew. He'd never be a dad. I'd never be a mom. Not that I'd ever thought I wanted to be, but . . . The idea that I couldn't, that I didn't have the choice, gave me a surprisingly sharp pang.

"They called them shotgun houses," Bobby continued, as ex-pected, "because from the front door to the back is a straight shot so that both doors could be opened to encourage cross-breezes. You could literally fire a bullet right through without hitting any-thing. In theory, anyway. The rooms are arranged one behind the next."

"And that one?" I asked, spotting one twice as wide as the others with a door on either side, one red, one green.

"Double-barrel or double-shotgun house," he said. "Really two houses sharing a central wall, like a duplex."

"Turn here," David said, as we came to the end of a street.

"What are all those Xs?" Imanyi asked Bobby.

Now that she mentioned it, there were Xs painted on many of the houses—all the ones that hadn't been renovated, in fact.

"Don't encourage him," I groaned, even though I was secretly wondering as well.

"FEMA markings," Bobby obliged. "I'm not sure what all the notations mean, exactly. I'd have to look that up, but I know they marked the houses to show they'd been searched for survivors and people in need of rescue. Pets too. I think the top mark is the date searched. Left is probably the crew that did the searching. Then maybe people or pets found, alive or . . ."

"Dead," Imanyi finished for him.

"Yeah."

We all fell quiet, a moment of respect for the immensity of the disaster and those lost.

David's phone suddenly piped up, loud in the midst of the silence, telling us to take the next left in five hundred feet.

"Turn here," David said, as though we all hadn't heard.

We did and a block down were greeted by a huge, gorgeously painted mural on the side of a building with floodlights illuminating it. The entrance was on another street, so we couldn't see what the structure was, but from the appearance, it was probably a school or a municipal building. The mural itself was a musical staff, winding almost like a road. There were notes interspersed with faces, instruments, notations, and all along the outside of the staff, in the background space, were overlapping children's handprints in every color of the rainbow and more. It was exuberant and cheerful.

"Beautiful," Brent commented.

We all agreed.

Not so long after, signs let us know we were headed into the city proper, though the increasing stoplights and traffic would have given that away. We turned down Canal Street, the main road separating the French Quarter from the business district, which we knew because Bobby told us.

There were people everywhere. Neon everywhere, Mardi Gras colors—purple, green and gold. Tourist shops, hotels, eateries, and an Insectarium, which freaked the bejeebers out of me. Why on earth would anyone *pay* to see bugs? I'd pay to keep them away! There were jewelry shops and clothing stores and more food and even more drink. It was a lot to take in.

"So where's this place we're staying?" Bobby asked.

"On the fringes of the Quarter," David said. "We'll head there after. Laurel thought it would be best for the five of us to go straight for Renata. Turn here," he added, after his phone chimed in with the information.

Here was Royal Street. One lane, one way, mostly pedestrian-free, except for one early reveler who swayed off the sidewalk in her four inch heels and caught herself on the car stopped in front of us. There were also bicycle cabs pedaled by girls in Hooters-length shorts and guys in man-buns. Okay, I only saw *one* guy, so I didn't know they were *all* rocking the man-buns, but this guy certainly was, streaking it though with bright purples and blues. His shorts were slightly longer than the girls, but his shirt was open, showing washboard abs. Not the big, bulky kind that came from lifting weights, but the kind from crunches and body sculpting. I was guessing that while the bicycle cabs would get a person from point A to point B, the big attraction was flirting with the driver.

This wasn't the big party street, and it was still early evening, so right now there were more browsers than carousers. Royal seemed to be a street of galleries, antique stores, thrift shops, jewelry and estate sales, but there were still the requisite bars and cafes.

"In 200 meters, turn left on Dumaine Street," David's phone demanded.

"Three blocks down on the left, it looks like," David said.

"Are you positive it's still open?" I asked.

Dumaine Street sported a lot of small shops, many of which looked closed for the night, gates locked over their front windows and entrances. There was a doggie clothing boutique, a skateboarding shop, a voodoo emporium. And there, on the left, the

Occult Outpost.

We all spotted the lit sign in the window at the same time, *Seekers Welcome*. There was no place to park on Dumaine, so Imanyi turned down a side street and pulled into the first available spot.

"Do we have a plan?" Brent asked.

"Well, Ophelia said to look for Renata, right, so I assume she's an ally," Imanyi said. "Aren't we just going to go in and talk to her?"

"Amateurs," Brent said under his breath. When Imanyi asked, "What?" he answered, "That would be great if we weren't wanted and Ophelia weren't captured. For all we know, the Feds have already gotten to Renata or are watching her at the least, waiting to spring a trap. So here's how it's going to go. Imanyi, you watch the front entrance. David, you look around to see if there's a back way out—fire codes probably demand a second exit. You watch that. Bobby, Gina and I are going in."

Since this was exactly what I'd propose, I didn't protest him taking lead.

"Vamps are here, so the humans get sidelined?" David asked, an edge to his voice.

"*I'm* human," Brent reminded him. "And it's not about that. You ever watch cop shows, FBI shows, anything? There's always someone at each exit, part of the team. I'm going because I can read objects. Bobby's going because he can read people. Gina's going because she can mist out with any information in case of ambush. It's all about what makes the most sense."

David didn't like that, I could tell. *He* wanted to make sense in the situation, but he couldn't argue Brent's logic.

"Okay," David said, getting out of the car first, leading that charge. "Let's go."

We did. "This would be so much easier if we all had those FBI earpieces so we could keep in touch," David grumbled.

"We'll requisition them for the next mission," I said wryly.

David shot me the side-eye, then broke off from the rest of us to duck into a cut-through between buildings that might lead to a back alley and the rear exit Brent had told him to look for. Imanyi trailed us, pretending to be preoccupied with her phone as we turned the corner so that anyone watching wouldn't connect her with us.

I didn't hold Bobby's hand, even though I could have, since we were walking in as potential clients. I wanted both hands free in case of trouble.

We passed one man on the street who smelled like a liquor store alley—all booze and piss—and one young woman trying not to look like she was wiping away tears as she hurried to her car, but other than that, the street was quiet. Imanyi took up position across from the Occult Outpost, still focused on her phone, apparently texting someone. Laurel, for all I knew, maybe with an update.

Bobby, Brent and I headed for the door, which chimed as we entered, warning of customers. The smell of incense hit us instantly, sandalwood and something. There were too many old and new scents at war with each other to pick out much beyond that. The lighting in the shop was no brighter than out on the street, so our eyes didn't take any time to adjust. As soon as we entered, there was a check-out counter to the right, nearly obscured by racks of merchandise—spiritual almanacs, tarot decks, new age art cards, voodoo and voo-don't dolls, astrological window clings, alligator claw backscratchers, preserved gator heads. The touristy stuff, I presumed. The deeper magic stuff was probably toward the back of the store, which seemed to open up to the left, where a series of hanging panels partitioned the room off for readings. One panel was already open to reveal a table with a beautiful dark-skinned woman with a nose-ring, dressed in a colorful batik dress, her hair in thick roped braids tied into a bundle at the base of her neck by a scarf that matched her dress in colors if not patterns. She was sitting at a table that, in contrast, was draped with a simple black cloth in the center of which was an actual crystal ball.

She'd looked up at the sound of the chiming door and her kohl-lined eyes studied each of us in depth before settling on me. "You come seeking answers," she said to me.

Which was a pretty good guess, given that their sign said "Seekers Welcome" and we were here during prime party hours in a spiritualist shop rather than a bar, but still, I felt like she actually *knew*.

I nodded, then wet my lips, which were weirdly dry. "I was told to ask for Renata."

"Told by whom?" she asked, cocking her head. "I like to know which of my clients to thank." Her voice had . . . not so much an accent as a cadence. Her voice rose and fell like waves.

"I don't remember," I said lamely. "A friend."

She nodded, though her gaze sharpened, and I had to force myself not to squirm.

"Well, your friend hasn't steered you wrong. I am Renata, and it appears my next appointment has not shown. Gemma," she called, and released me from her gaze as she turned it toward the check-out counter. I turned to follow it and noticed a girl I hadn't before, sitting behind the counter, all but hidden behind the merchandise.

"Yeah," she called back. In contrast to Renata's melodic voice, hers was sharp and bright, like light glinting off a knife.

"I don't have anyone waiting?" Renata asked.

Gemma looked around, as though to be certain. "No one who's checked in with me. Lady K——," she said, in such a way that I knew she was leaving off the rest of the name for client confidentiality, "didn't show. Didn't call either. Should I call her?" She sounded like she hoped for a negative.

"Please," Renata said instead. "Just to be sure she's okay. And to reschedule."

She turned back toward us . . . toward *me*. "Well, perhaps it is fate that you come to me at this time."

She gestured to the chair across from her, and I looked back at the guys flanking me.

"Why don't you browse," I asked.

"Actually," Brent said, "I'd like to watch, if I may. I'm fascinated." Despite the warmth of New Orleans, he'd kept on the jacket he'd been wearing since Ohio, hands tucked into the pockets so that no one would note the odd fact that he was wearing gloves. He'd take them off, I knew, if he needed to get a read on something, but until then all the input would be too much.

She studied him. "If she says it's acceptable, you may stay, but if you want to be read, it's two readings, two fees."

Brent looked stricken at the very thought. Marcy, I knew, would have eaten it up. She was probably kicking herself that she wasn't here right now. I'd have to absorb all the details to relate to her later.

Brent nodded at Bobby, and I assumed they exchanged some kind of mental speech as they traded places. I wasn't used to having Brent at my back. It wasn't that I didn't trust him, but he wasn't Bobby, and . . . it just felt wrong.

I preceded him into Renata's alcove and took the seat she'd indicated. Brent stood behind me, looming over us both. Renata looked up at him. "This won't do," she said. "There is another chair there, up against the wall. Perhaps you would use it?"

It wasn't really a question, and Brent didn't mistake it for one. He had to take his hands out of his pockets to grab the chair, and I watched for Renata's reaction when he did. When she didn't react at all, I looked over at him and realized that he must have nudged the gloves off in his pockets. His hands were bare. The look on his face didn't give anything away, but surely the chair had tales to tell.

He set the chair down beside me and sat without another word. Apparently, we weren't going to question Renata right away. We were still feeling her out. I was going through with the reading. A weird electric shock of excitement and fear went through me. After all, our own psychic Alistaire's predictions had been a pretty mixed bag. And according to him, I was chaos, which was kind of okay. On the other hand, he'd seen desolation and death all around us, which definitely wasn't. I wondered what Renata would sense, assuming she was the real thing.

"Do you prefer the cards or a palm reading?"

"What about the crystal ball?" I asked. It seemed like such a classic.

"We can do this, yes," she said. "Though sometimes seekers are disappointed that they do not see what I see. The mists reveal all, but only to me. I am the conduit through which the visions flow."

I looked over at Brent, wondering if he was buying this. Surely even seekers often came with doubts. I didn't think it would be out of line.

"Whatever you want," he said with a shrug. He wasn't interested in me and my fortunes. He was watching Renata.

"That's fine," I said, still curious. "I'd like the crystal ball."

"As I suspected," she said. But what else would a psychic say? She reached for my hand, presumably to guide it to the crystal, but as soon as she touched it, she screamed. Shrieked, really, dropping the hand like it was hot and backpedaling from the table so quickly she knocked her chair over and nearly took the table down as well. Brent grabbed the table to stabilize it, and his eyes rolled up into his head. He dropped the table like Renata had my hand and pushed away as well, the legs of his chair scraping across the floor, making a horrible high-pitched sound that nearly eclipsed Renata's scream.

"What?" I asked, trying for calm, but hearing my voice rise as well. "What's wrong?"

Renata's back was pressed up against the curtain separating her alcove from the next, denting it in.

"Hey, what's going on?" someone shouted from the other side.

The curtain was whipped back and Gemma stood in its place, Bobby craning to see from behind her.

"Renata, what the hell?" Gemma asked.

Bobby tapped Gemma's shoulder, and immediately her combative posture relaxed. Her eyes glazed over just slightly, and she said, "Never mind. Whatever. Just keep it down, okay. You don't want to scare customers."

"Clients," Renata said, like it was an automatic response she couldn't help, but she sounded strangled.

"Whatever," Gemma repeated. She let the curtain drop, and I lost sight of Bobby and whatever mental mojo he might be doing to calm down anyone else in the shop.

"You're dead," Renata accused, as soon as Gemma was gone. She stayed pressed up against the curtain, as if it was any protection, but she kept her voice down, either because she wanted to keep things calm or because she feared us and didn't want to draw any others we might hurt.

I didn't think denial would do any good. "Well, undead, technically," I said.

"And you?" Renata asked, spearing Brent with her gaze. "What are you?"

"Human," he said. "Like you."

"Not like me," she answered.

"No?" Brent asked. "Give me your hand."

She caught her left hand in her right and clutched them close to her body, physically shouting her refusal.

"You're a touch psychic, aren't you?" he asked. "Touch clair-voyant, I'd guess," he continued, despite the fact that she'd neither confirmed nor denied, "because true psychics are really rare."

"What do you want?" she asked. "Who told you to look for me?"

She was practically quivering, but despite the fear, she held her ground, stared us down.

"Ophelia," I said, dropping it like a mic.

She froze. All quivering stopped. All movement, even her breath. And then finally she gasped as oxygen became a desperate need. "Ophelia? You've talked to her? You know where she is?"

Renata leaned away from the curtain, closer to us, hope start-ing to overtake fear in her eyes.

"Yes and no. We were hoping you could help."

"How? She disappeared weeks ago. No call, no note, no . . ."

"Visitation?" Brent asked, gently.

"Yes," Renata said, miserably, righting the chair she'd knocked over and sinking down into it. She looked as if she wanted to drop her head into her hands as well, but didn't dare take her eyes off of us. "Why did she appear to you and not to me?"

"So that's something she does regularly?" I asked, confused. Brent had clearly made a logical leap and not taken me with him.

Renata gave a sigh that sounded like a sob and then con-sciously sat straighter to show determination rather than defeat. "How much do you know?" she asked.

Brent and I had stayed in our seats, the better to remain as unthreatening as possible when Renata panicked. Now we were back on the same level.

All clear out here, Bobby said in my head. Probably Brent's too. *I've made sure no one's interested in what's going on in there.*

I nodded, which was silly, because he couldn't see me, but I hoped he got the idea. I shared a look with Brent. How much to say? I figured as little as possible.

"We know she's been captured. We have a pretty good sense of who has her. We just don't know exactly where. We're working on that. She . . . took over one of our people. We got an image of the doctor who's been working on her, and she told us to find you."

"Doctor? Is she sick?"

"Who is she to you?" Brent asked, leaning forward. He hadn't said it, but the implication was that we'd already given out information and weren't giving away any more until we got something in return.

If looks could kill, Renata would have incinerated him where he sat. "She's my grandmere, and the only one I've got left. She raised me after my father abandoned us and my mother died. So if you want my cooperation, you'll tell me right now—*is she okay?*"

I put a hand over Brent's, forgetting it was a bad idea. He drew back right away, but he got the message. His way was going to antagonize. We were doing things my way.

"She's alive," I said. "Or rather . . ."

"Undead, like you," Renata finished, leaning forward so that she could whisper it. "I know."

Well, that made things a lot easier. Guess you couldn't hide that sort of thing from a touch-psychic.

"So, we'll call it alive, because that's how I feel. But the people who have Ophelia—the government," I said, leaning in as she had and dropping my voice, "—don't have her best interests at heart. They don't have anyone's interests at heart other than their own. We want to free her and others, but we need more intel. And manpower. I'm not sure how you can help. Maybe Ophelia just wanted you to know—"

"No," Renata said, voice full volume now. "She didn't want me to know. She wanted me to *act*."

Brent and I stared at her. She was taking this well.

"How?" he asked.

But Renata was shaking her head. "Not yet. I need to know more. I need to meet the person who spoke with Grandmere. I need to make sure you're for real. How do I know you weren't sent to draw me out and gain my trust. How do I know *you're* not from the government, building a list of the wyrd community? Or part of some hate group?"

"Weird community?" I asked.

"*Wyrd*," she said again, and this time I could almost see the spelling. "Eldritch, magical, supernatural."

Brent stared her down. "I can almost promise you the Feds already have a list, though I couldn't tell you how complete. Today they're coming for the vampires. Tomorrow . . . This isn't just about Ophelia."

That chilled me to the bone. It sounded like Brent knew about that list from personal experience. I wondered if he'd had some part in creating it.

Renata and I were both studying him now.

"Give me your hand," Renata said. It wasn't a request. It was a line in the sand. Anyone could hear it in her voice. Either Brent would comply or she'd be done with us. The problem was that Brent had so many secrets to keep. Years of working with the Feds—probably some secrets really were better left unsaid. I knew from my spy training that the Feds would have taught him strategies for hiding things, but I didn't know how well they would work against a trained psychic. Or, not a psychic. If what Brent had said earlier was the case, Renata didn't actually see the future so much as she saw into people's lives and knew what they wanted or needed to hear. Part power, part psychology, like warning a client off a guy who was no good for them or pushing them onto a more promising path. Which made sense, because if we believed in free will, then nothing was predetermined and the future was choose-your-own-adventure, not a book that could be read beginning to end.

It made what Alistaire did that much more amazing. And creepy. Maybe seeing all the possibilities at once, holding all that in your head, made you crazy. Maybe it hadn't been Mellisande's meddling at all. Maybe it didn't matter once there was no going back.

Brent didn't move, considering. He was a telemetric. Usually able to read objects, but I knew it was possible to read people as well, just overwhelming. It overloaded his supernatural circuits. He'd get as much from Renata as she'd get from him. Maybe more, depending on their relative strengths.

"Okay," he said finally, holding out one hand, but not yet resting it for her to take.

Now that he'd given in, Renata didn't look so sure she wanted to touch him. After her reaction to me . . . I wondered what she'd seen, what she'd felt. If she'd come across a vampire before—her own grandmother—it shouldn't have been that much of a shock.

And that nudged me past worried and into potential freak-out territory.

Renata tentatively reached across the black tablecloth and

took Brent's hand. Both her eyes and his rolled back into their heads and both tensed like they'd received an electric shock. It was disconcerting, and I called out to Bobby, *What do I do?*

I let him see through my eyes, or, at least, I hoped that's what I was doing. *Five more seconds,* he said. *Then stop it.*

That sounded like a good plan. I gave it a four-count. It was all I could stand, then I threw the tablecloth over their linked hands so I wouldn't add my touch on top of theirs, and I pulled them apart. Both slumped in their chairs, heads lolling back. I gave them half a minute to recover, worried I'd have to slap them back into awareness, wondering if I could reach in and grab Brent's gloves to do the job without adding to his overload.

Renata recovered first, blinking frantically as though the world refused to come back into focus.

Then she stopped, closed her eyes and forced herself through five slow, deep breaths before she opened them again. "I'll help you," she said, looking at me. "But, damn, the things he's seen."

Brent was starting to blink now as well, but slowly, as though his eyelids were so heavy that each motion might take the last of his strength.

"What did you see?" I whispered.

Her eyesight must have returned, because she narrowed her gaze at me. "That's private."

"You were going to let him sit in on my session," I protested.

"Because you gave consent."

"Fair enough. What did you see when you read me?" I asked, before Brent could be aware enough to take it in. In case . . . in case, what?

"I saw your death."

I almost couldn't draw the breath to ask, "Old or new?"

And then I remembered—she was a reader, not an actual psychic. I relaxed.

"Your first death," she confirmed. "But I've also seen the danger you are in. If I'd given you a reading, I'd have said that have set yourself on a dangerous path, surrounded by death. That if you stay on this route, the future is unclear."

I had chills despite myself. "The future is never promised," I said. No one would have guessed I'd meet my death on prom night in the most gorgeous dress my parents could afford and wake three days later after being buried in an outfit I literally wouldn't have been caught dead in. Life dedicated to fashion. Death to trashion.

"No," she said. "But we invite some outcomes closer while rejecting others."

I couldn't argue with that. We were back to free will. I was way more comfortable with that than the alternatives.

"I still need to meet the person Grandmere possessed."

"That ought to be fun," Brent muttered as he came around.

14

Renata let Gemma know that she would be out for the rest of the night. We collected Bobby, David and Imanyi, and insisted that Renata ride with us. Based on Brent's read, we trusted her, but only so far. Not far enough to give her the address where we were staying and leave her to drive herself, possibly with a few ill-advised phone calls along the way.

The boys tried to leave Renata and me the middle seats, but with Brent still half knocked-out, I insisted he take mine, which left Bobby and me bumping around in the back of the van. It turned out that the place we were staying wasn't too far away, just off Frenchman Street, a guesthouse rather than a hotel that could be rented by the week or weekend. It had a private, gated entrance with security and all the bells and whistles. Exactly the kind of place rich people rented for privacy and seclusion while still being close enough to take advantage of the Quarter. Leave it to my parents to know of such a place. They were the ones who'd found it, though they'd arranged it through a third party so that it couldn't be traced.

The wrought iron front entrance was almost obscured by vines. It led to a small circular drive around an age-darkened fountain of a barely covered sprite pouring water from an urn onto the flowers at her feet that formed the bowl of the piece. The house was built around the drive in a U-shape with the open side facing the street, so that there were verandas on three sides of us, all facing the fountain. The verandas had more of the wrought iron work and more of the vines. They also had lantern-like lights that made it possible to see the red flowers overflowing from baskets hanging at intervals along the buttery-yellow walls.

"Beautiful balconies," Imanyi commented as we drove up.

"Galleries, actually," Renata said. "See how far they extend and the pillars that hold them up from below? That makes them galleries. If they were cantilevered, they'd be balconies."

Oh, she and Bobby were going to get along great. I didn't want to admit I had no idea what cantilevered meant, but I guessed that if galleries had pillars and balconies didn't, that made all the difference. Probably balconies didn't extend out as far either, since that would be a lot of weight hanging out there with no support.

There was a code box hidden among the ivy. Imanyi lowered her window and typed something into it that she read off David's phone. The iron gates swung back to admit us and slowly shut behind us, locking us in.

"What are those spiky things at the top of the pillars?" David asked as we all piled out.

I'd noticed them as well—nasty-looking spikes at the top of the wrought iron columns supporting the galleries that looked like something you'd find on top of prison walls. Designed to take a bite out of crime, I guessed.

"We call those Romeo-catchers," Renata said, "supposedly they were installed on the homes with daughters so that suitors couldn't shimmy up the verandas and visit them in the night or steal them away."

"Ouch," David said. Brent and Bobby winced as well.

"They look effective," Imanyi commented, trying to cover a grin.

There was a code box at the front door as well, and Imanyi typed the numbers in again. This time there was a click, but the door didn't open for us automatically. We had to push our own way through. So pedestrian!

We entered onto a tiled foyer through which we could walk straight out to the back patio, which was sheltered from the neighbors by a high, stockade style privacy wall. It enclosed a soaking pool surrounded by greenery, so that it seemed more a grotto than a yard.

"I hope the rooms have a little less sunlight," I muttered. I could appreciate beauty as much as the next person . . . until it burned my eyes out.

"Black-out shades and everything," Laurel said, stepping into the foyer from the right, where apparently the hallway opened onto a beautiful chef-style kitchen. "You should see what this place rents for. Apparently, it's got everything for the hard-party-ing millionaire who doesn't want to be up with the sun or even know it exists, lest it hurt his hangover. Does champagne give you hangovers?" she asked. "I've never had the chance to find out."

"It's not the champagne that'll kill you," David said. "It's the caviar. Fish eggs." He shuddered, his face scrunched in a comic look of revulsion, tongue sticking out.

"Don't knock 'em til you try 'em," I said. They all looked at me. "What? There's a reason people pay the big bucks for caviar. It's tasty."

No one answered.

"Where's Alistaire?" I asked.

Laurel got a funny look on her face. "In the pool."

We'd just rescued Alistaire from a nightmare hospital with nothing but the clothes on his back. It wasn't likely he had a swimsuit stashed.

I forced myself not to look. Not that I *wanted* to look, but it was the natural sort of reaction, and I found my gaze wandering that way before I snapped it back lest I see something no amount of mental floss could make me unsee. "Is he—"

"Naked?" she asked. "Yup, naked as the day he was born."

My whole face scrunched in *yuck*. I did *not* want to think about that. Luckily, my brain gave me something else to chew on—vampires and water and how we didn't mix. Maybe it was just naturally running water we couldn't take? After all, we sur-vived showers and baths. Or maybe the rules didn't apply to Ali-staire. Nothing about him was exactly normal.

"Oh, Lordy," Renata said, pushing to the front of our pack. "Alistaire is the guy I came to see?" At our nod, she glanced out toward the grotto. "So I'll see more of him than expected. So what. The human body is what it is. He won't have anything I haven't seen before."

I didn't know about that. The extra joints were disconcerting enough when you couldn't get a good look at them.

"Laurel, meet Renata. Renata, this is Laurel," I said, hoping to head her off.

But Renata paid no attention, leaving the introduction in her wake as she made her way toward the back patio. She was going with or without us. I guessed if my grandmother were at stake, I'd feel the same way.

The French doors out to the patio were slightly ajar, and Renata flung them open entirely, and then stopped in the entrance, backing us all up behind her. I peeked around her to see Alistaire, just his nose, eyes and forehead above the water like a gator ready to snap someone up. Even in the dark, I could see that his abyss eyes were riveted on Renata, boring into her soul. I felt a wave of power go out, washing over her with just the dregs splashing up against the rest of us.

Her arms dropped where they held the doors she'd just flung open, and she stepped forward. One foot in front of the other, walking as if she was in a trance. I'd been there, done that. Didn't like it. Liked it even less for Renata, because she was human and Alistaire liked to play with his food.

"Stop it!" I snapped, stepping around Renata and into her path. I was short, and if Alistaire had locked eyes on her while he was standing, I'd never have been able to block the contact, but as it was . . . I waved my hands in front of Renata's face for good measure, but she took another step forward, and another, right into me. Alistaire didn't need the eye contact for control. I knew that, but I'd been hoping to break the trance or surprise him into bobbling the connection. I should have known better. I was going to get run down.

"No!" Bobby said behind me, and the blast of power he sent out matched Alistaire's in intensity.

Renata's raised foot came down almost on top of mine, backing me up a step so that we didn't occupy the same space, but then she stopped. Alistaire exploded out of the water, and I whirled around. I didn't like having my back to him. Alistaire lunged for the edge of the pool, ready to rush right out of it and . . . what? Challenge Bobby for control? But he crashed into nothing, as if an invisible wall had just sprung up between him and us.

"What is this?" Alistaire raged, banging against the unseen barrier.

I had the same question. I didn't know Bobby could do that. I knew he could move objects and cloud minds, but . . . Maybe the barrier was all in Alistaire's head? Could Bobby have turned him into a mime convinced he was trapped in an invisible box? Or, a mime who could speak, anyway. And colorfully.

"You need to calm down," Bobby said, and I thought or prayed to whatever deity existed and didn't have a hate-on for the undead, *Oh please don't let Alistaire kill my boyfriend.* Because Alistaire wouldn't be trapped forever, and he wasn't exactly the forgiving sort.

Alistaire seethed and glared, but he stopped beating at the wall and settled for glaring at Bobby, as though he'd incinerate my boyfriend if only he had laser-vision.

Now, that would be a cool power.

Then all of a sudden, Alistaire's body language changed. He dropped his shoulders, seemed to shrink into himself, probably settled back on some of his extra joints. I wouldn't know. I was trying to keep an eye on his, well, eyes. Watch his face and not drop below the neck. He cocked his head, like a bird, and flashed what was probably meant to be a charming grin. It was disconcerting instead, like a hawk smiling at a mouse. You know, if birds could smile.

"I just wanted to taste her," Alistaire said. "She smells like ginger. Ginger and nutmeg and— She smells like a spice cake!" he finished triumphantly, as though pleased to have figured it out. "Or a pie. Pumpkin. Sweet potato. She tastes orange." He smacked his lips together.

Bobby started to speak, but Renata talked over him. "Enough with all that," she snapped, meeting his crazy eyes when he shifted them from one target to the next. Her. "You talked with Grandmere? How is she? Why you?"

Alistaire's smile grew wider, almost splitting his face in half. Like a gator. "Tasted her too," he said. "They gave me her blood. Dark and dense. Spicy and sweet. Like ancho chilli chocolate, it bites you back."

Renata closed her eyes and breathed for a moment, like she was processing that pain. "That sounds like her," she said. "But why you?"

Her eyes were open again now, and she was staring right into Alistaire's, unflinching. "Gave her mine too, I think. Testing . . . But it was you she asked for. 'Find Renata.' And here you are!"

"Would you get some clothes on?" Laurel asked, unable to take it anymore.

Alistaire smiled, like he'd just won something. It was a shark's grin. As always, too many teeth, too pointed. The better to eat you with, my dear. But then he backed up and without even looking managed to step smoothly into the grotto pool and sink beneath the water until again only his head and snout were showing, waiting for unwitting prey. I shivered.

"So, you met him," I said, glancing at Renata. "Does that help or hurt our case?"

Brent gave me a sharp look, but I didn't see any point in dancing around the question we all wanted answered.

Renata turned on her heel and led the way back into the house. "Tell me everything now. All of it. I'll help. I can't leave Grandmere's rescue in his hands."

"Our hands," Brent corrected.

She whipped her head around and speared him with distain. "I've just met your guy. Do you really think *you're* in control?"

It was a good question. How did you fight your enemies when you had to guard against your own allies? I guessed we were going to find out.

Renata headed toward the kitchen and sat on one of the stools at the breakfast bar. "Do you have anything to drink?" she asked.

"The others went out for groceries. Right now, I can offer you fridge water."

"Fine," she answered.

Laurel looked at me, and I supposed that meant I was to wait on Renata. "Yes?" I asked.

"Would you mind?" she asked.

"Yes," I answered. But I went anyway. Someone had to. I found glasses in the second cabinet I opened, made sure they were dust-free, and pressed one against the sensor on the refrigerator for ice and water.

In the meantime, Laurel grabbed a sheet of paper off the island and set it down in front of Renata. It was the drawing she'd done when Alistaire had channeled Ophelia. "Do you recognize this man?"

Renata touched the paper to move it to a better position, but didn't react otherwise. I didn't think she could read objects like Brent, only people. I wondered if it was a strength and calibration thing—objects having to be drawn out, since they didn't have neurons constantly firing and thoughts swirling—or a difference in abilities.

"No," she answered, pushing the paper back toward Laurel. "Should I?"

"This is the man who has your grandmother," she said.

"One of them," Bobby added.

Renata pulled out her cell phone from the front of her dress, and it only occurred to me then that I hadn't seen her carry a purse. I wondered what else she had tucked down there. Money, almost certainly. Identification? Credit cards? Lip gloss? I'd had a friend like that in high school. Anything you needed, she had it tucked away somewhere. We called her cleavage the Incredible Boobs of Holding.

She typed in a code, pressed a few buttons and held the phone over the paper. I understood what she meant to do when a light from the phone illuminated the sheet. "May I?" she asked.

Laurel nodded, and Renata snapped a picture, then moved the camera into another angle and took a second. Then a third without the flash.

"I can send this out to my network, see if anyone knows," she typed furiously and hit a button before looking up at Laurel again. "Okay, now tell me everything."

"This just in," I said quietly to Bobby, "we need a network."

"You just want minions."

I looked at him from beneath my lashes. "Is that so wrong?"

He didn't respond, but it gave me an idea. I was going to mull it over, think on it, save it for later, but Bobby read my mind. "Gina," he said, even more softly than I'd been speaking, "what are you thinking."

"When I know, you'll know . . . apparently."

We left it at that.

The others came through the door at that moment anyway, bearing groceries and reeking of olives, salami, and seafood. Maybe it was the vampire senses making everything so much stronger, but—

"What on Earth?" I asked Marcy. She'd been in an enclosed space with the smells. I didn't know how she could stand it.

"I know, right?" she said, her face all scrunched so that her nose crinkled in classic *Ick* face. "Muffalettas and shrimp po boys," she announced. "I'm told it's classic New Orleans cuisine."

"Po boys?" I asked, hoping the answer would explain muffalettas as well.

"Sandwiches," she said. "Subs, really—"

Her face froze and she stopped right there, looking past me out toward the back patio. "What was that?" she asked.

I didn't turn around. I'd gotten enough of an eyeful earlier. "Oh, that's just Alistaire, having a swim."

"Not that, the light!"

Morsel! Alistaire shouted in my head right then. Maybe everyone's head, because Marcy winced too. *We've been found.*

There was a huge splash and then a blistering crack, like someone was using a battering ram on the palisade fence surrounding the grotto. The splash was Alistaire lurching out of the pool, unhinging all of his joints until he looked like a huge centaur spider, man body riding the jointed legs. He had too few limbs for the spider analogy to be apt, but no one was splitting hairs at the moment.

Another huge crack sounded from the front door, and I knew the Feds had found us.

Hands grappled at my arm, gripping me hard in fear. "What do we do?" Renata asked me, "You led me into a trap."

"Or you led the trap to us," I answered. Not that I believed she'd done it intentionally, but she might have been watched and followed.

But we'd been trained to spot surveillance. Even if Bobby and I missed it somehow, I had complete faith in Brent. We must have slipped up somewhere. Maybe the Feds had flagged last minute rentals, particularly those with privacy features. Possibly we weren't even the first vampires to use this place and it had already been on some kind of watch list. But blame didn't matter right now. Survival did.

Alistaire just made it into the house, sloughing water, when the fence behind him collapsed and soldiers poured into the backyard.

Bobby faced them down, sending a blast of power at them. The soldiers' infiltration suits lit up blue, and whatever Bobby had sent crackled against them, then seemed to fizzle out. The team kept advancing.

"Run," Laurel yelled, racing out of the kitchen and down a hallway and to a set of steps leading to the second floor.

"Up?" Bobby asked, even as he followed. There was nowhere else to go. Without a doubt, the Feds would have the first floor surrounded, but what were we going to do on the second? We couldn't very well fly out of there.

There was a huge concussion at the front door and the sound of splintering wood and groaning metal. That door was toast. We were about to have more company than we could handle.

Alistaire gave a blood-curdling cry from the back of our pack. Something must have hit him, but I didn't hear him fall as we clattered up the steps.

Another concussive blast came from above us, followed by the sound of shattered glass, then the metallic clang of canisters striking and bouncing across the floor and the immediate hiss of something unleashed. Garlic gas. Laurel choked and fell back, nearly knocking the rest of us down the stairs before David and Imanyi caught and steadied her. Only Renata's continued death grip on my arm kept me on my feet. At least the still-human among us were unaffected by the garlic. But that wasn't going to help us against the soldiers.

The gas burned like poison, like acid, seeping into my cells until they were on fire.

I had to do something, and I couldn't take anyone with me, not without the blood exchange, and there was no time for that. I forced myself to ignore the distress signals my body was sending out and let it go. Let the body go. Mist out.

Renata's startled cry was the last thing I heard before I was floating, misting up, up, and above the garlic gas, which hadn't yet made it all the way to the ceiling. But I felt it around the edges, where the burn wanted to pull me back into my body.

I misted until I felt movement, bodies disturbing the flow of the air. I went solid behind the upper-floor invaders, thumping to the ground and immediately bitten by the acid burn of the garlic. I ignored it as the two commandos in front of me swung their guns my way. I didn't know what they were loaded with, but I wasn't waiting to find out. Faster than they could react, I reached for the first gun and tried to yank it away, but it was strapped to the guy's neck, so all I succeeded in doing was wrenching it out of his grip.

No matter, I swung the stock for his head, but that gave the other guy time to aim for me. The wooden bullet hit the side of my neck at the same time the butt of my gun knocked the other guy in the temple, sending him reeling back, ripping the gun right out of my hand.

The pain brought blood tears to my eyes, but I was still standing. Unless the commando hit my heart or put enough bullets in my neck to sever it entirely, I would survive.

I dropped to the ground anyway. He'd expect that. He wouldn't expect the instant attack. I lashed out at his leg, catching him hard in the shins. If I'd still been merely human, it might not have had any effect, but with my vampire strength, bone snapped. He started to go down.

But a third commando was already taking aim at me over his buddy's falling body. As I dove and he pulled the trigger, something—someone—grabbed him from behind by the strap of his gun and yanked him off his feet, sending his shot into the ceiling.

There was a volley of fire from downstairs, and I heard cries of pain all around. This couldn't continue. We were outnumbered and outgunned. The others were trapped in a stairwell. And my neck where the wooden bullet had torn through was becoming a raging inferno.

Beneath me, the stairs gave a huge groan, like students at a pop quiz. Then something exploded into my field of view, blurry through the stinging blood tears brought on by the grenade. *Alistaire*. He had Renata tucked under one arm like a football he was running into an end zone. He encircled my waist with his other arm and pulled me tight to his body, where he held me trapped. Then he sprinted over the downed commandos, knocking aside a newcomer by swinging me as a battering ram into his solar plexus. My head delivered a solid blow, but the commando got a shot off as he went down, and I knew from Alistaire's hiss of pain that it had hit home. But then we were to one of the windows the commandos had blown out, jagged shards still at the top and bottom like predator's teeth.

Alistaire looked out, my head and Renata's going out over the grotto. My feet were dangling in the air, but Renata was taller than me. Hers must have been dragging on the ground. I squirmed to get loose, to go back to the others, but Alistaire might as well have been made of marble for all the give.

"Here!" I cried to the others. "Run!"

Alistaire's arm spasmed around me, squeezing me so tight I couldn't draw any more air to speak. If I'd needed to breathe, I'd have been dying.

The Feds had left a couple of commandos out in the courtyard in case any of us escaped. There were likely others in the front as well. But even with bogeys in the backyard, I knew what Alistaire meant to do. There was no other choice—with his arms full of us, he couldn't climb, so up wasn't an option, which meant . . .

Oh god, he was going to jump. We were vamps. He and I would surely survive the fall, but Renata was human and there was no telling how incapacitated we'd be once we landed. Alistaire was bogged down with Renata and me, and therefore unbalanced—something he was no doubt used to, mentally anyway.

I no sooner thought it than Alistaire leaped, going airborne. Another wooden bullet tore through me, my shoulder this time. Alistaire hissed in pain, so I knew he'd been targeted as well. Probably primarily. No telling how many wooden bullets had torn through him. But he didn't loosen his hold on Renata and me as he landed in front of a commando and bulled right through him like he was nothing but a paper soldier. He ran him right over, then dropped his center of gravity and swung Renata at the second commando, her legs flailing like nunchuks. Her feet hit him in the stomach, but not hard enough. The commando kept firing right over her at Alistaire.

I misted out of his grip. It must have been shock that kept me from thinking of it before. I reappeared right next to the shooting commando, yanking his gun up so that he missed this time, and whacking him in the head with his own barrel. At vamp strength, I felt a small crack of bone. Not enough to kill him, but enough for his eyes to roll back up into his head and for him to drop like a stone.

I turned back toward the house, but Alistaire said, "Stop." Gasped, really. His words were weak, but the compulsion he laid on was strong. Like back at the hospital, my body was suddenly not my own. "The others are lost. Have to save ourselves to save them."

He grabbed me then, put me back under his arm and sprinted

away, leaping the back grotto fence where it still stood like it was nothing.

I howled inside. Bobby! Marcy! Brent and Laurel and the gang . . . It felt like the worst kind of betrayal running from the battle, leaving them behind. I understood Alistaire's reasoning, but I didn't accept it.

We'd been ambushed. My friends were headed for the horror hospital and there was nothing I could do.

15

We landed in someone else's back patio area, thankfully deserted, but Alistaire sprinted out of there as well, running through yards, leaping barriers like the jumping spider he reminded me of, even without the extra limbs. By the time we'd stopped, Renata had fainted—or maybe had the air squeezed out of her—and we were blocks away. I had no idea where. I was sure Alistaire had no idea, but the house had an uninhabited, neglected feel to it. The weeds and riot of flowering vines were reclaiming the yard in the name of Mother Nature.

When Alistaire let me go, my feet sank into the overgrown grass. Renata sank into it as well, though prone. She looked like Sleeping Beauty or Rapunzel surrounded by a tangle of her hair, the briar wall hedging her in. I gave one glance to make sure she was breathing and then unleashed my full fury on Alistaire—screaming, punching, kicking, howling obscenities at him for leaving our friends behind until he too collapsed into the greenery.

Which was when I realized why he hadn't fought back. Or even stopped me. He'd used up all his strength getting us here and now the wooden bullets and the blood loss had knocked him to his knees.

"Oh, hell," I said.

My neck was on fire. I could only imagine how Alistaire felt. I could see six separate wounds in his check, neck, chest and shoulders alone. I had to get him healed. But first, I had to get him out of sight. I knew how the Feds worked from my time among them. They'd be cordoning off a perimeter. Probably doing house-to-house searches—questioning occupants and surveying the grounds at the very least. Like vampires, they couldn't bust into homes uninvited, at least not without warrants or a state of emergency.

Or so I hoped.

As long as we didn't give the Feds any cause to search this

place, we could lie low. But a naked man-monster carrying a woman under each arm was bound to have attracted witnesses. Security cameras would be useless for catching Alistaire, and if it had just been the two of us, we'd go unseen by security. But he'd carried Renata, and she wouldn't disappear with us. I could only imagine how it would look to see her bobbing about, making mysterious leaps without her feet ever touching the ground. If only the Ghouligans could get a hold of *that* footage . . .

"Come on," I said to Alistaire. "You've got to get up. I've got to get you inside."

His red-glazed eyes met mine. "Can't," he said.

I slapped him in the face. His teeth extended, and he showed them to me, snarling like a big cat.

"Fine," I huffed, extending my wrist. "Have a sip. Just enough to get your strength up. Then we have to hide."

I was pissed at him. But not pissed enough to desert him. Not after he'd saved Renata and me, even if I hadn't wanted to be saved. Maybe if we'd stayed and fought we could have rescued the others. We could have won the day.

I didn't really believe that, but I couldn't *know*, and the fact that I accepted the necessity of what he'd done made me mad at myself, which only made me angrier at him, which made no sense.

The pain of his bite into my wrist—no finesse—tore me out of that loop, and I had to watch carefully, monitoring us both so that he wouldn't take too much. If Alistaire used that mental mojo to keep me from tearing away, could I do it? I didn't know and didn't want to find out. As a newly minted vamp I'd had more resistance to compulsion than this. The only thing I could think was that the Feds or Ophelia's blood had done something to him. Changed him like Mellisande's assassination attempt had changed him. Apparently, the adage 'whatever doesn't kill you makes you stronger' worked double-time for Alistaire.

After half a minute, the wound on his cheek started to heal up. His neck and chest as well. I judged he'd had enough and told him so. Alistaire growled, muffled by his mouth still on my wrist, but he released, wiping his mouth with the back of his hand. "Blackberry, cherry, cinnamon spice," he chanted. I assumed he was naming my flavors and tried not to be icked out.

"Cinnamon, spice and everything nice," I said. "Yup, that's

what I'm made of. Whatever. Get your ass up."

I turned toward Renata without turning my back on him. Her I could lift with my super-vamp strength. Probably I could have carried Alistaire too, but he'd be ungainly and I couldn't handle them both at once. Plus he was still naked and *no*. Hell to the no.

Renata's eyes fluttered and she moaned as I got my arms under her, ready to grab her in a fireman's carry. As I started to lift, she came fully awake and spazzed out, kicking like a mule so that I dropped her feet to the ground. If I'd just been kidnapped by Alistaire and come back to consciousness trapped again, I'd have reacted the same.

Her eyes were the size of dinner plates.

"Good," I said calmly, "you're awake. Follow me."

I hoped she'd follow my lead and take things in stride. It seemed best to give her space. She'd run off or she wouldn't, but I didn't dare spook her any further.

I went to the back door of the house's patio and found it locked, of course, but the doors were sliding glass, and I knew from experience that if you mule-kicked them, in just the right place, they'd pop open. It was a failing. Unless they were high-end, of course. These looked builder-standard.

I did my kick and sure enough, the doors popped. I slid them open and only then turned to see Renata backing toward me, away from Alistaire, who she was watching like a hawk. He was getting to his feet, the remaining wooden bullets pushing their way out of his body. He staggered a step toward the back door and Renata suddenly turned and ran for it, blowing past me into the house. Alistaire was there seconds later, closing the door behind him. By that point, Renata had already found and locked herself in a bathroom. I knew it by the sound of the latch and the start of running water. Sink, not shower. The difference was clear.

Alistaire and I stood eying each other. But we were still where we could be seen from the back yard and that wouldn't do.

"Come with me," I said. We'd entered onto a small eat-in kitchen that opened through an archway into a hall that ran the entire length of the house to the front door. *Modified shotgun?* I wondered. You could certainly shoot through from the front to the back, but rather than one room leading into another there was a hallway opening onto each. Everything was compartmentalized.

The next room off the hallway was the bathroom Renata was holed up in. The room beyond was a small bedroom. About the last place I'd choose to be alone with a naked Alistaire, but maybe we could find him something to wear. The medical bed up against the wall and the old lady smell—cold cream and menthol—argued against that, but I lived in hope.

I headed straight for the closet and opened it onto not much of anything. Whoever had lived in this room hadn't for some time. There were a few faded house dresses, though, hung neatly on hangers, and one fuzzy pink robe. My mind momentarily boggled at the thought of Alistaire in it.

I pulled the robe off the hanger. "Here," I said, handing it to him. "Put this on."

He didn't take it.

"No," he answered, jutting out his chin and crossing his arms.

I gave him my death-glare. "Do it or so help me, Renata and I will leave you and go off on our own."

"With me unchecked to terrorize the town?"

I put my free hand to my hip. "You're terrorizing *me* right now. Take the robe. I'll search the rest of the house for something more appropriate, but you will be clothed when Renata comes out of that bathroom. *If* she comes out. You hear me?"

Alistaire's lips twisted in what I once again supposed to be a smile, or some cheap knockoff of one, anyway. "I have excellent hearing."

He held a hand out, and I handed him the robe. I stood with my hands on my hips while he put it on, just to be sure. Then, as promised, I went off to find him something else to wear.

The front room of the house was a living room area with a set of stairs oddly placed behind a half-wall. On the second floor were two bedrooms, shotgun style, one leading right into the next. The first had belonged to a petite woman, which worked out well for me, since I was petite (or fun-sized as my very *ex*-boyfriend Chaz would have put it). I was able to appropriate a cute, cap-sleeved red top to change into after I got cleaned up and things settled down. The second room was clearly for a toddler. The final space probably counted as a bedroom, but was currently serving as storage for boxes, banged-up furniture, exercise equipment, and a rack of clothes. Pay dirt! Whoever the clothes on the rack had belonged to—a man from the looks of it, outdoorsy from the style and durability of the clothing—had about a foot on the woman of the house. I grabbed everything off the rack rather than pick and choose, and as I did, the thing moved, and something scurried out from underneath it.

I screamed and bolted for the doorway as the biggest bug I'd ever seen—a black-red cockroach the size of my father's wallet—bolted for the wall. I met Alistaire halfway up the stairs, not looking quite so ridiculous in his pink bathrobe when he was headed to save me from the big bad bug.

"Cockroach!" I said, pointing. "Or palmetto bug or whatever they call them here. Mutant sized. Do *not* go in there." I thrust the clothes into his arms. "Here, I brought you these."

Alistaire stared past me, as though he expected the bug or other danger to be nipping at my heels. As though disappointed that it wasn't. But when I pushed again at the clothes, he took them.

"I'll be downstairs," I said, contorting to get past him without touching. If the bug was upstairs, I wanted to be downstairs. There were probably more where he came from. Hells, downstairs might not be safe either. I'd rather be fighting Feds than insects any day. At least those you could see coming.

A pang gripped me at that. My friends were in danger and I was worried about cockroaches and clothing. I needed to get a grip.

Back downstairs, I crept to the still-closed bathroom door and tapped.

"Yes?" Renata asked, after a pause. Her voice sounded raw.

"Renata, it's me, Gina. Oh, I don't think we were formally introduced. There wasn't time. Alistaire, the scary psychic, is upstairs getting some clothes on. He's really not that bad once you get to know him." By some definitions of the words *not* and *bad*. "He did what he thought he had to do."

"I know," she said. "It's just too much. Grandmere was taken. Then you show up and tell me she's alive and that you can rescue her. Then all of you are taken. It's—"

"Not hopeless," I said, as though I was having a psychic moment. "We've faced crazy-impossible odds before. Hell, we're vampires. Some would say *we're* crazy and impossible. But we're going to get our friends back. And your grandmother. Failure is not an option." It seemed like I'd heard that somewhere before.

"But how?" she asked. I could hear that she was right on the other side of that door, waiting for me to say the magical words to unlock it.

"That's what we need to figure out. Together. We evaluate what we're up against. We look at our assets, and we decide how best to utilize them. We need you as one of our assets. We need you to come out and plan with us."

"I have your word neither of you will feed on me."

"I promise," I said, even though I would have to eat, and the little bit of my blood Alistaire had gotten wasn't going to hold him. We'd need to go hunting. And it was going to be damned dangerous.

The doorknob turned, and a second later, Renata came out, holding a towel bar in her hands like a bat. I must have been upstairs screaming at the cockroach when she ripped it out of the wall for protection.

She laughed when she saw me catch sight of it, a near-hysterical sound. Then she relaxed her stance just a bit. "Yeah, I don't know how much good this was going to do. I just needed to feel I could do *something*. If it came to it, I wasn't going down without a fight."

"You're my kind of people," I told her.

We smiled at each other for a second before Alistaire came busting in. "I look like a freaking weekend warrior."

Alistaire clothed was far less fearsome than Alistaire unclothed. I'd noticed the wardrobe rack had tended heavily toward khakis and other earth tones, and sure enough he stood there in a pair of tan cargo pants with a camo T-shirt and bare feet. Only instead of looking soldierly, he looked silly. Alistaire was not made for earth tones, but for black and burgundy and other darks that hid the blood better.

"As long as you're ready to fight," I said.

"Always," he answered.

Always except for a little while ago when we'd bugged out. It ate at me.

"What about you?" he asked Renata, staring at her in that creepy way that made it seem like he wasn't looking at, but *into* her. "Are *you* ready?"

"Yes," she said. She held up her phone. "I wasn't just pulling myself together in that bathroom. I was putting out a call for help.

Emergency meeting tonight. I told them it couldn't wait."

Alistaire flinched like he'd been shot again, his whole right side jerking back as from a blow. When he righted himself, his eyes were black. All black. No whites showing. Shark's eyes. "No!" he said, firing it like a shotgun blast. "Phone!" He snapped his hand out for it, and Renata, whose eyes showed white all around them, slapped it into his palm without question.

Alistaire started to close his fingers around it, then dropped it like it had burned him. "No," he repeated. "It's a trap. The Feds might close in tonight, they might mark and wait, but they're watching. You're all targets. If there's a bug out code, use it. Now. So they know it comes from you. Then grab any contact you need —only people you absolutely know and trust—and we destroy this phone."

"But I'm a touch psychic," Renata protested. "I'd know if anyone had compromised my phone."

Alistaire looked ready to pounce and do what he'd ordered right then if she wouldn't. He shook with the effort to hold himself back. "It might not be your phone they've compromised, but your network. Your people. You think the government doesn't have psychics of their own? People who can twist your mind? *You* could be the mole and never know it."

"Am I?" she gasped.

I didn't like the way he was looking at her now. Before I could protest, he lashed out and grabbed her hand, the one she hadn't entirely retracted when she'd reached out with her phone. With it, he pulled her in until his lips rested on her forehead, like a mother might take a toddler's temperature.

I leapt in to peel her away, but it was like pulling at a locked door. I'd break off the handle—or more specifically, Renata's shoulder—before I'd budge her.

Just as I contemplated doing some serious harm to the psycho psychic to draw his attention away from Renata, he released her, and she staggered away.

"No," he said. His favorite word tonight. "Not the mole. Tasty, though." He licked his lips and Renata's face twisted up.

"You've got to get him under control," she said. She'd grabbed back her phone and was now furiously typing—the bug-out code, I presumed.

"It's been tried," I said wryly. "I don't know that there's any-one left to tell the tale."

She glanced up at me sharply, maybe to see if I was kidding. When I didn't give any sign of it, she returned to what she was doing. A second later, she handed the phone back to Alistaire.

"Here. Do what you've got to do. I have all the contacts I need in my head."

Alistaire snatched the phone, did an excited jump into the air and raced out of the room. With a baffled glance at each other, Renata and I chased after him into the kitchen, where he was rummaging drawers and countertops. He came up with a wicked look-ing metal hammer with a smooth face on one end and a bumpity one on the other that looked as if it could do some major damage. I hadn't spent much time in kitchens, but it was either for tender-izing meat or pounding the bejeebers out of pecans and such, maybe for pies. Umm . . . pies. I let my inner Homer Simpson out for an instant before I realized what Alistaire meant to do with the mallet and dashed to find a cutting board or something for him to pulverize the phone on before he settled for the counter.

Too late. Alistaire had the phone down on the kitchen island and was merrily smashing it to bits, parts flying like shrapnel. Then he chased down any parts bigger than a toenail and smashed them too. When he was finished, he looked at us with homicidal glee. "Hulk smash!" he said.

It was so unexpected it surprised a laugh out of me. Renata looked from Alistaire to me like we were both crazy. And maybe she was too for not running the hell out of there.

I got myself under control, and said, "I'll change, and then I'm going for burner phones. You two play nice."

Renata's expression went from accusations of insanity to downright fear. Every muscle tightened and stress lines showed like fractures around her eyes and forehead. "You can't leave me alone with him," she said, inching toward me.

Well, damn.

I didn't dare leave Alistaire unattended. There was no telling what he'd get up to. Finding himself a nice, tasty "morsel" at the very least. On the other hand, I couldn't leave Renata to deal with him. She might very well be the meal he craved. And anyway, her powers weren't meant for standing in the way of a determined mutant vampire of questionable sanity.

"Okay, you come with me. But no credit cards and stay away from video surveillance. I'll buy the phones and whatever else you might need." Because strictly human meant she'd need to be fed and all that jazz.

"Protein bars and bottled water. I can live on that forever if I have to."

"Yum," I said. Like blood was any better.

I fixed Alistaire with my glare from hell, the one I used to use to skewer handsy boys. He looked unimpressed. "And *you* behave. No murder. No mayhem. Nothing that will cause a stir or bring the police crashing down on us. Got it?"

Alistaire blinked, then grinned that crazy grin at me. "Got it! Don't get caught."

"I didn't say 'Don't get caught.' I said 'No murder.'" It was an important distinction.

He cocked his head at me, considering. "Okay," he said finally.

I stared at him. "Okay?" That couldn't be right. I didn't trust him as far as I could throw him.

He cocked his head the other way. "Morsel and Madness ride again!" he said, as though that was an answer. "Tally ho!"

Morsel and Madness . . . worst superhero names ever.

And he was gone. Disappeared out the back door the way we'd come.

"Tally ho?" Renata asked.

I lifted my shoulders, let them fall. I was baffled. "No idea. Sounded like agreement though, right?"

"I guess."

I sighed. "I think it's as good as we're going to get."

And if I found out later that we were wrong, what could I do? Had we let the devil loose when we'd freed Alistaire from the federal facility? Would the end justify the means? I thought about my friends being caught by the commandos, strapped down and drained of blood and free will. We couldn't let it continue. That wasn't even in question. But the Alistaires of the world . . . what did we do with them? With this one in particular?

For now the answer seemed to be "Let It Go," which put that damned Disney song in my head and didn't do much for comfort.

16

The first thing I did when we had our phones activated was check in on the digital drop site we'd set up with the Ghouligans. I didn't dare use any number I'd had for Ty in the past for fear the Feds would be monitoring it. Renata worked with her contacts and Alistaire . . . well, Alistaire stared creepily, licking his lips and singing a little song under his breath about blood. I thought it might be something from My Chemical Romance. It had a dark, catchy tune that I was pretty sure was going to get stuck in my head, and that I was going to hate him for it in very short order.

A half hour later, Renata announced that they had a meeting set up.

"Just like that?" I asked. "You didn't clear it through us?"

"Do you know the area?" she asked.

"No," I grumbled.

"Do you think you're now the boss of me? Is it the fangs you think gives you that privilege?"

Ouch. I was struck by the accusation, and even fell back a step as though it was a physical blow, but Alistaire was grinning like a fiend—a big, bloody grin with maybe a bit of flesh still attached to one of his fangs. "Blood is blood is blood. We're all the same beneath the skin."

Creepiest statement ever. True, but still.

Renata pointedly ignored him, though I could tell from the tension of her body that it was an effort. She still looked to me for an answer to her question.

"Fine, you lead," I said. "Where and when?"

"Coop's, the Quarter, one hour."

"Like in chicken coops?" I asked.

Renata heaved a sigh. "As in Coop's Place, the eatery. It's specialty is rabbit and sausage jambalaya, but they've got a lot of other good stuff too. Not that I suppose you two care about that."

Honestly, vampire senses and Cajun and creole seasoning didn't mix. New Orleans had been an olfactory overload so far, but I was getting used to it. I might not be able to eat real food anymore, but I could still roll the taste around on the back of my tongue, which shouldn't have anything to do with scent and yet . . . There were all sorts of things I'd learned since going vamp.

"It's secure?" I asked.

"It's public, it's small. There aren't a lot of windows for commandos to bust through. The owner knows all the locals and how to keep an eye out for trouble. He says he's even got a long table of folks who've overstayed their welcome that he can chase out when the time comes. He won't reserve tables, even for us. Bad for business."

Public was good. More witnesses, less chance of funny business. But Alistaire didn't blend. He was going to scare the crap out of Coop's clientele. Of course, this was New Orleans. People paid good money for that with all the ghost, cemetary and vampire tours. Maybe they'd just think Alistaire was part of the local color.

"How long will it take us?" I asked.

"At a slow walk, fifteen minutes."

"Let's go."

"So early?" she asked.

"We need to scope things out. Make sure no one's watching."

"Table won't be ready yet."

"That's okay, my pretty princess days are behind me. I can stand until I can sit. Not that I expect to do that anyway. We're security and surveillance. We'll stand and survey. But first, Alistaire, brush your teeth."

There was local color and then there was just *ick*.

There were two entrances or exits from Coop's, depending on whether you were coming or going. One faced the street and the other a back alley between businesses which shared a bathroom alcove. Enough space for an extraction, maybe, or the spill-over of a bar room brawl, but not enough for a full on commando invasion.

I knew about the front and back entrances, because I'd scoped them out, dragging Alistaire with me, even though the touch of his hand freaked me out. We were both vampires. Both dead—or undead. Both theoretically more chill than your average bar patron. And yet, somehow he managed to actually suck heat.

Inside, Coop's was all exposed brick, exposed wood, cement flooring, bar stools and trestle tables. In other words, a bar that served food rather than a restaurant that served drinks. But it had more the feel of a neighborhood place, the kind where everybody knows your name, than the party-palooza places on Bourbon Street.

It was full when we got there, but not standing room only. Everyone had a seat, unless they didn't want one, too intent on table hopping or flirting. Renata headed straight for the bar and the girl with the bottle-black hair behind it, sporting an unnecessary-in-the-heat red plaid flannel with the sleeves cut out over a black stretchy top. I couldn't see her bottom half behind the bar, but I'd have bet money on a black mini-skirt and black mesh or lace tights below it. It's what my alter-ego Geneva Belfry would have worn back when I was undercover in a New York high school's goth scene.

Alistaire and I held up the back wall while we waited and watched. Two people approached Renata at the bar. Then three. The goth girl serving drinks had moved on, but a guy in a Bob Marley shirt had taken her place and was chatting with the group. One more woman and they must have hit critical mass. Marley-shirt exited from behind the bar and led them to a long table near where Alistaire and I were lurking. In a dark corner, of course, because—vampires.

The group already at the table had been getting louder and louder by the minute. As far as I could tell, two of the guys were about to come to blows, one of the women was about to lose her liquor and one was at the "hold my beer and watch this," stage. Never a good thing.

The bar guy, probably the owner or manager, rousted them, though not without more raised voices and one swing, which he easily deflected, twisting the guy's elbow up behind him and using it to march him out into the back alley. He suggested the guy might need some fresh air. Aborted-punch guy had some suggestions for him as well. None were PG-13.

Renata's group filled the void left behind, settling at the table, after pushing everything left behind to one end for bussing and mopping up the remaining moisture with a pile of napkins. Alistaire was shooting glances toward where the rowdy group had disappeared.

"No," I said. "We need you as a look-out. You're fine. You've already fed."

His gaze snapped to me. "But I haven't *played*," he said, making it sound like a need and not a want.

"I said *no*."

We had a staring contest that could have gone on all night, but suddenly he bent down and licked my face. Licked it. Like a dog. Chin to forehead, right up over my eyes, which I squinched closed in a hurry, rearing back.

"What, *ewww*."

"No fun," he informed me. "Tasty, though."

I shoved back with both hands, and he didn't budge, though he did laugh, his creepy, skittery laugh. When I turned away, I saw two girls at the nearest table watching us, as though they might intervene. I was touched. They didn't even know me, but yeah, Alistaire was scary and they were *this close* to butting in anyway. To having my back.

I gave them a smile to let them know it was okay, and I walked away from Alistaire, ordering "Stay," and hoping he'd listen.

I wanted to join Renata's group at the table. I needed a sense of them to be sure they wouldn't betray us.

More had arrived, and we were now up to seven in total. A man with the most incredible dreadlocks I'd ever seen eyed me suspiciously as I approached. "Can we help you?" he asked, as though certain they couldn't.

"I'm with her," I said, tipping my head toward Renata.

"Nat?" he asked.

Renata looked up from her conversation and nodded at me. "Everyone," she said, raising her voice just slightly—enough for the others at the table to hear, but not all the patrons of Coop's. "This is Gina."

Someone gasped, and I looked over to see a man so slender he was almost skeletal with a shaved head and all-black yoga retreat wardrobe of drawstring pants and a simple tunic shirt that hung on his frame. He looked like someone had grabbed Jonathan Statham at the temples and stretched him out.

"You're—" he began.

Beautiful? Dead? All of the above?

"Yes," I answered, before he could say whatever it was out loud. "And I need your help."

I met each gaze. In addition to Dreadlocks and Stretch, we had Black-eyed Susan, who I so nicknamed because her bleached-gold halo of hair framed a mahogany face and fathomless eyes; Hoodie-ninja, who could have been male or female, sixteen to thirty, silently watchful; Sasquatch (self-explanatory); and two who looked so average as to defy easy nicknaming. T-shirt Girl and Cheekbones? Might have to work on those.

They had real names, of course, and if I was a better person I'd have remembered them all. As it was, I was pretty sure T-shirt Girl was actually Mila and Hoodie-ninja was Ahn, pronounced with a long aaah. Beyond that . . .

I explained why I needed their help, but Renata jumped in before I got more than a few sentences out. "The Feds have Ophelia," she told them. "That's where she's gone. And they've grabbed others. So far, it's been . . ." she lowered her voice and leaned in close to the others, ". . . so far it's just been vampires, but . . ."

"Wait, wait, wait," T-shirt Girl—Mila—cut in. "You're saying Ophelia was a vampire? I thought she was one of us."

Renata looked as if she'd been struck. "The two aren't mutually exclusive."

And then it was a free-for-all. Questions, comments, arguments, explanations.

I left them to it for a minute. They were going to need to get it all out before they could get down to business. There was a lot to deal with.

Then I cut across it all. "Renata," I said, "do you still have the picture of the doctor who has Ophelia?"

She looked up at me, because I was still standing. One of the few times in my life I'd ever gotten to loom over anyone. "I can find it."

Oh, right, because Alistaire had smashed the phone on which she'd taken a picture of Laurel's drawing. But she'd sent out the photo before he'd killed it, so surely it existed somewhere in the cloud, if she could log onto web mail or whatever.

"Take your time," I said, meaning *hurry up*. I wondered if anyone in the history of those words had ever meant them to be taken at face value.

She got out the burner phone we'd bought and activated for her, and played around with it for a moment while the others continued their discussion. When she found the pic, she called it up on screen and turned the phone toward the others, who leaned in to look and then took the phone to pass around. Renata had sent it to her contacts before Alistaire had smashed her original phone, but maybe not everyone had opened the attachment. Maybe they'd been out and about and not wanted to use data. Maybe they'd been busy or hadn't grasped its importance.

Cheekbones gasped. "That's Doctor Bannon."

Everyone looked at him.

"Doctor Bannon. He—" suddenly Cheekbones was staring down at his hands rather than meeting anyone's gaze. "He did a study at the university a few years ago. When I needed the extra money for Clarissa's surgery."

"You joined a study?" Stretch asked in disbelief. "Vin, you know better. Studies are for hacks. If anyone knew . . ."

Okay, so Cheekbones was Vin. Like in Vin Diesel. I could remember that.

"Relax," he said, "I knew better than to let on about my real power. I was just good enough—"

"Says you," Sasquatch cut in. "I'm sure they hooked you up to monitors and the whole nine yards. There must have been ways to register your power. It's the only way to weed out the fakes. I worked on hardware a few years ago—"

"Wait, you worked on hardware for this sort of thing and you're going off on me for throwing one small college study?"

"Where do you think the work is being done these day? Colleges, grad schools."

"Labs," I snapped out. "Like the one we're trying to close down. Look, we're not going to get anywhere fighting amongst ourselves. Save it. We have a name—Doctor Bannon. That's a start. With that we should be able to find him. The internet, faculty records, something."

"I can do better than that," Vin said, "if you can get me something of his, I can track him wherever he goes."

My heart gave a leap. If he could track Bannon, we could have the whereabouts of the federal facility by sun up. And we could start to plan.

"It didn't work with Ophelia," Renata said, settling my heart back to the lump of coal it had become. "Vin is a dowser," she added for my benefit. "A finder. When Ophelia went missing, I gave him something of hers so that he could track her. Three somethings, actually. There was nothing. Her trail went cold just outside of town. Wherever they've got her and the others, there's some powerful mojo disrupting magic."

Well, crap on a cracker.

I thought of the blue wands the Feds had carried at their checkpoints, the blue sizzle to their suits that neutralized whatever Bobby had thrown at them back at the house. Maybe the tech was like a magical EMP, electromagnetic pulse device, only instead of shutting down electronics, it shut down magic. If the whole place was shielded with it, there was no way I could mist in or out. All the apparent supernatural strength in this room could be meaningless.

No, I wouldn't accept that.

What happened to *Failure is not an option*? Or Yoda's *Do or do not; there is no try*? Or the fact that I was going to wring Bobby's geeky little neck the next time I saw him for the fact that these things were stuck in my head? (After kissing him senseless, of course, for joy that he was still alive.)

"We'll find a way around that," I said with more confidence than I felt. "First, let's see what we're working with. I'm Gina. I'm a vampire, and I can go ghosty, which means I can mist in and out of places." I'd been about to expose my secrets on network television with the Ghouligans. It wasn't hard to reveal them here. Weaknesses, that was a whole other thing. They didn't need to know how limited my senses were in my misty form.

I cocked a head toward Alistaire. "The creepy guy in the corner is Alistaire. He's like a vampire gone wrong. Typical strengths amped up until they're off the charts. Oh, and he's a psychic. An honest to Vlad psychic. Which makes him a little nuts."

Renata snorted, and I guessed it was at me minimizing his

level of insanity.

"Now you," I said, staring back at her to start. I figured the others would trust a lot easier if she demonstrated that she was willing to expose herself, figuratively anyway.

"I'm a clairvoyant," she said. "I get impressions off of people. Unfortunately, I can't dive deep. Or, let's say I can, but not without giving us both a migraine. I've done it once, and it's nausea-inducing. And usually not necessary. You'd be amazed at how much energy people expend thinking about the thing they're trying not to think about."

She looked at Dreadlocks to her left, and he glared back for a second. "You vouch for her?" he asked, even though it seemed obvious already.

"I do," she answered.

He turned his glare on me, the look promising *bad things* if I betrayed the trust. "I'm Rameses. Not Ramsey. Rameses, like the pharaohs. I'm a chemist. I specialize in potions with power."

Like Snape! I thought, but I didn't say that. *Damn* Bobby and his geeky influence.

"Okay," I answered, because he said it like a challenge and something seemed to be required.

He looked beside him, to Black-eyed Susan. "I'm Suzanne," she said, throwing me for a loop, because I'd pegged it. Well, close enough. "I feel electricity and I can manipulate it. Power surges, black outs, a jumpstart to the heart . . ."

I was fascinated. "How does that help you make a living?"

She looked at Stretch across the table on my side, though I didn't understand why. "I'm big at séances," she said. "People want to feel the energy in the air. They want the hairs on the back of their necks to stand up. They want to be moved."

There was a smile on her face, but a sadness in her eyes.

"All that power and you use it for parlor tricks?" It was out of my mouth before I realized how rude it sounded.

"What would you use it for?" she asked.

I didn't have an answer for that.

I looked to Hoodie-ninja, who was next at the table. He—she?—responded by lowering the hood. Beneath was night-dark hair long enough to be pulled back into a pony tail with a couple chunks of bangs falling lose over perfect golden skin, almond eyes with ridiculously luxurious lashes, the kinds celebs get extensions for and a pointed, elfin chin. Most importantly, *I recognized that face.*

"You're *that* Ahn?" I asked, stunned.

Ahn Kim was a famous street performer. On the level of Chris Angel. Commentary on Ahn's act generally used the stage name and didn't try for gender identifiers, though some defaulted to masculine. Ahn had never said how s/he identified. In fact, Ahn had never said anything at all. Whether it was a gimmick, mutism or what, Ahn never spoke, making it clear with body language what s/he wanted from the audience, aided sometimes with the help of an assistant.

"Wow," I added. Ahn's tricks were amazing. I'd seen Ahn walk through sidewalks and pop back up as though the sidewalk had been was a sphere rather than a straight line. It wasn't exactly what I could do—at least, I didn't think so—but the showmanship of it! Though now I wondered. "So, what *do* you do exactly?"

Ahn spread hands out in a way that seemed to indicate that I should name it and it would be done. I glanced at Renata, who shrugged. "Ahn won't say. I'd think it was mass hypnosis if not for the cameras. Harry is playing with the idea that he can fold time and space." I followed her glance to Sasquatch. No way— Sasquatch's name was Hairy? It was too perfect. Okay, so it was spelled with an 'r' instead of an 'i'. It read the same in my head. I fought a grin.

"What I actually said was 'pocket universes' or 'alternate dimensions' but same difference," Sasquatch said.

"Isn't that science fiction?" I asked.

"Aren't we?" he countered.

"More in the realm of fantasy, I think," T-shirt girl said. She reached a hand across the table, since she was next. "Hi, I'm Mila." She shrugged toward Sasquatch. "You've already 'met' Harry. He's a reader, like Renata, only he has a day job where he's Mister Fix-It. If you've got faulty gear or gadgets, he's your guy."

"I prefer computer engineer or hardware technician," he grumbled.

I gave him a startled look. "You're a reader and you work with computers? That must be . . . fun." Or not, knowing how many people surfed the web for porn and medical maladies they were too ashamed to bring to their family care doc.

"Why do you think I prefer hardware. Hardware is a tool. Software is the way you use it. And believe me . . ."

"We do," Mila said in a tone that implied they'd been over this before. "So back to me. I do spells in general. Most of us do, at least in a small way. But I specialize in the laws of attraction and repulsion. Two sides of the same coin. You want to draw some-one closer or push them far, far away, I'm your girl. But where Rameses is potions, I'm more about gris-gris and charms. He and I work out of the same shop."

That brought us to Stretch, who didn't shake, but instead waved overlong fingers in my direction. "Wyatt," he said. "I com-municate with the dead."

My eyes got wide. "Like Whoopi Goldberg in *Ghost?*"

He cringed, and Renata actually slapped my hip. "That's of-fensive."

"Why?" I loved that movie.

"Because in the film Oda Mae is a joke."

"But she turns out to be the real deal."

He gazed at me steadily, and I let it go. And then I thought of something else. "Wait, you communicate with the dead?" I said.

He looked confused at the question, because he'd already said as much.

"The *souls* of the dead?" I asked just to be sure.

He nodded again, brows starting to lower and face to close up as though he could see where I was going with this. But I was-n't sure myself. Did I really want to know the answer to my next question?

"Have you . . ." I swallowed unnecessarily and started over. "Do vampires . . . ?"

I couldn't bring myself to finish.

"I don't know," he said, putting me out of my misery. "When Ophelia first . . ." he glanced around the table, an apologetic look on his face, ". . . resurrected, became a vampire, she came to me. She wanted to know. We communed, just the two of us, trying to discover whether there was a part of her that had crossed the veil. We didn't find it. But that's not conclusive. Sometimes the dead don't speak, especially not right away. It takes some time to ad-just."

"Why didn't you tell me?" Renata asked.

"It wasn't my story to tell."

"And the but?" I asked.

It was Renata he answered, though. "It's not very scientific, I admit, but I don't think the soul came because it was already present. I don't know if it applies to all vampires or just Ophelia. She was an astral projector. It might be that her soul was so used to being parted from and returning to her body that death made no difference."

It was meant as a comfort to Renata, but to me it was a blow. I'd hoped I might have an answer. Or an impression, anyway, a theory based on more than my own wishful thinking. But Stretch —Wyatt—made sense. Generally vampirism was like flipping a switch. Life to death, power to none. Or, in rarer instances, no power to something like Bobby's mental mojo or my ghosting. But if Ophelia had projected before and after 'death' then . . .

Then what?

It was hardly conclusive. And Bobby was too much of a white knight to be soulless. I was holding onto that with everything I had.

Bobby! I called out into the ether, hoping against hope that he could hear me, tell me he was all right. That I could let him know we'd be coming for them, as if he could have any doubt.

But it was like Wyatt calling into the void. There was no answer. Emptiness yawned inside me.

17

We were in mid-plan when suddenly a commotion started out in the courtyard. I swung around instantly, looking for Alistaire and, sure enough, found him gone.

I cursed colorfully and told the others I'd be back, then flew like a bat out of hell toward the back entrance. I burst through the doors there into the alley to see Alistaire with a guy lifted by the front of his shirt, pressed up against the wall between the men and women's rooms. Red had bled into his eyes, and he now looked like everyone's nightmare. A petite woman in an even more petite red dress pulled at Alistaire's arm, claiming he hadn't meant anything by it. *He* apparently being the guy Alistaire held at the neck.

"A!" I said, afraid to give out Alistaire's name in public where it could be picked up and passed along to anyone on the lookout. "Put him down."

Alistaire glanced at me and peeled his lips back, showing his teeth. "He was disrespecting the lady," he lisped around his full-on fangs.

"It's okay," the girl said. "Please—"

"No," I said, "it's not. But neither is this." I stood up on my tiptoes and risked getting within biting distance of those fangs to whisper as close to Alistaire's ear as I could reach. "Alistaire, we need to be low key. You didn't rescue us just to get us captured again."

Alistaire seethed, and for a second I wasn't sure I was getting through. Then the fangs start to recede, though he didn't let the guy down yet and his breathing was starting to get rough.

"He was manhandling her. He called her a slut."

I looked up at the guy as he dangled there. "You do that?" I asked.

He choked something out, but it sounded like more profanity. Others were starting to pile out the back of the restaurant to watch. We had to end this fast.

"Drop him," I said to Alistaire. I could feel my fangs coming out now as well. Alistaire was turned away from the pair as he glanced at me, but I was facing them, and the girl, who was looking to me for help, gasped.

"Go," I told her. "Change your number. Hell, change your address, but if he's manhandled you once, he'll do it again. Maybe worse. Don't believe the apologies. Don't accept the flowers. Learn the warning signs."

She was staring at my teeth. I snapped in her face and she jumped half a mile. Sure, the vamp girl just trying to help is a threat, but the abusive boyfriend is okay. "Go," I repeated, putting a little snarl in it. I didn't like scaring her, but something had to get through.

She went, nearly twisting her ankle on her four inch heels in the effort to get away. I watched her push through the crowd, and that was when I noticed that the people in the doorway had their phones out. Of course they did. I looked around for our people and caught Suzanne's gaze. She gave me a nod, and I suspected that electronics were going to experience sudden inexplicable problems. I could almost feel a charge in the air from where I stood.

When I turned back, Alistaire had lowered the guy to the ground but not let him go. Instead, he got right up in his grill, nose to nose—only Alistaire's nostrils were flaring, as he made a point of going bloodhound on the boy.

"I have your scent, which means I can find you again at any time," Alistaire snarled. "The girl won't always be around to save you."

I bristled at being "the girl" but it was better than "morsel," and anyway, I wasn't about to quibble.

Especially when the sharp tang of urine hit me. The boy had peed his pants. Alistaire's message had been received. I just hoped the boy wouldn't take it out on his hopefully-former girlfriend. To be sure, I reached into a back pocket for his phone and checked the number.

"And I have your number," I said. "Which means I can get your name. Which means *I* can find you. Understand?"

He nodded. Not vigorously, but one quick jerk. He grabbed

the phone when I threw it to him, ducked under Alistaire's arms, which were braced to either side of him, and ran off down the alley, trying back doors until he found one that let him in.

There was applause behind us. Alistaire flashed his retracting teeth and then took a bow.

"See that," he said under his breath on his way back up. "I'm a hero."

I rolled my eyes. "You're a menace. We have to get out of here."

He swept an arm before him in an after-you gesture.

I figured we had a minute or two maximum before people tried and failed to replay the video they'd taken. Or would their phones work at all? How precise was Suzanne's power? I didn't know. There was too much I didn't know and would have to find out before we could put together a working plan.

We gathered again back at the table, but only long enough for me to say, "We have one lead, Bannon. I say we start with him. We've got the rest of the night to research, plan and decide whether you're in or out.

"We're in," Suzanne said, looking around the table to see if anyone would contradict her.

No one did.

I got Alistaire out of there just as I heard the first irate "Hey!" Someone had just checked their video.

It was a challenge to keep Alistaire from getting distracted and off course on the way back to the house. There was too much going on. Too many sights and sounds, conversations spilling out onto the sidewalk and streets. One hostess trying to lure people in and nearly succeeding with Alistaire.

"She smells like ink and roses," he insisted.

"And you thought the guy at Coop's was creepy?" I said.

At his look, I added, "Not that he wasn't. Or that I don't applaud you, but you sniffing people and getting up in their personal space? Not okay."

He blinked at me as though trying to understand.

"And the nudity thing is right out," I added.

He smiled.

"Wrong reaction."

"Clothing is synthetic. The body is all natural. How is it wrong?" He asked, but he was playing with me, I thought. He wasn't a child. There was no way he didn't know.

I grabbed his arm and hurried him past a girl wearing nothing but body paint on top in a fleur-de-lis pattern. As we hustled by, two drunken guys stopped to have their picture taken with her and she tucked their tips into the pocket of her short-shorts.

None of this escaped Alistaire, who gave me a sly side-eye.

I huffed. "First, not all clothing is synthetic. Second, nudity is distracting and we need to focus. And third, you can be naked all you want where everyone is in agreement. Hell, wear body paint and a banana hammock for all I care—Wait, forget I said that. But anywhere else nudity is unwanted and intimidating, if not downright abusive. Everyone has triggers. You don't want to be one of them."

"Banana hammock?" he asked.

"Look it up," I said, kicking myself for bringing it up. "And another thing, *morsel* is not okay."

His forehead scrunched in honest bafflement. "Then what should I call you?"

"How about my name?"

He looked at me, one eyebrow raised. "*Chickzilla*," was all he said.

It was my turn for bafflement. "That's not me, that's . . ."

It struck me like a clue-by-four. But . . . but . . . Sure, it was a nickname, but it was *her* nickname. I'd chosen it for her particularly, just like Dreadlocks and Hoodie-ninja. It wasn't like . . . Even my own rationalization machine, which was top-of-the-line, couldn't come up with anything convincing enough to put me in the right. I was naming people based on characteristics. Clothing. Hair. Cheekbones. Language had power. I'd taken away their names and imposed my own. But that was just until I knew, wasn't it?

"That's Carrie," I finished. Point taken. Maybe *I* needed sensitivity training. Marcy certainly thought so.

I put it out to the universe that if we got our friends back safely and took down the federal facility, I'd do better. Really. Cross my heart and hope to—well, not die; I'd already done that.

But something.

As soon as we hit the house, I got busy on my phone checking the drop site we'd set up with the Ghouligans. My heart nearly kicked into gear when I saw we had a message. I typed in the code and opened the message immediately, staring at the screen in surprise. We had an address. The Ghouligans had found—or thought they had—the location of the new hospital of horrors. I didn't recognize the address, of course, but on the map it looked to be just outside of the city, probably about where Ophelia's psychic trail had gone cold.

Beyond the information was a brief message: *On our way.*

I let myself collapse into a chair in the eat-in kitchen. "We have a location," I told Alistaire, who was typing furiously and paying me no attention whatsoever. "*What* are you typing?" I asked him.

His head shot up, and he gave me his feral grin before turning the screen of his phone my way, the photo of a banana hammock front and center—as in an actual hammock made to look like a banana, not as in a glorified jock strap. "Bookmarked!" he said.

He'd come a long way with cell phones since I'd first met him. Now if only I could bring him that far along on his sensitivity training.

I showed him *my* screen with the message from the Ghouligans. "Good," he said, his eyes getting that far-away look that said they were seeing more than what was in front of him. "It takes a village."

"What's that supposed to mean?" I asked.

"We need all the help we can get."

Only, the Ghouligans would be watched. It would be risky to meet up. We could be instantly captured, but . . . Something I'd been working on in my back-brain suddenly exploded to the fore, nearly blacking out my vision with the force of it.

We'd been doing everything by the federal playbook, turning the lessons they'd taught us against them. But that was the whole problem. They *knew* that thinking. They could predict it. They *had* predicted it, back in Ohio and once again when we hit New Orleans. We needed a new way of thinking—the Gina way. I was Chaos? Fine, I could work with that. Or maybe what Marcy had said back in Ohio had stuck with me. Maybe the problem was that I already thought I knew best. I squashed the part of me that didn't see any problem with that idea and tried to listen to the other voice trying to shout it down. I needed to be open to what the others came up with. I needed to listen.

Crap, this sensitivity thing was hard.

18

I jolted into consciousness, as always, not waking so much as the universe witch-slapping me into awareness. But this time there was something else to it. Something had sent me right into high alert, and—

Voices!

Oh my flippin' gods, there were voices! People were in the house. The front foyer, from the sound of it. We were seconds away from discovery.

I'd taken the kid's room, Alistaire the forward bedroom on the second floor. With our extra-sensitive vampire senses, we'd left the cold cream and menthol-scented room for Renata. Which meant she was in the most immediate danger.

I thought insubstantial thoughts and let myself fall misty through the floor into her bedroom, which was right beneath me, every room above stacked on the one below.

When I felt the air open up again, I went solid, but I hadn't exactly been thinking. I wasn't feet on the floor when I remater-ialized, which meant I fell straight onto the bed and half onto Renata, who let out a startled cry.

The voices in the front hall stopped dead, and so did we. Renata and I stared at each other in horror. We hadn't done the blood exchange. I couldn't ghost out and take her with me. And from the sound of the voices, these were the homeowners and not the police or the Feds. I didn't want to hurt anyone in our escape. Or for anyone to hurt us, gun ownership being what it was. I'd heal, but Renata wouldn't.

I shoved off her, not worried about noise anymore; we'd al-ready been heard. She rolled out of bed, and I was halfway there when I felt a blast of power from upstairs. It was meant for the newcomers at the front of the house, but it spilled over to us, and I knew instantly what it was meant to do because for a second I had the hardest time moving, as if the air had become taffy or my body was suddenly made out of stone, and then I shook it off. I had to grab Renata, though, and push her toward the hallway. When she didn't move fast enough, I slung her over my shoulders like a shawl and ran for the back entrance.

I didn't know if the homeowners had returned because someone had reported suspicious comings and goings at their place or if it was just bad timing, but we weren't going to stick around to find out.

I heard Alistaire sprint down the stairs into that front room and willed him not to do anything stupid when he encountered the people. I didn't hear any commotion. His compulsion to stop or freeze or whatever he'd blasted out must have held, because the next second he was behind us. Not having to fight his own compulsion, he quickly pulled ahead as the hall opened into the kitchen area. He raced ahead and reached for the sliding-glass door, yanking it so hard it went off its track with a horrible sound. We hit the backyard and plowed through the overgrown foliage. I had to toss Renata to Alistaire in order to leap the back fence, which came up to my chest. Even with the vampire strength, I didn't have Alistaire's double or triple jointedness, and given our relative heights, Renata really threw off my center of gravity.

There were one or two screams as we bolted through backyards with people enjoying the evening air, and then Alistaire stopped between houses to put Renata back onto her feet and slap her into motion much as the universe had done to me at sunset. Because the universe and I had that kind of relationship. She glared, but kept to her feet. We walked from between houses and joined the foot traffic along the sidewalk and around the corner onto a busier street.

"What the *hell*?" she asked when it seemed we were far enough away.

"We couldn't have predicted that," I said.

"He could." She shrugged in Alistaire's direction

"*He* was asleep," I answered. "What about you?"

"Asleep too," she said with less heat. "I heard the door open, but I didn't know what to do. I was downstairs. You were upstairs and the only way to get to you would have been through them. Then the next thing I knew, you landed on me."

"Yeah, sorry about that. Anyway, we're out. Have you heard anything more from your people? We need to meet up. We've got the address to the horror hospital. Now we can plan."

Renata had stayed behind at Coop's last night after I'd hustled Alistaire out of there. Her group had argued and debated and thrown out ideas, but in the end, they decided they needed more information. More input. And they'd gone off to get it.

That sent chills up my spine.

"Has everyone checked in?" I asked.

"Let's find a place to stop and I'll see. I've only just woken up myself. Coffee would be great."

"Uh huh," I answered, but my mind was a thousand miles away. Or, not a thousand, as it turned out, but however far it was to the address the Ghouligans had given us. To Bobby. Worrying about Renata's people brought back the worry I was trying to suppress for my own. Not just for Bobby. He'd be useful to the Feds; they'd be sure to keep alive, though in what state— No, I couldn't think about that. But what about Imanyi, David, Paige, even Silvio? They were human. What would Doctor Bannon and his crew do with people who knew too much and weren't any good for research purposes? Or were they? Would they be guinea pigs? What would that mean for them?

Or would they be turned over to Agents Sid and Maya or their counterparts and kept under lock and key, under some Patriot Act sort of charges that never had to go before a jury of their peers and held on mere suspicion?

If they were being kept somewhere else, would we ever find them again or would they be lost in a vast system? It was pretty awful when experimentation might be the best of all possible answers.

All of a sudden, Alistaire grabbed my arm and yanked me through a restaurant door. It was a long, narrow place with a swinging door at the back through which was probably the kitchen. There was an L shaped bar with the little part of the L laid out along the rest of the back wall and a good portion of the wall to our right. The rest of the place was taken up by tables. Small round tables, only one or two of which were occupied. The rest of the early-evening patrons were clustered at the bar. The design worked for us. Booths were too hard to vacate in case of attack.

We sat at a table up on the left-hand side, and Alistaire positioned himself so that his back was directly against the wall, so he could see in all directions. Renata chose the chair facing the kitchen, which gave me the prime view of the front entrance.

Renata waved down the waitress and ordered a carafe of coffee. Alistaire raised his eyebrows at that. Neither of us would be helping her drink it. Then, instead of looking at the menu, she focused on her phone, swiping, reading, typing. I pulled out my phone, which luckily I'd slept with, and checked the Ghouligans' drop site as well. There was a message waiting for me. *Here*, it said. And there was a number. I typed back *Talk soon* and left it at that for now.

Finally, Renata looked up from her phone. "Everyone is good. I've told them to meet us here. Ahn in particular has something to share."

"Great."

The waitress came back with the carafe and an order pad. Renata ordered shrimp and grits, told her Alistaire and I had already eaten and got back to her phone.

We didn't have long to wait for her cadre to arrive. Dreadlocks and T-shirt girl—Rameses and Mila, I corrected myself—were the first to arrive. Rameses had said they worked at the same shop, presumably in the French Quarter, so they wouldn't have had far to come. They pulled over an additional table, which brought the bartender flying out from behind the bar to caution us about fire codes, and before we knew it, she and the waitress were rearranging the seating themselves. The food and Vin (Cheekbones) arrived around the same time. Shortly thereafter came Wyatt (Stretch) and Harry (Sasquatch). With each new arrival came new food orders and new drinks until we were assailed by so many smells I thought I was going to have to retreat. Everything was spice, spice, spice except for the acidic tang of coffee, and even that came with the scent of something bitter I couldn't identify. Bitter even for coffee. It smelled something like dandelion root, but stronger. When I asked, I was told it was called chicory. Also a root, so I was close.

Suzanne and Ahn were the last to arrive. They entered together, Ahn in another hoodie—or the same one as yesterday, for all I could tell. They had the air of secrets to tell. All conversation stopped as they approached the table, as though someone had muted us but left the background sounds of the restaurant going.

"Show them," Suzanne said, nudging Ahn as soon as they were seated.

A smile broke across Ahn's face, half obscured by a curtain of raven hair. Ahn looked around the table, meeting each of our gazes, dark eyes dancing with glee. S/he unzipped the hoodie, reached a hand in, paused dramatically and pulled out . . . well, I had no idea what. All I could tell was that it was a box about the size of a switch plate or electrical outlet cover attached to a stake that would have been pounded into the ground. Only instead of a switch or plug, the top portion had panels. They looked a bit like solar panels or reflectors and yet different.

"Ta da!" Suzanne said.

"Um, what?" I asked, as eloquent as always.

"Ahn—" she started, falling off when Ahn laid a hand on her arm. I noticed that the nails were unpainted but perfectly manicured.

"I decided to case Doctor Bannon's house last night," Ahn picked up, in a soft voice that seemed to contain amusement and triumph in equal measure, "and this was one of the security devices guarding the entrance."

I was so shocked, I burst out, "Wait a minute, you speak! Why didn't you speak before?"

Ahn looked at me, eyes glinting merrily. "I had nothing worthwhile to say. You can't learn when you're talking, you can only spout that which you already know."

"Confucius?" Vin asked.

"What, you assume Confucius because I'm Asian? Racist much?" Ahn asked, head cocked, drilling into Vin with a look that made him go sheepish.

"Um . . ." Vin started.

"Nevermind all that," Alistaire cut in. "tell us about the device. What made you pick it up?"

"Here's the thing, there was no reason for it. It's not a motion detector or laser sight."

"So what is it, then?" I asked. "What did it do?"

"It glowed blue." Ahn said it with the weight of a great revelation, and we all took it that way. I thought of the wands the

Feds had held, their infiltration suits. Both had flared blue.

"Did it set off an alarm inside?"

"It did. Security panels stared to slam down—over windows, over doors. Sprinklers came up on the grounds and started spraying everything. I presume that if I'd been a vampire, I'd have been toast. With all that going on, I didn't dare try getting in. So I swiped the box and now I'm here."

Mila gasped. "You could have been caught. What about security cameras?"

Ahn gave her a *look* and a raised brow. "Really? It's like you don't know me at all. It's true that when the light flared, I couldn't do a thing with my power, but I was an illusionist even before I found out what I can really do. I simply employed my talents."

"What *is* it you do," I asked, hoping to get an answer this time, since Ahn was talking and all.

But Ahn just raised the other brow.

I blew out a puff of breath in exasperation. "We're going to be counting on each other now. This is need to know."

Ahn contemplated that for a second, glanced around to see if anyone else in the restaurant was close enough to hear, and then leaned forward, toward the very center of the tables. Everyone else leaned in as well. Ahn looked me straight in the eyes and said in a whisper hardly more substantial than me at my most ghosty, "I don't know."

I glared. I'd had a lot of practice lately with Alistaire, but as with the psychic psycho it had no effect on Ahn, who merely sat back again.

"How can you not know?" I asked.

"Do you know what you do?" Ahn said.

"Of course. I go ghosty. I mist through things."

"Okay, but *what* are you doing?"

"I just told you."

"You told me the effect. You didn't mention the cause."

"Does it matter?"

Ahn shrugged. "Not entirely, I suppose. But it does for these devices. We know their effect. They alert to and block magic. Like a firewall. But we don't know how or why."

"You're deflecting," I said. "We were talking about you."

"Yes."

"Gah! Whatever. So the blue blast. Do you have any theories?"

Ahn looked to Suzanne and gestured that the floor was all hers. "That's my area. Though, Harry, maybe you could weigh in as well. Ahn called me because the way the device was piked into the earth, Ahn wondered if it had to be grounded. If so, that would make it electrical."

"But we've seen it in wand form. In armor—" I began.

"And those people have probably been grounded. Rubber soled shoes or whatever. Anyway, I checked it out, and it seems like some kind of magic surge protector. Or firewall, like Ahn said. And yeah, it's based on electricity. There are a lot of theories of magic, and maybe there are as many paths toward it as there are theories, but there seems to be a special relationship with resonance, electricity, energy, if you like, given off by all living things. It's all around, latent, potential. Some places it's stronger than others, like the ley lines, where it pools." I had some experience of that back in New York where the vamps were using the ley lines, strong streams of power, to bump up their own mojo and create a whole town (to start) of mindless meals.

"Some of us," Suzanne finished, "can tap into it. And if it's energy or electrical impulses, it can be measured and it can be neutralized."

"And the Feds have found a way to do it?" I asked, horrified.

"It looks like."

I glanced at Harry. He had mentioned that he was a hardware more than a software sort of guy, but surely he knew both, and fixing systems that had been screwed with was supposedly his specialty.

"If it's a firewall or a surge protector sort of thing, it can be circumvented, right?" I asked him. "I mean, systems get hacked or fried all the time. We took down one of the federal facilities with an electromagnetic pulse."

I'd thought before this blue tech was something like that. Now it seemed I was right. It did give out an electromagnetic pulse, only instead of slagging electronics, it zapped magic. They must have isolated frequencies or sources or something. Whether we'd given the Feds the idea or they'd come up with it on their own, we were screwed.

Harry was shaking his head before I'd even finished my freak-out. But then he nodded, mixing his signals. "I mean we *can*," he said, as though finishing some thought that had started in his head. "Maybe. If they don't have safeguards against it. But if I were them, I'd have back-up or redundant systems. And definitely some kind of malware that would backfire on the user."

We were all looking at him now. "Just thinking like a hacker. Or an internet security specialist. I don't know how it works for magic. Give me a week and access to their system and maybe—*maybe*—I could figure it out. *If* I didn't get caught."

"But," Alistaire said, skittery voice doing it's trick, as I saw at least two people shudder, "they're doing experiments inside. They're doing all kinds of nastiness. Why would they create something that limits the powers they're playing with like gods?"

"They wouldn't," I answered. "That's why they must have made the gizmos directional, so that they can be pointed outward rather than in."

Something was starting to nip at my brain as I said it, the smallest spark of an idea.

"How does that help us?" Renata asked.

"Give me a second, I'm working on it." We couldn't get in without our powers. At least, I didn't see a way in unless we were going to take that week or more Harry mentioned to try to hack into their systems. But he wasn't a hacker. It didn't mean he couldn't get there, but learning to get into, let alone defeat, a secure system would take time. A week was ambitious. And the learning process usually involved trial and error. Mistakes could prove fatal for us. Meanwhile, horrible things were going on inside. Happening to people I loved. And Imanyi and the gang might be getting lost further and further in the system. No. Just no.

It wasn't only that I was an instant gratification junkie. Every moment we let things stand meant more torment. It also meant more time for the Feds to find us, and they were already looking in earnest. They had resources we could only dream of. More time too for them to tighten their security. Create more super soldiers. Close any gaps in their security, knowing or guessing that we'd be coming for them, as we had in the past. More time to set traps.

We had to move ASAP. And we had to surprise them. Stun

them. We had to do something they'd never predict.

And then the idea exploded in my head. Like nearly blew the top off the whole thing. I was a vamp, I'd probably heal. Probably. But I wouldn't be too pretty in the meantime. Although, the wigs I could buy . . . I always wondered how I'd look as a redhead.

My brain was babbling to avoid looking directly at my sheer terror of a plan. I shared it with the others, the beginning, at least, hoping they'd come to different conclusions on the only possible ending. I didn't want to bias them or limit their thinking.

"Okay, so—" I stopped when the waitress approached, but Stretch . . . Wyatt . . . quietly pressed some money into her palm and sent her on her way. "So we can't break in without our powers. At least, not without a buttload of planning and even then it's totally dangerous with no guarantees. And that's painting it rosy."

"Tell us something we don't know," Mila said.

"How about this. There's only one way in then, and it's to get captured."

Everyone started to protest, but I shushed them. "Not you. Me."

The protests started up again instantly, and I let them go. Alistaire met my gaze over everyone. His was piercing. "No," he said.

"Yes."

"Not alone," he continued.

The others, most of them, stopped to listen.

"No, not exactly. I can't do it alone, as fabulous as I am." It was feeble. I didn't feel fabulous anymore. I felt scared. The fact that vampires felt fear, experienced emotions had to mean something, right? Something good about our souls. I was hanging onto that. It might be important if this mission turned out to be my last. Because true death was a real possibility. "I'll need help."

I glanced at Rameses and Mila specifically. They created portable power—potions, charms. If the blue blaster—I could still nickname objects if not people—did work like an EMP, it only detected and countered the active use of magic, manipulation of energies, *whatever*. Which meant potential or stored magic shouldn't trigger it.

"Can you two, either of you, create something I can take in with me? Spells that will remain passive until I trigger them?"

I realized they were stupid questions as soon as I asked them. Mila and Rameses sold the charms and potions, which meant that it had to be possible for the end user to activate them.

They looked at each other. "It's possible," Rameses said for them both. "But what? You're only one person. The spells would have to be big or targeted. Something that would help you without hurting those you're trying to free . . ." He trailed off, thinking.

The others seemed to be as well, but Renata was studying me. "The bigger problem is how you'll get anything in with you. I'll admit that getting captured would get you in, but you'd be searched. Then you'd be restrained. The Feds know about your misting ability. They'll have found a solution by now. Stab you with a stake and leave it in, perpetually keeping you debilitated and tethered to your physical form; a holy water bath . . . If I can think of two things right off, they've surely considered all that and more."

"And that's if they let you live," Alistaire said ominously. "They need me for my blood. They don't necessarily need you."

I hadn't even considered that. If they killed me on sight, it was all over.

"But—"

"I know the *but*," Alistaire said without even a leer. He looked at the others. "The only way for her to take anything in is if it's inside her. We vampires can't ingest anything but blood. Swallow anything else and it will come right back up. Which means the spell tokens have to be implanted inside her. But the body will reject those too—if it's strong enough to heal."

Everyone was staring at me now, Ahn's gaze especially intense.

"So the only way to do this is if you're at death's door?" Ahn asked in that quiet voice.

Crap, I'd been hoping they would come up with some other conclusion.

I nodded. "Staked, like Renata said. I can't heal with wood inside me, and the Feds will never buy it if I'm not too weak to pull the stake out myself. It's going to be a very tricky thing. I'll have to be hurt enough to be convincing, yet somehow strong enough to do what they think I can't."

"So you—" Renata started.

"*We,*" Alistaire cut in. When I glared, he glared back and said, "Redundant systems."

I wasn't ready to concede, but I let Renata finish her thought.

"When you *both,*" she said, side-eying Alistaire as though daring him to interrupt again, "do this—if you do it—you'll use your own bodies as transportation systems and then unleash the horrors once you're in?"

"In a nutshell," I said.

"So, you're the Trojan vampires."

I didn't see what the plan had to do with condoms, but whatever.

Renata explained to me that the Trojan vampire comment came from the Trojan Horse, which was a giant wooden horse on wheels that the Greeks built and left outside the gates of Troy when they pretended to abandon their long, fruitless siege. It was only when the Trojans wheeled the horse inside, figuring it for a peace offering, that they discovered the horse was hollow and filled with Greek soldiers, who then overran Troy for the win. Hence (her word, not mine), the expression *Beware of Greeks bearing gifts,* which didn't make sense to me, because the Greeks didn't actually bear anything, unless it was ill will toward their enemies, but whatever.

I thought again that she and Bobby would get along like a house afire. They could compete to see who could out-info the other. I'd even be glad to keep score if it meant getting my boyfriend back.

Speaking of which . . . "And once I—"

"We," Alistaire said again, stealing my thunder.

"*Whatever.*" I continued, "Once I unleash my surprises and kick off the chaos within, is it possible for the rest of you to ban together for an assault on the outer defenses? You know, from a nice, safe distance? If you can overload the system from without, it will make escape that much easier. Getting in and getting everyone free is one thing. Getting them out is entirely another."

The group all looked at each other, brows furrowed. In some cases, lips worried between teeth. It didn't inspire confidence.

"Our powers don't work like that," Ahn answered for them all. "Maybe Suzanne's with the electricity, but not the rest of us. There's a reason I'm a street and not a stage magician. My stuff works up close and personal."

"And I don't think communicating with the dead is going to help you out a helluva lot here."

"Or dowsing," Vin said.

"But . . ." Renata said, drawing the word out as though she hadn't yet decided whether to finish the thought. "We know those who might help. If we get the whole community together we might have a chance."

She looked to Alistaire, who'd pounded her last phone to dust to prevent just such a thing.

"We can't do that," he said, his eyes flaring with an intensity that made me fear a little for what he might do next.

"Or can we?" I asked, drawing his fire, or at least the dark fire sparking in his eyes.

Before he could do anything stupid like blow up and inspire a flurry of 911 calls, I leaned in as Ahn had done earlier. Everyone leaned toward me as though I'd suddenly acquired my own gravity.

I sketched out the beginnings of my plan. We were going to need the Ghouligans as well. That meet-up was next.

19

When we parted from the others, I found a quiet patch of street, got out of the stream of foot traffic and dialed the number the Ghouligans had left for us. Ty picked up on the first ring.

I didn't bother with names or *hi, how are yous*, but got right down to things. "We have to meet."

"You read my mind," Ty said. "What about the outlet mall at the Riverwalk? There's a food court there that—"

"There's a *mall?*" I was flabbergasted. So far the only streets I'd seen were too congested for that, the shops too small. "An *outlet mall?*" I asked, just to be sure.

"Focus, morsel," Alistaire growled in my ear.

Like I wasn't focused. Like I wasn't thinking 24-7 about rescuing Bobby and Marcy and everyone else. But celebratory shopping afterward? I didn't see anything wrong with that.

Ty ignored my question and countered with one of his own. "How soon can you be there?"

I looked at Renata, who'd stuck with us and was standing in my personal space eavesdropping. "How far?"

"Tell him ten minutes."

I relayed it.

"Good," he said. "Might take us fifteen, but we'll meet you there."

"We?"

"Me and Bryson. We'll leave the others behind so that if anything happens, they don't have all of us. Someone stays to get the word out."

"Is your cameraman with you?"

"He is, but—"

"Bring him. I have a plan, and we're going to need his help."

"But you don't show up on film," he protested.

"I know, and that works out perfectly."

I hung up before he could ask any more questions. They'd all be answered in person. Between my new burner phone and his, I doubted anyone was paying attention, but I didn't want to take any chances. Brent had once told us that someone was *always* listening for key words, code phrases, things that set off surveillance. The important thing was to be discounted. Like the merchandise at the outlets!

Okay, down girl, I told myself.

Renata led the way, and I practically heard angels sing as we hit the waterfront and I spotted not one mall, but two. *Two beautiful malls. Wah-ah-ah*, I thought, channeling my inner Sesame Street Count. Hey, we were both vampires; it was only fitting. Oh sure, he was a Muppet, but I didn't hold that against him. That monocle, on the other hand . . .

With superhuman willpower, I resisted the siren call of sparklies and took the elevator with Renata and Alistaire up to the second floor food court. Renata had already eaten, but she told us to find seats and she'd go off to get a soda to justify our sitting there. Not that there appeared to be roving bands of mall cops waiting to hassle us.

Only two minutes later the three Ghouligans joined us—Bryson Seacroft, the crustier of their on-air talent with his tanned, weathered skin like an old-timey sea captain; Ty McClellan, who with his piercing blue eyes and dark, wavy hair was almost too pretty to be real; and their cameraman Kaleb Something-or-other with his eyes alway darting about as if he was always analyzing lighting and camera angles. He didn't have the camera with him now, and Ty had roughed himself up by growing a beard that was coming in as much salt as pepper, probably to obscure his identity. From the looks people were flashing him, it wasn't working. Or maybe it was. No one came over, though a few kept sneaking glances like they were trying to place him.

Good. Let them figure it out. Maybe they'd take pics and spread them about on social media—four of the six of us would show up anyway. It would all tie in to my master plan.

There were quick greetings and introductions and then I let them in on what I had in mind.

They looked at me like I'd lost my mind.

"If you've got a better idea, I'd love to hear it," I told them.

There was silence.

More silence.

Then Bryson piped up. "So you want us to let everyone know you're here."

"We put the word out tonight. I'm sure you have boards, Twitter feeds and all that you follow for news. Maybe you even have dummy accounts for lurking or spreading info. Use them. Use them all. We need the news to go viral. Vampire lovers, vampire haters. Deniers. We need everyone. As witnesses and as cover. It needs to be convincing that I—*we*," I said, looking at Alistaire, "have been jumped and that we're in the condition the Feds will find us in."

"I don't understand," Kaleb said, side-eying the woman a few tables away who was stealthily aiming her camera phone our way, "you're going to let yourself get beaten?"

"No, it's too surgical a procedure for that. It's going to be a set up, and you're going to help."

He didn't look so sure of that.

"Here's how." I told them the rest of the plan.

Tonight we were going to spread the news that vampires were about to appear in public. If possible, we'd send it viral. Give people time to mobilize.

Tomorrow, when we were ready, we'd reveal ourselves. We'd let everyone find us—Feds, fans and fanatics. And I was going to have a few surprises waiting.

20

It happened on Bourbon Street.

Ahn walked down the sidewalk, going with the flow of the crowd. We'd seeded the street with our people, but not too close. They needed to be present, but not block the performance. Not if we wanted to draw a crowd.

Up until Ahn reached the bar with the giant hand grenade as mascot—I kid you not—the magician was just any other pedestrian, except for being overdressed in the heat with that hoodie. But when the guy in the grenade suit danced out in front of Ahn, s/he made as though to step off the sidewalk to avoid him . . . and fell right through it.

People all around stopped and stared, gasping, grabbing others, asking if they'd seen. And waiting, waiting for Ahn to reappear or for something more to happen.

Ahn didn't disappoint, but appeared out of thin air right behind grenade guy, clapping him hard on the shoulder so that he'd feel it through the suit and then ducking behind his back and whirling with him as he spun, trying to find the source. The crowd went wild. Laughs, gasps. Phones were coming out. People were frantically texting or tweeting or whatever. Or hitting record buttons and holding the phones out in front of them. Our people included.

Ahn ducked out of grenade guy's orbit to face the crowd, arms up in a *Ta Da!* sort of gesture, then flicked thin wrists out to draw the attention to them before slowly, dramatically, lowering the jacket's hood. Hair fell immediately into Ahn's face, and s/he shook it out to more gasps and people telling each other in reverent voices that it was Ahn. *The* Ahn.

It was full night, but the neon all around seemed to spotlight Ahn's particular patch of pavement.

Suzanne pushed through the gathering crowd to act as Ahn's

hawker, motioning them in, promising them the real show was about to start.

Someone came out of the bar, locked on and headed straight toward Ahn, ready to move the show along somewhere else, probably, where it wouldn't block foot traffic into the bar. Suzanne went to intercept, but Ahn waved her off and turned to face the man. The audience booed at the fun they thought they were about to miss out on.

But the booing turned to laughter in short order, as the guy's wallet suddenly appeared in Ahn's hands, flashed behind Ahn's back so the gathered crowd could see. While the guy talked, Ahn fanned out the cash in the wallet, then tossed the credit cards into the air, where at first they froze as if time had stopped. And then, suddenly, they bunched up two by two and fluttered like birds. One set did loop-de-loops before racing toward the onlookers, doing a strafing run at one of the women, who screamed and batted at her hair. Her friend tried to catch the buzzing cards, but they flitted away and zipped back to their fellows.

The bouncer lunged for Ahn, trying to grab the hidden hands, and suddenly they were empty. The wallet disappeared. Ahn showed the bouncer that there was nothing to see there, then half turned, holding empty hands out for the audience to see as well. And in fact, when Ahn held them one way, there was nothing at all. When flashed another way, the guy's watch—or *a* watch, anyway—suddenly caught the light from the streetlamps, as it was meant to.

Everyone laughed again, and the bouncer's face got a little ugly, all scrunched and mean as he lashed out to grab Ahn.

And closed on empty air. Ahn was gone.

The crowd gasped again, looked around. Cameras swung this way and that, trying to find the performer. The bouncer dropped to the ground where Ahn had been, sweeping a hand over it as though he might find a latch or hidden door or some sort of trick.

There was a sharp whistle from the roof of the bar, and when we all looked up, Ahn was riding the neon sign with the bar's name as though it was a mechanical horse.

I didn't know how Ahn did it, but it was an impressive show. It was also time for me to put on a show of my own.

The crowd had grown to an impressive size, with people

standing on tiptoes or holding their phones far above their heads to capture the performance.

"Ready?" I looked at Vin, Harry and Mila, faces obscured by Mardi Gras masks to hide their identities. They were loaded up with stakes and, in Mila's case, a giant wooden cross, which hung around her neck so that I couldn't get any closer to her without third degree burns.

Instinctive fear kicked in my gut.

They all nodded stoically, but Alistaire licked his lips and grinned like an idiot. We were watching everything through the window of a souvenir shop half a block down, and the proprietress was starting to pay us particular attention. It was time to go.

Vin started the commotion right there in the store. It began with the name calling, as it so often did.

"Hey, bloodsuckers," he called, loudly, obnoxiously, slurring a bit in what I'd call a drunken frat-boy voice.

It was all downhill from there. All according to plan. When *bloodsuckers* didn't get a rise out of us, it escalated into more names, threats, and then quickly into the physical. Vin shoved Alistaire hard into a rack of keychain voodoo dolls, which started to fall like a lumberjacked tree. Alistaire made a fake grab as if to stop it, but missed. I dodged the falling rack, knocking into another, and soon we had a domino effect, with beaded necklaces, boas, masks and fans all crashing to the ground, and Alistaire and me dodging in and out of the obstacle course aisles with Vin and the others hot on our heels.

The proprietress yelled at us to stop. When that didn't happen, she yelled that we'd have to pay for everything and then quickly escalated to threats of the police, which was exactly what we wanted. The Feds knew we were in New Orleans. They'd be paying attention to everything, particularly disturbances in the Quarter where cries of 'bloodsucker' were loud and clear. Our uncertainty was not if they'd arrive, but when. We had to give them time. And we were about to take our show on the road.

Alistaire hit the exit before me. It was wide open for customers but at the same time cluttered with whirligig standees of postcards and other tourist crap that clattered to the floor as we ran. Alistaire crashed headfirst into one of the tourists checking out the rack and flashed his fangs. She screamed, and when her companion tried to get into his face, Alistaire snarled and he fell back. He wasn't the only one. Everyone on the street around them saw Alistaire and then saw me push him out of my way and keep on running. I nipped at one girl who thought she was going to stand her ground—intentionally missing, of course, though not by much.

We crashed into pedestrians who weren't paying enough attention despite the commotion we were causing behind them, blew through those who were aware and falling back before us, and then crashed right into the center of the crowd Ahn had gathered, who already had cell phones out and set to record. Those checking their screens instead of watching with their own eyes would see immediately that we weren't where we should be. That in fact, we weren't anywhere on camera. Combined with the cries Vin, Mila and Harry were sending up behind us, they should be able to put two and two together.

They should spread the word. One of my recent realizations had been that we'd gone about outing ourselves and the Feds the wrong way initially. The old fashioned way. We were still counting on television or news. We had to go viral. We needed social media.

We couldn't let Vin and the others catch us, though, or they'd be expected to carry through with their threats right on the spot. They weren't trained in stage fighting, and even if they were, to make it convincing up close? That took a master. But we had a plan for that too.

Mila did get close enough to throw a punch, but over-torqued her swing. I grabbed her by the arm, using her momentum to hurl her into the others like I was the hero in some kind of action film. I used the second they took to recover and sort themselves out to grab Alistaire and mist out. We'd already done the blood exchange in preparation for it. I went fast enough with the misting to escape, but slowly enough for everyone to get a good look. To tweet or Periscope or Vine or Facebook Live or whatever the cool kids were doing these days.

Cries of *holy sh*t* and *mother f*cker* and other startled expressions ringing in my now non-corporeal ears, I drifted us up, up, up, and over, until I was pretty certain the roof of the bar was beneath our feet. Then I let go of the ghosty and let us rematerialize. We dropped, but not far, and only a few feet from where Ahn had been when we'd interrupted the show. Where Ahn *still was*, because that was all part of the plan as well.

Alistaire darted forward, making sure to be seen down below, and grabbed Ahn from where s/he stood on the sign. He yanked Ahn up against him like a hostage or a human shield. It was perfect. The cameras wouldn't pick up Alistaire, but they would capture Ahn being ripped right off the perch. Given the street magic, some would chalk it up to a trick, an illusion, but there were enough who would believe.

"Get them!" Harry yelled from down below. Or maybe it was Vin. "They'll kill Ahn!"

"They'll drain Ahn dry!" Mila took up.

"Oh my God, call the police!" This from Suzanne, I thought, but it might not have been any of our people.

And then there were so many voices taking up the cry, I couldn't make out individual words. We'd successfully formed a mob. Now we had to create a crime scene. Our own attempted murders.

Ty, Bryson, Kaleb and one other Ghouligan, their director, Lloyd, were already up on the roof, though well out of the public eye. We retreated to where they were, and I said, very bravely, I thought. "Okay, let's do it."

They didn't ask if I was ready. We didn't have the time. We'd guestimated how long it would take people to get to the roof, but . . . variables.

Missions were won and lost on variables and how well they could be accounted for. Variables sucked.

Worse than vampires. And I should know.

"Go," I said, facing Alistaire.

We'd decided that we couldn't ask anyone else to do it. We were going to beat on each other and then, before the scars could heal, apply the stakes Ty and Bryson had brought so that it looked as if we'd been attacked by haters. Then came the real work, but not for us. We'd be out of commission.

"*Morsel—*" Alistaire started.

No time for niceties. I punched him right in the face. Or I would have, if I'd been taller. I aimed for the face, but ended up catching him in the neck.

He snarled the way he had down below, but this time for real. We might have planned this, but his inner predator was unconvinced it was an act. He slashed his stake at me, but more like it was a blade than a sharpened stick. Still, it ripped a furrow in my arm that burned like a thousand suns.

I slashed mine back at him, catching him across the chest. His shirt ripped open and blood spurted at me. My teeth snapped down with force at the scent of his blood, and I found myself snarling as well. We faced off, glaring at each other, trying to remember it was all for show.

He leapt at me with the stake out like it was meant to be used, going for my chest. Instinctively, I blocked, afraid that in the bloodlust he'd forget to miss the heart itself, but all vamped-out he was stronger than me, and I only managed to deflect. The sharp end of the stake pierced my right boob, and I had time for a flash of *Oh hell, I had* better *not go through eternity lopsided* before than pain blasted away all other thoughts and the sky tilted and the roof rushed up to smack me in the butt. Then my head came tumbling after, hitting the roof, sending up an explosion of blinding fireworks and crackling pain. The stake I'd been planning to use on Alistaire fell from my hand.

"Mmmfff," I said, meaning 'get it'. I didn't have the capacity for a second try at sound. I thought Alistaire's stake might have punctured a lung, which I didn't need for breathing, but did need for speech.

I tried to blink away the fireworks display behind my eyes, to center on what was going on, to make sure Alistaire wasn't feral enough to finish me off. There were dark spots swimming through with purple blotches, but between, around and through I saw Ty pick up the dropped stake and run it through Alistaire's back as he leaned over me. I couldn't see what expression Alistaire wore before the stake struck and he was all shock and pain, but then he fell on top of me, driving my stake deeper, and I blacked out for a moment.

Or maybe more.

"Gina!" someone was calling.

I opened my eyes halfway. It took all the energy I had. Kaleb leaned over me, face pinched, a study of concern. As soon as he saw me blink, his eyes flooded with relief. "Oh good, stay with me. I'm installing the camera." My tension was instantly back.

Kaleb had probably done a lot of crazy camera work in his time with the Ghouligans, but it was a good bet that had never included installing one *inside* a person. But it was the only way to hide a camera. I wouldn't record, so my flesh would be no impediment to filming. The lens could look right through me. We could get everything down in digital. Expose the whole shebang.

There were other installations too—the spells the New Orleans witches had come up with—but I never even felt them. The pain from the stake was all consuming. It kept my body from instantly rejecting the alien objects and from healing up around them, though I needed a certain bit of that. We'd already planned it. They were going to rub our vampire blood, mine and Alistaire's, around the wounds created. It ought to slow-heal the edges enough to hide them, even if it couldn't do anything internal.

It seemed to take forever, though that had to be the pain talking. If it had actually taken forever, the mob that Mila, Harry and Vin were leading would have reached us. So it couldn't have been long before we were finished. The Ghouligans donned masks to hide their identities and pushed us over the edge of the roof to fall, staked, into the crowd below.

The pavement knocked the consciousness right out of me.

21

Gina! Oh my god, Gina, are you okay?

Bobby?

I tried to call out to him, I tried to open my eyes, even, but nothing happened. No, that wasn't true. My consciousness had shifted, returning to me and bringing with it torturous pain.

And then I remembered. The stakes, the plan. Urgency! I didn't know how long I'd been out, but I did know I had to find a way back to superhero vamp status before someone strapped me down to a gurney and my window of opportunity fled.

"*There* you are," said a voice. Male. Not a particularly nice voice. It was the kind made for sneering, which was what the man behind it sounded like he was doing right then. "There's no point pretending to stay asleep. I can tell you aren't."

It was a bluff. It had to be. Vampires didn't breathe, so there was no tell-tale change in the rise and fall of our chests or anything like that to give us away. I hadn't so much as blinked, though I'd certainly given it my best.

He, whoever he was, grabbed hold of the stake through my chest and twisted. I convulsed in pain, which only put me in more pain, because the stake was in a bad place doing bad things. The spasms nearly split me in two as some things moved and others very pointedly didn't.

"Thought so," he said.

My eyes were open now. Once I blinked away the blood tears brought on by the pain, they even worked. The man swam into focus after only a second. White lab coat, hair wild and red, as I'd known it would be, aggressive nose looming over his lips, which were thin and right now twisted into, yes, a sneer. Laurel had been right—Beaker meets Sam the Eagle. A Muppet in man form. But evil. No doubt about that. If I could read auras, I suspected that his would be as black as night except where it was poison green and maybe snot yellow.

Now I was grossing myself out.

Gina! Bobby came again. *You're awake! Oh, thank gods. Who's there with you? Are you okay?*

A million thoughts mobbed me all at once—we were right, powers worked inside the facility, the mental ones anyway. Next thought: answer Bobby. Then activate the camera and get to the spells.

Bobby, I'm . . . here. I couldn't quite lie and tell him I was okay. *Gonna be distracted for a bit.*

I tried to twitch my fingers, to push the button on the small camera hidden in my palm, the kind someone might install in a purse or teddy bear for covert surveillance, but unfortunately, that was the side on which things weren't working. It must have been the side I'd fallen on when I hit the ground. Oh hells! We hadn't planned for this. My right hand was the dominant one. Everything had been put within reach of it.

I forced my head to turn, despite the pain, but it would only go so far and then it was as though something got stuck. I searched for Alistaire, but I could tell that I was alone in the room with Doctor Doom's Muppet equivalent.

A supercharged rush of fear almost overwhelmed my pain. Almost.

But thinking of Alistaire reminded me of something—his long-ago prophecy. I was chaos, but Bobby was the *key*. We'd never quite known to what. My heart, definitely. To most plans, yeah, especially with his powers. In this case, he was going to have to do what I couldn't, turn my camera on with his telekinetics. If he could. Surely the Feds would have hamstrung Bobby. They couldn't let him go unchecked.

They didn't, he said, reading my mind. *I bit one of their super soldiers. He must have had enough of Ophelia's blood in his veins—or whatever distillation the Feds are feeding them—to power me up. I'm strong enough to blast through this collar they have on me. Mentally, anyway.*

His words stopped, but not his powers. I felt a pressure in my palm, as though the camera button was being pressed by a phantom finger, and I prayed it was working the way it was supposed to. Kaleb said the camera would record *and* transmit, though I was pretty certain the Feds had the place wired so no signals would get out. If the Ghouligans received a signal, they'd cue Renata's team to start bombarding the external security. Otherwise, they were supposed to count down.

But that was their part of the plan. I had to focus on mine. I wracked my brain for the first, best spell to have Bobby activate when a nurse and one of the super soldiers joined Dr. Bannon in the room. The latter was dressed just like Mountain Man had been back in Ohio, in olive drab and khakis. (Apparently, I was only swearing off nicknames for good guys. Bad guys could continue to be objectified at will.)

The nurse had a tray in hand with a slim metal collar on it, hinged on one side and open on the other. Not for long, though. Fear hit me, as I wondered whether this was the collar Bobby had mentioned, the one that kept his powers locked down when he wasn't juiced with super-soldier blood.

"What are you going to do with that?" I asked, stalling for time. *Bobby, can you sense Alistaire? Do you know if he's awake and able to function? If not, he might need your help too.*

Evil Muppet—yup, apparently, I was all about the nicknames for the dastardly and destructive . . . *Evil Muppet* smirked evilly, swiped the collar off the nurse's tray and held it in front of my face. "You don't like it?" he asked. "Your dossier said you liked jewelry. Bling, I believe you call it. It won't hurt. Just make you magically impotent while activated. There might be times we'll want to trot you out and see your power in action."

I woke him up, Bobby said in my head. *A little plink to the cerebral cortex, and—*

Bobby!

Right. Alistaire's awake. Prepare for all hell to break loose.

"We'll just strap you down, put this on and *then* see about removing that pesky stake," Bannon was going on, smug that he had me and there was nothing I could do about it.

He was so wrong.

I clicked my tongue against the one thing I could do for myself, because we'd set it up that way, my exhale as the dispersal system. Immediately, Rameses' powder filled my mouth, and I blew it straight into Bannon's smug face, then swung my head as far as it would go toward the others. Bannon's head lolled toward his chest, his knees gave out and he crumpled to the floor with a loud snort-snore. The nurse crumpled as well, but fell sideways, landing hard on her shoulder. But the super soldier rushed me, Ophelia's blood apparently giving him some immunity.

My right side wasn't working; my left side was weak from the damage and the stake, but I didn't have any time to baby it. It hurt like hell, but I forced my hand up toward the stake and clasped it. My own blood made it slick, and the soldier was on me before I could do a thing, grabbing both my hands in one of his and reaching toward the back of his belt for something to tie me with.

And that was when the huge explosion hit down the hall.

The soldier's gaze met mine, and I could see the second of debate in his eyes, before he said under his breath, "Fuck it, you're not going anywhere," and he took off toward the real danger.

I silently blessed Alistaire, hoping blessings didn't burn like holy water, and I tried again with my good hand. This time I felt something almost pushing from down below as I pulled, and I knew Bobby was helping me with his telekinetics. The stake hurt as much on the way out as it had going in, only in slower motion, which made it that much worse. I could feel it ike a living malevolence, trying to suck out my tissue with it. My hand spasmed open with the pain, but Bobby was right there with me, pushing the stake the rest of the way out with a final pop, after which it fell onto the floor and rolled, leaving a trail of my blood.

I tried my right side again, but it wasn't obeying. Too soon. I could still feel the broken bits, but my pain had at least downgraded from *kill-me-now* to *maybe-don't-kill-me-at-all*. I made myself roll off the table, but with only half of me working, I fell to the ground, using my good arm to pull the doctor toward me. He had blood to spare. I was in need of it. It was a win-win. For me.

My teeth snapped into place, and I bit into his neck, not trying for gentle. Too angry. In too much pain. I gulped him down, not even focusing on taste, but Alistaire and his tasting notes somehow swirled into my head, and despite myself I did notice that he tasted like some kind of stew, but not beef or lamb. Something gamey. Deer, maybe. Coupled with the scent of decaying underbrush.

I might have lost myself, especially given how much blood I needed to replace, but that thought killed my appetite. I didn't want any of Bannon's rot to infect me like Ophelia's blood had the super soldier, although in his case he'd certainly gotten the better deal.

Pain flared again as my healing body forced out the spells we'd hidden under my skin. Two pennies from the days when they were still made of copper slid out from between the bones of each wrist, along with a small charm etched with the tree of life.

I gave myself two seconds to heal, just enough so that I felt the bones start to reknit. As soon as I could clench and unclench my good hand, I used it to push myself to my hands and knees and from there got to my feet. Dizziness washed over me, and I had to reach back and hold onto the gurney until it passed, but then I was on the jog. Not on the run, because I couldn't quite manage that yet.

Bobby, where's Alistaire?

Can't tell. Don't know the lay-out of this place, and he doesn't know right where he is.

But as soon as I burst out into the hallway, I could see where he was for myself. Alistaire was fighting off three of the super soldiers. A doctor or nurse stood outside the pack with a huge hypodermic needle just waiting for his chance to dodge in. My blood boiled. With a vampire, it wouldn't be a sedative. Those wouldn't work on us. It would have to be some kind of poison—holy water or garlic extract. Two bodies—one super soldier and another person in a white lab coat—already lay at Alistaire's feet.

I didn't wait to see what would come next, but launched myself straight at the man with the hypodermic. He spun, catching sight of me in his peripheral vision, and held the hypodermic out like a dagger, as if he hoped I'd impale myself on it. I dodged it with ease, grabbed that hand in both of mine and twisted until the needle clattered to the ground and the doc went down with it, his knee apparently hitting the needle before hitting the floor based on his sharp, startled cry of pain. I let go of his hand and grabbed his head instead, bashing it onto the floor to knock him into unconsciousness. He'd wake with a hell of a headache, but he'd wake.

I had to duck and roll then as Alistaire hurled one of the super soldiers he fought away from him. The soldier skid-bounced along the ground, stopping only when he hit the wall. I watched to see whether he was getting up again, but with no throat, I didn't see that as a possibility. I was about to go running to help Alistaire with the other two when a clattering of feet from the hallway spun me round. I didn't count heads, but there were enough soldiers to take us down, even if they just did a flying tackle and buried us in bodies. I hated to use up one of my explosive pennies so soon without a prime target in sight, like a control room or maybe mega vamp storage facility, but if I didn't, we might not get any further.

The pennies were already covered in my blood, which was part of the activation, so they were triggered to me and couldn't be used against me. I spoke the words I'd been given and lobbed a penny at the oncoming soldiers. It hit one of the guys in the lead, dead center of his forehead. I turned away to shield my face as the concussive boom shook the whole hallway. The heat of the blast was like a furnace and the force of it staggered me forward, but when I turned, the soldiers in the back were climbing over those in front and still coming.

"Alistaire!" I yelled. At least, I thought I did. My ears were ringing, and the sound of my own voice was like a distant bell.

He was down to one opponent now, but that one was hanging from a stake he'd embedded in Alistaire's shoulder. I lunged forward and pulled the guy off with a bellow no one heard, but he had another stake hidden on him and thrust it into my hip. The pain ratcheted up my anger, and I hurled him at his oncoming brethren . . . and sistren. Go Feds for equal opportunity.

I didn't wait to see him hit, but yanked the stake out of my hip, screaming at the pain. I grabbed Alistaire and took off down the hallway.

There was a *thwang* behind us, and a crossbow bolt or something flew close enough to graze my head and muss my hair. Damn projectile weapons.

Alistaire took one of his spelled objects out of a pocket, smeared it in my new blood—it was still coated in his—and breathed words across it. Immediately, there was a kind of weight to the air that settled around us and hardened, not like a shell, but like a membrane. A shield spell. The next bolt struck it and fell away.

We kept running.

"We need to find a control room or computer room or something," I said. I could even hear myself; my ears were starting to work again. "We can't keep running blind. They'll find a way through our shield or just overwhelm us."

And that was when I saw it, like serendipity—a stairwell, and right beside that an emergency evacuation map showing what to do and where to go in case of emergency. The Feds, complying with mandated fire safety regulations. There was no chance there'd be a room labeled "Do not Enter" or "Very Secret Stuff" but maybe . . .

I dodged toward it, and Alistaire had to dodge as well because of the nature of the shield. It wouldn't let me go in one direction and him in the other, but held us together like a rubber band.

I tried to take the sign in at a glance, but I wasn't that fast and the super soldiers were close on our heels. Alistaire growled and ripped the damned plaque off the wall, drawing it in through the shield bubble and handing it to me. Then he bolted, the bubble bumping against my butt to hurry me along. I studied the schematic as we ran. "Not on this floor," I said. "There's no indication—"

"Down then," he said. "It's never up. Not with the possibility of aerial attacks. They'd build down. Layers upon layers."

"Each one more protected than the one above."

And we hit a wall. Not a literal wall, but a fire door that had been locked shut between sections, probably when the alarms went off. There was no keycard reader here like in the last facility—not that we had a keycard—but instead what looked like a retinal scanner.

Alistaire and I glanced at each other. "Staircase," he said.

"Only way back is through." Meaning through the super soldiers arrayed behind us. Would our bubble hold if we rushed them? I guessed we were about to find out.

We spun, backs to the door. The soldiers were less than a body-length behind us. Not much room to build momentum, but we pushed off the door and launched ourselves at them. Our bubble hit the first row and knocked them back into their fellows, but then we were sunk. Surrounded. I tried to land blows, but the shield wasn't that versatile. It felt like punching through taffy, killing any momentum and power. The only way to fight effectively was to drop it and take away our protection.

But Alistaire lashed out with his mental mojo. I felt it go out of him and hoped it wouldn't bounce off our shield and come back at us. I knew it had hit home when the soldiers about to overrun us froze, as though someone had hit their pause button. I wondered for a second why Alistaire hadn't done that sooner and then realized that his power was probably finite, like mine, and he didn't want to spend it too soon and not have it when it counted.

We backed up again all the way to the wall and then took another running start. This time we took down a few more, knocking them over like dominoes, but it only went so far, and then we were lashing out like football players, blasting through the defense to get to our goal. Their goal? Anyway, the entrance to the staircase.

There was another retinal scanner, but Alistaire picked up one of the soldiers at the back of the pack and I got a sense of how weird things would look to those watching on camera, because the guy seemed to levitate in his arms, blocked from actual contact by the shield, which was pretty impressive. Alistaire had a bit of trouble manipulating him into position, but we got there and the scanner clicked the door open for us.

There were three more soldiers and two lab coats waiting for us on the other side. One of the coats shoved a wand straight into our shield and it lit up like blue fire. The shield popped and dissolved on contact.

Alistaire threw the man he held at the lab-coated woman who'd shut us down, but he hadn't gotten any momentum on his swing, and she only oophed and staggered as the man hit and dropped to the floor at her feet. Meanwhile, the other lab coat had come at me with a hypodermic. I blocked the swing and twisted his arm up beneath mine so that I had it trapped, but one of the soldiers stabbed me with a stake to the shoulder.

I let go of the doc to lash back with my elbow to his face but the soldier had already moved, taking the stake with him for another try. I tried to mist out, but that blue wand had to be messing things up, because nothing happened except that my expectation of insubstantiality left me open to the next blow. This time the stake got a lot closer to my heart, and I fell with it still inside me. The pain flared with the burn of a thousand suns, and when I rolled to lash out with my legs, I was careful not to roll all the way back and push the stake farther in. My legs connected with the soldier, but not solidly enough. He grabbed them and tucked them under his arms to lift me up and slam me back down to do what I'd just avoided—complete the impalement.

But I'd trained for this in the Feds' super spy training, and if they could predict us, the good thing was, I could predict them too. I used his bracing of my legs to bend at the waist, levering myself up so that we were practically face-to-face, given our relative sizes. I instantly latched onto him with hands viced to either side of his head and went in for the kill. My teeth were already down, and they sank into his neck like a knife through warm butter. His blood flooded my mouth. Hot, salty, and pulsing with power. It roared through me, but I was worried it would gush out around the stake as quickly as I swallowed it down.

The soldier dropped my legs as soon as my fangs hit, but I was latched on so tightly I dragged his head and neck down with me. Someone grabbed him and ripped him away from me, leaving a great gash in his neck. I snarled and swallowed down the last of him, his supercharged blood and the fire of the pain making me feel like I was flush with fever. Alistaire had downed the other soldier and lab coat, so now we both faced off with the dazed, wounded warrior I'd just bitten and his friend who'd pulled us apart. Even staked, I liked those odds.

Alistaire smiled that feral, creepy grin of his and grabbed for the guy I'd already marked. He was in no state to resist, and without his buddy in front of him, I lunged for the other guy. He jumped back, but rammed against the stair railing, and I caught him, pulling him in by the wrist. He grabbed for something at his back, and I knew another stake was coming. I didn't even think about it, I stopped pulling and pushed, hard, sending him up and over the railing in the time it took to regret it. Only I didn't. It was kill or be killed.

The soldier I'd bitten now sagged in Alistaire's arms as though he'd given all he could.

"Alistaire!" I said, in case I could still save him, but also because we had to get going. The Feds knew we were here. They'd been waiting. I couldn't believe they hadn't sent everything they had against us. Maybe they were trying to wear us down. Or maybe Bobby was causing trouble elsewhere. He'd been quiet in my head for a while now.

Alistaire looked up, his eyes blood red and totally inhuman. He didn't appreciate me interrupting his meal, but he dropped the soldier to the floor and stepped over him, ready to head downward like we'd planned.

"Wait," I said. Despite the infusion of super blood, the stakes and earlier beating had taken their toll. I was about ready to drop. I turned toward Alistaire so he could see the stake still sticking out of my back. "Maybe you could do something about this first."

Alistaire spotted the stake, and glanced at the soldier at his feet like he might do worse than he'd already done, but there was no point. The soldier was completely insensible. I tried not to think *dead*, but I was pretty certain I'd just killed a man and there'd be more bloodshed before this was all over. Alistaire grabbed the stake embedded in my back and pulled. Not gently, but I didn't want gentle. I wanted fast. I wanted the damned thing gone.

I bit my tongue to keep from crying out as he yanked the stake out and almost ended up gnawing my tongue right in half. Blood flooded my mouth, but I swallowed it back down. I didn't have any to spare.

Alistaire gave me a second to recover as he grabbed up one of the lab coats from the floor and flung her over his shoulder. At least he hadn't just torn out her eyes for access. Probably they needed to actually be in her head because of some light or heat or blood flow sensor in the retinal scanners. Now wasn't the time to experiment.

Then before I could bring myself to straighten my back, Alistaire was bounding down the stairs. I cursed and took off after him. We'd only passed two floors when the sound of clattering boots on stairs stopped us in our tracks. From above us, from below us. It seemed we were about to be mobbed. Alistaire dropped lab coat lady like she was hot, and slid into a fighting stance. I did the same. The soldiers from below pounded up the stairs, quick time, almost like they were running in formation. They ignored us entirely, not looking left or right or anywhere but up. The soldiers from above never reached us, but must have diverted at one of the upper floors. It was freakish.

Bobby, I asked in my head, mentally shouting in case we had a bad connection or Ophelia's blood was starting to wear off. *You okay? You've been quiet. What's going on?*

I did my best to send the mental image of the soldiers running past us.

There was a heart-stopping pause (or maybe heart-restarting) before Bobby answered. *It's Ophelia! They had her really out of it, but when you arrived, the team around her got called off and I was able to wake her. She knows about the rescue. She says she can feel her granddaughter outside.*

And the soldiers?

Blood calling to blood. Their soldiers are now ours. Well, hers.

Whoa, I bet that was a side effect the Feds had never anticipated. But it made sense. I was an exception, but generally, the vampire compulsion worked best on those who shared blood, which was why Bobby'd had such a hard time turning against the vixen vampiress who'd vamped him. With Ophelia's added strength and the super soldiers tied to her via blood, Ophelia had turned their army against them. Except we still had the lab coats and non-combatants to deal with, assuming none had taken doses of their own medicine.

Can they free you?

Some of us, probably, but they're headed for Ophelia, and she's got extra protections on her door. Maybe mine too. You still need to get to the control room and shut it all down. Can you do that?

No other choice. We'll get it done.

I relayed this to Alistaire, who got a gleam in his eye like he was contemplating his own human army. I shuddered to think of it. I hoped we wouldn't have to fight Alistaire when all this was over. If he and Ophelia ever got together, they could probably rule the world.

"No," I said.

Alistaire's head swiveled toward me and his eyes glistened, but he didn't answer except with one of his full face creepy grins, like he'd been hit with the Joker's J-juice.

"Come on," was his only answer. He grabbed lab coat lady back up in his arms and took off down the stairs, one more floor. Suddenly he stopped, looked out the small landing window and nodded. He shifted lab coat lady around and pried open her right eye to offer up to the scanner. This floor looked the same as the others from where I was standing, but whether it was some kind of intuition or psychic instruction, Alistaire seemed certain we were in the right place.

The door buzzed in response to the accepted retinal scan, and he readjusted lab coat lady's weight so that he could yank the door open and get through. The hallway beyond was eerily empty. No one waiting for us. I heard alarms going off somewhere to the left, but muffled, as though there was a fire door between us and them.

"That way," Alistaire said, indicating the direction from which the alarms were coming.

I thought he was probably right. I let him lead the way, but I kept watch on the rear. I didn't like the empty feel of things. It might just be that the soldiers had cleared out, answering to Ophelia's call, but . . . It smacked of a horror film where all the workers had already been zombified or possessed by aliens and were waiting to jump us.

There *was* a fire door between us and the alarm, and it was locked up tight, which made me feel only marginally better.

Alistaire held lab coat lady up to the scanner, but this time nothing happened. Nothing at all. He threw her aside and went at it shoulder first, bouncing back in pain, but angling like he was about to go in again.

"Stop," I said. "It's a fire door. You'll batter yourself broken before you break it down. We're going to try it my way."

I grabbed Alistaire by the hand, trying not to shudder again at the sticky feel of it, coated in someone's blood, maybe even mine from when he'd yanked out my stake. Then I focused on going insubstantial, hoping no blue light would suddenly flare to screw the whole thing up. It worked, and we misted out. It felt like the last of me to go insubstantial was the place I'd been stabbed, but it did go, and I pushed us toward the door with the idea of going through. The door seemed to pull at us, denser than it should have been. Or maybe all the blood I'd lost made this harder.

We hit the other side of the door and solidity smacked us to the ground. That blue light flooded the area, flaring as my vision returned with my form, and immediately sprinklers in the ceiling went off, droplets of holy water hitting us like hail, driving us to the ground. I curled up instantly, trying to protect what I could and inching myself across the floor to get my back against a wall, to spare that much of me at least.

Alistaire shocked me by throwing his body over mine, trying

to protect me. The burn was already burrowing into my skin, melting into the rest of my flesh. But Alistaire . . . he'd be completely burned alive.

Bobby! I called out, which was crazy, an instinctive reaction. My call would never get out through their magic-killing light, and even if it did, his power wouldn't penetrate back through it. The spells I still held wouldn't do me any good either.

The entryway to the control room was a trap.

Of course it was.

The blue light flickered as something happened—maybe Renata's people bombarding the place from without—but it wasn't enough for us to take advantage of.

We were dying.

Alistaire was going to die protecting me. If we lived, I vowed never to call him the psycho psychic again. Ever. Even if the shoe fit. Even if the shoe was Ferragamo. Even if I was disassociating from the pain and not making any sense.

The sprinklers above us petered out, but it hardly mattered. I didn't even know how long ago they'd stopped, because the pain didn't. It went on and on. Alistaire lay curled around me, unmoving. The blue light still blasted when I forced my eyes open. Just in time to see the fire door, which wouldn't open for us, swing inward. In the void left behind stood Doctor Bannon, glaring as though he could incinerate us with his eyes. But it was too late for that. We were already on fire. Far more intimidating was the crossbow in his hand.

He saw the fear in my eyes, and he laughed.

It must have hurt, because I'd done a number on his neck, but that didn't stop him. The laugh was deep and dark, and I wanted to shove it back down his throat, but I couldn't move. Alistaire was locked around me, frozen in pain or unconsciousness. *Not death*, I told myself. As far as I knew, we could only die by stakes to the heart or beheadings. Or, I suppose, a fire strong enough to burn us up and sever connections between our heads and the rest of our bodies, but as badly as the holy water burned, we weren't truly incinerated.

The blue light faltered again, longer this time, and Bannon's laughter cut off. I focused on going ghosty, taking Alistaire with me, but the light was back on before I could pull myself together,

or apart, or however things worked. I slammed back into full solidity, cursing that I wasn't strong enough to find a way through
like Bobby had. Maybe it was the combination of the blue light
and the holy water. Or my various stakings taking it all out of me.
Or the fact that I was trying to move two bodies at once.

Meanwhile, Bannon's crossbow hadn't wavered.

"Get up," he said.

"Can't," I answered, taking perverse pleasure in thwarting his
will, even while hating the weakness.

"Get up or I'll shoot him," he said, indicating Alistaire with a
flick of his wrist. Already he could probably impale us both with a
single shot, but I didn't point that out. I didn't think he was bluf-
fing and didn't want to set him off.

I tried. My whole body was aflame, but if I ignored every
warning klaxon in my body screaming at me to stop, I *could* move.
Slowly, I stirred, leaving skin behind me as the burn from the holy
water and the friction of sliding out from under Alistaire sloughed
it off. I didn't want to think about that.

When I was free of Alistaire, I got as far as my hands and
knees. I could feel the super charged blood I'd acquired via the
super soldier doing all it could to heal me, but I was still reknitting
from earlier wounds and I didn't feel steady enough to make it to
my feet. Which wasn't really where I wanted to go anyway.

It was do or die. I had nothing to lose. If I went along, I'd be
captured. Alistaire too. If I didn't get to that control room, Bobby
and Marcy, Ophelia and the others would stay locked up, captive
and bled for the rest of their unnatural lives. If I died, at least I'd
die trying.

I looked up at Bannon, gauging the distance, gathering my
strength, and then I lunged.

He fired the bolt he'd been aiming my way, but I wasn't
where he expected. It skimmed by back as I charged, burning a
gouge between my shoulder blades, but I hit him at stomach level,
shoulder to the solar plexus, knocking his breath out, my momentum carrying us both to the floor.

Bannon hit hard. He managed to keep hold of the crossbow,
but unloaded, it was no threat. He'd have done better to release it
and free up a hand, but he was a doctor, not a fighter. He tried to
use the crossbow to batter at me instead, trying to cave my head

in, but it was harder than that. His blows barely registered on the scale of overall pain, and in the meantime, the neck wasn't the only vulnerable spot on a human. With my fangs, I ripped the lab coat aside, and tore through what was beneath, shirt and all, ignoring the petrochemical taste of polyester, to bury my fangs in his gut.

I could taste his terror in his blood, in the fight or flight cocktail flooding into me. The burn of the holy water started to recede. The pain of his blows were almost nothing, until it *was* nothing. Until he was too weak to continue. I'd already bled him once. It didn't take long to finish the job. I stopped when I realized the rush of blood had slowed to a trickle.

I pulled back and looked down at the doctor, at the bone-white pallor of his skin, as though I hadn't left him enough blood to pink it up . . .

And I looked away. To Alistaire.

I was torn between using Bannon to get into that control room before anyone else came to stop us and feeding the blood I now had to spare to Alistaire to save him as he'd saved me. It might have been overdramatic. I didn't think Alistaire was in imminent danger, but one more stake could be his last, and if anyone arrived and decided he was too dangerous to live . . .

There was no contest. He'd saved me. And anyway, I might need him in that control room. Surely, I couldn't subdue *everybody* and bring down the shields alone. Alistaire had been right. I couldn't go it alone.

I knelt and rolled Alistaire until his mouth faced up. I could have been gentler, given time, but he was in no condition to appreciate it anyway. I ran my own fangs across my wrist and held it to his lips, letting the blood drip in until suddenly his hand grabbed mine and his over-sharp nails dug in to hold my wrist in place. Then he began sucking with a vengeance.

Fortunately, he pulled back on his own before I had to knock him upside the head.

"Take a second," I said, grabbing my wrist out of his grasp. "I'm going in."

The blue light flickered as I got my arms up under Bannon's armpits and dragged him into position at the retinal scanner. He was dead weight, and I was focused on other things, so I couldn't be certain he still breathed. I thought I might have felt his chest rise and fall, but I didn't confirm, too busy making sure his eye lined up with the sensor.

The door into the control room clicked open, and I dropped him back to the floor. No one came flying at me, so I rose, and stepped into a room full of people, heads down over their computer panels. Only the closest looked up, their eyes going huge when they saw it wasn't anyone they expected, when they saw my fangs, still red from Bannon's blood.

The blue light behind me faltered again, and this time it didn't come back. Renata and her people had done their jobs. It was time for Alistaire and me to do ours.

Behind me, I heard Alistaire get to his feet and lunge to the door. When I looked back briefly, he was hanging in the entryway as if he needed the wall to hold him upright. But his eyes were blazing, and he sent out a pulse of power with the words, "You're mine now."

Everyone looked up from their computer screens then, riveted by Alistaire, captured by his compulsion. "You," he said, pointing at a girl with glasses pushed so far up her nose it was a wonder they didn't dent her brows. "Unlock everything."

Her face was blank. Not afraid. Not anything, as she said, "I don't have those codes."

"Who does?" Alistaire asked.

She pointed behind her to a man who'd outgrown the hair on his head. "He does."

"You." As Alistaire's attention snapped to the man, he seemed to jump, despite the compulsion. Or maybe because of it. "Unlock everything. Now."

Sweat broke out on the man's forehead, as though he was trying to resist, but his hands flew over his keyboard.

I hurried across the room to see what he was seeing, to make sure he was doing what Alistaire had said. There was a dialogue box open, asking him to confirm the unlock order. His hand shook as it hovered over the blank for him to reenter his code.

"Do it," I said. I had the vamp mesmerism, but making people suggestible was a lot different from compelling them the way Alistaire and Bobby were able to. Still, it was the final push he needed with Alistaire's power already pulling at him. He reentered the code, and his computer flashed green and then red.

Warning. Locks disengaged. Warning, scrolled across his screen.

I nodded to Alistaire.

"Disable protections," Alistaire said to another. "All the collars and blue-light defenses."

I left him to it. I had plans for the balding, sweating man and his computer. I grabbed the chair that had rolled back when he'd stood up at our entrance, and sat down in it so that I was eye and chest level with the computer monitor—so that the camera now clipped to my shirt would record everything. And that's what I had him show me, everything he had access to. For good measure, I also rifled his area for a thumb drive and insisted he make me a copy.

"You'll never get away with this," the man said through clenched teeth, the words costing him. The sweat was starting to pool and drip off his brow and chin.

"Oh, *cher*, here's no one left to stop us," said a new voice from the control room entrance we'd come through. The voice held *power*. It was old and rich and distinctly feminine.

I looked over—*everyone* looked over—to see Ophelia, standing bent, but very much unbroken, in the entryway, the vanguard of her super soldier army just visible behind her.

22

"Where are the rest of the vampires?" I asked. I'd gotten as far as taking down the shields and unlocking doors so we could free them. I hadn't considered for a second they might be free already when the doors opened, potentially out of their minds with blood-lust. We'd brought Renata's people. We'd had the Ghouligans put the word out so that we'd have as many witnesses as possible when we got our signal and our people out. Enough witnesses that no scrub team could be sent to take us all out and burn the place to the ground. We hadn't brought them to be slaughtered.

Ophelia focused on me, a grim smile on her face. "It's not a problem, *cher*. I have people taking care of them," she said, indicating her soldiers. If by "taking care of" she meant "feeding" then the freed vamps would be okay for now. Hopped up on super-charged blood, but all right until the crash.

"What about—"

I'd been about to ask about my people when Bobby's voice came from out in the hallway calling, "Gina! You did it!"

My heart gave a great leap that I'd swear wasn't a metaphor or hyperbole or whatever. Bobby!

I tucked the thumb drive into my cleavage and left the balding man and his computer monitor behind, running for the hallway.

Ophelia moved aside rather than be run down, and her soldiers cleared a path as well.

"*We* did it!" I said, flinging myself into his arms.

Bobby caught me to him, buried his hands in my hair and kissed me as though we never had to come up for air, which, thankfully, we didn't.

If it hadn't been for the clearing throat and insistent tapping on my shoulder, we might have gone on like that forever.

"What?" I snarled, turning toward the mad tapper.

Oracle—Laurel—stood there, looking at least a little sorry for the interruption. "Shouldn't we take this outside?"

I glared. It seemed that, after all I'd gone through, I should get to enjoy my moment, but she was right. We should go, in case this place had a self-destruct button and someone had enough willpower to break free of Alistaire's compulsion to use it.

If we played our cards right, there'd be a lot more of these moments to enjoy. An eternity.

"The others?" I asked her first. "David, Imanyi—"

"Safe," she answered. "The Feds decided they needed donors to feed the vamps their subsistence level blood. I guess they preferred captive sources to mandatory blood drives. But we've got them. We've got everybody."

I nodded, feeling the last of my tension drop away and something like euphoria start to rise up.

"Okay then, let's go!"

"Gina!" Alistaire said, stopping me short. "What do we do about everyone here. We can't just leave them behind us, with the computers and data."

Right. One more thing I had to do.

"One sec," I told Alistaire. I went back through the path I'd created. "Hold them one more minute."

I brought out the tree of life charm the others had bespelled for me and tossed it into the center of the room, chanting the words Mila had told me. Nothing happened at first. Or at least, it happened in such a small way that we couldn't see it. And then something grew where the coin had landed, leaves unfurling, vines spreading across the floor from a big central bud, light purple toward the bottom, deepening to indigo at the very top. The vines wound around chairs, twisting up legs and over backs, creeping across desks and keyboards. Things popped or spat as tendrils pierced straight through monitors or speared through drives. The vines flowed right around the people, like a river flowing around boulders. The central bud began to unfurl, and it's stalk shot it toward the ceiling where it suddenly burst into full flower, showering the room and everything in it with pollen like pixie dust. It sparkled over everything as the vines continued to expand, bursting through windows, straining walls that wouldn't hold out much longer.

"Okay," I said to Alistaire, "you can release them." Nothing manmade was going to be working in this place for a long, long time. It was the opposite of salting the earth so nothing would grow. The earth was reclaiming this patch of itself. It was possibly the most beautiful thing I'd ever seen.

"You don't have to go home, but you can't stay here," I said to the techs. "This spell is going to grow and spread until there's nothing left but a garden on this spot, and you don't want to be the fertilizer."

I didn't like letting them go, but we couldn't lock them all up the way the Feds had done to us. For one, we didn't have the means. For another, just no. We needed checks and balances, not one group lording over another. The rebels were right about that.

The techs practically ran each other down to get past Ophelia and her super soldiers. We followed after them, meeting up with the others in the hallway. Marcy spotted me immediately, and waved a hand to be seen above the mob. There might have been squealing. And hugs. Definitely hugs. Brent and Bobby did the manly *hey man* head nod at each other. Very touching.

And then someone grabbed me from behind. I nearly came out swinging, but I pulled my punch when I saw who it was.

Chickzilla. *Carrie.* Her ponytail was gone, and with her hair falling around her face, excessively pale from blood loss, she looked softer. Her outfit on the other hand . . .

"Thank you," she said, looking as sincere as I'd ever seen her. "As soon as the lights started flickering, I knew it was you. No one else could cause so much trouble."

I grinned. It felt good. "Well, I didn't do it alone, but I might have orchestrated a thing or two."

"Whatever. I just wanted to thank you. You're right. We have to work together. We'll be in touch."

"Absolutely we will." I knew a finder now. There was no way we were scattering to the four winds again, every vamp or every council with a separate agenda that might endanger others. "But one question—how grateful are you?"

"What?" she asked, rearing back like I'd suggested I might kiss her.

"Not like *that*," I said laughing. "I was thinking miracle makeover. You, me, Marcy and whatever we want to put you through. Trust me, you'll thank us."

If I'd transformed into a snake before her eyes, I don't think she'd have looked more shocked.

"Oh, come on," I said, "I've been wanting to do this since we met."

I raked a gaze down her breaking and entering outfit and she did the same. She completed the inventory with a twist of her lips. "Fine," she said. The teenaged-version of fine, where it's really its the slash of an exclamation point and the pistol shot of a period all at once. "But no pink. And I don't do bangs."

"We can work with that," I said, smiling.

She disappeared into the crowd before I could make any other demands, and I linked arms with Marcy on one side and Bobby on the other, and off we went into the dark of night to meet the Ghouligans and our French Quarter friends and anyone who'd answered the shout out about us vamps being loose on the city. Hopefully everyone'd had phones at the ready, tweeting, Facebooking and Instagramming, Periscoping and whatever. Going viral, spreading the word like the vampirism. You turn two people, then they turn two people and so on and so forth. Only, with social media you could reach hundreds of thousands—millions of people. Which gave me ideas. So many ideas. I had everything I'd captured on camera and on the thumb drive to turn over to the Ghouligans. It was the least I could do for everything they'd done for us. But inevitably there'd be things they couldn't use, that their lawyers or whoever would advise against.

And that's where I'd come in.

I might not become quite the film and television celebrity like I'd always wanted, but that wasn't the only way to go. Not anymore.

"You ready?" Silvio asked two weeks later.

Thanks to Harry and him, I had a shiny new avatar who looked like me on my best hair day, a voice synthesizer, and all kinds of other things I let them handle, like super cyber security. And I had a great co-host. Not side-kick, because that was passé.

I looked glam. Marcy looked goth. Both of us wore our fangs with pride, at least on the screen.

We looked at each other, and our digital avatars, who'd been rigged to us with wires and sensors and such, did the same.

"Ready?" I asked.

"Ready," she said.

It was her turn to open the show. I let her take it. I'd done the first. The Feds had rushed to get us taken down, of course, but the Internet was eternal. By the time they got to us, the show had already been cached all over the place. It had been tweeted and retweeted, blogged, posted, shared about a million times. It popped up again as quickly as they could quell it. We were a sensation.

We'd pop up in new places each week. We'd alternate openings. We'd have special guests. Overall, we'd blow the lid off so, so many things. We'd become part of the checks and balances. The fourth estate. The free press.

Cyber-celebrities!

I smiled big for the camera as Marcy began, "Hello, and welcome to *The Vampire Report.*"

About the Author

Lucienne Diver is a literary agent by day, a writer by the dawn's early light. In addition to the *Vamped* series—*Vamped, Revamped, Fangtastic, Fangtabulous* and *Fangdemonium*—she writes the *Latter-Day Olympians* urban fantasy series, featuring a heroine who can, quite literally, stop men in their tracks. *Long and Short Reviews* gave the first in the series her favorite pull-quote of all times: "*Bad Blood* is a delightful urban fantasy, a clever mix of Janet Evanovich and Rick Riordan, and a true Lucienne Diver original." Sequels include *Crazy in the Blood, Rise of the Blood, Battle for the Blood* and *Blood Hunt*.

Her short stories have appeared in the *Kicking It* anthology edited by Faith Hunter and Kalayna Price (Roc Books), the *Strip-Mauled* and *Fangs for the Mammaries* anthologies edited by Esther Friesner (Baen Books) and the *Rogue Mage* anthology *Tribulations* (LoreSeekers Press). Her essay "Abuse" was published in *Dear Bully: 70 Authors Tell Their Stories* (HarperCollins).

Faultlines, a teen thriller dealing with the serious issues of cyberbullying and teen suicide, is her latest novel (Bella Rosa Books). Carrie Jones, New York Times bestselling author of the *Need* series, called it, "Vivid, suspenseful and charming . . . a must-read page turner."

She lives in Florida with her husband, daughter, the two cutest puppies in all the known worlds, and a second floor ever in danger of collapsing under the weight of all of her books.